UNRULY

UNRULY

BECCA MANN

Cover by Ashley Siebels

ISBN: 979-8-9925609-1-6 (paperback)

ISBN: 979-8-9925609-2-3 (ebook)

www.becca-mann.com

To Eva, for never letting me forget about this book.

CONTENTS

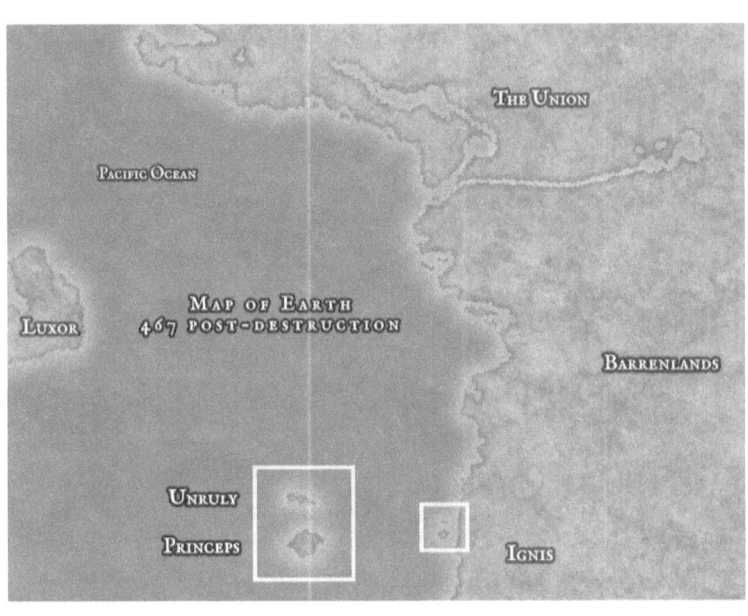

THE UNION

PACIFIC OCEAN

MAP OF EARTH
467 POST-DESTRUCTION

LUXOR

BARRENLANDS

UNRULY

PRINCEPS

IGNIS

I

A tendril of anxiety weaved around Charlotte Galvin's stomach, strangling her from the inside out. The world felt dead around her, the tension in her body all that electrified the air.

She shouldn't have been out here. Not now. Not this close to the end. But Charlotte was nothing if not a servant to her fear. If she was going to survive the next few days, she needed the fear gone.

Towering buildings frowned upon her as she crept through the alley. If they could speak, they'd be as cold and unforgiving as the stones they were made of.

There was a reason no one was out, and that reason was *her*.

Unease trickled through Charlotte's body. She willed herself not to think of it.

If anyone knew—if they saw her now—she would lose everything.

She should turn around. She should go back to the Academy, and finish her last day of schooling like the High-Pointer she was.

The High*est* Pointer.

But Charlotte never turned around. Not when it came to Dust.

And she never got caught.

Charlotte wiped a bead of sweat from her forehead. She couldn't look flustered when she returned.

Summer had come early this year. The air was hot and dry, the earth parched beneath the thick smog. If she happened upon someone, she was half-convinced she could disappear into the dirty air.

There's no one to hide from, Charlotte told herself.

Yet.

She walked through a "good" neighborhood, near the city center of Ignis. Physical harm didn't worry her as she hurried through the alleys of the cobblestone streets.

Charlotte was still a distance away from her destination when a figure stepped out from the shadows of an adjacent alley, only a few bounds away.

Charlotte's heart skipped a beat, freezing for a second before she spun away.

Maybe he didn't see me. Maybe I'm fine—

"Hey!"

It took Charlotte a moment to recognize the voice, and another for her body to sag with relief.

Jaxson Elling. Exactly the man she had been looking for.

Though he could hardly be called a *man*. He wasn't a day over twenty. His baby-face, scrawny body, and tight skin held a spry glow—but his eyes were focused, an intense glint giving him a wizened presence.

A presence that Charlotte was all too familiar with, that could have only come from Dust.

Jaxson put a comforting hand on her shoulder.

"Relax, it's just me."

"Don't touch me!" she snapped, shaking him off as she

recomposed herself and straightened her uniform. Charlotte despised being touched, regardless of the context.

If Jaxson was upset by her reaction, it didn't show. "Figured you were looking and I'd save you the time. How much you want today?"

"How much do you have?"

"How much do *you* have?"

She must've been Jaxson's best client. She was the richest teen in all of Ignis, even with her Dust habit.

"I want three ounces," Charlotte said.

Jaxson attempted to hide his excitement. If Charlotte had been anyone but herself, he might have even succeeded. But details, like Jaxson's tapping left toe, rarely escaped Charlotte's notice. Years of paranoia had instilled it within her.

Three ounces was more than Charlotte had ever asked for. She had no idea what the next few days would hold. All she knew was that she'd need Dust to deal with it.

"Gonna cost you..." He trailed off when Charlotte pulled out a wad of cash. A moment later, she had three ounces of pink Dust in her pocket.

"Pleasure doing business with you, Zandra." He disappeared back into the side alley like a wraith, just as he had entered.

Charlotte had *never* told him she was Zandra. She hadn't lied —she just hadn't corrected his mistake. Which made it okay, right?

Charlotte pressed herself against the corner of the building— an easy escape to either her right or left.

She unzipped the baggy, taking in the fine pink powder. Most would call Dust a *drug*, though to Charlotte it was medication.

She dipped her finger inside the bag and inhaled the powder. Within a few moments, the Dust reached her brain.

Charlotte closed her eyes, inhaled the smog, and allowed herself to *be*. These moments were few and far between—so she indulged herself, relishing in the feeling of Dust flowing through her veins.

She was fine. *Everything* was fine. She was going to be Paired with the best possible option, she would be admitted into High Society. She was almost there.

Her mind was clear and sharp, her body ready for anything.

"Hey, you! What are you doing out of the Academy?"

There was a reason she never basked in the relief of Dust. She'd failed to hear the tap of approaching shoes on the dry cobblestone.

A rookie mistake.

A patrol officer—one of the workers tasked with keeping all Ignis' teenagers where they were supposed to be—hurried toward her, having recognized Charlotte's blue vest, identifying her as a student of the Academy.

She looked down the other alley, but it was no use—the officer's eyes widened in recognition. Running would only hurt her.

"You're Two's daughter!" he exclaimed, confirming Charlotte's fears. "Charlotte's sister!"

He only saw what he wanted to see. What made *sense*.

Charlotte had spent enough time during her seventeen years searching for imperfections in the mirror to know exactly what the rest of the world saw when they looked at her.

It wasn't the deep ocean-blue, cat-like eyes that saw everything. It wasn't her orangish-brown hair that fell just past her pointy shoulders in a perfect wave. It wasn't the freckles that dotted her slightly turned up button-nose and her heart-shaped face.

It was her points. It was the way she carried her lithe frame—gracefully, her hands always folded, her posture always impeccable. Not just to make up for the fact that she was a few inches shorter than most women. Charlotte was the epitome of grace.

She'd never been caught with food on her face, even when she was a baby.

Which was exactly why—though Charlotte hated herself for it —she slouched and loosened her stiff joints before the officer could see *any* of it. Before he could realize that she wasn't who he thought she was.

Charlotte's elegance was absorbed into the dry air, as if it had never been there to begin with.

The reason *Charlotte Galvin* had never been caught was because her identical twin sister, *Zandra Galvin,* was the troublemaker.

"Please don't tell anyone," Charlotte said, deepening her voice in the way that Zandra spoke, "I was just taking a walk to clear my head, with Pairing so close."

The officer didn't budge, though his tone was kind. "Rules are there for a reason, Miss Galvin." Running into Charlotte's "delinquent twin" would be the highlight of this man's career. "You should be more like your sister."

If only. She'd give an arm and leg to be rid of the pressure that plagued her. Zandra didn't have to make choices—she would be given two potential Pairs to choose between, and one of them would be the man she would be with for the rest of her life.

Charlotte was going to have to choose while thousands of eyes scrutinized her every move, waiting for her to make a mistake. She was going to have to navigate the manipulation that came with her title, all while being a role model for younger women, shaped and designed by Ignis' leadership, The Council.

The Dust dulled the dread that this reminder usually wrought in her, keeping her mind focused on the task.

Getting out of this.

"Are you going to deduct points?"

The bag of Dust felt heavy in her pocket. Would he search her? Did he have reason to? Did he know that Dust dealers ran rampant through the streets between the male and female Academies?

"Actions have consequences," he replied. Charlotte's stomach sank.

"I'm so close to Pairing," Charlotte pleaded, "I'm on the verge of getting to choose between two options. *Please* don't do this."

Charlotte searched the guard's face—

He's starstruck.

"I'll tell my mom," she promised, "That you helped me."

Charlotte clenched her hands behind her back, hoping this man's ambitions were greater than his honor.

He hesitated for only a moment, before whatever future he'd envisioned was overpowered by his rational sense of duty. Charlotte would've respected it had it not directly impacted her. "I'm afraid I can't do that. Rules are rules. Fifty point deduction."

No.

Fifty points meant that Zandra would most certainly not get to choose between two Pairs. She'd be *assigned* one with no say in the matter.

That was what Charlotte was subjecting her sister to.

Charlotte had kept track of every single point that she had lost on behalf of her twin. And—Charlotte was the only one who knew this, because Zandra certainly wasn't counting—those points would have been the difference between Zandra being a Mid-Pointer, with several potential Pairs, and a Low-Pointer.

Though it would have been a lot for Zandra, Charlotte would still be in the lead without them. The Highest Pointer, though nowhere near the highest of *all time*.

Guilt ate at Charlotte's heart, but it was dulled enough by the Dust for her to think rationally.

"Please," Charlotte begged, "I'll do community service. I'll—"

"You'll empty your pockets."

He knows there's Dust around these parts.

Most teens didn't even know about Dust's existence. Ignis couldn't advertise the punishment for Dust if Dust didn't exist. How many points would get deducted?

Enough that they might figure out I'm not Zandra.

That wasn't to say that Charlotte *hadn't* been discovered with Dust before. Back when she was thirteen. Her mother had been able to cover it before news had gotten out. She'd believed it to be a one time thing, and had managed to get *Zandra* off with a warning.

That situation hadn't involved a patrol officer like this, though. If she spilled it out in her pocket, would the Dust dissipate into the air, lost to the smog?

The bag would give her away.

She needed to think like a Low-Pointer. No, not just any Low-Pointer.

Like her *sister.*

Charlotte met the officer's impatient gaze. She stuck her hands in her pockets, gripped the Dust...

And tripped over her own feet.

Charlotte broke the fall with her left hand, dropping the Dust with her other. Before the officer could react, she bounced back up, making sure to crunch the Dust under her right shoe, obscuring it from sight.

"Are you—?" the officer exclaimed.

"Fine, fine," Charlotte assured him, wiping the grime off her hands before turning her pockets inside out. "I just want to get back."

Her left hand was a bit scratched up, but she was otherwise unscathed. A small price to pay.

The officer nodded. "C'mon," he said, putting a gentle but firm grip on her shoulder and steering her back toward the Academy.

"Don't touch me. I know the way."

To her relief, the officer obeyed.

Charlotte made sure he was looking ahead before she took her foot off the Dust. She felt ill leaving it behind, especially after how much she had just spent on it. But there was nothing else she could do. And even though her soul mourned, her head told her she was lucky.

She should be grateful. *Should* be.

But Charlotte could never bring herself to do it. She could only acknowledge that she had what everyone else coveted.

Because, no matter how hard she tried, Charlotte Galvin was *not* grateful, and she doubted she ever would be.

2

Charlotte was escorted into the Academy's auditorium, where the rest of her class was gathering. In a few short minutes, the hundreds of students would be paraded over to Phoenix Square, where Charlotte would be honored before the nation as the Highest Academic Pointer.

Like the rest of the Academy, the auditorium was pristine and intricate—too nice and well-maintained for immature teenagers.

For others, it would have been easy to get lost in the crowd. To be just another face amongst peers.

Not Charlotte. No one openly stared, but plenty of people went out of their way to *not* look at her.

Let them look, her Dust-filled mind dared. A thought that wouldn't have appeared in her mind had she not been under the influence.

Glances were not what she needed. She had taken on something between her own body language and Zandra's, wearing it like armor. An in-between so people couldn't be quite sure which she was.

It only took a few moments to find her sister.

Zandra hated crowds. She hated anything that made her feel contained. She slouched against the wall of the auditorium, her eyes—usually glazed, as she was often in her own world—searched for Charlotte.

The easiest way to differentiate the twins after their posture was their hair. While Charlotte kept hers calm, Zandra's was an untamed mane of orange, presenting a lion-like appearance. Charlotte had attempted to mess hers up during the walk back, though it still wasn't quite as rabid as Zandra's.

The only difference that the twins had found in their appearances was the small mole that rested to the right of Zandra's belly button.

Zandra brightened when she met Charlotte's gaze. While it would have only taken Charlotte a heartbeat to notice the facade, Zandra wasn't as quick on her feet. She was already halfway to Charlotte when she straightened her back and combed a hand through her hair, sliding her signature shark tooth necklace beneath her shirt.

"We only have a minute before our names are called," Zandra whispered as she reached Charlotte.

Charlotte nodded. They headed toward the bathroom, where they could "change back" without prying eyes.

The stalls in the bathroom were individual rooms. No chance of being overheard as Charlotte closed the door behind them. "I'm *so* sorry. I lost you some points—"

"You're okay though, right?"

She didn't even *know* what Charlotte had done. How did Zandra care about Charlotte's emotional state over herself? Over her own *future*?

"Yeah, but I—"

"It's fine." Zandra was genuine, but Charlotte always wished that Zandra was half as furious as Charlotte was with herself. It would be much easier if the anger came from an external source.

"I get it. I've wandered off campus, like, a million times without even knowing."

Charlotte would never tell her. She couldn't bear the shame of Zandra knowing that she'd lost multiple potential Pairs to Charlotte's Dust habit.

"But I shouldn't have—"

"You know I don't care about points."

"But *I* do!"

Just not enough to actually take responsibility, a voice whispered in the abyss of Charlotte's mind.

"Exactly," responded Zandra, "So it works out perfectly."

While Charlotte's actions showed she cared more about points than Zandra, Zandra's proved the opposite.

Maybe it isn't true. Maybe the evidence was wrong—

But you don't act that way, the voice continued. Charlotte muted it.

"So it's all good," Zandra concluded.

"It isn't *good*. You're only going to have one Pair."

"Whatever." Zandra seemed so unconcerned that, for once, Charlotte wasn't envious.

She was *too* unconcerned.

A pit formed in Charlotte's stomach. They only had two days left, so Charlotte swallowed her trepidation and finally chose to address what she'd been too terrified to acknowledge. "You aren't thinking of going Unruly, are you?"

Zandra shrugged, and the blood drained from Charlotte's face. Deep down, Charlotte had suspected that Zandra didn't plan on getting Paired. But she'd been too terrified to acknowledge it—like if she ignored it, it would disappear.

She'd been naive to think that.

"Let's just see what Lynx says today," Zandra said, her voice emphasizing the name with a hint of excitement.

Lynx. The woman who would honor Charlotte with her

award today. Zandra's best friend until Lynx had graduated last year.

If going Unruly could be *called* graduating.

"You can't," Charlotte said, "If it's to get into High Society, there are *better* ways—"

"Forget I said anything," Zandra mumbled with a glassy look in her eyes, "I'm not actually gonna do it." She paused. "Probably."

Zandra could shut her up by going for the jugular. By saying that Charlotte had left her with no option. That it was *Charlotte's* fault with all the points she'd lost. But Zandra never stooped low.

Sometimes Charlotte thought her own perfect posture was to make up for the fact that she *always* stooped.

If Zandra "went Unruly," she would only have one chance to win her way back to freedom.

Why does Zandra have to make things so difficult?

Charlotte reverted to her usual self as she stepped out of the stall, the Dust quelling thoughts of Unruly from her mind.

The walk from the Academy to Phoenix Square wasn't far through the vendor-filled narrow streets. Ignis loved an event— the ceremony marked the commencement of a three-day holiday, *Pairing Season Commencement.* It was a holiday filled with gossip, betting, and entertainment.

Charlotte was the main attraction.

As the students paraded the streets in a jumbled line, she noticed the craning necks of the civilians.

They were looking for *her.*

The few eyes she met widened just before the jaws dropped. Charlotte offered each a polite, grateful smile, as fake as Charlotte's perceived flawlessness.

Zandra didn't notice the stares. She softly hummed to herself, glancing between the sky and the windows above. This street was home to shops on the ground floors, apartments for former High-Pointers above.

As Charlotte had suspected, most of the smog had burned off, making way for the unforgiving sun to beat upon them. Sweat dripped down Charlotte's back, beneath her blazer.

Her heart rate increased. *No one can see it,* Charlotte told herself, *The blazer is dark. You're fine.*

Charlotte's best friend, fellow High-Pointer Jayana Triller, fell in line beside her as they reached the square.

"This is my favorite spot in Ignis," Jayana declared, her lilting voice clear, "And soon we're going to see it every day."

Jayana had the second most points of their class. Like Charlotte, she would have a dozen potential Pairs to choose from.

Points weren't the only reason Jayana would be a sought-after Pair. Jayana was extroverted, smart, an interesting conversationalist—and beautiful. Her large brown eyes rested the perfect distance between her arched eyebrows and raven-black hair. She was several inches taller than Charlotte and Zandra, with a perfect body type.

Best of all, she was reliable. A reliable friend, with a reliable head on her shoulders.

Unlike me. Charlotte was reliable on paper only.

The land *was* beautiful—it sloped downward, dissolving into a cliff to the west, offering a stunning view of the Pacific Ocean. To the east spread Phoenix Gardens, a sprawling hundred-acre field of hedged labyrinths, stone statues, and glinting fountains.

But neither the ocean nor the gardens were the most entrancing view. In front of the students, beyond the clearing where Ignis' entire population currently gathered, was Phoenix Palace.

Or, as Charlotte would be calling it in two days, when the Top Twenty High-Pointers moved inside to get Paired, *home.*

The palace was an impenetrable fortress, having been

constructed completely of marble. It was almost too bright to look at—Charlotte squinted past the columns into the glass windows, trying to catch a glimpse of what her future held.

She saw nothing except the reflection of the square.

"It's going to be weird, personally knowing the speaker," Jayana whispered. Charlotte's blood froze. She glanced over at Zandra, hoping that her sister hadn't heard.

Unfortunately, the word *speaker* snapped Zandra back into reality, wide eyes fixed on Jayana. "I didn't know you two were friends."

"Well...more like acquaintances. It'll be interesting to see how Unruly changed her."

The only reason Lynx wasn't still banished on the Island of Unruly was because she'd won the singular annual ticket off of Unruly, *the Conquest*.

"It *won't* have," Zandra insisted.

"Zandra—" Charlotte warned.

"She's not going to do it."

"Zandra. Stop," Charlotte ordered.

The presenter of the Academic Award was always the winner of last year's Conquest, delivering the same message: *do not go Unruly*.

Lynx would do the same, warning all the soon-to-be graduates about Unruly from the palace's second floor balcony.

"Well you knew her better than I did, so I shall defer to you," Jayana said. She entertained Zandra despite Zandra's Low-Pointer status, though Charlotte was never sure if it was just because Zandra was Charlotte's twin.

Charlotte barely remembered Lynx from the Academy, communicating with her only when she'd needed to corral Zandra to class. Charlotte condemned the Unruly as much as the next Ignite, but no one knew what went on there—and if the Council decided Lynx had redeemed herself, who was Charlotte to disagree?

The women from the Academy gathered into their designated area, blocked off from the male students who were marching in to their right. The rest of the people gathered behind them.

Charlotte wedged between Jayana and Zandra. All that was left to do was *not think*. To not think about why this event in particular was so anxiety-provoking.

Yet, Charlotte couldn't stop herself from looking in the direction of the boys, trying to find the source of her unease. Maybe if she saw him first, his nearness would be less painful.

It didn't take her long to find him. She'd recognize that deep laugh anywhere. Charlotte's gaze followed the sound—there he was, his eyes squinted in amusement.

His shoulders were broader, arms more toned than when she'd last seen him. Despite that, he was the same.

A sour taste filled Charlotte's mouth.

Harris Alder. Charlotte's ex-best friend. The reason Charlotte no longer trusted *anyone*.

Avoiding Harris hadn't been a problem before now. The Academies never interacted, and were located on opposite sides of Phoenix Palace. With the exception of the occasional formal event—like this—they lived completely separate lives. She had always kept private tabs on him, of course, but they had never actually interacted.

Until today.

Charlotte had only seen him from afar three times in the past four years. Today, she would be forced to stand by his side as they both accepted their respective Highest Academic Pointer awards.

She would get through it. She was a professional.

Zandra must have followed Charlotte's glare. "I can't believe you have to go up with *him*."

Zandra had no idea what had happened between her and

Harris. She just knew that one day, Charlotte had decided she hated him. And Zandra was loyal to a fault—when Charlotte said she didn't want to explain, Zandra simply saw that he had hurt Charlotte, which labeled him *the enemy*.

"It's fine. I've dealt with worse."

"Still, *I* don't like it."

Charlotte just gave her twin a small smile, one that held no mirth, as she cast Harris from her mind, focusing on Zandra's wide eyes instead.

But Zandra didn't summon pleasant thoughts either. How could Zandra forgive her when Charlotte couldn't forgive Harris? And how could Charlotte forgive herself when she knew that she'd do it all over again, even with the guilt?

A trumpet played, signifying the beginning of the ceremony.

While everyone else sat, Charlotte stood, making her way toward the sectional dividing the Academies.

She hadn't realized just how difficult it would be to walk toward the person she hated most.

3

Charlotte avoided Harris' eyes—she didn't want to be forced into small talk as they journeyed to the balcony. She was acutely aware of the space his body inhabited. He was *actually there*, in the flesh.

She was glad he would see how well she was doing after all these years. How many points she had, how much the people loved her...

Did she *want* to interact into him?

It didn't matter that her persona didn't match her feelings, so long as he only saw the picture she had painted.

When she stole a glance, Harris was staring.

"Hi," he said, falling in step with her. His voice had changed, now a rich baritone. One that Charlotte couldn't help but listen to. But his dark hazel eyes and defined features were just as Charlotte remembered, only now more mature. He was on the shorter side, just as he had been his whole life, though still taller than Charlotte.

Charlotte offered a polite smile, surprised by the raw pain in seeing him. Her limbs felt heavy, physically feeling the rift. How could she feel so close yet so far from him at the same time? How could she want to speak with him and want to run at the same time?

Charlotte pushed it beneath the surface, making sure it didn't show.

"How have you been?" he asked warmly. It was a ruse. It *had* to have been.

"Well." She didn't reciprocate the question.

"You look well."

What was she supposed to say to someone who had known everything about her until just a few short years ago?

She said nothing.

They started up the center aisle toward the balcony, shoulder to shoulder. Harris cracked his knuckles as they ascended—a nervous tick. Never a good habit when everyone was judging every move. He should have ridden himself of it by now.

"Well, congratulations," he tried again, "You've been doing... great."

Charlotte kept her gaze ahead, used to flattery. People just told her what she wanted to hear. If she let her guard down and believed them, she was bound to make a mistake.

Harris had already shown his true colors, and Charlotte never made the same mistake twice. She didn't fall for the sincerity in his words, despite knowing he would gain nothing from it—even if they were potential Pairs, she would not be speaking to him on any of their outings in Phoenix Palace.

"Thank you." The few trickles she gave him threatened to open the floodgates. But she couldn't confide her worries to him like she used to.

"You're going to find yourself a great Pair."

Charlotte held back a scoff. The reason Harris had as many points as he did was because he had been hoping, until their falling out, anyway—that he would be Paired with Charlotte. It had been the unspoken tension of their friendship, one that Charlotte never addressed because she'd never reciprocated the sentiment.

"I'm sure you will too," she managed, speaking only because there were people watching his lips form words, while hers remained pursed.

"Or maybe something even better."

What did *that* mean? Before Charlotte could ask, they reached the base of the stairs. Harris took a step back, allowing her to rise first.

It irked her more than she cared to admit.

Charlotte wandered into her maze of thoughts as she ascended, despite the numbness of the Dust. She was grateful for its soothing affect, and didn't dare to imagine her state if she hadn't gotten a fix.

But since I'm thinking about it, does that mean that the Dust is wearing off? What if I needed to—

Charlotte's spiral was interrupted by the speaker of the event sweeping through the balcony's double doors.

Lynx Hillenbrand.

There was a moment of silence as Phoenix Square held its breath, taking Lynx in. This year's prodigal daughter of Ignis.

Even Charlotte was breathless. She was not at all what Charlotte remembered. The only ghost of her awkward teen self was her frenetic walk.

Lynx stood in an emerald silk gown that exposed her muscular shoulders, bare and obscured only by the few sandy strands of hair that fell from her up-do. There was a carelessness to it that Charlotte found perplexing—surely her stylist could have fixed it before she stepped forward. Was it purposeful? Was there still a hint of the rebellious nature that landed her on Unruly running through her veins? Had the Island of Unruly been so physically challenging that she'd put on that much muscle? Or had she been training since joining High Society?

Cheers and applause came a moment later. Lynx's wide green eyes barely squinted as her straight teeth flashed. The smile didn't reach her eyes, and didn't make her young heart-shaped face wrinkle.

Surprising Charlotte even *further* was the woman who flanked Lynx. Though the woman tried to remain inconspicuous, it was impossible with her built six-plus foot stature.

Five. The fifth member of the Council, and the fifth most powerful person in all of Ignis.

Charlotte and Five had known each other at the Academy, years before the nineteen-year-old woman had been Paired two seasons ago. As fellow High-Pointers, they had run in the same circles.

It was strange that Five was there—she was the Council member in charge of Pairing, and would be the chaperone of the High-Pointers who would be living in Phoenix Palace until they found their Pairs, but she didn't usually lead any events until the Season Opener.

Five's less-than-appealing face frowned upon Charlotte. Her left eye was slightly lower than her right, her forehead an odd shape, her nose crooked. But despite her looks, she carried herself with the confidence that only someone with more power than everyone else combined could muster.

Five made every person on the balcony look weak, which was impressive considering Lynx looked as if she could hold her own against the for-show-only guards. But Five...Five may have been the strongest woman—if not *person*—in all of Ignis.

Five tore her gaze away from Charlotte, fixing it upon Lynx, staring at her with something like pride. Something else was going on that Charlotte didn't yet have the information to explain.

"Thank you," Lynx's voice echoed through the square, "It's an honor to be here, speaking to all you wonderful people."

Charlotte glanced into the crowd, finding Zandra amongst their peers. Even from the distance, Charlotte could see Zandra's confusion in her clenched jaw. This was clearly *not* the Lynx that Zandra remembered.

"I'm here to address all of you, and but mostly those of you about to embark on your Pairing journeys, including the two outstanding students standing beside me."

This isn't even the Lynx I remember. Charlotte intellectually decided she hated this new Lynx, though her heart wasn't quite sold yet.

"I took the difficult road to Princeps. I urge you not to do the same. I'm speaking to those of you thinking of joining Unruly."

The commencement speech was always the same—and this year would be no different, despite what Zandra believed.

"Don't," Lynx advised. "You know I went Unruly. I thought I had it all figured out. Pairing felt like a cage, so I chose the only other path."

Another drop of water slipped down Charlotte's back as she found Zandra—her sister's jaw was unhinged, hanging on every word.

"But it was a hard, brutal experience—one that I needed in order to repent. And yes, I survived. But I almost didn't. Most *don't*. I thought I was choosing freedom, but really I was choosing *pain.*"

A baby cried, echoing through the square.

"The Council was gracious enough to forgive my sins. I got lucky," Lynx continued, "There are easier ways. Better ways. Pairing is going to happen. And even if you think you don't want it now, I promise you...you will regret it if you don't choose it. *Pairing* is freedom, not Unruly."

Humanity's future depended on Pairing and procreating since

the Destruction, when the nuclear war had all but destroyed the human race.

"So learn from my mistakes, and if you want to join High Society, take advantage of the yearly opportunities."

To Lynx's left, Five nodded.

"Before our ceremony begins, an update on the threat from the Union," Lynx continued.

The Union had been advancing for years, trying to claim Ignis' land as their own, since most habitable places had been ruined in the Destruction. Thankfully, Ignis had the military backing of the Nation of Luxor to keep them at bay.

"They are closer than ever, but our combined effort with Luxor is holding them off."

Murmuring.

"But enough of that," Lynx said, "Now I would like to present the young man and woman who finished their tenure at the Academy with the Highest Academic Points."

Charlotte fought the urge to straighten her uniform. She hadn't looked in the mirror since the bathroom with Zandra. Was it wrinkled? What if she flashed her scratched hand and the Academy Guard was watching? What if—?

"Please welcome Charlotte Galvin and Harris Alder."

The applause was deafening as she stepped out of the shadows, Harris at her side. Despite her worries, Charlotte was well-trained for the spotlight, having learned how to woo a crowd before she could walk.

The thousands of eyes didn't bother her. She was used to it. It was the powerful individuals ahead who created the pit of nerves in her stomach. A million people couldn't equal the powerful enigma of Lynx.

The sweat hit the small of her back.

Charlotte met Lynx's stare. Now that she was closer, Charlotte could make out each individual ring of Lynx's seaweed-green eyes, striking beneath her thick eyebrows. Her long nose was slightly crooked, but it suited her in a way that Charlotte couldn't explain. Like if it weren't crooked, she'd look *too* perfect.

It took Charlotte several long, uncomfortable seconds to pull her gaze away.

"Hey," Lynx said, holding the microphone away from her mouth. Charlotte almost flinched at the informality.

Making up for Lynx's causality, Charlotte replied, "Greetings."

Lynx smiled. This one crept to her eyes, though Charlotte couldn't believe it was genuine.

"Hello, Five. Lynx," Harris said, stepping beside Charlotte. Charlotte and Harris bowed in unison, as was required of citizens of Ignis to do when greeting members of High Society. Charlotte despised how easily they fell back into sync.

Lynx bowed in return, an optional gesture that members of High Society only gave as a sign of respect. Charlotte tried not to be flattered by it and failed.

"I hope you're well, Charlotte," Five said, not bowing. Likely compensating for her age, flaunting her power and letting all of Ignis know that she bowed for no one.

To Charlotte, it reeked of insecurity.

"And you, Five."

Lynx gestured them forward, putting a hand on each of their shoulders, and turned them toward the crowd. Charlotte swallowed the urge to shrug her off.

"Charlotte and Harris, High Society hopes to reward your hard work with a suitable Pair." Lynx said before passing the microphone to Charlotte.

"Thank you," Charlotte said, her voice rich, powerful, and confident as it reverberated through the square. "I'm honored to accept this award, and am eagerly anticipating Pairing."

It was polished. Uncontroversial. Normal. Boring, even to Charlotte.

But she didn't need to be anything except what was expected. Any rebellion they were craving they received from the mere existence of Zandra.

Charlotte glanced at her sister in the crowd. She did not applaud along with the masses.

Zandra was sad. Sad for *her*.

If only she knew what it was like to be the best. Then she would understand. She would realize that it was worth it.

Because it *was*.

…Wasn't it?

Yes. Charlotte would die on that sword. *And you won't worry about the fact that you doubted it, because that is your anxiety tricking you.*

Charlotte took a half-step back, allowing Harris to take the spotlight. The people weren't nearly as thrilled to see him.

"Fellow Ignites," he said, the microphone just a little too close to his mouth, "I am grateful for the opportunity to speak to all of you today."

Polished. Uncontroversial—

"Because I've had something on my mind that I've been wanting to share for a while now."

Abnormal. Riveting.

The crowd snapped to attention.

"I've been wondering. For a while. About why things are the way they are. And I'm going to find out."

The silence that met his words was deafening. Before Charlotte could stop herself, she calmly wrested the microphone from his hands and handed it to Lynx.

Harris knew that a mistake on the balcony could be the difference between multiple high-quality Pairs in Phoenix Palace and a few mediocre choices.

So *why*? Why sabotage himself like this?

As her mind raced and the silence morphed into murmurs, Charlotte pasted a disappointed expression on her face.

"Thank you all," Lynx finished, unperturbed by Harris' words. "And congratulations to Charlotte and Harris."

Five turned to Harris as trumpets boomed through the air. "A word."

She swept for the balcony entrance. Harris shot Charlotte an apprehensive look—which Charlotte did not return—before following.

"Well, that was interesting," Lynx murmured to Charlotte.

"And uncalled for."

Lynx studied her. Charlotte's skin prickled. "It doesn't seem right that you can't go inside the palace yet."

"Soon enough, assuming I hold onto my ranking."

Lynx tilted her head. It was almost impossible for her to lose her ranking, but her points wouldn't be locked in—and frozen forever—until the Season Opener.

She glanced at Harris out of the corner of her eye as he was scolded by Five.

"You really don't loosen up, do you, Charlotte?"

Charlotte's blood cooled, caught so off-guard that she wondered if she'd imagined Lynx's words. A thousand replies circled through her Dust-filled brain—

"That hardly seems like a fair question to ask of someone you barely know." Harris interrupted as he approached, thoroughly reprimanded by Five.

Charlotte's irritation grew, though her voice remained even. "I merely say what needs to be said, and nothing more."

"Touché," Lynx said, a hint of amusement in her voice. Lynx was *enjoying* this. "Tell Zandra I give her my best." She bowed low, her face close as she whispered, quiet enough that Harris wouldn't hear, "And tell her to keep the course."

Then Lynx strutted away until she was swallowed by Phoenix Palace, her dress billowing behind her.

Charlotte stared in silence, heart racing. *Keep the course?* What the hell did *that* mean?

Keep fantasizing about Unruly?

No. Lynx meant Pairing. She had just given an entire speech on it.

"That was...strange," noted Harris as they walked back toward the staircase.

Curiosity prickled in her gut—what was his game? But she would die before she let Harris think that she cared about anything to do with him.

Because I don't.

At the top of the staircase, Charlotte stopped. They were *much* steeper than she remembered. An image flashed of her tripping over her own feet and pummeling to her death.

Vertigo overtook her. It took all of Charlotte's willpower not to grip the railing.

Don't let anyone see. You're fine.

"Are you alright?" Harris asked, because of *course* he knew Charlotte was terrified of heights.

"*Fine.*" And, though they both knew she was lying, Charlotte said, "I just—I was thinking about how much Zandra would love the view up here."

Harris knew better than to argue as Charlotte carefully descended.

"Charlotte, I—"

Charlotte raised her hand for silence and stepped off the staircase. At ease now that she was on solid ground, she said, "Goodbye, Harris."

He knew better than to pursue her. Once again, Harris was gone from Charlotte's life. And she was better for it, despite the unexplainable desire to turn around and see if he was still standing there, waiting.

She repressed it, as she did with all uncomfortable feelings.

People were already dispersing, heading home to gossip with their Pairs about the upcoming Pairing Season.

It didn't take long to find Zandra standing with their mother, Imogen, and their father, Lawrence.

"You good?" Zandra asked. Charlotte nodded—and flashed a look that read *not now*.

Then she turned to Imogen, who she hadn't seen in a few months.

Charlotte and Zandra didn't look like either of their parents, but Charlotte certainly carried herself like Imogen did. Like *she* was in charge.

In Imogen's case, she *was*. Because Imogen was Two.

That was as similar as Charlotte wanted them to be.

Imogen turned her pointed nose—the only feature she and her daughters shared—toward Charlotte and smiled warmly. Charlotte didn't trust it.

Imogen was taller than both her daughters, with almost-black hair that Charlotte suspected was dyed, a narrow face, and a jawline that was sharper than her own tongue. She was a stunning woman, with an edge that warned she was not to be trifled with.

"Well done, Charlotte," Imogen murmured.

"Uh-huh." There was no one within earshot, so she allowed her facade to fall, "I got up on a balcony and waved like a show pony. It's almost like I've been practicing my whole life. Oh, wait."

"Well, I'm proud of you," Lawrence said. Charlotte nodded. She had nothing against her father, though she didn't feel particularly close to him either.

Zandra snorted, not quite holding in her laughter.

Imogen inhaled to protest, but a Pair from High Society interrupted their privacy, their status easy to determine with their loud jewelry, experimental fashion, and haughty expressions.

"You have quite a dynamo there, Two," the woman said. Charlotte snapped back into *Highest Pointer* mode and gave a grateful bow.

"She'll certainly get her pick of the Pairs," the man echoed.

"Thank you," Imogen replied.

With Imogen, Charlotte was a prized jewel rather than a human being. It was just one of the many reasons Charlotte despised her.

"Honestly, they should just ferry her over to Princeps right now," the woman continued. Charlotte grimaced—now she was *cargo*.

"You are very kind," Imogen said. She glanced at Charlotte out of the corner of her eye.

You're being rude. Charlotte could practically read her mother's thoughts. It was irrelevant that she hadn't been directly addressed. Not to mention that these snooty people hadn't acknowledged Zandra *at all*.

Sometimes remaining silent was the bravest thing of all.

But Charlotte wasn't brave. Not at all. "I hope to see you there."

Then they were gone.

"Hope to see you there, too!" Zandra called the moment they were out of earshot. Charlotte chuckled.

"Hush," Imogen scolded, making Charlotte and Zandra laugh harder.

"'She is quite the specimen,'" Zandra mocked.

"'Yes, but her identical on the other hand...'" Charlotte added.

"'Disgusting. An abomination.'"

"'Are you sure they're related?'"

"'Two, you should really fix that one,'" Zandra laughed, pointing at herself.

How Zandra felt comfortable enough around Imogen to speak with her that way, Charlotte didn't know. Imogen would never tolerate that kind of behavior from Charlotte.

But for Zandra, Imogen just looked mildly amused. "Let's go home before someone hears you two."

Charlotte wondered which was worse—having a mother who cared so much that she showed no love or a mother who cared so little that no matter what was done, her attention would never be captured.

Imogen won't protect her, Charlotte thought, *Zandra can't know what Lynx said. She's too close to choosing Unruly.*

The next time she saw Phoenix Palace, she would be allowed inside.

It didn't feel real. Maybe it wasn't—because Charlotte couldn't help but feel that something was going to go terribly wrong and keep her from it.

Was everyone else thinking that way? Charlotte glanced at the happy, laughing teens chattering about who their upcoming Pairs would be. Why couldn't she be excited like them?

And, not for the first and surely not the last time, Charlotte craved the reprieve of normalcy.

4

Zandra Galvin wondered what it must've been like to be normal.

She certainly wasn't it. But what even *was* normal? Was it just some subjective measure of a lack of oddity? Were normal people content? Did they enjoy what they had and not want more?

She didn't *want* to be normal—she was simply curious. It must've felt comfortable, like a house warmed by a crackling fireplace. But it wasn't for her—whenever Zandra was stuck in a place for too long, she felt suffocated.

That was what *normal* would look like on her.

As she walked *home*—as much as her parents' mansion in central Ignis could be considered home after twelve years at the Academy, during which only one month was spent there—she reminded herself that there was no one she'd rather be than her strange self.

Because, for the first time *ever*, Zandra had doubts.

What had Lynx been through? What kind of horrors awaited on Unruly? What exactly had she said to Charlotte?

Lynx just said that because she had to. This changes nothing.

She'd expected to get more information from Lynx's speech. Like a message. Or a sign.

But she'd gotten nothing.

Not that Zandra *was* going Unruly...though she couldn't deny the allure. She'd planned on going, winning the Conquest and joining Charlotte in High Society. Even though Zandra despised High Society.

Since she and Charlotte were High Society offspring, they'd spent their early childhood on Princeps, the luxurious island reserved specifically for High Society's people. Then, at five, they'd been shipped off to the mainland's Academy, never to return to Princeps again unless they earned their own way back.

Zandra didn't rely on her memory when it came to Princeps. Her recollections tainted and morphed every time someone spread another rumor about what Princeps held.

She recalled bright, glinting buildings and cobblestone streets, but whenever she focused on something specific, she felt as if she were sticking her hand into a pond full of fish. Just when she was about to grasp one, it slipped between her fingers, making her wonder if she'd been close to capturing it at all.

She could only confidently recollect the bunk bed she'd shared with Charlotte in their parents' mansion. Zandra had told Charlotte, who hated heights, "Bunk beds were made for us. So we can both be comfortable without having to be apart."

They made pillow forts on the bottom. They whispered secrets to each other late into the night. Sometimes Charlotte would stick two pencils with giant eyeball erasers that she had won at a carnival up to Zandra's bed to scare her.

The only thing that wasn't perfect was Harris. He'd never invited her on his and Charlotte's excursions, until Zandra stopped asking to be included all together.

Charlotte still hadn't even *mentioned* their falling out. It was the only thing Zandra didn't know about Charlotte. Thank you very much, Harris.

Princeps had been her normal back then. But when they moved to Ignis and kids at the Academy learned that Zandra and Charlotte had "grown up" there, they wanted to know what it was like. Only they didn't ask—they *told*. *What was Candy-land like? How many giants live there? Did you ever go down the slide from the top of the mountain into the ocean?*

And within a few years, the foundation of Zandra's childhood memories was shaken.

Zandra and Charlotte weren't the only kids from Princeps, but the fact that there were two of them made them peculiar. Some of the kids thought that one of them was a clone. Or that one of them wasn't real. The loss of individuality and taste of celebrity had launched Charlotte's obsession with becoming the Highest Pointer. Soon the twins were on different paths, and all Zandra had wanted was to go back to that bunk bed.

It wasn't Princeps she wanted back. It was her sister.

Zandra didn't just *want* to stay with Charlotte—Charlotte *needed* her. And, unless she miraculously convinced Charlotte to go Unruly with her, she only had two options.

Get Paired and live an unfulfilling life on Ignis, closed off to the majority of Charlotte's life since Zandra wouldn't have access to Princeps. Charlotte would have to visit *her*. And whenever Charlotte struggled, she didn't seek out support. If Zandra couldn't check on Charlotte, Charlotte would retreat into herself.

Or go Unruly and win a place in High Society via the Conquest.

Though Zandra didn't think the rumors about Unruly—or Lynx's words, for that matter—were true, she doubted it was paradise.

But what could be worse than a lifetime of wondering if she had missed out on something better?

Of course, if she didn't win the Conquest, she would be stuck on Unruly—just as she was stuck in Ignis—for an indefinite amount of time, and she might not see Charlotte for years.

Or ever again.

Who would look after Charlotte if Zandra were gone? The random man Charlotte got Paired with wouldn't even *know* he had to. Charlotte certainly wouldn't let Imogen either, and their clueless father didn't even notice when Charlotte got so anxious that her skin turned blue.

"It'll be nice to have you both home for a few days," Imogen said as they approached their mansion that was only occupied during the few months the twins were home.

No one in Ignis was destitute, but former Low-Pointers—people who had been like Zandra—lived in tiny houses, with just enough food to feed them for that day, and only what they needed to survive. High Society made sure that they were taken care of, though they rotated between the same two dull outfits.

But Ignis was not like the Union, where half the population lived in old disease-ridden shipping crates. Because there was no Pairing, most of the population was *Impaired*. The other half was enlisted in the military that was actively attacking Ignis.

Pairing and The Council of Five had saved Ignis from poverty and sickness. Ignis was slowly rebuilding the population, saving humanity by ensuring that its people genetically *couldn't* get sick.

So why did Zandra hate Ignis so much?

"Uh-huh," Charlotte grunted to their mother.

"I'm looking forward to it," Zandra chimed, trying and failing to ease the tension. She grabbed Charlotte's wrist after Imogen and Lawrence disappeared into the house. "Did Lynx say anything to you?"

"What do you mean?"

"Anything interesting?" Zandra paused. "Anything for me?"

"No. I'm sorry."

Zandra felt stupid. "All good, it's not your fault." She hurried away, through the foyer and up the marble staircase, stung that Lynx had passed up the chance to give her a message.

She rushed into the room she shared with Charlotte, the first door on the left. Even though the house had six bedrooms, she and Charlotte had always shared. Charlotte had night terrors and Zandra knew how to calm her without waking her.

Zandra dug for her notebook in her still-packed trunk from the Academy. The second she felt the coarse leather in her palm, she wrenched it out, spilling clothes all over the floor.

A pen was in her hand and a moment later she was scrawling on the first blank page she saw: *What happened to Lynx? What did they put her through to make her change her mind??*

Because they must have. Lynx had been as close a friend as Zandra'd had—and she'd promised she'd send Zandra a message, if she could. This had been her chance, and Lynx hadn't taken it.

Zandra stared at the page. She couldn't bring herself to write anything else. She wanted to think about something else.

A boy she'd passed on her way out of the square had mentioned a party. It had felt irrelevant, but maybe she should go. Give herself a break. Zandra sighed, ran her hands through her messy hair, and climbed up to her sanctuary—the roof.

Up here, the city surrounded her. Phoenix Palace loomed in the distance, and the ocean beyond it. She could see the tips of both the islands of Unruly and Princeps at the edge of the horizon.

As the sun dyed the clouds a brilliant mosaic of pinks, reds, and purples, her gaze couldn't help but be seduced.

Princeps' tallest point held sophisticated buildings that Zandra could tell were intricate even from miles away. Its contrast to Unruly was almost laughable—the cliffs that peeked over the neighbors' rooftops were jagged, dark, and dangerous.

What adventures do you hold, mysterious cliffs?

Zandra had been coming up to the roof for years to think. Charlotte never joined due to her fear of heights—it was a place *just* for her.

Most of the time, anyway.

Imogen rarely joined her. She generally respected Zandra's space and thinking time, though she did make the occasional exception.

Like that evening.

"It's beautiful out here tonight," Imogen murmured, climbing out of the window of her study, the only place in the house that was always locked and off-limits to the twins.

"Yeah, I guess."

"Is it Pairing?" Imogen asked, immediately picking up on Zandra's sullen mood.

Zandra wasn't sure how to verbalize her thoughts. "I just...I wish I could freeze time. And stay like this forever."

"Stay unpaired?"

"Yeah. And with Charlotte."

Imogen knew about Zandra's Unruly obsession. Though Imogen was Two on the Council, she was the twins' mother first. She was trying to change things for the better.

She was one of the good guys.

"What do you *want* to do?"

"I want you to tell me what's there," Zandra complained. The Council knew what was on Unruly. "I won't spill, I swear on my life."

Imogen would lose all her power if she broke confidentiality, so she didn't.

But Zandra could keep a secret. She'd never told a soul that she'd taken Charlotte's point reductions for years.

But if they'd be safe on Unruly...it was why she swore on *her* own life only.

"And Charlotte's life?"

Not her twin's. That was an oath too serious to swear.

Charlotte wouldn't be happy Paired. She wouldn't be so afraid if she believed she'd be happy.

Imogen gave her a pointed look.

"It's not fair," said Zandra, "I'm going to get a lame Pair and never get to do anything I want to ever again."

Zandra wanted *more*. She wanted to see Luxor. She wanted to go out on the sea. She wanted to see the Barrenlands. She wanted to see Unruly. She wanted to write about them in her journal— what they must've looked like before the Destruction and what they'd look like after she was gone. She wanted to be able to sit in peace on this rooftop for as long as she wanted, letting her mind drift to places far away.

"Would I be happy on Unruly, Mom?" Zandra asked when all she got from Imogen was a stoic gaze into the distance.

Imogen's eyes rested on Unruly, her stare far and vacant. Her mind was working—making a decision.

After the longest few seconds of Zandra's life, Imogen said, "I think you can make yourself happy anywhere, Zandra. Because you make the best of everything."

Zandra's heart skipped a beat. That was the most she had ever gotten out of her mother, and she was determined not to move, breathe, or even think in case Imogen continued on.

When she did, Zandra almost gasped. "And I think that you're too special to be Paired with someone unworthy of you."

Was that it? Did Imogen *actually think* Zandra should go Unruly?

Imogen stood, squeezing Zandra's shoulder on the way up. "I love you, Zandra. And I'm proud of you."

"Thank you, Mom," Zandra whispered, sure she was dreaming, "I love you, too."

Imogen climbed back toward the window. Adrenaline flowed through Zandra's veins and into her heart. She needed to talk to

Charlotte. To tell her everything Imogen had just revealed. They could both go Unruly together.

"Your father made dinner. It'll be ready in a few minutes," Imogen said as she disappeared into her window.

Zandra looked toward Phoenix Palace and watched the sun get swallowed by the ocean. Tomorrow it would rise, Zandra would awaken and, for the first time ever, she would know what the future was going to hold.

Sort of.

Zandra made her way down to the chandelier-lit dining room, her spirits lifted.

Charlotte was already in her chair, staring blankly ahead as Zandra slipped into the seat beside her. Their parents' voices were muffled and indiscernible from the kitchen.

"I have an idea," Zandra announced.

"You always have an idea."

"It's gonna take you a minute to warm up to it, so can you just, like, be open?"

Charlotte raised her eyebrows, knowing what was coming.

"What if I told you that Unruly wasn't so bad? And that we could stay there together?"

"I'd tell you you were wrong. *And* crazy."

Zandra had gotten swept up in her emotions. Charlotte wasn't going to give up everything she had worked for just because she was nervous. "What—what if I told you I got inside information?"

"From whom? Lynx? Or our dear mother?"

"Do I need to get you proof?"

"No. Because you're not going to find any." Anxiety crept into Charlotte's voice. "Look, I know you're nervous about Pairing—"

"I'm not nervous," said Zandra, "You're the nervous one."

Charlotte scoffed. "Then you really are crazy."

"Gee, thanks."

"Zandra, nothing good happens on Unruly! You heard Lynx."

"She didn't mean that! Someone—someone *made* her. What did she say to you? I saw her at the end—"

"Do you hear yourself?"

"Mom told me—"

"Mom is Two!" Charlotte interrupted, "And she's your hero —which means if someone *made* Lynx say that, it was *Mom*."

"But Mom isn't *One*."

"Yet."

"If Mom *did* make Lynx say that—if she has that power— then she won't let anything bad happen to us on Unruly," Zandra pointed out.

Charlotte rolled her eyes. Zandra puffed out her chest, ready to defend their mother, but Charlotte cut her off. "You're not listening. I don't *want* to go Unruly. And you don't either."

"You don't know what I want."

Lawrence and Imogen entered with dinner, bringing the conversation to an abrupt halt.

"We have two daughters who are Academy graduates," Lawrence announced, failing to read the room as he set a plate of flank steak on the table. "That's a Princeps-food worthy dinner if there ever was one."

Zandra perked in her seat despite the argument. If there was one thing tempting about Princeps, it was the food. She and Charlotte occasionally got to eat it when their parents transported it to their mainland home from Princeps.

"How was being honored?" Lawrence was acutely aware of ears in public, so he always stayed quiet until they were in the safety of their own home. He was a fashion designer on Princeps and Zandra had seen his work on several people from High Society when they visited the mainland—no commoners could afford his clothing.

Imogen's mouth twitched at Lawrence's question.

Lawrence and Imogen had been Paired for twenty years and had been one of the two Pairs selected for High Society in their year. Though Lawrence seemed to genuinely like Imogen, Zandra couldn't shake the feeling that beneath the pleasantries, Imogen despised their father.

It didn't give her hope for her future.

"Not that exciting," Charlotte replied, lifting food onto her plate.

"Did Five say anything to you?" Imogen asked, "Or Lynx?"

Zandra stopped her fork an inch from her mouth. The same thing she had asked.

"Just formalities."

"What kind of formalities?" Imogen pried.

"'Greetings and congratulations."

"Five's nervous about you joining. She knows that you're going to take her spot on the Council next election."

Charlotte grunted in response.

A lull. Imogen used it to pass Charlotte her anti-anxiety pill, which she'd been taking since she was four and hadn't been able to breathe.

The conversation turned boring.

Zandra barely paid attention, plotting instead. If Charlotte wanted proof, she'd find proof. She needed to do something different. Something outside the box.

And when Zandra couldn't think of anything that would work, she realized she needed something desperate.

I could make proof, a voice in her head said.

But there were lines that Zandra wouldn't cross, and that was one of them.

I'm just going to have to tear this house apart until I find something.

She would start with breaking into Imogen's office. It didn't matter if she was caught. She and Charlotte were going Unruly, after all. May as well act it.

≈

She waited until everyone was asleep, careful not to disturb Charlotte as she jumped off the top bunk and climbed to the roof.

Zandra picked up the pretty rock she'd found and stashed there a few years ago, then climbed toward the study window. If she was going to find something, it would be in there.

Zandra laid on the side of the roof, dropped her head over the edge, and peered inside.

Dark.

Zandra tried the window. Maybe she'd get lucky and Imogen hadn't locked it.

Nope.

So Zandra took a deep breath, praying that her parents' room was far enough that they wouldn't hear.

Before she could overthink it, Zandra bashed the rock into the window.

It shattered upon contact. Zandra brushed the glass fragments away and hopped inside, ripping her pajamas on the way in.

This was Zandra's first time in the study. If she had more time, she would have taken in the mahogany desk, the antique art, the shelf of old books. But she didn't. She had to assume the sound had awoken Imogen.

Zandra ran for the desk. The first drawer she tried opened immediately—

It was empty.

So was the second.

Come on!

The third drawer held useless files of blueprints of new buildings on Princeps.

There was going to be nothing important here. Zandra had been stupid to think that there might be.

Lawrence yelled in the distance. She didn't have much time.

Zandra rushed to the door and shoved a chair under the handle, hoping it would buy her a minute. Then she darted back to the desk and tried the fourth drawer. One of the lower ones.

Folders. Zandra took the top one off the pile and opened it.

The first page was a picture of a smiling boy. Atticus Marquez. Seventeen, with enough points to make him a High-Pointer.

Zandra furrowed her brow at the picture. She turned to the next page.

Another smiling High-Pointer boy. Mace Phillips.

And another. And another.

They all looked the same. The same smile, the same white teeth.

Charlotte's Pairs, Zandra realized, her mouth falling open.

She glanced back at the drawer. Would there be a file with *her* Pair just below? The person she would have no choice but to be with?

A *bang* rattled the door. Zandra didn't look up.

"Don't worry," Zandra said, "It's just me, not a burglar."

"Zandra!" Imogen's voice called. She wasn't quite yelling, but she was stern. No panic in her voice. "Come out *now*." That confirmed it—there was nothing here top-secret. Nothing that was going to help her.

But she needed to make sure. She looked down to close the file...

And found herself looking at a picture of boy who looked different from all the others.

His warm brown eyes matched his skin, which matched his

hair. A single curl fell perfectly onto his forehead. He gave the camera a shy smile, like he wasn't exactly sure of why he was being photographed.

Prince Tiberius of Luxor. No points.

Zandra gaped down at him. *Luxor?* Charlotte might be Paired with a *prince* from *another land*? She'd get to travel to Luxor. She'd get to see the world. To live a life that didn't just consist of having a child and sending it off to the Academy.

Proof no longer needed to be found.

Zandra stopped when Imogen burst into the study and fixed her with a glare. Now that there was a worldly prince on her horizon, Charlotte *shouldn't* go Unruly. It would be selfish of Zandra to convince her otherwise.

Charlotte would get the life that Zandra had always dreamed of, with the foreigner with the kind brown eyes, and Zandra would get Paired to make sure Charlotte lived it.

5

Prince Tiberius of Luxor fixed his warm brown gaze on the palace guard, knowing it would melt her heart. "I'll only be out for a moment," he told her, "And I'll make sure you get paid double for this shift."

Tiberius wasn't sure *why* everyone loved his eyes so much. He just knew that when he widened them and tilted his head, people had trouble saying no. Did he use it to his advantage? Yes, of course. Did he hate that he had the power to get whatever he wanted with a single glance? Just a little.

But Tiberius always used his eyes for good. Like now. The guard motioned him past and he strutted outside the palace walls, giddy with a hint of melancholy.

The stroll had two purposes, the first of which was saying farewell to his homeland and its people. Today was the last full day in Luxor for who knew how long. Maybe ever.

His excitement grew from the exact same place—he was *leaving*!

Tiberius was buying the love of his life a little piece of Luxor —a crwth. Though this one wasn't the typical bow used on the instrument. The blacksmith collaborated with the music shop owner to design a bow that could be used on an instrument like a crwth and *also* shoot darts. Because his future wife deserved to hear music whenever her soul craved it, and have the safe feeling of a secret weapon.

Tiberius' lanky, too-long arms swung as he headed down the hill at the base of the palace toward the market. His crwth, a lyre-like instrument, was slung over his back, it's bow secured behind it. Inspiration could strike anywhere—it didn't wait to see if he had his crwth on hand or not.

He was excited to teach Charlotte Rachel Galvin how to play. As he did, the greatest love song written would form in his mind, gushing out his fingers and through his instrument, soaring through the world and into every ear blessed enough to hear it.

Tiberius had known he was going to marry Charlotte since the day his father, King Akil of Luxor, had showed him her smiling picture on his twelfth birthday. The entire palace had been brought into the Grand Ballroom to celebrate. He had gotten a new crwth that year—the same one he currently wore on his back—and was allowed to play with the palace's orchestra. It had been one of the greatest days of his life, even before Akil had pulled him aside.

"There's something I want to show you," he had said.

"What?" His father's face was serious. Tiberius felt that his entire life was about to change.

And it did.

"You're my fourth son."

"I know."

"Which means you're going to be married to a woman in Ignis."

"Right." It was his duty as the fourth son. Abram, the eldest, was heir. Timur led the navy in Luxor and Ignis' joint fight against the Union. Alex was a professional jerk who shirked all his duties.

And Tiberius had been promised to Ignis at birth, something that he'd been neither excited nor upset about. It was his duty, and a better life than most people post-Destruction could ever dream of.

"Would you like to know who your future wife will be?" Akil had said.

"You—you already know who I'm going to marry?"

"They call it Pairing there. There's a girl who's not unlike you. She's the daughter of one of their leaders."

"Like me."

"Like you. And she excels in all areas of life."

"Does she play music?" Music made sense. Music was the only thing he thought he could possibly have in common with a girl from the other side of the world, who lived in a strange nation.

"This file has everything on her," Akil had replied. He handed it to Tiberius and said, "There will be other young men vying for her affection, so learn what will make her choose you."

No pressure.

Tiberius had been overwhelmed until he took a deep breath and opened the folder.

It wasn't Charlotte's beauty that won him over—though it certainly didn't hurt. It was the confident smirk on her face, as if she knew she was the best and she didn't give a damn if anyone else was aware of the fact. Because *she* knew.

He could write a song about that expression. The pursed lips, the challenging eyes.

Akil's words echoed through Tiberius' thoughts. *Like you.*

Charlotte had a sister, something that they would bond over. Children were uncommon post-Destruction, siblings even rarer. It was one of the reasons Ignis had a Pairing system to begin with.

They tested people's genes and only Paired them accordingly. Tiberius' had been tested as well, and were compatible with Charlotte's.

Luxor didn't have that system, though Tiberius suspected his father was thinking of instituting it. Luxor fought off the Union in the north on behalf of Ignis for Ignis' knowledge, technology, and drugs.

Though Luxor had a higher birth rate than Ignis, almost half of the children born didn't make it past a few months. Most of the population was what Ignis would call *Impaired*—unlike the citizens of Ignis, they could catch and spread diseases, and had more difficulty fighting off the toxins that still plagued the earth from the Destruction.

Charlotte and his children wouldn't have to worry about that, though, since Tiberius' parents had been genetically compatible.

Tiberius' fascination with Charlotte had only grown. He looked forward to every picture—every update—he received about her. He remembered when she spoke in front of all of Ignis when she was fourteen about the benefits of Pairing, and when she won the Academy's yearly sport tournament. He only had one *bad* memory, which was when Charlotte had been caught sneaking out to see some boy named Jaxson when she was thirteen.

It had been covered up well. The only reason Tiberius even knew was because Luxor's *spies*—also known as the people who kept tabs on Charlotte and Tiberius' other Pairs—had discovered the situation before the patrol officers had.

It had taken him a while to get over the jealousy, but she and Jaxson weren't potential Pairs. Jaxson had been Paired with a fellow Low-Pointer two years before.

Now Tiberius' only worry was getting Charlotte's crwth.

Tiberius left the palace grounds, nodding at the gate officers as he passed. If he didn't sneak, people didn't stop him.

The narrow alleys of Luxor were crowded, covered by low awnings of vivid blankets for maximum shade. Lots of people lived out on the street, and sickness spread through the city quickly. Since he wasn't *Impaired*, Tiberius was at no risk of catching whatever seasonal disease plagued the people.

The viruses were often stopped with drugs supplied by Ignis —and sometimes accompanied by their Impaired, since Ignis needed to keep the number of Impaired down for Pairing to work.

Within two seconds of walking through the streets, people greeted him. Even in the heat, they were happy to see him. Tiberius always came to town with more than a little change to give to the people he passed. It wasn't their fault society didn't have a better place for them.

He'd made friends, including an old woman whose memory was long gone—something that could only happen to an Impaired—who believed Tiberius to be her nephew. He spotted her on a corner and folded her fingers around some coins.

"Thank you, Samuel," she said, brushing a strand of his dark, floppy hair off his chestnut forehead. "Things are well at the shoe shop?"

"Yes, they are," Tiberius said, "I'll see you next week." He wouldn't, but the woman would not remember.

He continued, the alley widening. He nodded at some boys his age who kicked a soccer ball, always stopping it inches ahead of their fellow alley-dwellers.

He was halfway to the store when a hand gripped his shoulder. He jumped, crwth rattling against his back.

"What do you think you're doing?"

"Let go of me!" he ordered, shrugging the hand away, though he relaxed at the voice.

Abram, Tiberius' eldest brother. Though Abram was eight years older, Tiberius was already taller than him. But not stronger. Abram tightened his grip.

Abram looked much more weathered than Tiberius, Abram's narrower eyes not holding the same charm and innocence as Tiberius'. As the crown prince, Abram had seen too much.

"I'm picking something up," Tiberius said, once more managing to squirm out of Abram's grasp.

"What?"

"A gift."

"For whom?"

"None of your business."

Abram narrowed his eyes, taking him in. It took all of Tiberius' strength not to twitch. "Is it a girl?"

"Maybe."

"You've been promised to Ignis—"

"I *know*, Abram! Can't you just let me be?"

"You can't go outside without security."

If only Abram knew how many times he had.

"Especially," Abram continued, "When the whole city is Impaired."

Tiberius scowled, troubled that Abram had adopted Ignis' language. A few years ago, they had just been *their people*.

"Oh, please. I'm just going to the blacksmith's and coming right back." Luxor was not a dangerous city. Tiberius was more likely to be murdered by a snake.

"If you die, the alliance dies," Abram reminded him.

"Dad would just give them Alex."

Abram snorted. "Come on, we're going back."

That was the end of it. Tiberius was going to have to send one of his servants to pick it up for him. Tiberius was upset—he'd wanted to personally thank the blacksmith and musician for constructing it. They had worked so hard!

When he voiced his concerns to Abram, he scoffed. "They're our people. They should be *honored* to make it."

Abram would not be a good leader. It wasn't that he didn't

care—it was that he didn't make the space to care for individual needs. He would keep the population safe, and that was it.

But maybe the only reason Tiberius cared was because he had no job except to be married off. He had plenty of energy for other people.

Paired. I need to start calling it Paired.

Despite that, Tiberius didn't have any close friends. Just a few acquaintances, but it was hard to find people who wanted to be his friend because they enjoyed spending time with him, rather than because he was a prince.

But Charlotte would change that. He would finally have a best friend. She was *like him*—she understood what it was like to be treated differently.

And until he met her, he had his crwth.

The Palace of Luxor sat on a barren, dirt hill. Many people found the brown exterior stones hideous, but Tiberius found the earthiness of the stones beautiful.

"I know it's your last day," Abram said as they climbed, "But that doesn't mean you get to throw caution out the door. If anyone's going to try something, it would be today."

Tiberius was silent. No one wanted to hurt him. The people loved him *because* he was one of them.

When they passed the guard back into the palace, Tiberius slipped her the money he had brought for the blacksmith and mouthed a quick, "Thank you."

She couldn't hide her grin.

"I have a meeting," Abram told him in the hallway. "I'm going to be standing in as king, so I don't have time to babysit you. Don't run away again."

Abram motioned to two sentries who hurried into place behind Tiberius. *As if I have a choice.*

"Okay," Tiberius muttered, annoyed at being treated like a child.

"And Father wants to see you. Something about preparations."

"Okay." He'd been staying away from Akil since they were about to be trapped on a ship together for two days.

The interior of the palace was more conventionally beautiful than the outside, though it was darker than Tiberius liked. Unfortunately, the hot Luxor sun demanded the palace not have many windows.

Tiberius found Akil in the Throne Room, consulting with several nobles. Akil had the same build as Abram and the same skin tone and eyebrows as Tiberius. That was all Tiberius had in common with him. He was told that he looked much more like his mother, who had died in childbirth like many women post-Destruction.

"We need to discuss what color you'll be wearing when you disembark onto Princeps," Akil said as Tiberius approached.

Tiberius wanted to wear periwinkle, Charlotte's favorite color, but he doubted his father would approve of that. Instead he said, "I don't care."

"We're trying to decide between the red of Luxor and the purple of Ignis," Akil said. Tiberius would have appreciated that his father was trying to include him if he hadn't been stuck on one thing—

"I want to go straight to Ignis' mainland."

Akil frowned at him. "We will go to Princeps first—"

"I thought I wasn't allowed on Princeps until I was marri—er, Paired."

"One said he would make an exception for your arrival."

"So we're going to sail in and say the rules don't apply to us?" Tiberius asked, "What will my Pairs think of that?"

His schooling had included extensive studies of Ignis. Charlotte would not be waiting for him on Princeps, and he wasn't going to go a second longer than he had to without seeing her.

"The rules *don't* apply to us," Akil reminded him, "You will live on Princeps in High Society regardless of what happens and who you choose."

Tiberius resisted the urge to roll his eyes. He didn't think that Charlotte would like his father much. Tiberius wasn't even sure if he did.

"Well, we don't need everyone to know that."

"Ignis would appreciate the gesture," one of the nobles that Tiberius had forgotten was there interrupted.

Akil looked annoyed, but gave in despite himself. "Fine. We'll land at the marina at Phoenix Palace."

Where Tiberius would live for the three months of Pairing—unless, of course, he proposed before that and Charlotte said yes.

"Thank you, Father."

"You're wearing red."

"Okay," Tiberius said. He had been leaning toward purple.

"The boat leaves in three hours."

Which meant there were only two days and three hours left until he got to meet and woo the love of his life.

6

"I expect you all to be on your best behavior for the king and prince," One told the Council, "Unless you want the Union to kill us all."

The months that Imogen Galvin had been preparing for her entire life were upon her. They would be stressful, but if she got everything right, it would be worth it.

The Council of Five gathered in their chamber on Princeps, each in their assigned seat at the singular round table. There were no windows and only two doors—no one could hear or see what they were doing.

It was the basement of a pre-Destruction church, one that now sat above a highly secure labyrinth of locked rooms and hallways accessible only by the Council and hand-chosen security.

Imogen kept her hands folded before her. She took in Three, Four, and Five. Like Imogen herself, Three—or as Imogen called him, Maddox—gave nothing away, his oval-shaped face neutral, blue eyes emotionless. He'd been at this as long as she had.

"Of course," Five said, ever the One-pleaser. Perhaps she knew that the moment Charlotte was admitted into High Society, she'd be giving up her seat to Imogen's daughter. Maybe Five knew she needed One on her side.

"Five, Tiberius must find a suitable Pair," One said, "That is the entire goal of this Pairing season."

Five glanced at Imogen out of the corner of her eye while Maddox stiffened.

"Shall I single any of the women out for him in particular?" Five asked.

"Jayana Triller would be acceptable," One said.

Imogen would be accused of bias, but she had common sense on her side. "Charlotte Galvin has more points. Surely we should be Pairing her with him instead."

Five scowled. One shook his head, "We should Pair her with an Ignis boy."

Maddox jumped to Imogen's defense. "Charlotte is a once-in-a-generation High-Pointer, and Tiberius a once-in-a-generation prince. Not at least *attempting* to Pair them—respectfully, One—is ludicrous."

One fixed Imogen with a glare. He was easy to hate—his beady black eyes, pale complexion, heavy frame, cropped white hair. Not to mention his personality. There were things Imogen admired, things she respected...but nothing she *liked*.

He had been One since she was born. She—and everyone else on the Council, for that matter—had never known another leader. He'd been One for forty-eight years, the longest One of Ignis. They held re-elections every year and, since only High Society was able to vote, and life on Princeps was virtually perfect, the people worshiped One.

She wished she could kill him, but his death would have a snowball effect—a re-election that would not end in her favor, an angry population, and instability in their alliance with Luxor would follow. None of which would benefit Imogen.

One looked away. Imogen and Maddox were unstoppable

whenever they were on the same side. Unfortunately, it was a rare occurrence.

"True," Four agreed, her face a stoic mask, "The story writes itself."

One was shoved between a rock and a hard place. Charlotte getting Paired with Tiberius could be the beginning of his downfall, but revolting against the Council and singling out Two's daughter could be just as catastrophic.

He wouldn't put it to a vote. Yes, One was *One*, but majority of the Council still ruled.

"Very well," One finally relented. "Are all the preparations set for the Season Opener?"

Five nodded. Imogen didn't trust that she would treat Charlotte fairly, which meant it was going to be on her to make sure that Charlotte got everything she and Imogen had worked so hard for.

"I wanted to propose a small adjustment to the Conquest," Five said, a hint of apprehension in her voice.

Silence greeted her words until One laughed. "So you don't interfere as you did last year? By all means, Five, entertain us with your proposition."

Imogen often couldn't believe Five's stupidity. "Never mind," Five mumbled.

One rolled his eyes. "*Anyway*. King Akil sent notice that the prince would prefer to arrive at Phoenix Palace and stay on the mainland until he's admitted into High Society." One paused, then added sarcastically, "Assuming, of course, that he is."

Tiberius certainly would be, but they had to keep up pretenses. Two Paired couples were chosen to join High Society, chosen by the people of Princeps themselves.

This year it would be rigged. Even more than it usually was.

One continued, "Our ferry to the mainland will depart in an hour. Dismissed."

One didn't wait for questions or concerns. Four and Five followed a pace behind him.

Imogen stood to follow, but Maddox stopped her with a cool, "Two, did you have a chance to look over the security report I sent you?"

Four and Five continued walking.

"Not yet," Imogen said. But she was only halfway across the chamber when the others exited, leaving no one in earshot.

"We need to talk—"

"I don't have the time, Three."

"You can't just ignore—are you serious?"

She kept walking. She hadn't even bothered to turn around. Three would criticize her—and she needed a clear mind.

Imogen fled the chamber just to find One waiting for her outside. "The prince requested to meet Charlotte immediately upon arrival."

It pleased Imogen even more than it displeased One, which was an impressive feat.

"Have her join you at the dock," One grumbled, "And don't let this mean more than it does."

"Understood," Imogen said evenly, despite the *great* news that Tiberius had already decided he would pursue Charlotte.

Imogen exited Town Hall and hurried down the stairs into Main Square, not bothering to appreciate the gothic architecture built into the hills of Princeps before her. It was an incredible island, with lush foliage encircling the cobblestone streets.

Before Imogen could take a step away from the building, a pack of people hurried toward her. Imogen plastered a smile onto her face as she had taught Charlotte to do, resisting the urge to blow past them.

"Good afternoon," Imogen said. She recognized only one of them—the sole man in the group, Daniel Solace.

Daniel had won the Conquest four years before, meaning he

had one year remaining to find a Pair in a Princeps widow or another Conquest winner. It was his prize for the victory—five years to recover before Pairing.

He stood a head above the women, and opened his mouth to respond—but a woman beat him to it. "Your daughter is gorgeous," she said, "Her skin—it glows."

She knew most people on Princeps—their population was just over two thousand, after all—but she couldn't recall the woman's name.

"When she joins us, I'd love to have her try out my new line of facial cream. It's perfect for her complexion."

Everyone wanted to capitalize on Ignis' soon-to-be golden girl. Imogen would expect nothing less. The woman was practically bouncing on her feet and the rest of her posse held their breath.

Imogen lowered her voice. "Will I have your vote for One, come election time?"

"Oh, of course!"

The election was only a few weeks after Pairing Season was over—and campaigning wasn't going to be Imogen's top priority.

"And mine as well if she wears my jewelry!" another woman squealed.

"I'll be in touch. Thank you," Imogen said, walking right through them.

"Two—" Daniel began, but Imogen didn't turn, pretending not to hear.

She hurried into the city, about to use her daughter for yet another scheme.

It will all be worth it in the end. She won't hate me when she knows why.

7

Charlotte couldn't sleep. She and Zandra hadn't spoken in sixteen hours—before Zandra had broken into Imogen's office. Zandra had been grounded for the day in a spare bedroom, and every time Charlotte had walked by, Lawrence had been lurking.

As the day wore on, the final day of freedom, Charlotte grew increasingly anxious. She was furious she'd dropped her Dust. She *needed* some. But she wasn't to leave unchaperoned—the few days between graduation from the Academy and the start of Pairing Season was to be spent with family, and no graduates were permitted to leave unsupervised.

Tomorrow was the day that Charlotte's entire life would change.

If her anxiety let her live that long.

She could barely breathe and she still had twenty-four hours. She half-suspected she'd have a heart attack before then.

Especially without Dust.

She couldn't even talk to Zandra. Zandra, who very well might go Unruly tomorrow.

Who Charlotte very well may *never see again*, if their parents didn't let her out of that damn room.

Charlotte paced the hallway, Lawrence reading a fashion magazine in a nook beside the door. On the third pace, Lawrence sighed and closed it.

"Are you going to do this all day?"

Charlotte stopped, but the dread in the pit of her stomach intensified with no movement. She wrung her hands instead, something she only did when she wasn't in public. "When is she getting out?"

"Whenever your mother has decided she's had enough time to think about her actions."

Lawrence always listened to Imogen. They were a good Pair in that way—they never argued, they deeply cared for each other, and they were always on the same page. They gave Charlotte hope for herself and her future Pair.

"Hey, Char," Zandra's muffled voice called from behind the door. Lawrence rolled his eyes, a hint of amusement behind them.

Zandra didn't sound upset. Just stir-crazy.

"You know the rules, kid!" Lawrence returned.

Even if Charlotte hated her mother, she couldn't deny that Lawrence was perfect for her. He made her better with his calm and kind demeanor. And Imogen made him more ambitious and certain.

"When is she even—?"

"Charlotte!" a voice called from the floor below. Imogen's voice.

Charlotte scowled and stomped down the stairs, frustrated and scared and worried—

Imogen waited at the base. She did a once-over. Charlotte looked perfect, per usual. Even when she had nowhere to go, she dressed to impress. Just in case.

"Your presence has been requested at the marina."

"By whom?" She was cool with Imogen, even though her curiosity was piqued. Only High Society was allowed into the marina.

"The Prince of Luxor."

Charlotte gaped, not quite comprehending. There were four princes of Luxor. What would one of them be doing here? Why? What? And *her*?

"I—huh?" she said, her voice dropping to her deeper register, sounding much like Zandra's, in her confusion.

"I'll explain on the way."

Stunned, Charlotte simply followed Imogen out the door. It only occurred to her when they were a block away from the house that she should've negotiated Zandra's release in exchange for her presence.

Zandra wouldn't have forgotten, had their positions been switched.

"Confidentially, Prince Tiberius is one of your Pairs. Though he demanded arriving on the mainland to meet you, so it won't be a secret for much longer."

"Okay."

"Okay?"

"Yes, okay."

Charlotte's mind reeled despite her even voice. Tiberius was the youngest prince. Her age. His mother had died birthing him.

That was all she knew. But *he* obviously knew something about *her* if he wanted to meet. She was at a disadvantage.

"You have no questions?"

"I'm *processing*."

Of course Imogen hadn't told her there was a prince in the equation. Terror flowed through her body. She was unprepared. For *all* of Pairing. She didn't even know what life in Phoenix Palace *looked like*.

"How long has he known of my existence?"

Imogen paused. "I don't know."

"I doubt that. What does he want?"

"To meet you."

"What does he *really* want?"

"That's all I know."

"I doubt that as well."

"Charlotte," Imogen said, a hint of condescension in her voice that made Charlotte prickle. "I'm not your enemy."

"But you're not my friend, either."

"Just...be on your best behavior."

"I always am." And she hated it about herself.

Ignis' streets were quiet as everyone prepared for the holiday of Pairing Season. It was the calm before the storm. Tomorrow the city would be crowded with people, all hoping to catch a glimpse of the High-Pointers.

Of *her.*

That would continue throughout the next three months. Whenever she left the palace on an outing with a potential Pair, people would ogle at her as if she were from the pre-Destruction world.

No, her months in Phoenix Palace would *not* be fun. Not at all.

Rumor had it that Pairing Season was an even bigger deal on Princeps, the holiday lasting three months since High Society had access to footage from security cameras in Phoenix Palace.

Charlotte couldn't remember whether or not it was true. She prayed it wasn't—she couldn't deal with the idea of constant surveillance.

The Luxor ship pulled into the harbor as Imogen and Charlotte arrived. Boats were the only mode of transportation to both Princeps and Unruly, so a concrete wall surrounded the marina where cliffs did not, with barbwires at the top and around-the-clock guards.

If flight technology from pre-Destruction times hadn't been lost, would High Society fly to Princeps instead? Charlotte couldn't picture it—it seemed much too terrifying for pampered High Society.

The only boat that didn't seem to belong in the harbor—maybe because it was the only one that wouldn't be transporting its passengers to the island of wealth and beauty—was the Unruly ship. It was ready to bring all who decided to go Unruly to the island. It was jet-black and barge-like, with an open deck and barbwire at the top of the railings that matched the wire at the top of the harbor walls. It made Charlotte want to glue her feet to the land, because surely nothing good could happen on the water in *that* vessel.

Charlotte stared into the indigo water, trying not to picture Zandra on that boat, cutting herself on the wire as a wave crashed over the ship and sent her sprawling toward the edge.

Charlotte tried to avoid looking at both Princeps and Unruly, but she could only stare into the water's reflecting light for so long before she compulsively looked up. If Princeps looked inviting, Unruly looked intimidating. The barren, jagged peaks jutted into the air as if warning birds to steer clear. Because not even birds should dare fly too close.

Charlotte tried to make herself feel drawn to Princeps, but she just wanted to stay here. Alone. Forgotten. No name. No expectations.

No. It's the anxiety talking. You want Princeps. You want this.

Charlotte and Imogen were escorted to the end of the dock, exactly where the Luxor ship was heading. It was easily the largest she'd ever seen—it had to be, to traverse the Pacific in only two days. Charlotte suspected it had upwards of six engines.

Charlotte could make out the shape of a tall, gangly man and a broader, shorter figure beside him. The sun silhouetted them, their details impossible to make out. Even so, Charlotte could feel their eyes piercing into her heart like four tiny arrows.

One stood waiting as Imogen and Charlotte approached the end of the dock. Imogen bowed. Charlotte mimicked her, bending just a little lower than her mother.

"Two, Charlotte," One greeted with a frown.

"Thank you for inviting me, One," Charlotte said, though he'd likely fought to stop the meeting.

"The prince is anxious to meet you."

Anxious in a much different way than she was, Charlotte was sure. "I'm honored to greet him."

One looked at Imogen, hatred radiating off of him. "You trained this one well."

A flash of hot anger blinded her. Before Charlotte could stop herself, "I know how to sit and stay, too."

Charlotte came to her senses a moment too late. Imogen and One gaped.

"And she bites, too," One growled. "You're both dismissed."

"One—" Imogen began.

"*Dismissed*," One repeated, his voice deadly. "You'll meet the prince when he meets the rest of his potential Pairs."

"I'm sorry," Charlotte squeaked. What had possessed her? *Why* had she said that?! "It won't happen again, I swear. I—I don't know what came over me...."

One kept his eyes on the ship. Charlotte took a step forward, but Imogen put her hand on Charlotte's shoulder, "We've been dismissed."

What have I done?

Imogen led her off the dock and through the marina. An icy cold swept through her body, and her skin began taking on a blue hue, as it did when she was overwhelmed with stress. Not a single thought crossed her mind until they were safely in the streets and Imogen released her hand.

"I don't know what came over me—"

"It's okay," Imogen assured her. But based on the expression on Imogen's face—which, to her mother's credit, she was trying very hard to mask—Charlotte had seriously screwed up.

"I can fix it. Just tell me how and I'll fix it."

"The damage has been done," Imogen said calmly. Factually. As if she were reading a report.

Charlotte wished she would yell. Scream. Give her something —*anything*. Why couldn't Imogen react? Why couldn't she show her true colors?

Why was it that, no matter what Charlotte seemed to do, Imogen didn't care?

"Will I lose points?"

"There would be too much explaining about you meeting the prince before the season. Just be ready for the Opener."

No dwelling on the good nor the bad. No celebrations, no wallowing.

Charlotte's thoughts looped. She timed them with her steps. As each foot hit the pavement, a new worry sprung to mind, just to be replaced with another the next step. The wheel spun, around and around...

When they finally arrived back home, Charlotte took the stairs three at a time and beelined for the locked guest room. She needed Zandra. Zandra would understand—she screwed up like this all the time. She would get it.

Lawrence tried to stop her, but Charlotte barged past him. She shook the door handle. Still locked. She bared her teeth at Lawrence—

But Imogen calmly maneuvered past Charlotte, key in hand, and unlocked the door herself.

Charlotte didn't waste time thanking her mother. She rushed inside and threw her arms around Zandra.

"Hey, what's—"

"I messed up, Zandra. Badly."

"That's okay. You're allowed to mess up."

How could Zandra be so uninhibited? How could she think it was that simple?

"Not if I want to—if I want to…" Charlotte trailed off, trying to remember what it was that she wanted—

"Get the best Pair and join High Society?"

"Yeah." *That.*

Charlotte glanced back. Imogen was standing in the doorway. Watching. She stared at Zandra with a glint of warning in her eyes, but Charlotte glared at her until she retreated, Lawrence in her wake.

"What were you thinking yesterday, breaking into her study?"

"That I could find answers."

"And did you?"

Zandra started for the door. "No."

Charlotte sensed she was lying, but she wasn't sure if she trusted her own judgement in her current headspace.

"Actually, Charlotte," Zandra confessed, heading down the stairs toward the back door, "I think you were right. I think you need to be Paired."

"And you?" Charlotte prompted, a step behind her.

"I mean, I…yeah. I'm not leaving you to the sharks."

She couldn't tell her sister that she had the opportunity to be Paired with a prince. Not when Zandra wasn't going to have an option because of *her*. It felt too cruel.

"Thank you," Charlotte said. And she meant it.

She expected her sister's revelation to alleviate some of her fear, but it seemed to only grow. Now there was the pressure of Zandra doing what she didn't want to do—even if it *was* for the better—added to the pile.

Why was she like this?

"And look, I know this is a long shot, but..." Zandra trailed off, listening for their parents.

"What?"

"There's a party."

Charlotte pushing through her shock and dismay quickly. "I'm sure there is, and I'm sure you're not about to tell me you're attending."

"I *will* be. And I would ask you to come with me, but I know you're going to say no, so can you cover for me?"

There was absolutely *no way* she was letting Zandra leave the house tonight, especially after her office break in the night before. It didn't matter how much she "owed" her sister.

"And I *do* want to convince you to come."

"How did you even find out about this?" Charlotte said in disbelief.

Zandra shrugged. "Some guy approached me in Phoenix Square when you were walking up to get your academic award thing."

"*Some guy?*" Charlotte could hear the blood pumping between her temples.

"Well, one of the girls called him Jaxson, so he has a name, at least."

The blood froze. Jaxson would be there. *Dust* would be there.

She wouldn't have to go through Pairing without it. She could get more.

"Charlotte?"

Charlotte was gaping. She blinked and closed her mouth.

Was she idiotic enough to actually do it?

Yes. She had made up her mind the second Zandra had uttered, "Jaxson".

"Is there anything I can do to stop you?" Charlotte asked.

"No. I mean, you could tell Mom, but I doubt you're going to be doing that."

"You know I can't let you go."

"You're not *letting me*—"

"Let me finish...*without me.* To watch out for you."

Zandra searched Charlotte's face, unsure if she was kidding. "Are you serious?"

"You promise you'll get Paired if I go with you? No last minute tricks?"

"Yeah, I promise."

"And you'll behave until graduation? And actually try in Final Chance?"

Zandra stopped walking, realizing that Charlotte was serious. "Yes, anything you want! This is going to be *so* fun! And there's nothing to worry about—"

"Zandra—"

"If you get caught, just pretend you're me again. I'm already getting assigned. I've got nothing to lose."

"And if they find us *together*?" Charlotte said, trying to shed light on the utter stupidity of the suggestion.

"Then we just say that you were trying to stop me. Or I forced you against your will or something."

Zandra threw her arms around Charlotte's shoulders, much like how Charlotte had done moments before.

"I'm so excited! We're gonna have so much fun!"

Charlotte feared that Zandra's words had just cursed them.

8

Once Zandra's elation of Charlotte joining elapsed, unease settled.

Charlotte needed to keep her points so she could get Paired with Tiberius. She couldn't get caught.

There hadn't been a chance in hell of Charlotte joining—Zandra had merely been warning her that she wouldn't be around tonight.

Who is Jaxson? Who was this mystery boy who could convince Charlotte to risk it all?

Pushing Charlotte would get her nowhere. If she wanted answers, she'd have to find Jaxson herself. She wished she'd studied him more closely. All she'd noticed was his scrawniness—the rest of him had been too average for her brain to compute.

Charlotte made an elaborate plan that Zandra only half-listened to. Her thoughts circled the future, Charlotte, Pairing...

Tiberius' face.

How much she wanted to go somewhere. Anywhere.

Did Imogen remember how much she despised confined spaces? Had she locked her up all day despite that?

Tiberius' smile.

Stop.

She forced her thoughts away. Should she find a former Unruly and ask if she could win the Conquest?

Every year, an Unruly or two were plucked *off* Unruly and brought back to Ignis to be Paired with Low-Pointers who either didn't have a genetic Pair from the pool of their year or to be Paired with new widows. They were sworn to secrecy, branded with a red *X* on their left hands.

She needed to be with Charlotte—but why not see what Unruly was all about first, then win the Conquest?

She'd tried to converse with a former Unruly before, but the woman had told her, with a blank look in her eye, that she'd "never speak about that place again." Was it the vacancy of unendurable trauma?

She'd spoken too neutrally for Zandra to be convinced.

The party, which was in the Low-Pointer Corner—the LPC, as everyone called it—would be a great way to get those answers. It wouldn't be hard to sneak away. Pure freedom with former Unruly nearby.

She had forgotten about it until she had too much time to think in that room—between wondering if Tiberius had a personality to match his face and when he'd arrive.

Charlotte was already in disguise, her hair pulled into a messy knot atop her head. She wore a baggy hoodie and loose-fitting pants, looking like someone from High Society failing to make a fashion statement.

"You look ridiculous." Zandra said, determined to ease Charlotte's stress. This was supposed to be *fun*. Their last fun moment.

"Do I look tough?"

"No."

"I *am* tough, though," Charlotte said, a hint of insecurity in her voice.

"Duh. It's your secret weapon. You fool them all."

"Just like how no one knows you're one of the smartest people in Ignis."

"Exactly."

"I look like one of those Princeps hipsters."

"The ones that Dad hates?"

"He doesn't hate *them*, he just hates their fashion."

"We better not get caught, then. He might disown you if he sees those pants."

"We have to make sure we aren't seen *together*," Charlotte said, pacing, "I'll introduce myself as Kathy and hope that no one recognizes me."

"Kathy's a dumb name."

"Do you have a better one?"

"What about Star?"

"Star?"

"Yeah."

"You think *Kathy* is dumber than *Star*?"

"Star is the name of a Princeps hipster wannabe. Kathy is the name of a boring Mid-Pointer who has a boring construction worker Pair and a boring four-year-old named Johnny."

"We're going for boring!" Charlotte protested.

"Why are you even going if you're not gonna have fun?"

"To keep you out of trouble."

"But it doesn't *matter* if I get in trouble," Zandra said, "I'm not stupid. You just said so yourself."

"Maybe I want to get outside of my comfort zone."

Maybe you just want to see Jaxson.

"If they *do* catch you, you're me. And I got cold, so...the hoodie."

"And if one of us gets caught, the other flees."

"Uh-huh," Zandra said, "Can we go now?"

"We haven't gone over the path yet."

Zandra groaned. Charlotte gave her a stern look. "This is serious."

"I know, I know," Zandra muttered. She hoped Charlotte wasn't going to ruin the vibe the whole night.

After going over the route—Charlotte was going to follow just within earshot of Zandra—they were ready. Zandra cracked the window.

A mighty oak stood outside their window. It was an easy climb down and they weren't very high but, of course, Charlotte was terrified. Zandra gave an encouraging nod—she'd be the same if they were facing a tunnel. "I'll be with you the whole time. Just don't look down."

Charlotte nodded. The fact that she was still intent proved that *something* was going on with this Jaxson kid.

Zandra jumped onto a branch, then offered her hand to Charlotte. "C'mon, Star."

"Shut up."

"It's a *good* name!"

"I kinda feel like one right now. But not in a good way."

"I'll make sure you don't streak through the sky to the ground, don't worry."

"You promise?"

"I promise. I won't let you fall."

Charlotte took a shuddering breath and leapt for the tree. Zandra grabbed onto her. "I've got you."

Charlotte wrapped an arm around her neck, not loosening her grip as Zandra led her from branch to branch, and staying quiet when Charlotte cut off her airway. When they reached the ground, Zandra breathed a sigh of relief.

"Lead the way," Charlotte murmured, recovering immediately.

The walk went without a hitch. Zandra had to dart into alleys a few times when people strolled onto their path, but it was easy for her to sidestep them. She trusted that Charlotte did the same behind her.

The LPC was less patrolled by High Society's law enforcement since they didn't particularly care what went on there. It wasn't exactly dangerous—nowhere in Ignis truly was—but it was grimier. Grittier.

A *little* freer.

Not free *enough*, but...better. She wouldn't be upset about it becoming her new home if she weren't getting assigned a random strange man to procreate with for the rest of her life.

All Zandra had been instructed was to go to the big redwood tree. There was only one in Ignis, and it was the LPC's claim to fame. The party wouldn't actually be there—the kids throwing it probably had someone waiting to escort them the rest of the way to make sure that word hadn't gotten around to unwanted ears.

Zandra found a few others waiting at the tree. She recognized some faces, but didn't know any of them by name.

There were two boys amongst the group. Zandra wondered if they were Low-Pointers like herself.

Will one of them be my Pair?

She hoped not. Even in the darkness, one of them had a face covered in cystic acne and the other refused to look her in the eye.

"What's your name?" Acne Boy asked, sizing her up, clearly aware of her identity.

"What's yours?"

"You're Charlotte's sister, aren't you?"

Zandra ignored him. "Is someone gonna come get us? Because I'm happy to dance under the redwood, if not."

That got a few laughs, easing Zandra's inner tension. Was Charlotte watching from behind one of the long gray living complexes? Would she be able to follow them?

"I think so," a girl whose name Zandra should have been able to remember replied. "There are definitely a lot more people coming. And we're not exactly early."

A moment later, an older teen—past the age of Pairing—materialized out of the shadows. Edgy. Purposefully messy. Someone she was sure lived in the LPC.

Maybe someone who knew Jaxson.

He scanned the area. None of the partygoers said a word. No one dared breathe.

Zandra forced air into her lungs as he met her gaze.

"C'mon," he said, "Let's go have some fun."

9

Tiberius was livid.

Charlotte hadn't been sent away by choice. He'd been too far to see One's expression, but his body language was easy to read. The way his body puffed imposingly over Charlotte. The way his hands had flailed as he spoke.

She'd done something to upset him.

When Tiberius laid eyes on her—even though she'd barely been more than a shape in the distance—ecstasy had overtaken his body. A piece of his soul he hadn't known was missing had finally been put into place. For a moment, he was whole.

He almost took out his crwth and started playing.

But when she'd started back down the dock and disappeared into the marina, his glee fled with her. He was broken again. How had he lived his whole life without her?

"Where is she going?" Tiberius demanded to his father, who stood beside him at the bow. He didn't care to look up at the beautiful Phoenix Palace, the mansions that must have been the second homes of the people in High Society, or the slums of the Low-Pointers beyond.

He didn't even care to look to his left at the colorful city on the Island of Princeps. He had vaguely noted its beauty before he could see Charlotte, but he had been too apprehensive to admire the lush green mountains, the stone palaces, or the glinting beaches.

Not even the Island of Unruly had perplexed him.

"I don't know."

"I wanted to speak to her!" he complained like a child, "I didn't just want to see her *from afar*!"

"I negotiated a conversation with One. I'm sure there's just been a misunderstanding."

Tiberius jumped down to the lower deck before Akil could stop him. The ship was nearing the dock...

Before Tiberius had time to think, he leapt off the ship.

But when his feet touched the dock, he stumbled. Sea-legs.

"Where is Charlotte?" he demanded of One, so furious he forgot his civility *and* his father, who—in his older age and rational headspace—couldn't launch himself off a moving ship.

"Welcome to Ignis," One replied. "We are very pleased to have you, Prince Tiberius."

He bowed, a sign of respect in Ignis. Tiberius didn't bow back. He couldn't make himself.

Akil finally disembarked, his scowl bringing Tiberius back to reality.

"It's good to see you, old friend," Akil murmured, bowing even lower than One had. He glared at Tiberius from beneath his arm. The message on his face was clear: *Get the hell down right now.*

Tiberius saw his own stupidity through the fog of anger. If One sent Charlotte away, he had the power to *keep* her away.

Tiberius was slow on the uptake, but he usually got there eventually. He bowed the lowest of all, hating himself for it. "Apologies, One. I was just...very excited to see her."

When Akil straightened, he and One embraced, genuinely pleased to see one another.

"Charlotte had a personal matter to attend to, but you will see her soon. As well as the *rest* of your potential Pairs," One said.

Tiberius made a fist behind his back. When Tiberius was ten, his youngest older brother Alex had snapped his crwth bow as revenge for Tiberius borrowing—*not* stealing—his training shield. Tiberius used it as a drum, a common pre-Destruction instrument that had lost its popularity in the years following. People had needed soothing instruments after the warfare, not the loud banging of drums.

Of course, Tiberius had dented Alex's shield with his fork-drumstick during his rehearsal. Which, when Tiberius brought the broken piece of metal to his brother, he explained meant that the shield was defective. If a fork was able to wreak havoc on the shield, then a sword was going to slice right through it.

Alex had thrown a tantrum. Tiberius had fled, but when he returned to his room, he found his bow snapped in half.

At dinner, the moment that Tiberius took his seat beside Alex, the tears began pouring, until his entire body shook with fury. Alex was pleased. What kind of monster took pleasure in watching someone suffer? But he couldn't confront his brother. Alex was much bigger than him, and there was a strict no-fighting-at-dinner policy.

Akil dismissed Tiberius, ordering him not to come back until he pulled himself together. Thirty minutes later, Abram had come to get him, with advice that Tiberius heeded to the day.

"Whenever you're angry, make a fist, channel all your emotions into it, and put it somewhere no one can see. Move all the emotion into your fist until it's the only angry part of your body, and then hide it from view."

"So only my fist is angry?"

"Exactly. You have an angry fist and nothing else. Now are you ready to go back?"

When Tiberius returned to his place beside Alex, he had transported all the anger in his body into his fist, clenching it under the table.

Now, facing One, Tiberius did the same. He stored all his feelings in his left hand, clenching it behind his back. His fist was angry, the rest of him calm.

"Thank you for welcoming me to your beautiful homeland." He was pleased to learn that his voice was even.

"We are elated to have you," One said, "May I show you to where you'll be staying in Phoenix Palace?"

"That would be wonderful." One gestured them down the dock as servants began unloading Tiberius' belongings from the ship. Akil would be staying on Princeps—Tiberius had given up that opportunity by trying to see Charlotte immediately upon arrival.

One and Akil struck up a conversation about One's visit to Luxor a decade ago, then the ongoing battle against the Union as they walked through the marina. Tiberius paid no attention, already planning how to find Charlotte before Pairing. He couldn't meet her with all her other Pairs. He needed her to know that they were meant for each other. She needed to know just how much he cared.

Phoenix Palace wasn't far from the marina. Tiberius took in the winding streets as One led them toward the impending building. There were no vehicles besides boats—Luxor had a few from pre-Destruction times, but it seemed as though Ignis hadn't been so lucky. Either that or all cars and motorcycles were kept on Princeps.

He marveled at the city. The pictures he'd seen had been gorgeous, but he realized that those pictures had only been of

Princeps. Not the mainland. Ignis was no where near as conventionally beautiful, but Tiberius found it extraordinary anyway.

The only thing he didn't like was the lack of people in the streets. It was the opposite of Luxor, creating a lonely, uneasy atmosphere.

The landscape got more luxurious with every step toward Phoenix Palace. When Tiberius finally got an up-close view of it, he realized just how different it was from his palace in Luxor.

This one was breathtaking on the outside, with manicured gardens surrounding it and countless balconies overlooking the greenery. The entire five story marble structure was elaborate, from the columns to the doors.

Inside, Tiberius found it just as exceptional—brighter and airier than Luxor's palace, holding an aura of comfort and safety. This was a place where nothing bad happened.

Would Charlotte be as amazed as he? Or had growing up seeing the marble palace every day desensitized her?

Tiberius was led up four flights of stairs and down many confusing hallways to the wing that would be his home for the next three months. It was ridiculously large for just him—even larger than his quarters in Luxor.

He hadn't comprehended the economic disparity between the two nations. Ignis was a place of wealth. The type of wealth that even the royalty of Luxor couldn't dream of.

"Would you like us to send in a servant to help you freshen? Or perhaps you would like a full tour of the Palace?" One said as Tiberius stepped into a room with a four-poster bed, three sofas, pre-Destruction art, and a bathtub in the center of it all. He even had a balcony with an ocean view.

"I would actually like nothing more than a nap." He could think of nothing less pleasing than a tour guided by One. "The journey has...drained me."

Akil didn't look pleased at this, but he didn't argue.

One remained neutral. "Of course. Your Majesty, it would be my honor to escort you to Princeps if you're satisfied with your son's arrangements? All palace workers are aware of his presence and will help him with anything he needs. And Five will be moving into the palace for the season tomorrow with special instructions to look after him."

"Go, Father," said Tiberius, unstrapping his crwth—the only thing he had personally taken from the ship. "I'll be fine."

"Rest up. I'll see you before the Season Opener tomorrow," Akil said.

Tiberius took a quick shower in the washroom. When he returned to the bedroom, he was pleased to see that his trunk had been placed just outside the walk-in closet—which, like the washroom—was as big as a normal bedroom. The rest of the Luxor crew would stay on the ship, minus his personal guard, Leon, who would also reside in Phoenix Palace.

He opened the trunk. On the top was Charlotte's bow. After a long moment of indecision, he put it aside. He wasn't sure he would find her. He didn't even know where to start.

But he would try. He would stay out until the Season Opener if he had to.

Tiberius changed, strapped his crwth onto his back, and headed out. He doubted he'd be stopped. He'd flown under his father's radar his entire life—as far as Akil was aware, Tiberius was a perfectly-behaved son. He had no reason to believe there'd be sentries outside his door. With the exception of the marina, Ignis' guards were only for tradition.

Two Luxor guards outside Tiberius' room, one of whom was the burly Leon, armed with spears. Yikes. "Oh, hi."

"Your Highness," Leon said.

"I'm just, uh, going out."

"Then one of us shall accompany you."

"No, that's okay."

"We've been given strict instructions—"

"Okay, never mind." Tiberius shuffled back into his room and shut the door behind him.

He was on the fourth floor. That couldn't be that bad. Right? He could probably jump and land—

One look down immediately stopped that train of thought.

But a crane of his neck revealed another balcony resting directly below his.

For Charlotte. He swung his legs over the side before his courage could leave him.

It was easier than expected, even with the crwth on his back and his sweaty hands.

No one seemed to be in any of the rooms. The palace must've been mostly empty since Pairing Season hadn't started.

Tiberius wiped the sweat from his brow when he reached the ground.

He had always thought Luxor was beautiful, but Phoenix Gardens...they were breathtaking. How was it so green here? Luxor was much too dry for birds of paradise, ferns, and water lilies.

He basked in the view, grateful to be here.

Stay focused.

Tiberius ran for the outskirts. When he reached the stone wall, he scrambled to the top like a squirrel.

The drop to the street was significant. He could get down, but he had no idea how he'd climb back up.

A problem for another time. Tiberius dangled his legs over the side, then lowered his body until he was hanging down.

He let go.

The impact jarred his knees and he stumbled backward. He felt himself falling—but his crwth—

Tiberius landed on his crwth and heard the deafening splinter of wood. *No!*

He hoped—prayed—that it was just a small crack. That the wood connecting the instrument to the back strap was the only thing that had been broken.

Tiberius jumped to his feet and unslung his instrument to assess its damage before he even assessed his own body's damage.

It was exactly what Tiberius had feared. The crwth had been shattered into four pieces.

No. No, no, no.

Tears sprang into Tiberius' eyes. How was he supposed to woo Charlotte without his crwth?

Someone would fix it. He could get it fixed by tomorrow. He would ask his father to find someone immediately. He wouldn't have to go long without it.

It was the only thought keeping his tears in this strange alley from progressing into sobs. Was this an omen for what his life in Ignis would be?

You're okay, he told himself, *You'll be fine once you find Charlotte.*

Would Charlotte wonder what it was? Would she think it was weird? That *he* was weird?

Maybe he would see if people gave him looks as he walked by, then figure out if he should leave the pieces elsewhere.

But there weren't any people in the street, just like during the walk from the marina to the palace.

It's a holiday.

How were there no Impaired? Yes, Pairing had likely decreased the amount of Impaired, and some were sent to Luxor, but there should still be *some* rejects wandering. Right?

It would make finding Charlotte harder. He needed directions. He had no idea where to go.

Tiberius meandered with no plan. Charlotte was probably home. Even if he found the house, Two or her father would probably send him away.

Tiberius turned down another street. Still no one.

Another.

The farther he got from the palace, the less *nice* the buildings got. It started looking a little more like Luxor.

Still no one.

The sun was setting when Tiberius ran into the first person. A tall, scrawny man.

"Excuse me!" called Tiberius, speaking with his best Ignis accent.

The man raised his eyebrows when he saw Tiberius running with his four splinters of wood and strings. "You getting Paired?"

"Yes, but—"

"Where are your folks?"

"What?"

"You better get home before a patroller deducts points," the man warned, turning away.

"Wait!" begged Tiberius, "I'm lost. I need your help."

The man raised his eyebrows, clearly not believing a word out of Tiberius' mouth.

"Don't tell me you're off to one of those delinquent gatherings."

Tiberius had no idea what that meant. "No, I swear I'm not. I'm just looking for—"

"The patrollers always bust those, kid. Go home. And be grateful I'm not calling anyone."

"I'm just—I'm looking for my friend. Charlotte Galvin."

"What do think you're up to?"

"Um—"

"Charlotte Galvin doesn't consort with people like you," the man growled, "I suggest you go before I call the patrollers."

Tiberius heeded the man's advice and ran, broken crwth and all.

Of course men weren't supposed to associate with women before they were married. *Paired*. He had known this.

But the disgust in the man's voice—the certainty that Charlotte was better than him—made Tiberius quiver. What if he was right? What if Charlotte gazed at him with the same disgust?

Tiberius shook his head. He had never doubted they were meant to be, and he wouldn't now. Charlotte was his future. And he was hers.

So he ran, with no idea where he was going. He spotted a redwood tree in the distance and headed toward it, if only to keep from going in circles.

Long shadows added to his unease as the streets got grimier. He clutched his crwth pieces closer to his chest. The buildings swallowed the top of the redwood. Phoenix Palace was long gone.

This had been a terrible idea.

"Hey, you!"

Tiberius turned slowly. He could use one of the splinters as a weapon if he had to.

But it was just a slight teen with short jet-black hair flopping over her eyes.

"You going to the party?" She wore a leather jacket, had a nose ring, and walked with a swaggering confidence that Tiberius immediately admired.

Or he *would have* admired if he weren't freaking out. "Yeah. Yeah, I am. Are you?"

"You look lost," she said, tossing her head to get the side-bangs out of her eyes.

"I'm, uh, I—"

"Come on, I know the way," she said, strutting past him.

Tiberius hesitated. Should he ask about Charlotte? But he had a feeling that this girl didn't run in the same circles as his beloved.

The girl turned and raised her eyebrows. "You coming? I don't bite."

And, because he had nowhere else to go, Tiberius raced to catch up.

"I'm Rae," she said, "Who're you?"

"Tiber..."

"Tiger?"

"Uh, yeah," Tiberius said.

"Cool name."

"Thanks."

"Did Jaxson invite you?"

Jaxson! Was it *the* Jaxson?

"Yeah...you?"

"Uh-huh. This party's gonna be lit."

"Yeah. Um...I'm trying to figure out if my friend's gonna be there. Do you—"

"A girlfriend?"

"Um...not exactly."

"Good. The odds of you getting Paired with her...best not make connections, you know what I mean? Who you looking for?"

"Zandra's her name," Tiberius said. This was a Low-Pointer thing and, well, Charlotte's twin was a Low-Pointer. If he could find her, she might take him to Charlotte.

Rae laughed at him. "How many Pairs are you gonna get to choose between, Tiger?"

"Um..."

"That girl's getting *assigned*. So, like...basically no chances there."

"I just...this is the last night, right? Let me live it. I didn't get to ask her if she was coming."

"She never leaves her pompous sister's side."

"Don't talk about Charlotte that way!" Tiberius snapped, surprised by the venom in his own voice.

"Bro, chill," retorted Rae, "I'm sure she's fine or whatever, but Zandra's, like, the only Low-Pointer that none of us really *know*."

"That doesn't mean you get to speak badly about her sister."

"I said no one knows *Zandra*. Everyone knows that Charlotte's a prick."

Tiberius almost screamed, heat rising into his face. He clenched his crwth and felt splinters poke through his skin. He couldn't make a fist while holding the pieces. "You're wrong about her."

"She parades around as if she's better than everyone."

"Maybe she *is*."

"Look, feel free to get lost again. I'm sorry that I insulted your girlfriend's sister or whatever, but I'm just telling you what I've seen every day for the past twelve years at the Academy."

Tiberius refused to believe it. He knew Charlotte better than anyone. He just couldn't let Rae's words get under his skin. "So. Zandra," Tiberius said, "Do you *think* she'll come? Since you know her and Charlotte so much better than I do?"

Rae snorted. He liked that she didn't hold a grudge. It was more than he could do. But the fact that she wasn't doing it for Charlotte...

"There's no telling."

"So...who all *is* coming to the party, then? From your Academy," Tiberius asked, trying not to sound as clueless as he was.

"We'll know soon enough."

"Are you excited for tomorrow?"

Rae laughed at him.

"Why not?" Tiberius asked.

"Don't tell me you are."

"I am, though."

"Why? You're not going to be Paired with Zandra."

"I know."

"Then what is there to look forward to?" Rae took a closer look at him. "Don't tell me you're actually a High-Pointer."

"I'm not," Tiberius assured her. But Rae shook her head.

"Pathetic. You're seriously risking this when you're going to be able to have your pick?"

"I'm *not* a High-Pointer."

Rae didn't get the chance to argue before they emerged into a square—and Tiberius was astonished to see the redwood in the center.

A group of ragtag 17-year-olds was being led away into an alley. Rae rushed toward them.

Tiberius kept to the rear, taking in the backs of the teens' heads. As far as he could tell, none were Zandra.

They zigzagged through several side streets until Tiberius was even *more* hopelessly lost, each one got a little smellier, a little scarier. No areas of Luxor were this dirty.

The leader of the pack stopped outside a nondescript door in a narrow alleyway. He knocked in a specific pattern that Tiberius memorized—though only because of his musically inclined brain.

He was sure that no one beside him was able to memorize it, but Tiberius was already constructing a melody out of the pattern. He just wished he could write it down, or play it on his crwth.

The group filed through the door one by one. When Tiberius' turn arrived, a buff twenty-something stopped him with a firm hand to Tiberius' shoulder. "No weapons."

"I don't have a weapon."

The man—who Tiberius assumed was a guard—nodded at the pieces of his crwth. When Tiberius took a closer look, he realized they did, in fact, look like stakes.

"I, uh, it was a crwth. That I shattered."

"A root?"

"No, a *crwth*."

"What the hell is a *crwth*?"

They didn't have crwths in Ignis?! What else had Tiberius' studies overlooked?

"It's like a lyre," Tiberius tried to explain, "But also a violin."

"We already *have* music."

The beat was already reverberating through his body. Tiberius personally wasn't the biggest fan of this type of music, but he could appreciate it nonetheless. "No, I mean—"

"Give it." He gestured for Tiberius to hand it over. But Tiberius just gripped it harder. "Or you can go home."

"Will I get it back when I leave?"

The man heard the fear in Tiberius' voice. "Sure, kid." He may as well have told Tiberius to leave his leg at the door.

Tiberius was ushered down the dark hallway. At the end was a door, behind the door was a staircase, and at the bottom of the staircase...

Was pure chaos. Or, as other people may have called it, *the party*.

The music pounded into his temples. The pain in his hand from his crwth's splinters pulsed. He couldn't take in his surroundings. The lights flickered on and off—whenever they flashed back on, the people standing in front of him were different people, in different positions. There was a lag in his brain, like his consciousness was flickering as well.

He looked down stupidly at his hands. He needed to get the splinters out. But if he took them out, then he would actually, *fully* be without his crwth. And he didn't think he could face this without it.

He froze on the dance floor, scared, wide-eyed, unprepared. Then a hand on his shoulder dragged him through the people away from the noise and the flashing lights and the kissing teens.

Where the hell had he taken himself? And who the hell...?

Tiberius turned to get a better look at whomever his savior—or captor—was.

A small woman in a hoodie that obscured her face. She led him into a quieter room—one that wasn't as overwhelming. "It's too much for me in there, too. It's better in here, don't worry," she said.

She put her head down and started back toward the chaos. But Tiberius touched her shoulder in gratitude as she passed. "Thank you."

She looked up at him.

Wait, he knew those eyes.

He'd spent five years looking at them.

He almost said *her* name. But then he remembered that it wasn't Charlotte. No, Charlotte wouldn't be here.

But Charlotte's sister, Zandra Galvin, had found and saved him.

10

Z andra couldn't enjoy the party as much as she wanted to. She hadn't realized how tightly packed the room would be. How, if she were to dance amongst her peers, she wouldn't be able to escape.

If patrol officers arrived, she would be smashed amongst the pressing bodies until the air was squeezed from her lungs and she collapsed to the floor, trampled with no escape.

When Zandra was twelve, Imogen made her swear to never tell anyone about her claustrophobia. Imogen said that weakness could—and would—be used against her. Zandra had raised her eyebrows—Charlotte was the one who had to be careful about exploiting vulnerabilities. Not her. But she'd agreed anyway.

The party *was* fun when Zandra hugged the walls. Yes, she wanted to be in the center of it all, experiencing it for herself, but she was much more comfortable with space to move as she pleased.

She'd caught a glimpse of Charlotte early in the evening before she'd melted into the crowd. So Zandra was on her own tonight.

The walls were a good place to see a rotation of people. It was easy to forget about her immediate quest to find Jaxson, and her later quest to find an Unruly.

Especially when an attractive boy with a square jawline and squarer shoulders joined her. An energy passed between them, and soon they were dancing in sync, his facial hair inches from her cheek. Butterflies flapped in her stomach, adrenaline rushing through her veins.

The boy was swept away by one of his friends, but soon another replaced him.

Zandra felt exhilarated. Alive. Like she was finally experiencing what life was supposed to feel like—but what Pairing made it impossible to be.

After a boy with rancid breath screamed into her face to be heard over the music, she decided it was time to take her search for Jaxson a little more seriously.

A loop around proved finding Jaxson fraught. Zandra pulled several people aside. Some gave her blank stares, others shrugged or shook their heads.

Zandra finally got an answer when she pulled a put-together girl aside. Zandra had seen her a few times before—a Mid-Pointer.

"Hi, do you know where Jaxson is?" Zandra shouted over the music.

"Just left for a deal."

Zandra had no idea what that meant, but she didn't dare reveal her ignorance. "Is he coming back?"

"Doubt it!" she said, disappearing back into the crowd.

Time was running out. She'd been at the party for several hours and she had nothing to show for it except the experience.

It took all of Zandra's willpower to walk through the back exit and step into the cool pre-dawn night. A cool breeze caressed her face, a soothing contrast to the heat of the dance floor.

The city was beginning to wake. She had a better chance of

finding a former Unruly now that the sky was lightening in the east. The LPC started their days early running Ignis' trash system.

Zandra turned onto a larger street, walking down the dirty cement amongst a few dozen Low-Pointers. She pulled her hood over her eyes.

The Low-Pointers headed for the center of Ignis to clean the roads before the city sprouted to life. It was ironic—and cruel—that their own home was caked in dirt and debris, yet they survived by sweeping the streets of those with better fortune.

We, Zandra corrected herself. She was going to be living here —well, later in the day.

Maybe it would be okay. She *had* just enjoyed herself at a party in the LPC, after all. But Zandra had a feeling that living there would be much different than visiting when something fun was going on.

Her privilege would be stripped away soon.

At least I'm not in the Union.

She'd been lucky to live on Princeps at all, and have been born into the Galvin family. She had enjoyed it while it had lasted. That would have to be enough.

Zandra blended into the crowd, weaving between the graffitied cement walls and the scattered people, glancing at everyone's left hand as she passed. Searching for the mark of the Unruly. For the X.

Zandra was found instead.

"Charlotte?" a woman's voice sounded behind her.

Zandra instinctually turned. Behind her stood an imposing woman. Zandra did a double take.

The woman was Five's doppelgänger.

Upon a closer inspection, Zandra realized they weren't *quite* the same. Though just as tall, this woman wasn't nearly as muscular or intimidating as Five. And there was kindness in her eyes—eyes that happened to be perfectly symmetrical, unlike her daughter's.

Because Five *had* to have been this woman's daughter. She appeared to be about forty, double Five's age. It immediately made sense.

She was dressed in worn Low-Pointer clothes, a hole in one of the armpits.

Zandra always forgot that Five had come from the LPC.

She wanted to stand and gawk, but she didn't need to get involved in...whatever this was. "I'm not Charlotte." She pulled her hood lower and turned.

"Wait!" Five's mother begged, grabbing Zandra's arm before she could flee. "Please. Please just give me one moment."

Zandra glanced at the hand gripping her forearm. A red *X* was tattooed into her skin. *Branded*.

Zandra gasped.

A raw vulnerability bled through the woman's voice. "I just need you to pass on a message to Samantha. I'm her mother. Greta."

It had been Five's name less than a year before. Five had done everything in her power to erase it from Ignis' collective memory.

And, apparently, the fact that her mother had been Unruly. How had she managed to hide *that*?

"What was it like?" Zandra whispered, "Unruly?"

A shadow of suspicion crossed Greta's face, though she didn't release Zandra's sweaty arm.

"Tell your sister to relay it," Greta said, her face inches away from Zandra's.

Hell would freeze over before Charlotte passed a message onto her rival, but Zandra had both enough pity and curiosity to ask, "What is it?"

"Tell her we miss her. And we just want to talk to her again. She always has a home here. With us."

"I will...but only if you tell me about Unruly."

Zandra would pass it on regardless—sympathy for Greta broke her heart, but Greta didn't need to know that.

"You don't want to go there."

"That's not what I asked."

"But it's what you need to know. You don't want my life."

"I'm going to get your life regardless."

Greta wasn't going to elaborate further, just like every other former Unruly she'd spoken to. There was no deep trauma in Greta's eyes, but also no uncertainty. Exactly the same as the last Unruly she had spoken to.

What was she missing? What had the Council done to these people to keep them from talking? And how had they done it without damaging the Unruly?

"I won't pass the message unless you tell me."

Zandra could feel Greta's frustration through the strengthening of her grip. "Don't have an Impaired. You wouldn't want to send them there."

"What?"

Why *would* she have an Impaired? She didn't even *know* anyone to have an Impaired *with*!

"Please. *Please* pass on my message. That's all I can say."

"Can or will?"

"Can. But you *can* speak to my daughter. I know you don't know me, but...if you have any goodness in your heart, *please bring my daughter back to me.*"

Of course she would help this woman. How could she not? But Greta—or any Unruly, for that matter—would not be helping her. That much was clear.

She wanted to keep trying, but the sun was beginning to rise and Zandra saw a patrol officer in the distance.

"Okay. I will. I'll try."

Tears flooded Greta's eyes. She released Zandra's bicep and

threw her arms around Zandra's shoulders. "Thank you. *Thank you.* Tell her that we're sorry. We want her back."

I will see this through, Zandra decided, *Somehow.*

"You love your family?" Greta asked.

"Yes," Zandra affirmed, "More than anything."

"I do too. I swear it."

"I'm, uh, sure you do," replied Zandra.

"High Society—it's hard to compete with that. Especially when you've made mistakes."

"We all make mistakes."

Greta steeled herself and said, "Tell her I'll get Upgraded. For her. Just to see her on more than the screens."

She wouldn't. Low-Pointers never won the Upgrades, the lottery spots that admitted a few lucky Ignites into High Society each year.

Zandra nodded and stepped away, unease building in her gut. Was this going to be her fate with Charlotte? Was Zandra going to stop passersby in hopes someone with more resources would be gracious enough to pass along a message to her sister?

If she went Unruly, didn't win the Conquest, and was eventually sent to the LPC and assigned to a Pair, would Charlotte be so ashamed of the red *X* that she'd never speak to Zandra again? Would Imogen? Would Lawrence?

No, Zandra assured herself, *They would never. They love me.*

But deep down, Zandra knew that if she even had to ask the question, her bond with her family wasn't as strong she desperately tried to convince herself it was.

II

Charlotte hated everything about the party. The lights. The noise. The people.

The boy—Phillips.

He sauntered over as she scouted for Jaxson from the side-lines, trying to glimpse his silhouette when the flashing lights allowed for it. She'd found a backroom that she used as a refuge when she started getting overwhelmed.

But instead of finding Jaxson, she found Mace Phillips.

She knew who he was before he introduced himself, and he knew her. He'd also grown up on Princeps, on the other side of town. Their parents hadn't interacted much, so neither had they.

She immediately judged him for being there. It was so careless. He didn't even have the excuse of a sister.

Or Dust. Charlotte assumed, anyway.

"You're Charlotte's sister," he said, sidling up. He was a fellow High-Pointer—the highest in the social category and near the top in the physical. He was notoriously charming, attractive, and seemingly everything a girl could want in a Pair—or so Charlotte's friends believed.

But as he stood just an inch too close, Charlotte didn't get it.

"Yep," Charlotte declared, "And who are you?"

"Mace Phillips. An acquaintance of Charlotte's."

That was pushing it. "Cool."

"Cool? Me? No, you're the cool one."

"Really?" Charlotte asked as she resisted the urge to scowl at him. Phillips leaned against the wall beside her, his pinky finger brushing hers for a fraction of a second. Charlotte crossed her arms, repulsed.

"Yeah. You don't give a damn. It's sick."

He did nothing threatening. He just stood there, looking at her with a glint in his eyes.

Charlotte wanted to run.

"This party's sick too. I feel like we're in the Union or something."

How could this idiotic boy compare this to the Union? The LPC was *Princeps* compared to the Union.

"You got a message for Charlotte or something?"

"I think we're potential Pairs," he drawled, "Which would mean that *you* and I are too, wouldn't it?"

"That's not how it works," Charlotte told him, stepping back.

Phillips got the message. "Got it, sorry."

Then he was gone. Charlotte exhaled.

This whole place was disgusting. The sweaty bodies that came too near. Everyone trying to touch each other.

Before Charlotte could find a place to retreat to, another boy approached. Had her conversation with Phillips given her identity away?

Scrawny and twitchy, with a long nose, greasy hair, and an endearing smile, this one radiated nervous energy. "Hi," he said, his voice barely audible.

"Hi," replied Charlotte, emotionless. Unlike Phillips, this boy was not looking for anything more than a conversation.

"You're Zandra, right?"

"Yeah."

"I'm Wade."

Charlotte waited for him to say more, but instead he just bounced on his toes.

"So what—" she began.

"I don't know why I'm here! I don't usually do stuff like this, and—and I'm not really sure I want to be here at all."

"Well, you *are* here this time."

"I live around here. And I heard the noise, and my friends are here, and I figured I'm not going to get to pick a Pair anyway, so what do I have to lose?"

Of course he was a delinquent. Any sympathy Charlotte felt for him vanished.

There was so much she wanted to say, but Zandra would say none of it. She plotted a way to get out of the situation.

"I'm just so scared, you know? I'm not ready for a Pair. I'm not ready for any of it."

That Charlotte could relate to. Wade leaned a little closer, as if people could hear him over the loud base. As if they actually cared about his words. "I thought that coming here would give me some courage, you know? Maybe if I could come here, then I could face a Pair."

"But you don't want to be here," Charlotte finally said, "So how is going somewhere you don't even want to go, for no purpose at all, courageous?"

Wade's eyes widened, as if she had changed his entire world. Charlotte looked for a way out. Any way.

Then she spotted the other boy.

He looked so overwhelmed that he must've just arrived. Charlotte could see a little of herself in him in his confused expression. Sensory overload, which looked a hell of a lot like panic.

Against her better judgment, she said to Wade, "Excuse me."

A moment later, she was pulling the boy away, into the backroom. Only when the beat was muffled did Charlotte realize it had brought on a headache.

Charlotte made to leave the boy in the back room after a quick exchange, but he stopped her with a hand on her shoulder. Charlotte shrugged him away before realizing he was gaping. Not in the same way the others did—as if she were a long lost relative returned from the dead.

Though he looked nothing like Phillips, the boy was also generically attractive, with kind, wide brown eyes and a tall, lanky —not *not* muscular—frame. He radiated gentleness in a way that Charlotte didn't often see. She felt safe despite the shoulder grab.

"Are you okay?" Charlotte asked when his mouth didn't close, dropping her voice in her best Zandra-impression.

He slowly recovered. "Yes. Yes, I am now. Thanks to you," he said, awkward.

"No problem." She flashed a smile and turned. She needed to get back to her mission.

"Wait!" The boy gently grabbed her wrist and Charlotte yanked it away, repulsed again. Why did people think it was okay to touch others? Didn't they all hate it as much as she did?

If he wasn't about to flirt with her, he probably wanted to know what it was like to be the Highest Pointer's clone.

"I really—"

"My name is Prince Tiberius of Luxor and I'm going to be Paired with your sister."

Charlotte forgot how to breathe.

"And I know this is going to sound crazy," he continued, not bothering to wait for Charlotte to turn back around, "But I didn't get to meet her earlier today and I just...wanted to. Before all the eyes are on us. Which sounded a lot less stupid before I was face-to—well, face-to-back—with her twin."

What was she supposed to say? What *could* she say?

What did she *want* to say?

Her heart pounded in her chest.

She may not know what she wanted to *say*, but she knew what she wanted to *do*. She needed to get her hands on Dust. Now.

But she couldn't leave Tiberius there. This could be the man she spent the rest of her life with. Leaving him—walking away—that wasn't an option. She couldn't let him think Zandra a fool.

She turned to face him. He was bouncing on the balls of his feet with a childlike hope in his eyes.

"So why did you come here?" She tried for the bold curiosity of Zandra, but her voice felt small. She tried to feel something for him—anything—but found herself empty. She wished she were anywhere but here.

"I got lost, actually." Charlotte would have laughed if her emotions had been working. "And then a girl found me and said there was a party, so I figured I'd come here and see if I could find *you*. And then I'd ask you to bring me to Charlotte—just so I could let her know my intentions. Again, before the eyes of the country are on us."

"I'm not usually at these sorts of things," Charlotte muttered, a hint of defensiveness creeping into her tone.

"It's okay even if you are, I don't care. Would you—I know this is a lot to ask...but can you take me to her?"

"That isn't a good idea," Charlotte mumbled.

"Why not?"

"Do you—if you have something to say to her, I'll make sure she hears it. I promise."

"I just...I want her to know that I'm all in. On her. I don't care about anyone else. She deserves a respectable, loyal Pair, and I want to be that for her."

Charlotte gaped. He was all in on *her*?

She should have been thrilled. This was good news. But a pit of nausea built in her stomach. He didn't know her. How did he know what she did or didn't deserve?

She needed to find Jaxson. *Soon*.

"I—I will. Thank you."

"No, thank *you*, Zandra Galvin. Charlotte's lucky to have a sister like you."

"Thank you," Charlotte said. *I am*. She anchored her mind to that thought. She could sort through the rest of them later.

"And, uh, you also deserve a loyal, respectable Pair! And I'm sorry if I overstepped. I just needed her to know."

"She will. She's really going to...appreciate you making this effort."

Tiberius bowed low, glowing at the praise. He was so polite. So kind. He was everything she should have wanted.

So why did she feel sick to her stomach?

Charlotte bowed in return.

"Thank you, Zandra Galvin. I'm sure I'll be seeing much of you in the future."

If only he knew.

"I'm sure you're right."

Tiberius made to leave, then stopped in his tracks. "But before I head back to Phoenix Palace...something has been troubling me."

Charlotte nodded for him to go on.

"Where are all the Impaired? I haven't seen a single person in the street since I've been here."

Charlotte was thrown. "What do you mean?"

"I heard you don't...integrate them into society. In Luxor—well, we don't call them Impaired there, they're just the people. But I'm sure you must have some here."

They were *integrated* there? Charlotte couldn't imagine it.

"They're sent Unruly when they're ten." She had sympathy for them—they were grotesque and unwell, since they'd been born outside of the genetic Pairing system. But she felt anger toward their parents—they should've known better than to procreate outside of Pairing.

"Oh. And then are some of the Unruly sent to Luxor?"

"What?"

"Some of the Impaired in Luxor are from here."

Charlotte gaped—that was the first she'd heard of that.

Unruly must be *bad*—overpopulated—if the Council were sending Impaired to Luxor.

It didn't make sense. Why wouldn't they send the genetically healthy Unruly to Luxor instead? Wouldn't that be more beneficial to the human race?

Perhaps the Council was afraid that if the Impaired population got large enough, they would try to reclaim Ignis.

It made Charlotte's head hurt. "I don't know—"

A yell interrupted her, followed by screams.

The patrol officers had found them.

"We have to go," Charlotte said. She'd scouted out the exits—there was the entrance in which they had arrived and a back door. Unfortunately, they had to go back into the party to get to both of them.

Tiberius offered her his hand. Charlotte didn't want to grab it, but she forced herself to. Tiberius couldn't be captured, and she didn't trust him to get out himself.

They ran and burst into the party. Pure chaos ensued. The flashing lights and music made it impossible to see which silhouettes were patrollers and which were teens. Charlotte pulled Tiberius toward the back, running blindly. But everyone was rushing that way, and soon they were trapped by shoving bodies. Panic built in Charlotte's veins. If they got trapped, they were going to get taken. And if Zandra wasn't out—

Charlotte pushed the person in front of her out of the way. The dread in her chest didn't allow her to feel bad about it.

She shoved with her right hand, her left gripping Tiberius' sweaty palm, as she fought to escape from her personal hell. People were everywhere, their skin pressed against her own, but she was almost there...

Until she found herself face-to-face with Jaxson. Jaxson, who was going *against* the crowd.

Jaxson collapsed to the ground as a patrol officer appeared behind him, taser in hand.

And now the officer was directly in front of Charlotte.

"Back!" Charlotte shouted. The officer stepped over Jaxson. Charlotte watched, turning in what she was *sure* was slow motion, her eyes on the ground...

A bag of Dust lied beside Jaxson's hip pocket.

Charlotte didn't even have to think about it. She pushed Tiberius away, into the pack of teens, and dived for the Dust. Jaxson met her eyes, but could do nothing to stop her as she snatched it off the ground and dumped it into her mouth.

The taste of the Dust centered her. It cleared her head. It made her whole.

She could get out of here now. She could do anything.

But before she could so much as stand, numbness spread from her back into the rest of her body.

"No!" she heard Tiberius yell from behind her. She couldn't turn to see if he got captured as well. If he were smart, he'd run.

He didn't strike Charlotte as the sharpest knife in the drawer.

Getting released from the patrol officers didn't take very long. After being loaded into a van and transported to the Juvenile Authority Center, someone glanced at her and, naturally, knew who she was. "The Highest Pointer's sister."

Someone grunted in response. "She's being assigned anyway."

"Still need to deduct before Final Chance."

"Copy that."

Charlotte may have felt guilty if she hadn't just taken triple the amount of the most Dust she'd ever consumed. But all she felt was relief.

This meant that Zandra hadn't been caught.

"Question her when she regains movement, then walk her home. Can't have anything happening to Two's kid."

Charlotte mumbled at the greenest looking patrol officer when her mouth regained movement. "'Elp."

The man eagerly rushed to her side.

"Can't 'oove. Clausss-cho'—foe—"

"Claustrophobic?" the patrol officer asked, unconcerned as he opened one of the manilla folders in his hand.

"Yah."

The patrol officer furrowed his brow as he flipped through the pages. Charlotte's eyeball regained enough movement for her to see *Alexandra Julia Galvin* typed out several times.

It was her Pairing folder.

"You'll be able to move soon. Then we'll get you home. We're not cruel here."

Fifteen minutes later, Charlotte was outside her house, her hair tousled like Zandra's. Her parents wouldn't know she wasn't her sister by looking at her. It was going to come down to the acting. Charlotte didn't know if her Zandra-impression was up to the challenge. She'd find out soon enough.

The patrol officer—a young, ambitious woman—rang the bell at her house.

Charlotte didn't worry. The Dust was doing its job.

Imogen and Lawrence answered together, Lawrence bleary-eyed, though Imogen looked as if she'd been awake for hours.

"Zandra?" Imogen asked.

"Hey, Mom," Charlotte said, the carelessness surprising even her. She'd pulled up the collar of her shirt so Zandra's shark tooth necklace could be hidden beneath.

"There was an underground gathering in the LPC and your daughter was discovered there," the officer declared.

"I tried not to get as many points deducted, but—"

"Thank you for bringing her home. C'mon, Zandra," Imogen said, putting a hand on Charlotte's shoulder and pulling her into the foyer before slamming the door in the patrol officer's stunned face.

"I had to have *one* night of freedom—" Charlotte began.

"Those parties can be unsafe, Zandra," Imogen murmured. Lawrence nodded in agreement.

"I *was* safe."

Zandra appeared at the top of the staircase. If she hadn't been filled with Dust, Charlotte might have cried with relief.

"What happened?" Zandra demanded. Charlotte was amazed by her sister's ability to impersonate her. The rigidity. The higher voice. The meticulously combed hair.

"Go back to sleep, Charlotte," Imogen ordered.

"*No*," Zandra responded, contempt in her voice.

"Charlotte," Lawrence said, "Please."

"I've got this, Char," Charlotte called, "I'll see you up there."

Zandra glared at Imogen—as if to let her know that it was her sister she was obeying rather than Imogen—then turned back toward their room.

"You too, Lawrence," Imogen murmured, motioning Charlotte toward the kitchen. She turned on the lights and got the blender out of a cabinet.

"Sit down," Imogen said, grabbing some fruit out of the fridge. "Do you want a smoothie?"

"Uh...sure." Weird. Imogen never made *her* smoothies.

Imogen threw some ingredients inside and turned it on. The Dust was like a protective shield around Charlotte—neither the loud blender nor anything Imogen was about to say could pierce it.

Imogen poured them both glasses and pushed Charlotte's toward her.

Charlotte didn't touch it. Imogen took a long drink of hers as she studied Charlotte.

"Did you do anything that—?"

"Of course not!"

Imogen nodded, taking her word for it. Another thick pause. Charlotte considered asking about the Impaired in Luxor. But before she could take a breath, Imogen said, "I've tried pulling strings."

That could mean anything, but Charlotte had a feeling what was coming—

"Your Pair...he isn't great."

The shield of Dust cracked.

"And I'm so—I'm so sorry, Zandra. I'm sorry I haven't been there for you. I'm sorry that I put you into this position."

If Imogen had treated the twins equally—if she hadn't let Charlotte become so obsessed with becoming the Highest Pointer—it all could have been avoided. She and Zandra would both have multiple options—*good* options—to choose from, and everything would have been okay. They both could have lived on Ignis, and gotten houses next to each other, and their children would have been best friends, and they would have been happy...

But no. Imogen had ruined that for them.

Charlotte had ruined it, too.

She wanted to tell Imogen that she could be sorry, but she wasn't forgiven.

"It's not your fault," Charlotte said instead, "I could've tried a little harder—"

Then Imogen shattered Charlotte's world with three simple

words. "Go Unruly, Zandra," she whispered, "You can win the Conquest and then you'll be with me and Charlotte."

Charlotte blinked, her brain refusing to process. She gazed into her smoothie. A chunk of strawberry levitated halfway down the glass. Or was it halfway *up*? She couldn't have been sure.

Why did Imogen leave out Lawrence? was Charlotte's first thought. Was that weird? Or was it only weird because Charlotte was high on Dust and was hyperaware of every syllable out of Imogen's mouth, and every hair on her head?

"Okay," Charlotte said after what felt like an eon but was only two seconds.

"Okay?"

"Okay," Charlotte repeated.

Imogen gripped her hand from across the table. "Okay."

Charlotte stood. She didn't remember telling her legs to do that.

"And Zandra?" Imogen said, "Don't tell Charlotte any of this. She won't understand."

"Okay," Charlotte said yet again, "Then that's what I'll do." Imogen was right about one thing. She didn't understand. Not at all. "Good night, Mom."

"Good night, Zandra."

Unruly wasn't as bad as everyone claimed. That, or Zandra's Pair was a completely different level of awful.

What am I going to tell Zandra?

Thank the heavens for Dust. Charlotte certainly would have lost it by now without it.

She knew what she had to do, even though she didn't want to.

Charlotte was at her room much too soon. Had that flight of stairs aways been that short?

She stepped inside. The door had barely closed behind her when Zandra's arms were around her.

"Did you do it?!"

"Yes."

"You're freaking incredible! What did she say? Are you—am *I* —in trouble?"

Charlotte didn't respond. She couldn't let Zandra go Unruly. It was too risky.

Charlotte would just have to make sure she left Princeps to visit Zandra often. And when she got Paired with Tiberius... maybe that would give her the power to let Zandra travel to Luxor. Maybe it would give the power to offer Zandra an Upgrade.

None of that would be possible if Zandra were stuck on Unruly. If she didn't get eaten by a wolf her first day, that was. Yes, Lynx had done it, but Lynx was physically stronger than Zandra.

Imogen didn't know what was best for them. If she was going to pull strings and use her as a puppet, Charlotte could do the same. Zandra would never know, and Imogen wouldn't get away with shipping her "embarrassing" daughter off to Unruly.

"No," Charlotte said, "You're fine. It's all fine."

"What happened?"

"I got captured. How did *you* get out?"

"I left right before that. And—okay, hear me out—"

"Oh no."

"It's not bad—"

"Nothing good has ever come after *hear me out*."

"I ran into Five's mother on my way back."

Charlotte furrowed her brow.

"And she wanted me to tell you to tell Five that she misses her."

Charlotte snorted. "That would go over well."

"Can you just *try*—?"

"Five *hates* me. She'd think I was trying to manipulate her."

Zandra bit her lip. She was leaving something out, but Charlotte let it go as Zandra bounced on the bed and changed the subject. "That was so much fun. I just wish we could've spent it together!"

The Dust relaxed her again. The twins' swap had saved them. Charlotte could rest in her victory.

"The lights were *so* much, though," Charlotte said, collapsing beside her sister.

"I loved them!"

"But you couldn't see anything."

"It was beautiful," Zandra said, "And look." She pulled a handful of wrapped chocolates out of her pocket. "I raided the dessert table."

"Of course you did."

"Should we pull a prank on Mom and Dad?"

"Why don't we just enjoy our last night together?"

"It's weird that I'm gonna be with some random guy tomorrow."

Charlotte swallowed.

"I hope he's not trash."

"You're not still thinking about Unruly, are you?" Charlotte whispered, not looking at her sister as she ran her fingers over the quilted blanket, "Because you promised—"

"No. I can't risk never seeing you again."

No hesitation from Zandra. Charlotte nodded and turned until they were lying facing each other. Even in the darkness, Charlotte could make out the freckles dotting Zandra's face, each placed in the exact spots as Charlotte's own.

They were so alike, yet so different.

"I'm going to be Paired with the Prince of Luxor," Charlotte whispered to Zandra.

"I know."

"You know?"

"Yeah."

"How?"

"When I broke into Mom's office. He's cute."

"I guess I'm lucky."

"*He's* lucky," insisted Zandra.

"Why didn't you tell me?"

"Because you're always living in the future. I thought I'd let you think about him when it was time to think about him."

"If—*when*—we get Paired, I'll make sure you get to travel with us to Luxor. You should get to see the world, too."

"Really?" Charlotte could hear the guarded excitement in her sister's voice, like she didn't quite want to get her hopes up, but couldn't help herself. "Would he even let me?"

"I met him tonight."

Zandra's mouth dropped, "At the party?"

"Yeah. He thought I was you."

Zandra guffawed. "Did you like him?"

"I think so?"

"You *think* so?"

"I mean, I would be friends with him. I think. He was nice."

"Nice?"

"Yeah. Nice."

"But, like, can you see yourself being Paired with him?"

Can I?

"I—I don't—I don't know what that means."

Zandra tilted her head, like *she* didn't know what *Charlotte* meant. "Did he, like, give you butterflies?"

Charlotte had never felt butterflies. She'd heard it described like the *reverse* of the fear that often rippled through her body. She couldn't imagine a *good* feeling overtaking her being, making her giddy. She didn't believe it was real.

The feeling in her stomach—the one she had gotten when Phillips touched her pinky and Tiberius grabbed her wrist—felt more like *moths* than *butterflies*. "No."

"Has anyone?"

"No. Has anyone made *you* feel that way?"

"Well, it's not like we know any boys," Zandra said, not answering the question.

She doesn't want to make me feel like there's something wrong with me.

But there is, a voice whispered in her mind.

So Charlotte said, "Yeah, I guess I did...feel butterflies. Beneath the stress."

"That's good. Really good." There was no jealousy in Zandra's eyes—just relief.

"I'm gonna miss this," breathed Charlotte. Things were never going to be the same. She was never going to share a bunk with her sister again. She wasn't going to see her at all while she lived at Phoenix Palace the next three months.

They'd never gone a full day apart.

"Me too. You have to come visit me when you're on Princeps. Every day you have to come back to the mainland."

"I'll try," said Charlotte. Visiting every day was going to be difficult. It was a half hour ferry from Princeps to the mainland. That would be a lot, especially if she was going to try to get on the Council.

"You have to do more than try. You have to *promise*," insisted Zandra, a hint of desperation in her voice.

"Okay," Charlotte said, "I promise."

"Then everything will be okay. It always will be, as long as we have each other."

Charlotte fell asleep beside her sister, still high as a kite on Dust, knowing that she had made yet another promise that she would not be able to keep.

12

Zandra couldn't fall asleep. The fact that Tiberius had been at the party should have been in the *background* of Zandra's mind. But Charlotte meeting him—he was "nice". What did that mean?

No. She needed to stop.

Charlotte was snoring. Charlotte was going to be Paired with Tiberius—Zandra couldn't comprehend *why* she didn't seem more excited about it—and Zandra would be Paired with... whoever.

Her fascination with Tiberius was simply because he was from another land. He hadn't grown up indoctrinated with points and Pairing. He was a freethinker.

Maybe she would get Paired with a freethinker, too. Maybe her Pair would be someone like her. Someone who refused to mindlessly follow the system.

Imogen wouldn't let her get Paired with someone beneath her. She would have used *and* abused her power to keep that from happening.

Even so, she wanted to stay in her bed with her sister forever.

She wasn't ready. It had come far too fast. She wished she had another night. Another year. Another *lifetime*.

She didn't want to fall asleep. She wanted to savor every last moment. Because when the sun rose, everything would change. Life as she knew it would be over.

At least Charlotte had promised that they wouldn't become like Five and Greta. Zandra mostly believed her.

This will just be another grand adventure, Zandra lied to herself. She already knew what happened when people like her got Paired.

At least she'd get to see Luxor one day. That would be enough to keep her hopeful through the years. And she would *always* have the sanctuary of her mind. She could always disappear into the palace she had built there.

Zandra didn't know when she had drifted off, just that she had. Because soon Lawrence was shaking both her and Charlotte awake.

"Rise and shine. Today's the day!" He was carrying two hideous, glinting white Pairing uniforms. Zandra glanced at Charlotte. She looked horrible, dreary...

Afraid.

Zandra grabbed Charlotte's hand and squeezed it. Charlotte let go immediately, as she always did.

"Mom said you have to brush your hair after you shower, Zandra. Get ready, kiddos."

Soon the twins were at the breakfast table in their loose uniforms, which was the most comfortable thing Zandra had ever worn.

Neither twin touched the pancakes Lawrence made. Imogen didn't either. Lawrence made small talk, seemingly to himself, as no one responded. And Zandra wasn't sure if she was just imagining it, but Charlotte appeared to be glaring at Imogen extra hard today.

When Lawrence finished eating, Imogen broke his monologue. "I suppose we should go."

It was a half mile walk to the stadium in which Final Chance and the Season Opener would occur. It was the only stadium in Ignis and sat twenty thousand.

The moment Final Chance was over, the points of the graduating class were finalized. So, assuming that Charlotte excelled in Final Chance and kept her place, she would be honored as Highest Pointer of the year.

Zandra was pretty sure that Charlotte getting caught at the party meant that Zandra was currently the Lowest Pointer of the year, but she wasn't certain.

Though they were early, the whole city was already alive with people heading for the stadium. Food vendors pushed carts over the cobblestones. Parents with teens in the comfy white uniforms hurried forward so they could get good seats. Kids zigzagged through the crowds.

The festivities would have looked joyous to an outsider. Zandra wondered if that was how Tiberius saw it. But her thoughts of Tiberius were abruptly interrupted when she saw another merchant—this one selling Pairing merchandise— holding up a shirt.

With *her* face on it.

It wasn't supposed to be *her* face. But there was no way to tell whether it was her or Charlotte. Highest Pointer or Lowest Pointer—pick your poison.

Charlotte hadn't noticed the shirts yet. Good. She positioned herself between Charlotte and the vendor, blocking him with her body.

Unfortunately, Lawrence was as oblivious as ever. "Girls, look! You're famous."

Zandra could have killed him. Charlotte followed his gaze

beyond Zandra's body, darkening when she saw it. Her respiration quickened. Her fingers tapped against her thigh.

Great job, Dad.

"They got my eyes wrong," Zandra said to lighten the mood, "Totally the wrong shade of blue."

The stares began next.

Women elbowed their Pairs and nodded at the twins. Men murmured under their breath. Kids gaped until their parents whispered for them to stop, but not before stealing a few glances themselves. Everyone tried to guess which of the twins was which.

Charlotte's skin began taking on a blue hue. Like her head wasn't getting enough blood. Zandra had seen it happen a few other times. Once when she'd gotten points revoked for whispering to Jayana in class when she was twelve. Zandra had thought she was dying and had made an emergency call to Imogen.

She'd been blue for three days after whatever had happened with Harris.

It had "just" been stress. Even on her anti-anxiety medication, Charlotte still had the ability to turn blue. But it was "all okay" because nothing was physically wrong with her.

That was when Zandra realized *she* was going to have to be the one who looked after her sister. Because everyone else had decided that she was fine as long as her heart was beating and she kept racking up points. She was apparently the only one who cared about Charlotte's blue skin.

"Hey," Zandra whispered to Charlotte, "You can do this, okay? I'm gonna be right there with you."

"I'm fine."

"But it's okay if you're not. It's scary. I'm scared too."

Charlotte kept her gaze forward.

When they reached the stadium, Imogen sent Lawrence to

their seats while she led the twins into the tunnel where hundreds of other graduates were flocking.

"We don't need you to come with us," Charlotte snapped. Even now, hours away from Pairing Season, she couldn't resist going after their mother.

"I know you don't *need* me, but I'd like to stay until you've been been checked in."

Zandra didn't blame her with all the looks they were getting.

Moments later, they were cutting the line for their faces to be scanned and their IDs to be taken by the mousy woman at the desk. "Ahem, Charlotte Rachel Galvin?"

She clearly had no idea which was her. Charlotte took a step forward.

"Please step toward the scanner."

Charlotte did just that. A light shone over her face, taking in every millimeter.

The mousy worker furrowed her brow. "It seems that your face matches both Charlotte Rachel Galvin and Alexandra Julia Galvin."

"They're twins," Imogen stated.

"Right, let me just override...Alexandra Julia, can you please approach the facial scanner?"

Zandra stepped around Charlotte and was immediately blinded by the scanner.

"Okay, two matches for your face as well. Give me one moment."

This delay was *not* easing Charlotte's nerves. She glared at everyone who looked at her too long, rolling her tongue around her mouth, growing bluer by the second.

"Okay, you're all set. Charlotte, you wouldn't mind if I put a name tag on you, would you? Just so they don't mix you two up."

"Not at all," Charlotte said. The mousy woman wrote out her name with a smelly marker and gingerly stuck it onto Charlotte's chest. She began writing out Zandra's name, not bothering to ask if *she* minded having a name tag.

"Can you put *Zandra* instead of *Alexan*—?" But the mousy woman just slapped the sticker onto Zandra's chest before she could even finish her question.

"To the left. Take your IDs and you will be escorted to your seats."

Imogen pulled them off to the side and enveloped them into a hug. "You're both so brilliant that I know you don't need good luck and I'm so proud of—"

Charlotte shoved her away.

"Charlotte!" Zandra exclaimed.

"Don't act like you care about us!" Charlotte snarled.

Imogen glanced at Zandra, a hint of betrayal on her face. Was she supposed to know what was going on? She couldn't for the life of her piece it together—

Unless...

Her gaze darted between Imogen and Charlotte.

Unless something happened last night. When Charlotte was *her*.

Imogen came to the same realization simultaneously.

"You two—"

"C'mon, Zandra," Charlotte said, dragging Zandra away by the hand.

Zandra yanked her hand away. Charlotte was never rational when it came to their mother. "What happened? What did you do?"

"I will tell you later," Charlotte said through gritted teeth.

Zandra would give up her entire life for her sister, but she needed to know *what* she was sacrificing. And why. Imogen's mouth was open, but no words came out—picking her words carefully, so only Zandra would understand.

"Do it, Zandra," Imogen whispered, "Go." People stared.

Listened. It was as direct as Imogen could be without people knowing. *Go Unruly.*

Zandra's brain was ten steps behind her body. She felt the eyes on her, felt Imogen begging her to listen, felt the tug of Charlotte's arm, trying to get her away from their mother.

Imogen nodded at her. Telling her to go. To go to Final Chance and to choose Unruly.

Zandra nodded back. *I will.*

She let Charlotte pull her away. Through the door. Away from the eyes.

The second the door was closed behind them, Zandra turned on Charlotte. "What the hell was she talking about? What did she say to you?"

"Nothing that you want to hear."

"You don't get to decide that!"

The door swung open and two girls strolled past, trying to hear a snippet of the unfolding drama. Charlotte continued onward, but when Zandra made no move to join her, she sighed and turned back. "Can you just trust me?"

"Can't *you* trust *me?*"

"She doesn't care about us! We are her *pawns.* We always have been! We're just ways for her to get more power!"

"She told me to go Unruly, didn't she?"

Imogen believed she hadn't been clear enough on the roof, so she'd blatantly told Charlotte—as *her*—to go Unruly.

"Zandra—"

"Tell me the truth!"

"She doesn't—"

"You know why you hate her, Charlotte? Because you need someone to blame for being so unhappy. But the only person you have to blame is yourself and your stupid obsession with points!"

Even in her most intense moments of rage—which didn't

come often—Zandra didn't go for the jugular. She'd regret hitting where it hurt most the second her rage subsided.

But this—this was just the truth. And Zandra had let Charlotte hate Imogen her whole life because she didn't think it was her right to get involved. So why did Charlotte think she could interfere with Zandra and Imogen's relationship?

"I'm not obsessed with points, I just—" A group of four giggling girls entered through the door, stopping Charlotte's words in her throat. She cared more about what they thought than defending herself.

Unfortunately for her, Zandra *didn't*.

"Charlotte, I swear if you give me some crap about how you've done it all for Pairing, I'm going to kill someone."

The girls stopped to listen, too curious to be afraid of falling victim to Zandra's promised murder. "You've never given a damn about Pairing. You've never even cared to *try* to see the boys' Academy! You like points because they make you feel powerful. But they *don't*. I've let you do whatever you've wanted—and supported you—your whole life. And you won't even tell me what Mom said to *what was supposed to have been* me?"

"Get the hell away!" Charlotte spat at the eavesdroppers. They scattered. A part of Zandra hoped that they would go and tell all their friends that Ignis' twins were at each other's throats.

"Fine. You really want to know?" Charlotte hissed the moment they were out of earshot, "She said *you* should go Unruly so you can win the Conquest and come take care of *me* on Princeps. Because *she* doesn't want to be stuck doing it. *That's* what she said. You happy now?"

She was far from it.

"And I think," Charlotte continued, her blue body frozen in her anger, "You deserve to live your own life. With your own Pair and your own dreams. I think you need to leave me alone and try to do something on your own for once in your life, instead of breathing down my neck to make sure I haven't tripped over my own feet or choked on my own saliva."

Charlotte went for the jugular. She always had.

But Charlotte was right about one thing. Zandra did deserve to live her own life. And she would live it right now, in this very moment. In this very argument.

"Fine. I'm just gonna go live and die on Unruly, then. Or maybe I'll get Paired with some idiot. I haven't decided yet. Either way, you won't have me breathing down your neck anymore. Have a good frickin life."

Charlotte reached for Zandra's wrist, but Zandra snatched it away. "Zandra, wait!"

She didn't.

The drab white hallway seemed to go on forever, but Zandra couldn't comprehend anything except her anger. Her fear.

But even now, it was Charlotte she felt for, even in her fury.

Zandra's mind didn't change. She was still going to get Paired. She had to now more than ever. She couldn't go Unruly while she was in a fight with Charlotte. It simply could not happen, and she was too mad to make amends now.

At the end of the hallway were six doors, three on either side of another table with two women. Zandra slapped her ID onto the counter.

"Alexandra Julia Galvin...please proceed to Door 4 to begin Final Chance."

"This is Final Chance?"

"Final Chance will commence—for you—behind Door 4."

Zandra turned. She'd passed the group of eavesdropper. They now trapped Charlotte behind them and were too deep into dissecting the sisters' fight to notice.

Zandra took her ID and proceeded to Door 4.

Ten dentist-like chairs lined the room, each with a helmet attached to the top. Nine were filled with other women in her class, so Zandra figured she'd go for the empty one. Two workers oversaw the operation—one paced between the chairs with a tablet while the other helped a teen lift her helmet.

What the hell even *was* Final Chance?

The pacing woman hurried toward Zandra and took her ID. She pretended not to recognize her.

"Alexandra, please be seated."

"What *is* this?" Zandra asked, much too emotional to want to sit with her head under a tiny helmet. She was already feeling enclosed in the building.

"This is Final Chance."

"I know, but...*what* is it? Exactly?"

"There's nothing to be worried about. You're just going to put on the helmet and answer a few questions."

She gave Zandra a gentle push into the seat. A light scanned her body.

"But why do I need the helmet?"

Before the woman could answer, the helmet was over Zandra's eyes and all the light faded.

A wave of panic flowed through Zandra's body. Why couldn't she see? "Hello?!"

"Hello," a robotic voice responded, "Please confirm your full legal name."

"Alexandra Julia Galvin," Zandra said, "Is it supposed to be this dark?"

"Welcome to Final Chance, Alexandra Julia Galvin. Please answer all questions honestly and to the best of your ability."

"Will that get me out of here?"

No response. Zandra took a deep breath, calming slightly as she closed her eyes.

"Do you believe in the ethics of Pairing?" the voice asked.

"What?"

"Do you believe in the ethics of Pairing?" the voice repeated.

"What do you mean by *believe*?"

"You may interpret the question however you see fit. Do you believe in the ethics of Pairing?"

"I don't know."

"Why?"

"I just don't...know," Zandra said, not in the mood to explain herself.

"Will you support Ignis' point system as the next generations of Ignis come of age?"

"Absolutely not."

"Do you pledge allegiance to Ignis and Pairing, in good times and in bad, in order to preserve the human race?"

"Hell, no."

A long pause as the voice processed *that*. Finally, it said, "You responded to the question with the answer, '*hello*'. Is that correct?"

"No! I said, '*Hell. No.*' No. No, no, no, no. And in case you didn't get that, *no*."

The voice must have understood, because it immediately continued, "Will you procreate with your Pair in order to preserve the human race?"

"If I want to, I guess, but I don't see how that's your business."

"Do you vow not to procreate outside of Pairing?"

She had to promise not to birth an Impaired? What kind of messed up test was this?

"Screw off."

"Do you consent to attending monthly fertility appointments?"

"Absolutely not."

"Please disconnect and proceed. May you be happily Paired forever."

"Unlikely."

Then the same woman was lifting the helmet away from her head, her tablet on the table beside the chair. Zandra wanted to run, but curiosity got the better of her. She stole a glance at the tablet.

And gaped at the number beside her name.

She had never seen a point total so low. She'd never even *heard* of a number that low. Because it was even lower than the Lowest Pointer of All Time from ninety-six years before.

No. The *second* lowest. Because Zandra had stolen the title.

She was the new Lowest Pointer of All Time.

13

"Do you believe in the ethics of Pairing?"
You've never given a damn about Pairing.

"I do."

"Will you support Ignis' point system as the next generations of Ignis come of age?"

You like points because they make you feel powerful.

"I will."

"Do you pledge allegiance to Ignis and Pairing, in good times and in bad, in order to preserve the human race?"

"I do."

But they don't.

"Will you procreate with your Pair in order to preserve the human race?"

"I will."

The only person you have to blame is yourself and your stupid obsession with points.

"Please disconnect and proceed. May you be happily Paired forever."

Charlotte ducked under the helmet before it was off her head and ran. She needed air. She needed to breathe. She needed to be *free*. Free of the points. Free of the expectations. Free of her potential Pairs.

She wanted to hide. From the people. The stares. The pressure.

Zandra was right. Points gave her something to do. She didn't *want* to be Paired.

Even Dust, which she had woken up *very* much in need of, even though she could still feel it in her system, couldn't help her. She needed a change.

But it was too late. She should have figured this out ages ago. But she hadn't. So she would do what she had always done. She would smile and wave, then meet all her potential Pairs.

Where was Zandra? Was she going to go Unruly? Charlotte cursed Imogen under her breath. If Zandra went Unruly because of Imogen, Charlotte would never speak to her again.

The only thing that might keep Zandra from making that terrible decision was the fight. Zandra couldn't even go to sleep if the two of them were fighting, but Charlotte had never seen Zandra so enraged. What if this time was different?

She needed to find Zandra again to make sure. She had to.

The next life-suckingly blank hallway was shorter than the first. At the end, after showing her ID, she asked, "Has my sister already come through? Alexandra Julia Galvin? Looks just like me?"

"She's already been escorted to her waiting room. Allow me to bring you to yours."

"Can't I go to the one that she's in?"

"Unfortunately not. Right this way."

"But I—"

"It's not possible, I apologize."

Charlotte almost screamed as they walked her into a luxurious suite. Four other girls, including Jayana and fellow High-Pointer Priscilla, were already inside.

She tried the door the moment it closed behind her, but it was locked. Of course. She ripped off her name tag in frustration and crumpled it into her hand.

Jayana rushed toward her. "Charlotte, darling, are you alright? You look a little...blue."

"Yes, fine. Just...fine."

Priscilla motioned them toward the velvet couch on which she sat. "This is where the Top Twenty Highest Pointers wait. Isn't it divine?"

Zandra certainly wasn't in a similarly adorned room.

"Yes." *I'm a pig being fattened before butchering.*

Could no one see that she was drowning on the inside? Why were they all acting *normal*? As if *she* were normal?

"Look up there," Jayana said, nodding at the far wall. On it was a screen with a leaderboard—and all four thousand three hundred fifty-nine of their classmates ranked. Ranked and, for those who had gone through Final Chance—*locked*.

The points were locked. *Charlotte's* were locked.

Her quest for points was over.

Charlotte had gained a sizable sum from Final Chance. She was now easily the Highest Pointer of All Time. She would've been marginally behind Jayana if she hadn't been able to pretend to be Zandra every time she did something wrong.

She'd likely be a Mid-Pointer if anyone knew about the Dust.

Charlotte expected to feel something, but she felt only emptiness. An emptiness that had only been filled by the goal of becoming the Highest Pointer. By her ambitions.

She shouldn't even *be* the Highest Pointer. Jayana should be.

Jayana does Dust too, Charlotte reminded herself. But it did nothing to dull the guilt.

Charlotte's eyes darted to the bottom of the list. Zandra was at the bottom, as expected.

But Charlotte's jaw dropped when she saw her sister's point total. Zandra had lost over *half* her points in Final Chance. How...? What had she *said*?!

She was the Lowest Pointer of All Time.

"Screw you, Zandra," Charlotte muttered.

Unfortunately, Jayana was close enough to hear. "Honestly, it's going to make you both more famous. It'll certainly help *you* and it might even help her."

"This isn't going to help her!" Charlotte shouted. Everyone in the room turned to look at her. "*I* don't know how to help her!" She didn't even know how to help herself.

Jayana put a hand on her shoulder. "It's okay, Charlotte. You've been a good sister. There's nothing more you could have done."

Charlotte scoffed, shrugging Jayana away. Would Zandra still be the Lowest Pointer of All Time if Charlotte had taken accountability? She did some quick mental math...no. She wouldn't. She'd have two Pairs to choose from.

"You know how you help her?" Jayana said, "You do well these next three months, and then you use your resources to make sure she's looked after. Okay?"

Jayana made it sound so simple. If only she knew that it weren't that easy.

Charlotte brooded in the corner of the room. Jayana followed and sat across from her, which Charlotte supposed was kind, though it irked her.

Jayana let her sulk for a few minutes before whispering, "Listen, I was thinking...if we have Pairs in common and one of us takes a liking to one of them, we should let each other know. I'll step back if you're really into one of them."

Her words sent a wave of nausea through Charlotte's stomach. "Okay."

"Will you do the same for me?" Jayana asked.

Jayana could have *all* the Pairs for all Charlotte cared. She just wanted to go back in time. "Sure."

"We're both gonna get to High Society," Jayana said, "You're a shoo in, so one of us just has to get Paired with Atticus Marquez. If we're genetic Pairs with him."

Charlotte looked up at the male board. Atticus Marquez was the Male Highest Pointer, though he had nowhere near the point total of Charlotte.

Charlotte compulsively looked for Harris.

He wasn't second. Or third.

Her eyes scrolled. 20th, but not yet locked. There was a good chance he'd be in Phoenix Palace.

Another wave of nausea would have made Charlotte heave if there'd been anything in her stomach.

"Because if you and Atticus get Paired," Jayana continued, "then I'll be the next Highest Pointer, since my total's higher than Benji Cohen's."

Tiberius was going to throw Jayana's whole plan off. If he hadn't been captured at the party and sent back to Luxor, anyway. But Charlotte didn't have the capacity to wonder about him.

Zandra. Harris. Pairing. Unruly.

"Hey," Jayana said, " You're very...blue. Are you alright?"

"No."

"It's okay. We'll look after each other in the palace. We always have. You're the best of us, Charlotte. Everyone's going to want you."

"Thank you," Charlotte said, "I think I need a minute alone."

Jayana left her to it. The remaining girls of the Top Twenty had all filtered inside. Charlotte glanced up at the screen—there were only a few names that weren't locked.

It was almost time.

Before she could see if Harris had fallen out of the Top Twenty, the screen faded away, replaced with a shot of green grass and lush mountains as the video that opened the ceremony each year began.

A voiceover began, "Over four hundred years ago, disease ravaged our beautiful earth."

People coughing. Dying.

"Tensions rose. People grew afraid. And soon, nations began to war in hopes of reaching uncontaminated land."

An explosion rattled the screen. The people disappeared into the inferno.

"The world as we knew it was gone, and the human race nearly went extinct."

Smoking buildings disintegrated until there was nothing left.

"But one country vowed to make sure disease never destroyed us again. Ignis devoted itself to creating the technology that would ensure our offspring were strong and healthy. And thus, Pairing was born."

A woman popped into the room, drawing Charlotte's attention away from the video. "Line up, ladies. Pairing Season is about to begin."

No.

Charlotte's legs were lead. She hid within herself, the outside millions of miles away.

Her body betrayed her, following the orders of the woman. Charlotte didn't look at her. Or if she did, her appearance didn't make it from Charlotte's retinas to her brain.

"Charlotte Rachel Galvin, follow me. The rest of you, wait here."

Once again, Charlotte's body obeyed.

You don't want this. You don't want to be Paired. You don't want to be the Highest Pointer.

It wasn't the anxiety this time. It was her soul talking. Yelling. *Screaming.* The voice inside her head had been gently trying to convince her to choose another path for her entire life, and it couldn't afford to be gentle anymore.

She was back in the white hallway, a door straight ahead. Right at the end. That was where they were going. Out the door.

They reached it. It opened.

Blinding light. Charlotte squinted. The woman gestured Charlotte through.

She wanted darkness. Invisibility.

But Charlotte's body obeyed the woman's order.

It took a moment for her eyes to adjust. When she could see, she wished they hadn't.

People. Eyes. Stares. All perceiving her in thick silence.

She was alone on a stage that was much too big for her. If she could feel her body, she would have been overly conscious of her posture. Of her expression. But she couldn't. She felt nothing except fear eating at her from the inside out.

Somewhere in the back of her mind, Charlotte noted the deafening applause. Her ears rang. The gaping audience acted as if she had just concluded an incredible performance.

Five stepped onto the stage, approaching from a section in the audience. Charlotte zoned in on it. The entire Council was there, including her mother. Along with an older man that looked somewhat like Tiberius.

Imogen met her eyes. She looked concerned, as if she could *see* Charlotte's inner state.

She probably could. How did *everyone* not?

Or did they?

Five was walking toward her, like a lion stalking her prey. She stopped when she towered over Charlotte.

"May I present," Five spoke loudly into the microphone she

carried, though it was quiet to Charlotte, "The Highest Pointer of All Time to this date, Charlotte Rachel Galvin."

More applause. Charlotte didn't smile. She didn't wave.

She met her mother's gaze and begged with her eyes, *Save me. Please save me.*

Imogen looked around. She leaned over Lawrence and whispered something to Three.

Five asked Charlotte something, shoving the microphone into her face. Charlotte opened her mouth, but no words came out. She shook, dread weighing her body. Tears gathered behind her eyes.

She was going to throw up.

Charlotte pushed the microphone away and ran toward her mother, the only person who *might* help her.

The crowd murmured. Imogen stood, her hands on the edge of the stage as Charlotte leaned down.

"I can't do it. I can't. I can't," whispered Charlotte, "I don't want to. I don't want this." Lawrence and Maddox clung to every word, the only two in earshot.

"Calm down. You just have to stand there and then—"

"I want to go Unruly."

"Charlotte—"

"Send me Unruly, Mom. Me and Zandra. I don't want to do this anymore."

A vein was popping out of Imogen's forehead. "Get off the stage and follow me," she murmured.

Charlotte jumped down like the stage was on fire. Imogen whispered into Three's ear. He nodded and jumped onstage.

Charlotte vaguely noted One's eyes on her back as she was led away again, this time by Imogen, through the front row and into yet another hallway. The last thing she heard before she came back into herself was Five announcing that there would be a slight delay in the ceremony.

14

Imogen knew how to behave in dire situations. She found a storage closet out of view of security cameras, put Charlotte inside, and ordered her to wait. There was no way to lock it, but Imogen didn't think that would be a problem.

Her child was a basket case.

She couldn't believe she was doing this. But it was the only way.

The clacking of Imogen's heels cast a wave of fear down the hallway. Everyone looked away and focused just a little harder on the task they were tending to.

She stopped outside the Low-Pointer waiting rooms and addressed the woman guarding the door. "Can you please direct me to the room with the Lowest Pointers?"

The worker straightened. "Yes, right this way, Two."

The monotonous hallway did not calm Imogen's racing mind, instead echoing words from Zandra's journals. Imogen had read *all* of them over the years, making a day of it when Zandra's trunk was delivered home from the Academy for holiday break.

She didn't feel bad about it. It was her duty as a mother—the mother of the two most famous children in the nation—to know what was going on. To solve problems before they arose.

Every time I'm in a tight space, I can't breathe, one read.

Why does everyone like Charlotte so much better than me?

Other people can't just tune out the world around them and disappear into their own minds. That must be boring.

What happens if I don't like my Pair options?

All this Pairing stuff is kinda dumb. I'd get thrown out of the palace in a day.

This was a terrible idea.

Imogen strutted into a silent room with fifty girls in chairs—speaking was strictly prohibited. Zandra fidgeted at the end, in the spot reserved for the lowest of the low.

"That will be all," Imogen said to the woman, "You may return to your post."

Imogen walked through all the Low Pointers to get to Zandra. It would be a problem later. But if her twins could fool her, they could fool anyone. *Every*one.

Zandra's brows furrowed with worry when she spotted Imogen. "Is Charlotte—?"

"Fine. Come with me."

"Where?"

Imogen just led her back toward the stage. People would wonder, but there was nothing she could do about it.

When they were alone in the hallway, Zandra whispered, "What's wrong?"

Imogen swallowed, choosing her words carefully as she tore off Zandra's name tag. "I found a way to keep you and Charlotte together."

"What?" She hated the hope in Zandra's voice. She lifted the shark tooth necklace off of Zandra's neck. "You just need to pretend to be Charlotte for a bit, okay?"

Zandra stared, trying to piece the puzzle together.

"Trust me, Zandra. Okay? This is what's best for both of you."

Zandra nodded. Believing her. Placing her life in Imogen's hands.

Imogen was going to drop it.

They reached the door to the arena. Imogen tidied Zandra's hair, giving her a once-over as Zandra fixed her posture.

She could have been Charlotte.

"You had digestive issues if anyone asks. The excitement of Pairing got to you."

Charlotte would have been appalled if she heard that, but Zandra nodded.

Imogen opened the door and nudged Zandra into the lion's den.

15

Zandra squinted into the lights shining in her face, just as Charlotte would have done.

She was beyond confused. Something had happened, and all Zandra could do was trust her mother.

People whispered as they stared. Zandra didn't care. A part of her even enjoyed it.

Five waited before her.

Zandra felt as if she'd lived the rivalry between Five and Charlotte with just one glance at Five's wolfish smile. She felt like a lamb approaching slaughter.

How could ruthless Five have come from a sweet woman like Greta?

"Are you feeling better?" Five asked Zandra through the microphone, before proceeding to throw it into Zandra's face.

Yes, now was *certainly* not the time to mention Greta.

It wasn't hard to channel Charlotte—she knew Charlotte better than Charlotte knew herself.

"Yes, much. I just had some...digestive issues. It must have been the excitement of Pairing."

The audience ate that up as Charlotte went from unattainable perfection to a girl with G.I. issues. It made her even more lovable, somehow.

This is so dumb.

"That's great to hear. For a second there I thought you were going Unruly."

Laughs from the audience. Zandra smiled politely through her teeth, her brain racing, trying to figure out what had happened. Where had Charlotte *gone*? Had her anxiety done even more than turn her skin blue?

Zandra's gaze flickered to the crowd. Imogen was gone again, probably to get Charlotte and switch them back once Zandra was done with this stupid interview.

"I'm honored to be Paired," Zandra told the audience, hating every word out of her mouth, "I would never give that up."

Five smiled condescendingly. "What are you most looking forward to this Pairing Season?"

Charlotte had probably prepared these answers years ago, so Zandra stuck with the generic. The people of Ignis *loved* generic. "Finding my Pair so I can have children of my own."

It made Zandra want to vomit, but when the audience *awwww*'d she decided to have some fun.

"And what are you looking for in your Pair?"

Someone interesting. Someone weird.

"A kind man who loves Ignis."

Five almost rolled her eyes. Zandra's hatred ebbed just a little. "You know that an invitation to High Society is on the line."

That wasn't a question, so when the microphone was shoved into her face again, Zandra just grinned.

"Do you feel a lot of pressure?" Five goaded. Zandra took half a second to think—she could take liberties with her Charlotte interpretation, right?

"No, I feel honored. I face the same pressure as every other person about to be Paired—nothing more, nothing less."

When had she gotten so good at this? It was as if her brain was suddenly running at the same speed as Charlotte's.

Five flashed her sharklike smile. "Thank you, Charlotte. Ignis is lucky to have you."

Zandra waved as the crowd roared. She didn't particularly *like* being the "good twin," but she was surprised that she didn't *hate* it either.

Zandra walked through the audience to the exit, nodding her appreciation at everyone lucky enough to meet her gaze. She had no idea what the future held, but if it meant that she and Charlotte got to be together, she would play any part they needed.

16

Charlotte quivered in the corner of the supply closet, her knees pulled to her chest. She had never felt like this before. Not even the thought of more Dust could quell the ache in her stomach.

The lingering Dust in her system didn't even help. Nothing could. Her terror was past the point of no return.

She only knew the darkness of the closet and the aching in her body. She didn't have the ability to wonder what Imogen was up to.

Charlotte wasn't startled when the door of the closet opened, showering her with painful light, and Imogen stepped inside. "How are you?"

Charlotte shook her head.

Imogen closed the door and knelt beside her, putting her arm around Charlotte's shoulder.

Charlotte sobbed into it until Imogen took Charlotte into her arms, and rocked her back and forth. "It's okay. I've got you."

Piercing through the fog of Charlotte's pain came the question—was this what it was like to have a caring mother? Had

Imogen been that Charlotte's entire life, and Charlotte had just been too stubborn to see it?

This touch—a mother's touch—Charlotte did not mind. Imogen's warm body melted the cold that had spread into Charlotte's soul, more comforting than the initial rush of a Dust dose.

Soon the shaking subsided, and the sobs settled into tears.

"Do you want to talk about it?" Imogen whispered.

Charlotte was too afraid she'd return to her previous state if she moved, so she kept her face pressed against her mother's collarbone. "I don't know."

"It might help."

Charlotte summoned all her courage. "I don't want to be Paired." A weight lifted off her chest, only to be replaced with fear and guilt.

"You would have the best of the best. Any option you wanted."

"But I *don't* want that."

"How do you know if you haven't tried?"

"I just do!" Charlotte said, getting upset again, "And I—I'm scared!"

"I know." Imogen held Charlotte tighter. "But is there something—?"

"*No.* I'm not doing it," Charlotte swore.

Imogen was quiet. "So what *do* you want to do?"

Charlotte didn't know. She had never known what she wanted.

She only knew what she didn't want. It didn't matter if it was Phillips *or* Tiberius. She didn't want *either* of them.

But everyone knowing was only slightly less unfathomable than getting Paired.

She needed to get out of here. Out of Ignis.

Charlotte lifted her head and looked into Imogen's reflective eyes. "I want to go Unruly."

Imogen wiped the tears from Charlotte's cheeks. "Okay," she said, "Then you'll go Unruly."

"I'll be okay there, won't I? It's not as bad as everyone says?"

"You'll be fine."

Charlotte sobbed again. She couldn't help it—the dread, the relief...it was all overwhelming. Her entire life was about to change.

"Okay."

"We can stay here until you feel better."

"Aren't they waiting for me?"

"Don't worry about that."

Charlotte had underestimated Imogen. She did care. She had probably just taken Charlotte's lead—Charlotte had only ever cared about points and ambition, so that had been the extent of their relationship.

She found comfort in that. She sniffled and steeled herself.

"Okay," she told Imogen, "I'm ready."

Imogen kissed the top of her head like Charlotte was still a little girl living on Princeps.

Charlotte exhaled. She would announce to the whole world that she was going Unruly. Zandra would watch on her screen and follow suit. It didn't matter what was on the island—they would have each other.

"They continued with the ceremony, so you'll be last. Don't speak to anyone until then, okay?It will make things worse."

Charlotte nodded, having no intent of speaking to anyone, anyways. Imogen put her hands on her shoulders. "I'm very proud of you, Charlotte. You're so brave."

"I'm sorry I've been so awful, Mom. I really am. I—I was just unhappy—"

"Charlotte. I'm sorry for all the pressure." She looked it even now. "Let's go, shall we?"

They went. The hallway was no longer imposing and never-ending. It was just a hallway. Charlotte was just a girl. Not the Highest Pointer—not in her mind.

Imogen led her into a room filled with the Lowest Pointers. All except Zandra.

"Where's—?"

"She already decided to go Unruly, so they brought her into a different room so she wouldn't *infect* the others." Charlotte shivered, but found relief knowing they'd be together soon. "Keep your head down. You are strong. I'll see you out there."

Before Imogen could walk away, Charlotte grabbed her hand. "I love you, Mom."

"I love you, too." Her stilettos clicked on the floor until she was gone.

The Low-Pointers were silent. They sat in their chairs, moving when they needed to. The line was going fast, which meant that all of the Top Twenty had already been interviewed. Now they were just calling each graduate's name and asking them if they were freely choosing Pairing.

Soon it was just Charlotte and the girl before her, who finally looked at her when they were alone.

"Nice necklace," she said.

Charlotte looked down.

She was wearing Zandra's shark tooth necklace. Since *when*?

Had Zandra put it on her when they'd argued? Was it a parting gift?

"Rae Hollis!" the woman called.

Rae stood. "See ya, maybe."

Had *Imogen* given the necklace to her...?

No. She gripped the tooth, centering herself. She was going Unruly. She couldn't let doubts creep in now. The necklace was a reminder—a reminder of the courage that Zandra would have in this situation.

The worker at the door beckoned Charlotte forward. She followed her back into the hallway, back toward the door.

When she stepped through it and the lights shone in her face, she barely squinted.

Five was gone, having only introduced the Top Twenty.

Charlotte froze. But *she* was Top Twenty. So where *was* Five?

A random member of High Society approached with the microphone. "Alexandra Julia Galvin, do you freely and willfully agree to be Paired, now and forever, to whomever your genetic Pair, chosen by the Nation of Ignis, is?"

Imogen. Imogen had done this.

She looked into the crowd. Her mother was in the same spot as she'd been before. Her eyes were wide. She nodded her support.

Imogen wasn't sorry.

Instead of being consumed by the betrayal, Charlotte looked directly into her mother's eyes and said, with all the hatred and coolness she could muster, "No. I'm going Unruly."

17

P rince Tiberius of Luxor was more concerned about the broken crwth he abandoned at the party entrance than the fact that he was being hoisted into a wagon, tased and immobile.

But what—or rather, *who*—he was *most* concerned about was Zandra. He hadn't been able to help her.

What kind of future brother-in-law was he?

Does Ignis even call them brother-in-laws?

Tiberius felt naked without his crwth and his motor skills. His father was going to *kill* him. Would One try to take Charlotte away as punishment? Sweat dripped down his skin.

After a quick wagon ride, someone lifted Tiberius onto a cot and rolled him inside. He had no idea where he was or how far he had gone. Not that he would've known even if he *had* been able to take in his surroundings.

They—whoever *they* were—didn't give him a good view. Instead, he got to stare at a white wall.

Wonderful.

At least he could hear. They talked about Zandra, arguing

over who would get to take her home. Everyone wanted the chance to impress Two.

It made him sick.

Footsteps approached and he was turned over. A bright light scanned his face. Tiberius wished he could squint.

He was still seeing spots when someone muttered, "This one's not in the system."

"Scan him again," another voice shot back.

They did, the second time no more pleasant than the first. "Uh, still isn't showing up."

"Give it to me. You're doing it wrong."

The third time wasn't the charm. Neither was the fourth.

"Try it on someone else."

"Works on him."

Tiberius was flipped onto his back and both faces peered at him with a mixture of annoyance and curiosity.

"Wait till he can move and figure out who he is," the one in charge said.

"I've never heard of someone not being in the system."

"That's because nobody *isn't* in the system."

"Could he be Impaired? Somehow escaped going Unruly?"

Mutters.

"He would still be in the system. And he wouldn't look like *that*." He walked away to deduct the other kids' points.

Tiberius' jaw began tingling a few minutes later. "My— father."

His babysitter hurried forward.

"What's your name, kid?"

"Ti—Tibeer—"

"Tiger?"

"Tiberius!" Tiberius gasped.

"Why aren't you in the system?"

"Let me send a message to my father. He will explain."

"We're not calling—"

"He's on Princeps. *Please*," Tiberius begged. His body was slowly regaining mobility and he tried to sit up, but the man pushed him back down.

"That isn't how this works."

"But it's like you said. I'm not in the system."

There was a long debate until finally a message was sent to Akil. At least, he hoped it was. He gave his father's first name and the patrol officers claimed he would be found. Tiberius wasn't so certain. His father wasn't even a citizen.

Tiberius had hours with nothing to do but think. What had Zandra dived for on the floor? What had been so important that she had been willing to get captured to retrieve it? He was sure she hadn't tripped.

And was his broken crwth still lying in pieces behind the door?

His father appeared an hour after dawn, fire in his eyes, along with a ruggedly handsome well-dressed man that looked vaguely familiar.

"We'll be taking him from here," the man said to the meaner patrol officer.

There was anxiety on the officer's now-mellowed face. "I didn't realize they would be calling you, Three. We could have—"

"This never happened. We will be putting a good word in for the next Upgrade for your discretion. As well as anyone else who saw him."

Akil stepped toward Tiberius while Three dealt with the workers. "Everyone who saw you—we need to know all of them. How many?"

"I only saw the two," Tiberius whispered, nodding at the other worker in the back.

"You're sure?"

"No."

"You were childish tonight," Akil grumbled before prowling off to help Three.

Three and Akil escorted him to Phoenix Palace in silence. Tiberius didn't dare to ask to go back to find his crwth.

The sun was up by the time they returned. Three excused himself, and Akil accompanied him into his room.

The second they were alone, Akil exploded. "What were you thinking?!"

"I was trying to find her."

"What?"

"Charlotte. Since I didn't get to meet her."

"Do you know how much trouble you got us into?"

Tiberius didn't. He had no idea what had happened.

"The entire Council thinks you're some—some Low-Pointer delinquent now!"

A flutter of panic. "Are they not going to let me be—?"

"They were gracious. They aren't going to punish you, but you have a lot of work to do to get back into their good graces, boy."

Tiberius ran is hands through his hair. He had one job—had only been there for *one day*—and was already failing.

"You will be on your best behavior for the rest of the season. And Leon will not be letting you out of his sight."

Tiberius nodded. He was getting off easy. Arguing would just make it worse.

"You look awful. Bathe and sleep for a few hours. You'll meet the women at noon."

Akil headed for the door. Tiberius opened his mouth, then closed it, then opened it again. "Father?"

"Yes?" Akil responded impatiently.

"I broke my crwth. And lost the pieces. Is there a way...?"

Akil sighed. But he knew how important the instrument was to Tiberius, so he said, "I'll see what I can do."

Tiberius sighed in relief.

F ive hours later, Tiberius waited in a line of twenty men at the bottom of a double staircase in an elegant ballroom. Gold adorned the marble walls and light cascaded through the floor-to-ceiling windows, beyond which extended a balcony.

Tiberius was first in line. Or *last*—he wasn't quite sure. The room was occupied by only the boys, Leon, and the orchestra.

No crwth players prepared to play. Based on the instruments that Tiberius could see, they were going to need one or two. If only he hadn't broken his instrument.

The men had been given strict instructions to remain exactly where they'd been left until the women and members of High Society arrived.

The man three down from Tiberius muttered something to his friend, then stepped forward. "You on the end, who the hell are you?"

Tiberius clenched his fist. This boy—it had been a mistake to think of him as a man—spoke with more than a hint of aggression.

"Do you talk?" the boy continued.

"Do you *stop* talking?" Tiberius replied. If he'd learned anything from having three brothers, it was how to handle provocation.

Some boys chuckled—a few in appreciation, a few in outrage. The only one Tiberius could make out was, "Maybe this guy took the extra spot after *he* went Unruly."

Tiberius had no idea who "*he*" was and didn't particularly care.

"You obviously don't belong here," the boy said.

"Shut up, Phillips," the unassuming guy standing next to Tiberius said.

"Really, Atticus?" Phillips shot back, stepping out of line in an attempt to assert his nonexistent authority. "You're just gonna let some stranger stroll in here and take all the good Pairs? *Your* good Pairs? Aren't you supposed to be the Highest Pointer? Aren't you supposed to be our leader?"

Yet *another* thing his training had been insufficient in—who he was going to be up against. Tiberius' fist tightened. Were men in Ignis raised to believe that a woman's worth was all about the number of points she had? Did they believe that about themselves? Perhaps the point system was more toxic than Tiberius originally believed. In Luxor, love was built on mutual respect for the *person*, not how "good" society deemed them.

Atticus shook his head. Everything about him looked *average*. Average height. Average built. Average skin tone. Average hairlength. Average brown eyes. But when he opened his mouth to speak, Tiberius could see that his thoughts were greater than average. "You're all embarrassing yourselves. Get back in line, and if you have a problem with this guy being here, bring it up with One."

Unable to stop himself, Tiberius added, "And show the women respect."

"Don't think they aren't talking the same about us," Phillips shot back. He gave Tiberius a once-over. "Well, the rest of us." Phillips turned to face the other twenty in line. "Charlotte Galvin's *mine*. If you so much as look at her, you'll answer to me."

"You can have her," someone else said, "That girl is crazy."

Tiberius laughed mirthlessly, so angry that it could no longer be contained to his fist—it flowed up his arm and into his shoulder, until it burst out of his mouth. "*Do not speak* of Charlotte

Galvin as if she can be *owned*." Even Tiberius was surprised by the poison in his own timbre as he stared Phillips down.

"Who even is this kid?" Phillips said.

"I can't believe you still want Charlotte after she flew off the handle at the ceremony," another voice added, "Maybe she caught some of the *unruliness* of her twin before she got shipped off." There were a few murmurs of agreement, and some laughter.

What was wrong with these people?

"Well, Charlotte is too good for all of you," Tiberius murmured.

"What the hell is your problem?" Phillips said, sauntering toward Tiberius.

"People like you are." But he needed to calm himself. He was about to meet Charlotte—he couldn't do it in this state.

So he left the line and started for the balcony, hoping he could get his head on straight before he met his soulmate.

18

Zandra wasn't allowed to watch the rest of the ceremony. She was placed in a horse drawn carriage and told to wait. Patience wasn't a virtue Zandra possessed, and she didn't even have her necklace to play with.

"How *long*?" she asked the random adult who escorted her.

"Until the rest of the Top Twenty have declared their intentions to Pair."

"Right, but how long is that?"

Her escort just gave her a look and left to retrieve the next girl. Zandra sighed. That question was very un-Charlotte-like of her. She had to be better.

Zandra turned to the horse, a tall mahogany mare, and reached over the carriage to pet her. "We're both prisoners here, aren't we?" Then she stopped, because Charlotte certainly would not have been conversing with the horse.

Jayana arrived a few moments later, glowing. Zandra liked her well enough—she was a decent friend to Charlotte and had been kind to Zandra herself.

"Are you okay?" Jayana said, peering into her eyes, "What happened out there? You look a lot better."

"I was just nervous."

"Are you sure?"

"Yes."

"Well, you know I'm here for you if you need anything."

Jayana seemed like she meant it, but a person could only *truly* be there for a few people. Zandra was basically capped out with herself and her sister.

"Thank you."

"Can you believe it?" Jayana said, attempting to brighten the mood, "We're actually about to get Paired!"

"I know. It's all happening so fast."

"I can't wait for the luncheon. To finally know who our potential Pairs are!"

Zandra nodded. Charlotte was going to have more potential Pairs than there would be men in the palace. Based on her point total, she would get twenty-two options. Which meant that she would have options as "low" as the Top Fifty. She would have to leave the palace for those outings.

"I wish we could see what was happening in there," Zandra said.

"It isn't really fair, is it?"

"I would like to watch Zandra."

"I'm sure we'll be at the palace by then. Maybe they're showing it there, like they were in our waiting room."

"Right." They hadn't had one of those in the Low-Pointer rooms, that was for sure.

Zandra grew antsy. A million years passed before a beaming Priscilla joined them. Then the next girl, and then the next.

When everyone was loaded into the carriage, the driver exited the stadium with a bright smile. "Next stop, Phoenix Palace. Five will be joining you there as soon as she finishes up with the men."

The carriage rolled forward. Zandra didn't like the distance this put between her and Charlotte, though she suspected it would be another hour before Charlotte stated Zandra's intentions. Was Imogen going to make her announce that she was going Unruly before she switched them back? Zandra doubted her sister could be convinced to do that.

The carriage moved slowly. The experience felt unreal, as if the world was ignoring that Zandra had no control over her destiny. As if each *clink* of the horse's hooves weren't taking her further away from her ability to choose.

You did *choose this.* And she would again. She always chose her sister, even to her own demise.

Zandra had never been angry at Charlotte for the points her sister had lost her. She knew she *should* be, but her soul was unable to arouse it. It would only make Charlotte's anxiety worse, and Zandra's entire life goal was to alleviate it—she certainly couldn't *cause* it.

But now, a flare of frustration shot toward Charlotte. It would have been nice to choose between two Pairs.

Alas. It was her own fault for enabling it.

Zandra glanced at the sky with a sigh, blocking out the other girls, willing time to go faster.

Her eyes were drawn to a skull-like cloud a few shades darker than the others. It scowled, like it too didn't approve of Zandra's lack of initiative.

"What are you looking at?" Jayana asked, following Zandra's gaze.

"That cloud that looks like the harbinger of death." The moment the words were spoken, Zandra's chin snapped down. Her posture was loose, her legs much too far apart for the girl who had just graduated as the Highest Pointer of All Time.

Everyone stared. Zandra recovered quickly. "That's what my sister would have thought."

A few nods from the girls. They didn't know what it was like to have a sibling, so they brushed it off as that. "She'll be fine," Jayana said.

"I hope so."

Jayana lowered her voice. "You just need a fix when we get there."

Zandra had no clue what that meant, so she just replied, "Yeah, I do," and thought nothing more of it.

Zandra wanted to bowl over the other girls and jump out of the carriage first when they *finally* reached the palace. How did Charlotte always retain such composure?

An old ghostly-pale woman approached her at the gate. She wore a servant uniform and had her gray hair pulled back in braids, out of her sky-blue eyes and plain, wrinkled face.

She bowed. "Miss Galvin, my name is Eloise and I will be your beautician during your stay at Phoenix Palace."

Zandra bowed in return. "Nice to meet you, Eloise."

"I'll show you to your quarters."

"Thank you...is there a way to watch the rest of the ceremony?"

"We'll project it in your room as I bathe you."

"Uh...okay." But Zandra was too relieved to care much about the concept of getting *bathed*. She followed Eloise into the palace, not noticing her surroundings until they demanded to be.

She gawked at the grand archways, the marble flooring, the gold-flecked walls. The entrance hall alone was large enough to fit twenty LPC houses inside. Zandra enjoyed it while she could. "Have you been doing this your whole life?" she asked Eloise.

"Fifty-three years," Eloise announced proudly, "I've seen many pass through this palace. Your mother included."

It was strange to think of her mother as a teenager in this palace, going on outings with various men while the entire population watched and gossiped.

"What does your Pair do while you're here?"

"He actually works here as well. With the boys."

"That's nice."

Zandra was in awe the entire walk to her—*No*, Zandra corrected herself, *Charlotte's*—quarters on the third floor. The moment the doors swung open, Zandra learned just how seriously these people took Pairing Season.

The main room was two-stories tall and open-plan, with a kitchenette, a king-sized bed, and a bathtub overlooking the ocean.

"Allow me to give you a tour," Eloise said, "And please take off your shoes. Periwinkle is your favorite color, yes? We designed this space specifically for you."

Everything *was* periwinkle—the curtains, the tablecloth, the couches. Zandra hated the color—her favorite was maroon—but she supposed Charlotte would've been happy.

"It's lovely."

Did they really think Charlotte was going to need all of it? She'd never even had her own room. She slept on a *bunk*.

They walked past the closet, which was bigger than the twins' room back in the mansion. "And the gowns—the gowns are a mixture of colors from your preferred palette as well as the colors that best match your skin tone."

"Great, thank you. You really outdid yourselves...I'm very grateful. About screening the ceremony—?"

"Let me show you the washroom first."

Zandra smiled through her pain, but the washroom transformed it to wonder. There was a shower with jets on all sides, mirrors covering three of the walls, a sauna, and a mini pool that, like the bathtub in the main room, also had an ocean—and a marina—view.

Warmth crept through Zandra's feet. She frowned, then realized the floor was heated. Of course.

"This is how you work the shower," Eloise said, pressing a button on the remote.

Water spewed every which way. It was all *so* much. Too much. Yet Zandra couldn't help but covet it. Envy it. Long for it.

She needed to watch the ceremony. She needed to see what was going to become of her, before she became used to this life. She couldn't settle in, then have it taken away. "Got it—"

"If you want to increase pressure, you hit this button." The water spewed harder.

"Alright—"

"And to decrease, you hit *this* button—"

"Great—"

"And I can tell you might try to drown me in the pool if I don't put the ceremony on immediately." Eloise turned off the shower and motioned Zandra into the main room.

"Sorry. I just want to watch my sister."

"Do not apologize. But we are on a schedule, so I will prepare the bath as you watch."

"Thank you." Eloise picked up yet another remote and hit a few buttons.

Suddenly, the girl who had been in line before Zandra—Rae —was projected onto the wall.

"There you go, dear," Eloise said, turning on the water in the bath.

Over the water, Zandra could hear the words of whichever pompous High Society idiot had received the honor of commentating on the ceremony. "We've heard from personal inside sources close to Rae that she may be thinking of going Unruly."

Another voice piped back, "Let's see if those sources were correct."

Now the voice of the new ceremony host—Five didn't bother tending to the Low-Pointers—filled Zandra's room, this time with a moving mouth to match. "Rae Tatum Wilmer, do you freely and willfully agree to be Paired, now and forever, to one of your pre-selected genetic Pairs chosen by the state of Ignis?"

The audio bleeped out the first part of Rae's response. It came back when Rae said, "Over my dead body!"

The crowd, which had significantly thinned since Zandra had been there—was stunned. The commentator said, "And there you have it. It's sad to see such troubled youth."

"And Rae doesn't strike me as the type who's going to win the Conquest."

"Well, she's off to Unruly."

"Such a waste."

Zandra was too nervous to roll her eyes. *She* was up next.

But first the Lowest Pointer male needed to walk the stage. Greasy Wade Pollocks. He stared at his feet as he shuffled forward, softly rejected Pairing, and was sent off to Unruly.

Zandra wasn't surprised. Five to ten teens usually went Unruly per year, and the ones at the bottom were much more likely to reject Pairing than the others.

The commentators didn't have much to say about him.

When he stepped away, they brightened.

"Now, the reason the spectator section is still so full is for this year's Lowest Pointer."

"The Lowest Pointer of *All Time*."

Zandra held her breath. Even Eloise stopped filling the bath, unable to resist giving the projection her full attention.

"And also the twin sister of the *Highest* Pointer of All Time, who we saw declare her intent to Pair earlier this morning."

"The question on everyone's minds is—how could one twin turn out so right, and the other so wrong?"

Zandra bit her lower lip. They still showed Wade, building the anticipation.

"There's never been anything like it in the history of Ignis."

"I'll be honest, I thought twins were a myth before the Galvin sisters."

"Well, let's see if Charlotte Galvin's doppelgänger chooses the path of good or evil."

Zandra scoffed. The stage went dark. A spotlight appeared at the tunnel door.

And Charlotte appeared.

As she stepped forward, Zandra was surprised to see that she didn't seem to be playing her usual version of Zandra—though she didn't seem herself, either. There was a hint of terror in her eyes, but she wasn't masking it. She wanted the world to know how she felt.

Charlotte's stance was neither rigid nor loose. It was powerful. As if Charlotte were living in her body rather than thinking about how others perceived it.

"I know that they're twins," the commentator said, "But Alexandra certainly doesn't possess the same poise as her sister."

"That's for sure."

Zandra dug her fingernails into the arm of the periwinkle couch, violated on Charlotte's behalf. A thread ripped. She didn't care about people having ignorant opinions about herself—she didn't care enough to be offended—but they weren't allowed to have them about Charlotte.

A flash of confusion crossed Charlotte's face as the host approached.

"And here's the moment. A lot of people are going to be losing money today."

"Speak for yourself, Pace."

Disgust unsettled Zandra's stomach. Eloise tutted in disapproval.

"Alexandra Julia Galvin, do you freely and willfully agree to be Paired, now and forever, to whomever your genetic Pair chosen by the Nation of Ignis, is?"

He thrust the microphone into her face. But Charlotte didn't even look at him. She was glaring into the crowd. And, though Zandra couldn't see *what* she was looking at, she knew.

Imogen.

But there was no anxiety. No uncertainty. Just pure intensity.

"No. I'm going Unruly," she declared.

Zandra forgot how to breathe. She was going Unruly. Charlotte had sealed Zandra's fate.

When the initial shock subsided, Zandra clenched her jaw in outrage. Charlotte claimed *they* were Imogen's pawns, but Zandra felt a hell of a lot like Charlotte was the mastermind behind the chess board.

Imogen had probably already sent a lackey to collect Zandra. Imogen and Charlotte would be waiting in the shadows of the stadium for the swap back. No harm, no foul.

The periwinkle couch ripped beneath Zandra's fingertips. She hadn't realized how hard she was clenching it.

"Sorry—" she began.

But she quieted the moment the commentators began speaking again. "No surprises there."

"It's a good thing. I'm sure this will help Charlotte to be distraction-free in the palace."

Eloise's voice startled Zandra. "Oh, shut up!"

Charlotte walked down the aisle, glaring into the crowd. They closed in on her face. Her eyes were wide and determined. Zandra's anger evaporated as quickly as it had come, concern for Charlotte overtaking it.

Charlotte's skin had returned to its normal hue, so at least she wasn't *super* anxious any more. It calmed Zandra just enough to say to Eloise, "I need to speak with my mother."

"I'm sure she'll be here soon, honey. After she..." Eloise trailed off, but Zandra didn't need her to finish the sentence. *After she sends your sister Unruly.*

"I need to see her now." There was no way in hell she was letting Charlotte go Unruly in her place.

"I'm not allowed to let you leave."

"I don't care," Zandra said, jumping to her feet. Acting before thinking as she always did.

"There are guards stationed outside. You will not get far."

"So I'm a prisoner?" *Of course* beneath all the marble and beauty, Phoenix Palace was just a gilded cage.

Eloise put a hand on either of Zandra's shoulders. Though petite, her grip was firm. "I didn't say that," she said, "But I didn't *not* say that. Let me help you get ready and you can talk to your mother when she gets here."

Zandra went over her options. She could escape—and likely be captured and jeopardize Charlotte's place in the palace. Or she could trust that Imogen had the situation handled.

Charlotte would go Unruly over Imogen's dead body. Imogen knew about Charlotte's anxiety. She wouldn't send her there to fend for herself. Zandra just had to trust her mother.

"Okay."

The next hour was torturous. Eloise scrubbed her scalp with a soap that made Zandra sneeze. After the bath, Eloise started on her hair. Zandra kept glancing at the clock, trying to figure out how soon the boat would leave. She worried about what Eloise was doing to her—she couldn't look too clean or put together. People would know. And what about the smell? Would she have to jump in the ocean after she boarded to get rid of it? But if she did that, would they even care to fish her out of the sea?

She was a trapped animal, helplessly entangled with no hope of escape.

Imogen won't let anything bad happen to her.

Eloise started on her makeup. Zandra barely noticed the brush against her skin. Where was Imogen? Where was Charlotte? Why had no one come to get her yet?

Eloise brought out a periwinkle gown. Zandra didn't even scrunch her nose as Eloise helped her into it.

Imogen *wouldn't* let anything bad happen to Charlotte.

Would she?

"Can I send a message to my mother?"

"One second..." Zandra's eyes were closed, the final touch of makeup being administered to her face. "Open."

Maybe her mother needed backup. Maybe Zandra was supposed to have still been at the stadium.

"Perfect." Eloise motioned Zandra forward, toward the washroom.

It was taking too long. She'd lock Eloise in and make a run for it. It would make Charlotte look bad, but desperate times called for desperate measures.

But when Zandra saw her reflection in the mirror, her mind stopped.

Her face was contoured. Her cheekbones looked like they were jutting out of her face. Her hair was curled and her eyelashes long and dark, accentuating her deep blue eyes. The dress draped off her shoulders, loose and tight in all the right places, her midriff lightly exposed.

She didn't recognize herself.

The pronounced femininity felt *wrong*. Yes, she looked generically beautiful, but she didn't feel like herself. Or even Charlotte.

She was a doll. An avatar of who Ignis wanted her to be.

She *hated* it.

"Do you like it?"

"I love it," Zandra replied, not wanting to insult Eloise, who'd objectively done a good job.

Then she noticed her mole—the only thing that differentiated her from Charlotte—was exposed.

"You look beautiful," Eloise said. A compliment to them both.

"Thanks. Um. Actually—do you have something...more modest?"

Eloise frowned. "Yes, of course. Let me take a look."

Zandra tore her gaze away from herself, resisting the urge to mess up her hair. She couldn't think while staring at herself. She looked toward the window. How would she switch back with Charlotte in this state?

Her heart stopped in her chest when her eyes focused on the marina.

The Unruly Ship. It was leaving.

No. It was already *gone*.

"No," Zandra whispered.

"What was that, dear?"

Zandra raced to the pool of water pressed against the ceiling-to-floor glass window, lifting her dress and rushing in.

"Charlotte!" Eloise exclaimed.

She let her dress drape into the water, shading her eyes at the window. She could just make out tiny figures on the deck, about ten in all. She squinted. Charlotte *couldn't* be on the ship.

But when the sun peeked through the clouds, a head of orangeish hair set aflame.

Charlotte was en-route to Unruly.

Zandra's heart froze. She couldn't remember how to breathe.

"What are you doing?" Eloise cried, "I know you didn't like the gown, but you didn't have to ruin it!"

Zandra rushed out of the water, leaving a trail of water in her wake as she pushed past Eloise. She needed to get down there. She needed Imogen to get them on a boat to intercept it. They could still stop this. She would find her mother—

Imogen was already in her room.

"They're taking her!" Zandra cried, rushing forward to grip Imogen's shoulders. "She's on the ship, they're—"

"It's okay, Charlotte."

The facade was no longer important. What was the point of being Charlotte if Charlotte wasn't coming back to reclaim her life? "But—it's not! She can't go!"

"Hello, Eloise," Imogen said with a collectedness that chilled Zandra's bones.

"Two, the pleasure is all mine," Eloise said, bowing lowly.

"Would you please give us a moment?"

Eloise frowned at Zandra's dripping dress as she exited.

"How could you have let her go? *How could you?*"

"She wanted to."

"You told me we were going to be together!"

"I thought that you *were*, at the time—"

"She needs me! She needs someone supporting her! And now she's just off to fend for herself?!"

"She'll be *fine*," Imogen said, a drop of condescension in her tone.

"Tell me. How. You. Know." Zandra trembled with so much rage that she believed she could swim to Unruly herself—and had half a mind to try it.

"You are in just as much danger here, Zandra. The less you know about Unruly, the less likely you are to slip."

Zandra scoffed.

"She'll win the Conquest," Imogen murmured, "And you'll earn your place in High Society. You'll be together there."

"You mean *Charlotte's* place! Was this what you wanted all along, *Imogen*? To get us both into High Society?"

Imogen didn't flinch at the accusation. Her face remained passive. Emotionless. Unsurprised.

It *had* been. Having two daughters on Princeps would increase her status. "Charlotte was right about you," Zandra whispered, horrified. "She's always been right."

"Everything I've done has been out of love for both of you. So you can *both* be happy."

"Did Charlotte *seem* happy to you?!"

Imogen remained unshaken. "You both deserve Princeps. And I will make sure you get it."

"What is she facing there?"

"I told you," Imogen said, patience beginning to fray, "She's going to be fine."

"That isn't an answer."

"She *will* be."

"Well, I don't believe you. You have to take me to her."

"Can you please just trust me?"

"I don't. I don't trust you."

"Please—"

"Get out."

"Zandra—"

"Get out!" Zandra shouted.

A tear rolled down Imogen's cheek, but Zandra couldn't find sympathy as her mother reached the door. "You should start taking Charlotte's anti-anxiety medication," Imogen said.

"*What?*"

"This is a hard life."

"And you think my life has been easy?" Zandra snapped, now angry *and* offended.

"No—"

"So you think that I can't handle it?"

"I just want—"

"Imogen, I never want to see you again. Okay? I'm going to find a way to get to Charlotte and nothing you do is going to stop me." The words were a promise on her lips—to do everything in her power to right the wrongs of her inactivity.

Imogen nodded, though still she hovered. "You have to keep pretending. It's the only way to keep her safe."

Zandra swallowed. She gave the tiniest nod. She would do it for Charlotte.

19

The reality of Charlotte's situation didn't settle until the boat was halfway to Unruly.

The land on which she'd spent the last twelve years grew smaller and smaller. It was Charlotte's first time seeing mainland from the ocean since she'd been ferried off of Princeps at five years old. It was stunning—not as shocking as the lush Princeps or the powerful Unruly, but there was something alluring about the towering palace, the ocean mansions, and the average houses behind. The Barrenlands encircled it, an oasis on a horizon of emptiness.

Meanwhile, the jagged cliffs of Unruly grew more terrifying the closer they sailed.

What have I done?

She'd had a nervous breakdown caused by her fight with Zandra. She hadn't *meant* to choose this.

It was the anxiety. You never wanted this. You can get back.

A pit formed in Charlotte's stomach, so she forced her attention to the boat. The Unruly teens were not allowed to speak to one another. So Charlotte, a stickler for the rules even in her exile, obeyed.

But didn't stop her from taking stock of her companions—or rather, her *competitors*. Because Charlotte was finally realizing what a *massive* mistake she had made. The only way forward, the only way to get back to her old life, would be to win the Conquest. If there was any way to keep herself stable, it was through the mission of winning. Then she'd be able to switch back with Zandra, who was hopefully in the process of getting Paired with Tiberius on her behalf.

Across from Charlotte was Rae, who watched the ocean with wide eyes. Next to her was the tallest, most muscular man that Charlotte had ever seen—she had heard Four, who captained the ship, call him Killian. Then there were a few others, and apparently even more who had gathered belowdeck before Charlotte had boarded.

Charlotte was surprised to see the shy, twitchy Wade aboard. She had been certain that he would get Paired. Her speech at the party must not have—

Charlotte stopped functioning.

There, on the other side of the boat, was *Harris*.

Charlotte's mouth fell open. Her blood went cold—so cold it couldn't reach her brain. She clutched Zandra's shark tooth necklace.

What the *hell* was he doing here? He would have had plenty of potential Pairs. Did he think he could brave Unruly, easily win the Conquest, and join High Society?

Or maybe something better, he'd said at the ceremony, just a few short days ago. Was *this* what he had meant?

How could the two Highest Academic Pointers, best friends turned enemies, be together enroute to Unruly?

Harris wore a curious expression, as if he were absorbing every detail his senses could reach. He kept glancing toward Princeps as the ship steered past. Sunlight reflected off the colorful houses on the hills, flaunting the beautiful and unattainable land.

Charlotte could only vaguely remember where her house had been during the first five years of her life. It was on the ocean, but it hadn't been facing the mainland. Even after she'd learned that the world was round, Charlotte still feared that if she ever went for a swim, a current would sweep her out to the horizon and she would fall off the edge of the earth.

As Princeps faded away, Charlotte turned her gaze toward Unruly.

At least no one will be watching me there, she thought darkly.

Except, perhaps, during the Conquest—whatever that entailed. She would have time to herself, to figure out what had gone wrong. To figure out how to *not* make it happen again.

Maybe there was a silver lining. Maybe it would be good to hit the pause button on her life while she worked through her issues.

Despite the nearness, Unruly still looked *very* uninhabitable. How many people lived there? *Where* were they living? Were they perched amongst the boulders, hiding out in the occasional cave? Or was the other side of the island—the side they couldn't see— completely different, with lush forests and pristine beaches?

She thought about the Impaired, and what Tiberius had told her. Would it be overrun with them? Charlotte had never seen an Impaired before. Were they as violent and unstable as Ignis had led them to believe? But Tiberius hadn't seemed afraid of them. So they couldn't be *that* bad, could they?

Stop wondering. But was it was even *possible* not to wonder? Could she just turn it off?

A hint of panic nuzzled into her body.

Charlotte took a deep breath and focused on the impending cliffs of her new home.

"You okay?"

Charlotte started.

Harris stood a pace behind, glancing down at her white knuckles. His smile was warm. His presence...comforting.

No. She hated him. She hated him, and she was about to be stuck with him.

"We're not allowed to talk to each other," she snapped.

"What are they gonna do? Send us Unruly?"

When Charlotte didn't laugh, he sobered. "You just...look like Charlotte does. When she's freaking out. So I was making sure *you* weren't freaking out."

He couldn't have known. No way.

"Don't act like you know her."

"Sorry. It's just, you're even more alike than I remembered."

"Maybe you remembered wrong," Charlotte said, using the word *wrong* rather than her preferred choice of *incorrectly*.

"I just...haven't talked to you in so long. I expected you to be more different...with the Highest Pointer and Lowest Pointer thing and all."

"I got the fun personality, she got the palace." She subtly lowered her register.

"She has a fun personality, too."

"I *know*," Charlotte snapped, brushing it off to hide that his flattery had worked.

"Well, I'm glad there'll be one person I know on this island."

"Can't say the same." He winced, and Charlotte kept the momentum going. "So why'd you come here? Decided if you weren't in the Top Twenty, you weren't gonna get Paired at all?"

What answers do you seek, Harris? What questions are you asking?

Harris frowned, crossing his arms. She'd offended him.

Good.

"I did, actually. Make the Top Twenty. Good to see you."

She wanted to say more, but Zandra wasn't callous. Unlike Charlotte, Zandra never crossed the line to *mean*.

Charlotte had hoped she wouldn't have to worry about coming off too much like herself since these people didn't know her. But with Harris around, she'd have to be careful.

He wanted to win the Conquest. That was the only explanation. Harris could outsmart her. He had scored more Academic Points than she.

Charlotte gripped the railing, her knuckles white as she wrestled with a new wave of unease. She was going to have to work harder than she'd originally anticipated. She couldn't *lose*. Especially not to *Harris*.

The boat slowed as it lurched into the shadow of Unruly. A chill raced up Charlotte's spine that had nothing to do with the island blocking the sun. Because one rumor could be confirmed—had she wanted to climb, the cliff would have sliced through her skin. If she weren't impaled on the rocks by the current first.

The fear spreading through her body was just further evidence that she had made a rash decision during her breakdown. She didn't belong here.

Four steered the boat around the side of Unruly—the side opposite Princeps. The side that none of them had ever seen.

It was more of the same. The landscape didn't change when the boat began idling. All the teens exchanged looks, bewildered. Except Charlotte, who peered ahead, trying to make sense of it all. There was no docking place in sight.

"Where are you taking us?" Killian demanded, looking up at Four.

Four didn't answer, messing with some buttons.

"They're killing us, aren't they?" Wade whispered, "She's gonna throw us overboard and we're gonna crash into the rocks—"

"They're not killing us," Harris reassured, "I've seen Unruly in the LPC."

"So have I," Killian said, throwing a dark look at Harris, "And I actually grew up there, not pampered on Princeps like you."

"Then maybe they're really taking us to the Union," Wade said, "It's way worse than Unruly. Everyone knows that.

It was much more likely they'd be sent to *fight off* the Union in the north.

Killian growled, "Grow up, dude."

Zandra would have comforted Wade with an empowering sentence, but Charlotte was having similar fears herself. All the bravery she'd felt as she'd declared her intentions to go Unruly had long abandoned her.

"If they take us to the Union," someone added, "they'll sell us as slaves. And if we don't get sold, they're gonna leave us to rot in a crate."

"They're going to feed us to the Impaired!"

"I should've gotten Paired," Wade said, hysterical, "I knew I should've—"

A loud *click* interrupted him.

Everyone froze in the silence that followed. Adrenaline pumped through Charlotte's exhausted body.

The hum of a loud motor came next.

A portion of the cliff rose into the air like a garage door. If Charlotte had known what she was looking for, she would have seen the seams in the cliffside.

Behind the faux-cliff was darkness.

Was *this* Unruly? Was it actually *inside* the island?

Tension rippled through the boat. The new Unruly didn't like the idea of being underground. They'd come here to escape, not to be contained.

It was good Zandra wasn't here. She wouldn't like this.

Charlotte reigned her thoughts. They were going to dock underground—then they'd be released above. Imogen wouldn't have let Zandra go to an underground island. Even *she* wasn't that cruel.

It can't be that bad. It can't be that bad. It can't be—

Four reversed the ship and steered them toward the mouth of the cave. Charlotte glanced at the sky in case this was the last time she saw it. Then at the blue water that sparkled in the sunlight.

The ship passed through the mouth of the cave. Charlotte's eyes began adjusting as the boat jolted to a stop. She could make out shapes...

Until the light was chased away by the descending garage door.

The ship was enveloped in darkness.

"Where are we?" Wade screeched.

"We're inside Unruly, idiot," Killian shot back, "Now shut up."

"You shut up, Killian," Charlotte snapped. She wasn't sure if it was for Wade or herself—so she could think. She didn't like going into situations blind, literally or figuratively.

The cavern came into focus as Charlotte's eyes adjusted. The cave was only big enough to fit one ship—all the cavern's black stone walls were uncomfortably close. The only way out, minus the way they had come in, was through a lit tunnel carved through the stone, which rested at the top of a single flight of stairs.

"Deck Unruly, come with me," Four ordered, descending the staircase. She stuck her head into the galley and called down, "I'll be back for you lot in a few minutes," before locking the door behind her.

"Up."

No one moved until Harris took a step forward, leading the charge. Killian was a moment behind, a frown on his face that told Charlotte he was angry his fear had stopped him from jumping into action.

Charlotte lagged until she was the only Unruly remaining on deck. Four raised an eyebrow when she didn't move. "I'm not taking you back to Ignis."

"Who's belowdeck?"

"The Unruly who got here before you did. Mid-Pointers. So we could fit you all."

"Then why was Harris up here?"

"Because he needed to stick around for some administrative work since he was a Top Twenty-er."

"What's going to happen to them?"

"The exact same thing that's going to happen to you. It's easier to keep track of you in small groups. Are you coming?"

Charlotte stalled, her new world no longer looking so enticing.

"You chose to come here, Zandra," Four reminded her, not unkindly.

Charlotte debated asking how to win the Conquest, but no one would believe Zandra would care. So she nodded and jumped off the boat, setting foot on Unruly.

It felt no different than Ignis.

Charlotte raced up the stairs, hoping the release of her adrenaline would drown her terror. She focused on her heavy breathing instead of the eery lapping water that echoed throughout the cavern, and the burning in her quads instead of the instability of the stairs. She caught up with the rest of the group before they reached the top.

Another person—a woman from High Society with white hair that practically glowed—waited at the top with a creepy smile pasted on her face. Half of the Unruly from the boat had already disappeared into the plain, brightly lit tunnel ahead.

Four caught up with them. She took stock of the situation and said, "All good?"

"Yes," the woman said.

"Then I'm going to get the rest."

"Copy that. Children, come."

Charlotte walked beside Rae, Wade, and a boy she didn't recognize. None seemed inclined to follow the creepy woman into the creepy tunnel.

Charlotte took a step forward, giving Wade an encouraging nod as she passed. But Wade fell in step with her. "You're the reason I'm here."

Alarmed, Charlotte asked, "How so?"

"You told me that going somewhere I didn't want to wasn't brave. I didn't want to get Paired. So here I am."

Charlotte internally cursed herself. But there was nothing she could do about Wade's stupidity now. "Well, I'm glad you're here."

"I'm glad you're here, too. I'm a little freaked out, to be honest. So it's good to know I have a friend here."

Friend was pushing it. But she went with it, giving him a nod before setting her gaze ahead.

The tunnel was similar to the hallways in the stadium, though Charlotte's unease was now quieter. She willed herself to be calm. To cling to the possibility that hope lay at the end of the tunnel.

"How are you so okay?" Wade asked, studying her.

Because I'm Ignis' greatest actress. "Because we're about to see what everyone else only *dreams* of. It's exciting."

Rae nodded in agreement, Charlotte's presumed fearlessness giving her strength. *Bravery is contagious. Maybe all emotions are. Good and bad.*

The group passed a window and a door. Charlotte slowed to gape. Inside was one of the groups of Unruly, Killian included, getting ushered toward chairs similar to the ones from Final Chance.

"What are those chairs for?" Charlotte asked, careful to keep her voice low and calm.

"Just a brain scan to make sure you're healthy before we leave you," the creepy woman replied.

That made sense, but she doubted Zandra would have been satiated. "Healthy how? And before you leave us *where*? In this weird hallway?"

"It's just procedure," she replied, "Nothing you children need to worry about."

"But why—?" Her question was cut short when the woman opened a door—labeled Door 19—to a room similar to the one the other group of Unruly had been ushered inside, and motioned for them to enter.

The sterile room smelled of antiseptic and bleach. There was another door opposite the one they had entered from. Four of the dentist-like chairs were placed in a diamond between them, the backs to one another. It must've been on purpose, so the Unruly wouldn't be able to see each other.

Electrodes were connected to the top of each chair, where the Unrulys' heads would be. "Please take a seat in whichever chair you'd like."

Charlotte spent half a second weighing her options. Did she really want to do this?

No. But who was she kidding? She had made her choice. There was no backing down now.

Charlotte moved first, repressing all fear and trepidation. She sat in the chair closest to the door they had entered from, in case a quick escape needed to be made. Rae and two others followed suit, none of them too happy about it.

Wade and three others, including Harris, were stopped outside to be taken into the room across. Wade met her eyes, and Charlotte gave him an encouraging smile before he was led away.

There was something meaningful about spreading courage. It felt just as addictive as a rush of Dust.

Charlotte had never thought of Zandra as a leader, but

perhaps she hadn't paid enough attention. Because Charlotte was certain that her sister would be jumping in head first, trying to make the other Unruly feel comfortable. And if *that* wasn't leadership, what was?

The woman attached the electrodes to Rae's head. She flinched, and Charlotte almost felt the urge to reach out and grasp her hand.

Almost.

"You're likely going to get drowsy," the woman said, making her way over to the boy whose name Charlotte hadn't gotten, "It's perfectly normal. The electrodes slow your brain activity. The full scan takes between ten and thirty minutes, depending."

"Depending on what?" Charlotte asked.

"Your brain waves. You wouldn't understand."

"Try me." But the woman just shook her head and decided that Charlotte would be up next.

Charlotte didn't protest as the electrodes were placed on her head. Or when they began vibrating. Or when they emitted a high pitch that Charlotte was certain only she could hear.

The woman didn't hover over her. She just went to put the electrodes on the final Unruly. Charlotte felt the world slowly drift away, until she was only semi-conscious.

20

Zandra couldn't believe she had to go to a ball after the day she'd had. And it wasn't even midday.

The moment Imogen left, Zandra asked Eloise, "May I please have a blank journal if you have one? Or even a piece of paper?"

"Of course. One moment, please." Eloise hurried over to the room's desk and pulled one out of the drawer.

"I would like a moment alone to collect my thoughts."

"Of course."

The moment Zandra was alone, she began scribbling words onto the pages.

Why would Imogen do this?

Where is Charlotte right now?

How am I going to do this?

I hate— Zandra stopped. She wanted to write "Imogen", but she couldn't bring herself to do it.

—that I have to do this. I hate that I didn't get a choice.

Eloise knocked. She hadn't even left Zandra alone for a full minute.

"We need to get you ready. You still have a ball to attend."

Zandra scribbled over the paper—over anything that could be used against her—then ripped it to shreds.

Fifteen minutes later, she was following Eloise down the many hallways, struggling to orient herself.

Eloise had changed her into another periwinkle dress that was just as distasteful as the first, but covered her mole.

Zandra was determined to hate everything even though she knew, as someone who loved *new* experiences, her curiosity would eventually get the better of her.

As Zandra's anger toward Imogen faded, it directed itself internally. How could she have just let Eloise dress her up like a doll when she knew Charlotte was in danger? She could have stopped it. Instead, she'd sat around getting pampered in a palace.

She was imprisoned in Charlotte's life until she could figure out how to save her. She needed to be both smart and speedy— she'd start by picking the brains of everyone at this stupid party who was from High Society. She hoped that Lynx or one of the other previous Conquest winners would be there. *They* would know how to save Charlotte.

The problem would be getting them to share.

Zandra heard the voices just before they were about to turn into the ballroom entrance. Eloise put out a hand to stop her. "You can't be seen until you are announced."

But Zandra's curiosity got the better of her and she peeked around Eloise's arm anyway.

Of course, as if the universe were playing a cruel trick on her, the first person Zandra saw was Imogen, Lawrence on her arm, strutting inside.

Zandra stepped back, overwhelmed. It was surreal—she was *here*, in Phoenix Palace. She was about to get *Paired* with someone *as Charlotte*. And she was completely, utterly alone.

You can do this, she reminded herself, *You are smart and brave and know Charlotte even better than she knows herself.*

"Are you alright, dear?" Eloise asked.

"Yes, I just need a moment."

"Dear—"

Zandra exited the nearest door, which just so happened to lead onto a balcony with a view of the Barrenlands.

Zandra didn't notice that she wasn't alone until he was clearing his throat. "Excuse me, Miss—?" His tenor was musically rich. When she turned to meet his eyes, they widened in shock.

Prince Tiberius of Luxor.

Zandra gaped. He was even more beautiful in person. There was an innocence to his face—a curiosity that Zandra didn't often see.

"Charlotte," Tiberius breathed. He bowed so low his forehead almost touched the ground. "The pleasure is all mine."

Zandra bowed as well, her mind bombarded with questions.

She tried to form words, but nothing came to her. What should she say? What would *Charlotte* say? Was she supposed to know who he was?

The lengthy pause encouraged Tiberius to say, "I...I've been dreaming about meeting you for five years."

Zandra had absolutely no clue what to say. She settled on, "Hi."

"I—I'm sorry. My name is Prince Tiberius of Luxor. You're probably really confused. I, uh, we're genetic Pairs, so I'm...I'm one of your suitors."

He was blushing. He was so sure of himself, but he still couldn't help but blush.

Zandra composed herself and smiled. Not in her usual way, with the grin consuming her whole face, but in the way that Charlotte did. The way that made people always want more, because they weren't sure if her smile was genuine.

"And I'm *only* pursuing you. We're the same, you and I."

Zandra's sense returned to her. This man didn't even know she wasn't Charlotte. "Thank you," she said, slightly unsettled, "I appreciate the support."

She made to turn, but Tiberius said, "Wait, I'm—that was really weird of me. I'm just—I've had one role my entire life. And I always knew that I was going to be sent off to Ignis, but I didn't know what it was going to hold. I just knew that you were going to be here. And that you know what it's like to be...isolated from your peers. So you've been something of an anchor in a stormy sea."

Charlotte didn't even talk like that.

This is her life, Zandra reminded herself, *And she met him. She liked him.*

"I imagined I'd have my crwth here and I'd play you a song, but I suppose I'll do that later."

Yet another sentence that made no sense to Zandra. She let Tiberius continue, "I don't know anyone else. And I don't *know* you, either, but...but I do know you. I know that your favorite color is the color of your gown, and I know that your best subject at the Academy was politics, and—and I know that you care more about your sister than anything in the whole world."

Zandra's face fell, her mind back on Charlotte crossing the ocean to Unruly. What was she going to face when she arrived? "I do care about her. More than anything."

"She chose to go to Unruly, didn't she?"

"Yes." She waited for him to scoff. To look down upon her sister—or perhaps it was Zandra herself, she couldn't keep track at this point—for choosing to go against Pairing.

But Tiberius was full of surprises. "That must be really hard for you."

"I'm afraid it's harder for her."

Tiberius nodded. "I met her, you know. Last night. Did she—"

"She told me."

"She saved me."

"She did?"

"From the flashing lights and the loud noise. Parties in Luxor are quite different," Tiberius said, making Zandra chuckle. "I liked her."

They were speaking of Charlotte as if she were dead. "I don't know if I can do this without her." Maybe Charlotte had been *Zandra's* rock just as much as Zandra had been Charlotte's.

"You can!" Tiberius insisted, "You're the most capable person I've ever had the pleasure of not knowing."

Zandra cracked a smile. One of her own—one that consumed her whole face—as he continued, "You're a master of all five categories. You're smart, you're brave, you're resourceful, you're good at thinking on your feet, and you're a good sister. There's nothing you can't do."

He was right. Charlotte was exceptional. Maybe Zandra just needed to trust that she would be fine until Zandra could save her on Unruly.

"Thank you, Tiberius. I'm looking forward to getting to know you."

Tiberius flashed a goofy, lopsided grin, "And I am as well. For real, this time." He paused. "We should probably go back inside."

He offered her his arm, but they had only taken two steps away from the railing when a servant rushed forward with a box. He stopped in front of the pair of them and bowed, presenting the box to Tiberius.

"Your Highness," he mumbled, "A gift from your father."

"Thank you," Tiberius replied, bowing and taking the box from him. Most nobles didn't bow to servants.

Tiberius' face lit when he saw what was inside—a string instrument of some sort that Zandra had never seen before.

"He found me a new crwth."

"A new what?" Zandra asked, peering at it. He'd said the word before, but she had never heard of such an instrument. Tiberius positioned it in the crook of his arm.

"This is for you, Charlotte Rachel Galvin."

He lifted the bow and began to play.

Despite the size of the instrument, the crwth emitted a loud, hearty noise. Tiberius' fingers moved swiftly, with deadly precision. The notes held a longing in them, and even someone as musically ignorant as Zandra could tell that it was a hopeful melody.

It was sweet, but Zandra couldn't say it touched her soul, as she was sure Tiberius was expecting it to.

After listening to a few more chords, Zandra decided that Charlotte would have appreciated it more than Zandra did—the soothing lilting of the melody. If Tiberius had known that Zandra wasn't Charlotte, would he have written something faster paced?

When he finished, Zandra applauded. Tiberius blushed and gave a small mock-bow.

"Did you like it?" he asked, trying and failing not to sound too apprehensive.

"It was lovely."

Zandra could tell he was pleased.

"Ahem, Charlotte," Eloise's voice called. She could tell from the way Eloise didn't look directly at them that she'd been listening to the whole conversation, and from the way she twitched that they were short on time.

"I'll see you inside," she told Tiberius.

"You certainly will," he said with a bow.

Zandra hurried toward Eloise, only remembering when she

was halfway across the balcony that she hadn't bowed. She awkwardly turned, tripping in her stilettos in the process.

But Tiberius had already gone back through the sliding door into the party, a large man—his guard, yet another person that Zandra hadn't noticed—trailing behind him.

"Come along now," Eloise urged.

All of the partygoers must have entered, because the hallway in which Zandra had seen her parents was empty. But instead of going through the main doorway, Eloise led Zandra up a staircase to a set of double doors.

"Jayana just entered," Eloise said, "You have about one minute. Just walk down the stairs and you'll be introduced to your Pairs."

Zandra nodded. Was she supposed have something prepared? Was she supposed to know what to do?

When the doors swung open, everyone applauded. Why did they think that her mere presence deserved applause? She hadn't *done* anything except shown up.

Five waited at the top of the steps to escort Zandra into the throes of the golden ballroom, another artificial smile pasted on her face. Did the woman even know how to smile for real?

She glanced into the crowd. She spotted Imogen, whose brows were furrowed with worry. Worry for *herself*, Zandra was sure. Zandra wasn't foolish enough now to think that it was for *her*.

It was a double-staircase, so Zandra didn't know which way to go. At the bottom, a line of men—her potential Pairs—waited for her, all adorned in various suits and robes. They all wore white, and Zandra couldn't help but feel that she was about to be sacrificed in a cultish ceremony.

Until her eyes met Tiberius'. He gave an encouraging nod.

Zandra did her best to keep her footing as Five led her down the stairs at a rapid pace, as if she were *trying* to make Zandra trip and fall to her death.

Not the time to pass on Greta's message, she decided.

Zandra reached the bottom in one piece and exhaled. Surely the hardest part of the day was over. Charlotte had gone Unruly and she'd made it down the stairs in one piece. Things could only get better.

Five escorted Zandra to the line of her potential Pairs. Most, anyway. The ones outside the Top Twenty she'd have to venture out of the palace to meet.

The first boy in line bowed and kissed her hand. She decided not to bow back, mostly because she was certain she would fall in her stiletto heels again if she tried.

The next boy did the same. And the next. They all gave her their names, which Zandra immediately confused with the names she'd heard moments before.

Their faces were no better. All of them looked similar, sounded similar, *acted* similar. Surely one of them would get wise and realize that he needed to do something different in order to stand out.

The first to do so was Phillips. He bowed and kissed her hand like the rest of them—Zandra couldn't *wait* to wash it—and said, "Mace Phillips. Allow me to accompany you while you meet the rest of my friends."

Phillips had grown up on Princeps as well, though he and the twins hadn't run in the same circles. He offered Zandra his arm. She took it, appreciating the variety. It was only after she gripped his forearm that she realized that Charlotte likely would have declined and carried on the *proper* way. She would have to be more careful.

Next in line was Atticus Marquez. Like several others in the line, she and Benji Cohen—the second Highest Pointer—weren't a genetic Pair, so he got skipped.

Atticus ignored Phillips as he bowed. Zandra had heard a lot about him—that growing up in the LPC had made him a force to be reckoned with. And through the firm grip in his hand as he clutched her own and kissed it, she sensed that the rumors were correct.

"Charlotte," he said. "I'm Atticus. I'm looking forward to getting to know you." He said it in a way that the others hadn't— he wasn't trying to impress her. Was it a trick? Was it his way of standing out? Did he *actually* not care?

Regardless, Zandra liked him. Charlotte would too. "Thank you, Atticus."

Atticus bowed, then stepped back, behind the line.

Tiberius was the final man who had to kiss her hand before everyone could enjoy the party. Zandra hadn't cared about her audience until now. She already *knew* Tiberius, even if their interaction had only been a few moments. This wasn't a fake show she was putting on—this was a conversation with someone she already *knew*. Having listeners felt wrong.

So she released herself from Phillips' arm and nodded, dismissing him.

Instead of kissing her hand like the rest, Tiberius said, "May I accompany you to the ball? Even though we're already here?"

"I suppose I haven't had any other offers," Zandra said. Tiberius laughed.

"What a strange ceremony," Tiberius whispered as the party began around them. Some of her suitors cast Tiberius murderous looks. As if *that* would somehow win her over.

"And what jealous competitors you have." She was doing it again. Being herself. Though she supposed it didn't *really* matter around him since the only time Tiberius had met Charlotte, she'd been pretending to be Zandra.

She would have to decide if it was worth the danger.

But as she and Tiberius turned toward the rest of the people, the season was cast from her mind.

Lynx Hillenbrand stood across the room, conversing with Five.

Zandra turned to Tiberius. "Excuse me for a moment."

Tiberius' face fell, but Zandra didn't care. Charlotte—and Zandra's vow to never be inactive again—was all that mattered. In her peripheral vision, she saw King Akil step forward and put a hand on Tiberius' shoulder, leading him into another conversation.

To the naked eye, Zandra would simply be going to converse with her new acquaintances from High Society. She passed Jayana, who spoke with Benji, but Zandra didn't take her eyes off Lynx.

It had been so long since she'd seen her up close. What had she been through? What had she seen? How had she gotten here?

If only Zandra could openly ask her.

Five spotted her a moment before Lynx did. Five's face fell as Lynx's rose.

"The woman of the hour," Lynx said warmly. She was radiant. Though she had grown up in the LPC, Lynx had always been self-assured. But unlike Atticus and Five, she hadn't made it her mission to get out.

Until now, apparently.

High Society seemed to have only increased her confidence. She looked good—she had put on muscle and makeup, and she had a glint in her eyes that made Zandra think she knew more than the rest of the people at the ball put together.

"It's good to see you again," replied Zandra evenly. Carefully.

"I hope you're more impressed with your batch than I was," Five said with a tone that claimed the opposite.

Five's Pair was halfway across the room, speaking with one of the boys. Most Pairs stayed together at social events, but Zandra appreciated when they weren't glued together at the waist. It made her respect Five, though she didn't *want* to respect anything about her.

"I'm looking forward to getting acquainted with them."

"You could be getting *acquainted* with them now," Five pointed out. Lynx flashed Five a warning look—one that only people who were familiar with each other dared to give.

Five had been a year above Lynx—two above the twins—and Zandra had never seen them of them speak. Five had been elitist even back at the Academy, and Lynx hadn't bothered trying to fit in with the High-Pointers. Or *anyone*, for that matter.

So why was she rubbing elbows with them now?

But all thoughts of Lynx's rise to fame were forgotten when Lynx said, "I see that passing on my message to your sister didn't do much good."

Zandra's blood froze.

Lynx had given *her*—Zandra—a message. Through Charlotte.

And this was the first Zandra was hearing of it.

Lynx had *told* her. She'd told her before going Unruly that she'd try to give Zandra a message. And she had. Through Charlotte.

And Charlotte hadn't even passed it along. Zandra had *asked* Charlotte—she had directly asked.

Charlotte had *lied to her face.*

"I'm sorry," Lynx continued, "I know how close you and Zandra are."

Zandra's head spun. She couldn't focus.

"We are," Zandra said, the only thing she could manage. How was Charlotte so quick on her feet?

This was the perfect segue. She just needed to seize it—

But Zandra missed her opportunity when Lynx asked, "How are you liking the palace?"

No. She could still do this. Charlotte would find a way to get back to what *she* wanted to talk about.

"More than Zandra's liking Unruly, I'm sure." Zandra glanced at Five out of the corner of her eye, making it clear she would like to speak to Lynx alone. "I'm worried for her. Her attention has a tendency to wander. If there really *are* wolves, well..." Zandra bit her lip, the concern not an act.

Lynx frowned, hands behind her back, her internal battle peeking onto her face. She wanted to say something, but she didn't dare. "Zandra's stronger than you think," Lynx said, "She'll hold her own."

"I'm not reassured."

Five cut in, "It doesn't matter whether or not *you* are reassured. Alexandra made her choice."

Zandra flared her nostrils at Five. *She* had power now. "I'd like to speak to Lynx alone."

Five took a step forward, looming over her, and Zandra was suddenly aware of how much taller and stronger Five was. But Lynx lightly touched Five's arm and said, "It will only be a moment."

Five muttered under her breath as Zandra exhaled in relief. The moment they were alone, Zandra said, "How bad is it there? What is she up against?"

Lynx's green eyes stared. Lynx *wanted* to tell her. Lynx was a decent person. That didn't just change, no matter how bad Unruly was.

"Please, Lynx. Anything."

"Trust that she can look after herself," Lynx said, looking away, "People are going to wonder why you aren't entertaining your men."

"And I'm wondering if my sister is already dead."

"Charlotte. That's all you're going to get from me."

Zandra almost screamed. She wanted to tell her that it was

her. It was *Zandra*, the person she'd spent hours discussing the world and its ridiculous expectations hour upon hour with!

But there was a chasm between them. One that, even if Zandra revealed her identity, would not be crossed. Lynx had walked the walk—she had taken on the unknown. She had seen it. Lived it.

And, at some point in the process, Lynx had changed. Zandra was still the young dreamer, fantasizing about a world she'd never see.

So Zandra just bowed and went back to her party.

21

Charlotte woke to beeping.

Woke was the wrong word. She had never fully drifted off. Everything had just seemed slow and strange. She remembered Rae and the others leaving. She remembered the feeling of her electrodes vibrating. She remembered her brain being only half on, incapable of emotion or reaction.

The electrodes were what was beeping. The scan was complete.

The creepy woman gently peeled off the electrodes. "You're done, Zandra."

Charlotte wasn't groggy. The moment the electrodes had turned off, her brainwaves had gone back to normal. So she jumped to her feet and demanded, "Where are the others?"

She motioned toward the door—the one Charlotte had watched them exit through—and said, "They've gone Unruly."

Charlotte was slightly offended that they'd gone without her. But she supposed it *was* Unruly. They would have to fend for themselves.

"You're dismissed." This was it. Unruly was behind that door.

Charlotte stepped toward it and put her hand on the knob. The metal was cool in her palm, exactly as a door leading to Unruly should be.

But before Charlotte could open it, she asked the woman, "When does the Conquest start?"

"I know nothing about what happens behind that door."

Charlotte furrowed her brow. She should have demanded answers from Four. She needed all the information she could get. "How long was my brain scan?"

"Thirty two minutes. The longest we've ever had, actually."

"What does that mean?"

"I suppose that you have a complex brain. Goodbye, Alexandra."

Charlotte thought about standing there just to spite her, since it was clear she had no intent of leaving until Charlotte was gone. But she didn't particularly want to be in the nameless woman's company any longer, so she opened the door.

On the other side was a narrow obsidian black tunnel. Charlotte cast one final look back, then stepped through.

The woman closed the door behind her.

Charlotte was immediately overpowered by the lack of sound. She heard nothing, except a faint ringing in her ears she was certain her mind created so there wasn't *nothing*. Her brain couldn't comprehend *nothing*. Maybe it wasn't as complex as the woman had thought.

Torches lit the way in one direction, so that was where she would go.

Charlotte felt a sliver of anxiety returning. The rest must've rejuvenated her. It was quite the double-edged sword.

Would the tunnel lead to a staircase to take her to the top of the island? Or was Unruly just a series of tunnels and caverns and artificially-lit hallways?

A sound interrupted the rhythmic pattern of Charlotte's feet hitting the ground, and she turned to see a silhouette running toward her, torch in hand. Charlotte braced her knees. Was this one of the rabid strangers who had been on Unruly for years? Was it an Impaired? What if the rumors were true and they sacrificed a few unlucky new Unruly?

"Hey!" A feminine voice. As she approached, Charlotte could make out her features. She was long and lanky—awkwardly so—with a long face to match. Her sandy hair fell to her boney shoulders and her wide hazel eyes were steely.

Charlotte took a few steps back and grabbed her own torch in case she needed to use it as a weapon. She didn't recognize the girl from the boat and wasn't about to get killed—or tricked—five seconds into being on Unruly.

"Who are you?" Charlotte demanded.

"I know you. You're Zandra."

Shoot. Had this girl known Zandra? Was it dark enough to pretend she couldn't see her? "I'm Enid."

But knowing someone's name didn't mean *knowing* the person. She had no idea if Enid had come in with the kids on the boat or if she had been on Unruly for years. Though Charlotte supposed she didn't look old enough to have been there for more than a year.

Enid had a hyperactive force to her, her physical awkwardness extending to her personality, but she owned it all the same. Charlotte got a sense that she was someone who would thrive in an uncomfortably long silence, and be irritated if someone broke it.

Something about the way she moved felt familiar. Charlotte must've seen her in passing at the Academy. "Did you just get here?"

"Like five minutes ago," Enid said.

"Were you—?"

"Belowdeck."

Charlotte opened her mouth to ask if she had been a Mid-Pointer or a Low-Pointer, but then decided not to tip her hand.

"Were there any more people in your room?" Enid asked.

"Three others, but they were all gone when I left."

"Same here. Have you seen anyone else?"

"No. You?"

"You're the first."

There was an awkward pause. Enid grinned, and Charlotte had the odd sensation that Enid had read her thoughts about lengthy silences. Finally, Enid said, "We need to find the rest of them. There's nothing back that direction, I already checked."

"Why?" asked Charlotte. She could think of plenty of reasons, but she kept her cards close to her chest. That was how she was going to win the Conquest, and old habits died hard.

"We don't know what we're going to be up against," Enid said, "People could get hurt if we don't stick together, and there are some scared kids who aren't going to be able to fend for themselves. Are you with me?"

"Yeah."

"Good. People listen to you," Enid said.

Charlotte had underestimated Zandra, and she doubted Zandra had known her own influence. "Do they?"

Enid raised her eyebrows, like she wasn't sure if Charlotte was being self-deprecating and wanted Enid to stroke her ego. Enid seemed like she had no patience for that. But when Enid realized that Charlotte was serious, she laughed. "You're kidding. People said you didn't pay attention, but I didn't realize it was *that* bad."

Charlotte didn't like how much Enid knew when she knew nothing about Enid. At least Zandra's weaknesses couldn't be exploited because they wouldn't work on her. "Thanks?"

"It's because you're an enigma. The other Low-Pointers don't really know you."

Charlotte decided that was an insult disguised as a compliment.

"Let's find the others," Enid decided.

Charlotte and Enid began the walk down the narrow tunnel. "So what's your story?"

Enid shrugged, trying to brush off a deeper wound with nonchalance. "I was a Mid-Pointer in a family of Mid-Pointers. Didn't want to get Paired. My parents weren't happy, so they told me I should come here. So...here I am."

"Why didn't you want to get Paired?"

"Because I'm *Unruly*."

"I see," Charlotte said, even though she did not, in fact, see *anything*. Was it a lack of context? An inability to understand subtext? Or because she had a guarded, privileged upbringing surrounded by only fellow High-Pointers and her sister?

"What about you? Why're you here?"

"I don't know. I just kinda...freaked out, I guess."

Enid tilted her head. Charlotte felt the urge to elaborate. To talk it out. To deny her instinct to keep herself from saying more than three words at a time. Because she didn't *know* what had happened, and she could feel all the horrible reasons stuck in the web of her brain, ready to obsessively weave through her thoughts the moment she wasn't distracted.

"I know it's not a very good answer," Charlotte murmured.

"It's not a very bad one either."

"I wasn't even planning on going Unruly until I was on the stage. I panicked—but, like, worse than I ever have, and I knew I couldn't do it. I don't want to be Paired either."

"Did you *ever* want to be?"

Charlotte swallowed, thinking. "No, I don't think so." Shame kept Charlotte's gaze rooted ahead. She'd had what *everyone* wanted. She should have been *grateful*. She should have been *happy*.

Instead, she had run away to an island of misfits and, potentially, monsters.

"Yeah," Enid said, her vocal cadence slowing, "It's rough out there for people like us."

"I guess it is." Though she didn't know if it was true, because she wasn't sure there was an *us* that she was capable of being part of.

"At least we can look out for each other here."

We. What an intriguing word.

They walked in silence before Charlotte remembered she was supposed to be Zandra and loosened her gait. "I wonder what this place is going to be like."

"It's home now, is what is it."

"Do you think it's all going to be underground?"

"I hope not," Enid said, "But maybe. It's not like there's much on top."

"Do you think there'll be a lot of Impaired here, too?"

"Dunno. But it's not like there were that many to begin with, right?"

"I wonder if they're as easy to spot as everyone says they are," Charlotte said.

"We'll find out soon enough, won't we?"

They settled into their thoughts as the tunnel widened. Soon, they heard bickering voices and Enid said, "You ready?"

Enid began running toward them.

Charlotte trailed a pace behind. Enid was fast, but Charlotte had scored the most physical points, so she had no trouble keeping up.

The tunnel had widened into a cave where the other Unruly came into view. There seemed to be an argument ensuing. "We wait for everyone," a familiar voice—Harris—was saying. "And we stick together—"

SLAM!

The moment Charlotte was out of the tunnel and in the cavern, a concrete wall dropped from the tunnel opening, sealing it off completely.

Sealing off any hope of going back the way they came.

"What the hell?!" Killian roared.

"We're doomed!" Wade cried.

Charlotte inspected the wall. There was no getting back through—it likely weighed a few tons, and there were no noticeable gaps or weaknesses.

"Come on," Enid whispered, putting a hand on Charlotte's shoulder. Charlotte was too preoccupied to even think to shake the hand off as she turned back toward the group.

The top of the cavern was several stories high and three tunnels ran off in various directions. Charlotte was glad she and Enid had taken torches from the walls, because the only light came from three other Unruly who had done the same.

Enid hurried through the gapers to get a better look at the argument, cutting a path for Charlotte.

"Well, that seems to be everyone, genius," Killian was saying to Harris. "You can wait all you want, I'm getting out of this hellhole."

He started toward the left tunnel. Charlotte wondered if there was a reason behind his choice. He held no torch and was soon swallowed by shadows.

"We should at least do a head count," Harris called, swinging his torch in Killian's direction.

A few kids started talking over each other, but no one could get a word in. No one had authority.

Enid turned and gave Charlotte an encouraging nod. If only she knew that Charlotte was *more* than used to being a leader. If anyone could get a bunch of Unruly in line, it was her.

"Stay where you are, Killian," Charlotte ordered. She kept her voice low and ran her fingers through her already messy hair. Zandra was never still, so she used her whole body to speak.

Killian scoffed, taking a few steps toward her. He was much bigger than Charlotte, but like with Five, it didn't faze her. If she could do this like herself—without pretending to be Zandra—it would be so much easier. No one listened to someone who was twitching all the time.

"You think you're better than us because you're the Lowest Pointer?" demanded Killian. Charlotte had no idea how it'd even be possible for someone to feel superior for being the worst.

"No, I think we're scared and have five torches and no idea what we're getting into."

"I'm not scared," Killian said, though Charlotte could tell by his darting eyes that it wasn't true.

"I said *we*, as a collective," Charlotte said, inspired by Enid's use of the word earlier, "Which *we* are now. And you don't have a torch."

Harris tilted his head, then stepped up to her side. "What if we took a quick head count and then split up into three groups? We'll explore the tunnels and meet back here. And you can lead your own group."

"That's a great idea," Charlotte said. Harris looked at her, surprised by her agreement. Enid nodded, as did a few others. Several of the Unruly visibly relaxed at Charlotte's words. Her initiative.

A proud feeling warmed Charlotte's chest.

Killian glanced around and quickly realized he was outnumbered.

"Fine."

Harris did a quick head count. There were sixteen of them in all, and Enid confirmed that the numbers added up with how many had been belowdeck. Killian decided to take the largest team

—the one that would have six—and hand-picked the largest, strongest-looking candidates.

Harris looked at Charlotte. "You take one group, I'll take the other?"

Charlotte needed to figure out how to put their feud aside until she'd won the Conquest. She needed to keep a close eye on him so he didn't get ahead. And that started with clearing the air between him and *Zandra*. "Let's stay together, Harris. Enid, will you go with the others?"

Harris opened his mouth to protest, but not before Enid replied, "Works with me."

Enid took half of the group, leaving Charlotte and Harris with a person Charlotte didn't know, plus Rae and Wade. "Shall we?" Harris asked hesitantly.

It felt right walking beside him, but also very, very wrong. His presence alone was like rubbing salt into an open wound. He was the reason she couldn't trust anyone. Because if *Harris* could betray her, anyone could.

But she had to do this. To get back to her old life. *Not* because she wanted to reconnect with him, that was for sure.

Charlotte gave her torch to Rae, who was bringing up the rear.

"I don't like the dark," Wade said nervously, fidgeting between Charlotte and Harris.

"It's going to be okay," Charlotte said. She wanted to speak with Harris alone, but Wade didn't seem inclined to leave her side.

"I'm just going to stay in the torchlight," Wade decided, walking too close to Charlotte, even in the narrow tunnel.

"That's a great idea—actually, I think you should be our flame-bearer and hold Harris' torch."

"Really?" Wade asked. Harris just raised an eyebrow.

"Yes, and it's getting a little narrower ahead—maybe you fall back so the others have enough light? I don't think we're going to be able to go three across."

"Yeah, I can do that!"

"So," Harris said when Wade had fallen into place, "What did you want to discuss?"

"Was it that obvious?"

"Either that, or you're trying to put me in my place."

"We *don't* have places. Isn't that why we're here?"

"I suppose so."

"Look," Charlotte said, "I know stuff went down between you and Charlotte and—even though I don't know what it is—I am forever on Charlotte's side. But I wasn't fair on the boat, and I know that you're a good leader and have a good head on your shoulders...so I don't want to be your enemy. Actually, I think you could maybe even be a sorta-friend."

"I appreciate that," Harris said, "And I agree."

Charlotte flashed a lopsided grin. "You're smart, so I figured we'd be a good team. To look out for these people."

Harris sized her up. "You want to win the Conquest, don't you?"

"*Harrison*," Charlotte drawled, knowing full well that wasn't his real name, "I'm the Lowest Pointer of All Time. The LPAT doesn't go for the Conquest."

"The LPAT?"

"It's what I've decided to call myself."

Harris knew how close Charlotte and Zandra were. Charlotte had a first class ticket to Princeps. Zandra hadn't spoken to Harris in years. It didn't take a genius to figure out her plan.

"So I assume that means *you're* trying to win," Charlotte continued, "Sizing up the competition, are you? Is that why you're here?"

Harris kept walking, giving nothing away. Charlotte scoffed, matching him step for step. "You're not going to give me anything at all? After everything?"

"I didn't want to be Paired like everyone else here." His nose scrunched up the slightest bit when he said it, giving Charlotte her answer.

"If you say so."

"Why do you assume I'm lying?"

"You have a terrible poker face." He always scrunched his nose when he lied. But she gave him a smile to show she harbored no ill will. He was going to be a problem. Only one of them was going to Princeps and Charlotte sure as hell was going to make sure it was her.

And not just because she had to get back.

This was personal now. She would play nice just to keep her enemies close.

"Charlotte always said that, too," Harris said, a hint of amusement in his voice.

"We need to put up a united front," Charlotte said, clearly changing the subject with a pointed look, "We can't let Killian convince the others to do something stupid."

"You want my help?"

"We both know you're the smartest one here," said Charlotte. "It'll be a lot easier for everyone if we step up and lead together."

Harris nodded. "It's not like I have anything else to do."

Except win the Conquest. But those words, though palpable, went unspoken.

"Neither do I."

Harris held out his hand and Charlotte shook it firmly, then subtly wiped her palm on the back of her shirt. She wished these sort of things could be agreed upon with a simple nod.

"So what do you think we're gonna find?" Charlotte asked. "Give me your craziest rumors."

"How about I give you the one that I think is the most accurate first?"

"Deal, but I want a crazy one after."

"I think it's a reprogramming camp. To make us *want* to be Paired."

Charlotte had suspected that may be the purpose of the island, but it was a rumor unspoken by her—to talk about it with others felt disrespectful to Pairing. She didn't *want* to know what that would entail, so she tried to lighten the mood in the way that only Zandra could. "Maybe we'll be forced to go to grand balls. And have manner-learning classes."

"Manner-learning?" Harris asked with a laugh.

"That's right."

They walked in silence for a moment before Harris said, "The craziest one I've heard is that they drain our blood and give it to High Society to drink. The boys at the Academy said that that's how Five is so strong. It's her whole diet."

Charlotte burst into laughter.

Harris grinned. "And she's actually fifty, but that's why she looks so young."

Charlotte couldn't remember the last time laughter had brought tears to her eyes. She couldn't even fight it. Soon Harris was laughing at her, until the others finally asked what was so funny.

It felt too natural to talk to him, even as Zandra. She internally berated herself even though she couldn't wipe the grin off her face at the thought of Five drinking chalices of her blood.

As the tunnel twisted and turned, Charlotte regained composure. It was similar to the one Charlotte and Enid had trekked together, only the top incrementally sloped downward, until Wade, who Charlotte hadn't realized was so tall, had to hunch. Charlotte and Harris were both on the shorter side, but it was only a few inches above their heads.

"I don't like this," Wade said, "What if we get stuck? What if there's a cave in behind us and we're trapped in here until we die?"

"I won't let that happen," Charlotte said, though she had no clue how she'd prevent it. Zandra would be nervous right now—about having no idea where the sun was—but no one needed to know that. Maybe Charlotte could take the best parts of herself and the best parts of Zandra to create a force that couldn't be reckoned with.

A force that was sure to win the Conquest.

"Look," Harris murmured.

A stalactite protruded from the ceiling ahead, leaving only a small gap. Charlotte narrowed her eyes.

"Do you think it's worth it?" Harris asked, "Someone could get stuck." The others murmured anxiously.

"I'll check it out," Charlotte decided, "I can fit through."

"I don't think that's a good idea," Wade said. But before anyone else could protest, Charlotte strutted toward the gap. Not only because she was half convinced there would be someone waiting to award her Conquest points if she was the first to the other side, but to build trust and leadership with the Unruly so it would be easier to get any information they learned about the Conquest.

And, Charlotte reminded herself, *to keep the others safe*, like Enid had said. Charlotte had a blank slate now. She was going to be better than she had been before. She wasn't just going to care about points and winning.

She was going to win and *also* do some good.

Harris would pass a torch through the gap when she was on the other side.

"Are you sure?" Harris asked, "We can go back and see what the others found."

It was going to be a tight squeeze, tighter than she had initially expected—but there was no backing down now. "I'll be fine."

Charlotte took a deep breath and squeezed into the gap. Earth pressed into her front and back. She exhaled, because she needed every millimeter of space she could get.

Her nose brushed against rock. She shimmied her hips and kicked her leg.

"Do you want me to push?" Harris called.

Charlotte didn't want to rely on *Harris*, but she supposed the Unruly couldn't be choosers.

"Let me move my nose."

"What?"

Charlotte folded her nose back with her hand and freed her head. "Okay," she told Harris, "My shoulders need a push."

He gripped it, giving her a comforting squeeze. "Tell me when."

Charlotte couldn't flinch at his touch. It physically wasn't possible.

But maybe she didn't even want to? His push was likely the only thing that was going to free her.

She soaked up the feeling of neutrality—a rare time that touch didn't feel repulsive—for a moment. It was just a shame it had to be Harris. Then she called, "Now."

His hands were gentle, but forceful enough to dislodge her shoulders. Skin scraped against the jagged stone...and then she was free.

Charlotte stepped onto the other side, giddy. She didn't even care to inspect the scratches. "I'm out! Pass the torch."

The torch popped through a second later. Charlotte grabbed it.

"I don't think anyone else is going to fit through," Harris said, "Is it more of the same?"

The tunnel snaked to the left up ahead. "You all stay there. Let me see if anything's around the bend."

There was a hesitation from the other side before Harris' voice called back, "Don't be too long."

"I won't be," Charlotte replied, already jogging ahead. Wade said something indecipherable in a high-pitched voice, but Charlotte kept walking, leaving him to Harris.

There was peace in this solitude—different than what she was used to in Princeps where, even when she was alone, someone was always judging her.

The eyes of the other Unruly held no scrutiny. They were united in their goal to survive. Charlotte had never considered herself a *team* person, but she supposed it wasn't so bad. Especially when she was the leader.

After the bend, the tunnel snaked in the opposite direction. Charlotte strutted toward it. Even if a dragon waited around the bend, she felt confident she'd be able to slay it.

Charlotte found a dragon *wasn't* waiting around the bend. No. Instead, she found something much more horrific.

A wall of debris towered hundreds of feet high, nearly touching the top of the massive cavern. Charlotte gaped at its magnitude. It surely *couldn't* have been man-made by the Unruly —it was constructed from old pre-Destruction tech and antiques, piled so oddly that Charlotte was convinced that if anyone tried to climb it, they would collapse the entire thing.

It took Charlotte a few moments to realize that she could see farther than her torchlight reached. This cavern was lighter than the tunnels, though she had no idea of the source.

Charlotte walked around the edge, trying to discern if it could be passed—

She rammed into something.

"Zandra?"

It was Enid, just as lost in the wall. "How did you—?" Enid's entire group was behind, all staring at the wall in various shades of awe and fear.

"Our tunnel led us here. But...where's the rest of your group?"

"There was a tight squeeze," Charlotte explained, "I offered to scout it out for them."

"Isn't this crazy?" Enid spoke quickly, her excitement palpable. "Do you think the other Unruly are on the other side? Is it some kind of test?"

"I don't know."

"And look at all the things. Like, what do you think *that* is?" Enid pointed at a circular device that had a long cylindrical piece attached to it via cord.

Before Charlotte could stop herself, she said, "It was a telephone."

"How do you know?"

Zandra wouldn't have. "Uh, Charlotte talked about it, I think."

"But...it's giant. How did people carry it?"

Charlotte shrugged.

"Weird." Enid stepped toward the mountain of things, the rest of her group mesmerized by it as well.

"We need to get the rest of my team here. And figure out where Killian's group went."

"I think I figured it out," someone from the back of the group said.

Killian and his people were heading toward them. Charlotte turned to Enid, "Can you go through my tunnel and tell Harris to go around? I'll walk the perimeter and see if there's a way through."

Charlotte's inspection brought little success—the wall continued until it kissed the sides of the cavern. When she returned to the others, the rest of her group had joined.

"So are we climbing?" Harris asked, squinting at the top of the structure.

"We can't," Charlotte said, "Not all of us anyway. It looks too unstable for more than one."

"I'll go," Enid offered, "I'm good at climbing."

Based on the odd way she walked, Charlotte didn't believe her. But she wasn't confident in her own ability, either. The tower climbing portion of the Academy's physical exam had almost lost her the physical category title. It was the only thing Zandra had ever beaten her in—Zandra had somehow placed in the top five of the tower climb. Charlotte had been thirtieth, but she'd made up for it by winning the running, archery, and agility portions of the tournament.

"I can do it, too," Harris said.

"No," Charlotte said, not about to let her fear of heights potentially give him an advantage in the Conquest, "I did alright on the climbing wall. I can handle it."

Charlotte hoisted herself up before anyone could protest—and before she lost her nerve.

She would be fine. This was different—there'd be something solid beneath her feet.

Going up was easier than down. She could pretend the bottom was just beneath her, not thirty or forty or fifty feet below.

She resisted the urge to look down as her head began throbbing.

Stop. Do not look down. Be calm.

The world began to spin.

Charlotte was navigating between an old couch and a rusty table when she had no choice but to look down for a foothold.

Instead of seeing the ground, she saw a pair of flickering eyes just below her.

Enid.

"I don't think two of us should be up here," Charlotte whispered, even as she wanted to scream, *What do you think you're doing!?* "I could dislodge something and it could fall on you."

"Just don't dislodge something," Enid said, "You shouldn't face whatever's on the other side alone."

Charlotte was both annoyed and touched. She did her best to ignore her dizziness as she made her way up the final stretch, careful not to disturb something that could kill Enid.

Then she was there. Charlotte peered over the top, careful to keep hidden.

At first she couldn't quite tell what lied below. More rubble of ancient pre-Destruction artifacts, with tiny creatures—rodents?—moving between them.

No. Those weren't rodents. Her mouth fell open when she realized—they were *people*.

"The forgotten Unruly," Enid murmured, climbing up beside her, "You were right. They don't live *on* Unruly—they live *in* it."

"And the Impaired," Charlotte said, nodding toward them, trying not to stare.

They were even *more* grotesque than the rumors had led her to believe. Humanoid rather than human, with boils on their skin, their features offset, bodies disproportionate.

It was clear why the Council had wanted them exiled.

"Do you think they know we're here?" Charlotte asked, pulling her gaze away. Like Enid, she kept her voice down, taking in the people with awe and horror.

"Everyone knows it's the first day of Pairing season, I'm sure." Enid whispered, "So probably. Should we just go down and introduce ourselves?"

"No. We need to make sure they're peaceful first."

"You sound like a High-Pointer. They're *our* people."

"*We're* our people," said Charlotte, "They're strangers who've been underground for who-knows-how-long."

"Fine," Enid said, "I'll go alone."

"You told me I should step up and take charge. This is me doing it."

"No, I said the others would listen to you. I didn't say *I* would."

"Well, it's not happening."

But Enid was already getting ready to hoist herself to the other side. Charlotte grabbed her leg before she could swing it over the top. "Stop, Enid!"

"Let go of me!" Enid whisper-scolded.

"Not until you promise to—"

Enid kicked at her and dislodged an old toaster, sending it tumbling down the mountain of knick-knacks, creating an avalanche of junk in its wake. Before Charlotte could process—and she was a *very* quick processor—the clunky desktop computer she was standing on gave way under her.

Charlotte felt herself falling. But before she had gone more than a foot, she was yanked upward by the wrist.

She was suspended in the air. She glanced down and terror consumed her.

"I've got you, Zandra," Enid gasped.

There was nothing beneath her feet. If she fell, it would be to her death. Why had she volunteered for this? What had she been thinking?

"Get me up!"

"I'm—trying," Enid panted. But she was barely able to maintain her grip.

"Try harder!"

Enid grunted and lifted Charlotte enough for Charlotte to get her other hand onto some object. She had no idea what it was. "Is this stable?"

"I—think so?" And without supporting Charlotte's full

weight, Enid was able to grasp under Charlotte's armpit and heave her to safety.

Charlotte immediately grabbed Enid's hand again, desperate to cling to her for fear of falling again. As she lied there, panting, her heart racing a mile a minute, she realized she had never willingly grabbed someone's hand before. Like with Harris, she didn't hate it. "Thank you," she breathed to Enid.

"Sure." She gave Charlotte a moment to catch her breath and get back into position.

Charlotte wanted *down* and she wanted it *now*. The throbbing in her head intensified, making its way from her temple into her eye.

When Charlotte was upright again, Enid said sheepishly, "So I think they know that we're here now."

Charlotte swallowed her fear and looked down again. A squad of people were gathering below. Nothing from the avalanche seemed to have hurt anyone, though Charlotte couldn't be sure from her position. Were these Unruly seriously stupid enough to live in a place that could be crushed and buried at any given moment?

"I'll go," Charlotte said, "You return to the others and wait for me to come get you. And be ready to flee."

"Flee where?" Enid asked, "All tunnels led here. They can wait for us."

"*Fine.*" Charlotte couldn't spend another moment on top of the mountain arguing. "You can come with me."

"I'll go first. Try to take the path I take."

"Fine," Charlotte repeated.

Enid waited, an expectant look on her face.

"What?"

"I need both hands to climb."

Charlotte released Enid's hand like it was aflame, heat rising to her cheeks. "Sorry," she mumbled. Enid flashed a grin. How was she so comfortable in awkwardness?

Charlotte disassociated for the climb down, following Enid's path. She couldn't decide if she liked or hated her.

When her feet finally hit solid ground, Charlotte released a breath. Her legs shook as she looked around, ignoring the pain in her head. *It must be from the crazy day.* Sleep would cure it.

Crevices were built into the garbage mounds. Eyes peered from the darkness, guardedness reflecting off their pupils that could have only been the result of getting hurt too many times. Charlotte couldn't quite figure out how many people resided there, but there didn't seem to be so many to have to send Impaired to Luxor.

A malnourished Impaired woman waited, eyes narrowed and arms crossed. Bumps covered her pale skin, some of which oozed —her hands were deformed, one of her arms several inches longer than the other. "Are there only two of you this year?" she asked.

"Are you the Unruly?" Charlotte asked.

"Yes."

Charlotte tried not to stare.

"I'm *obviously* Impaired," the woman said, a hint of annoyance in her voice, "But we're one and the same here."

"We're Unruly, too," Enid said. Charlotte threw her a warning glance.

"Are you." *Not* a question.

"Yes," Enid affirmed.

Charlotte took back control, "What's your name?"

"Jeri."

"Enid. And this is Zandra."

Enid was too excited to be here to stay guarded. She thought she was finally amongst her people. Maybe she was, but they knew far too little to let their guard down.

"Welcome," Jeri said lukewarmly, "Feel free to stay wherever you can find a spot." She turned away—

"That's it?" Charlotte said, "You're not going to tell us anything else?"

"What else is there to know?"

"I don't know," Charlotte said, her patience wearing thin, "How about if we're stuck down here? Or how many of you there are? Or where to get food and water? And do we have to climb that freaking mountain of junk every time we want to get out?"

Jeri's voice was monotonous. "You won't need to get out. There's nowhere to go."

Nowhere? Nowhere at all? Charlotte's heart skipped a beat and she heard Enid inhale sharply.

"This is all there is. If you don't like it, you should've gotten Paired."

And with that, Jeri disappeared into the tower of things.

22

When Imogen stepped off the ferry and into the golden-lit Princeps Harbor, Maddox hurried to her side. "We need to talk," he said, "*Now.*"

Imogen turned to Lawrence, who gave her a sad smile—he was still upset about *Zandra* going Unruly—and said, "I'll see you back at the house."

Maddox waited until Lawrence was out of earshot. They continued toward Town Hall, across Main Square. A lukewarm breeze ran through her hair. The night was far too pleasant for this.

The tension between Imogen and Maddox was palpable, stronger than anything Imogen's senses could perceive. Greater than any taste, smell, pain, joy—yet invisible to the naked eye.

They passed the statue of First One in the center of Main Square, the founder of Ignis post-Destruction. Imogen had always hated it, from its life-sized form to its haughty expression. She despised it almost as much as she despised the current One.

Maddox waited until there were no people around to even

read his lips. "You've put yourself—and the twins—into a dangerous situation."

"It's none of your concern."

Maddox scowled. His dark face had a permanently pensive expression, but when he frowned, it morphed into sadness. "I'm trying to *help* you."

"If commenting on my choices is *helping*, I think I can manage on my own." she asked. She sounded like Charlotte. Her daughter had inherited her sharp tongue.

She was treading perilous waters—it would be much easier if she had someone on her side, but with Maddox...with Maddox, it was personal. "I don't agree with your methods," Maddox finally murmured, "But I understand *why*. You were pushed into a corner. I'm reminding you that I am your ally."

"You want to help?" Imogen said as they began climbing the steps to Town Hall, "Don't let them crucify Charlotte in this meeting."

As Imogen had suspected, the moment they had all taken their places around the table, with King Akil joining as their honored guest, Five said, "We need a new champion."

"I wasn't aware that we *had* a champion," Imogen said.

One glared at her. Hatred radiated off of him.

"King Akil," One said, using a theatrical tone, "We want your son to be Paired with the woman who best exemplifies Ignis and our beliefs. Charlotte Galvin is, of course, our Highest Pointer ever, but she may not be..." he threw a look at Imogen, "*stable* enough to be worthy of your son. We want him to be Paired with the best, and not just as thanks for all you do for us in the north."

Imogen kept the string of profanities to herself. She threw Maddox a side-eye. This was his time. *She* was biased.

"The people loved the show," Maddox said, "You heard them —it made her more...relatable."

Five opened her mouth, but Akil leaned forward and she

wisely closed it. "My son will decide for himself. I want him to be with someone he loves. Or at least can tolerate. Not who would best suit him politically. We've narrowed his options enough."

"Hear-hear," Maddox said. Four nodded her agreement.

One didn't want to leave the subject so quickly, but there was nothing he could do. Akil seemed to be at least a somewhat decent parent.

A better one than I am.

"I suppose we should move on," One said slowly, buying time for someone to object. But even Five wasn't willing to openly quarrel with the King of Luxor. "Four, you're back quickly. Have all the Unruly been delivered?"

"Yes. Boat docked, tunnel locked."

One nodded, but Imogen clocked Akil's subtly tilted head. The tunnel was *not* information the king should have access to. One breezed over it, drawing attention away. "King Akil, I do hope you enjoy the party tonight. I believe it will give you a taste of what Ignis truly celebrates."

"Thank you, Council," he said, "And thank you for being so discreet about my son's misbehavior. It was not representative of his true character."

When they were dismissed, Imogen hurried away from the chamber. She needed to figure out how to best proceed.

As she walked back through the winding streets and various passersby congratulated and sympathized with her, her plan began to form. She eyed the back of Maddox's head.

He wanted to help, he would help.

The Princeps Opening Party was one of the two biggest annual parties of the island. Not everyone was invited— and every year, the attendees bragged and exaggerated tales of great drama and scandal, gossiping and betting on what the season would bring as they watched recaps of the Top Twenty's introductions to their potential Pairs.

Imogen would be watched like a hawk. But the longer Imogen waited to speak with Charlotte on Unruly, the greater the chance her daughter had of ruining everything. The party was something that *no one* wanted to miss, so only Maddox would be keeping watch in the security room this year—none of his hand-selected crew.

She could have just have Maddox do her bidding, but the less he knew, the better. No one could know what she had to do. Or *why*.

When Imogen and Lawrence returned to their ocean-view Princeps mansion, Lawrence gave Imogen space. It was one of the few things she appreciated about him.

Imogen went over the plan as she readied herself. She applied her makeup—any beautician would have been honored to have her drop by their salon, but she preferred to do it herself—and slipped into a sleek black dress.

Despite her children being in their late teens, Imogen was still young. Only thirty-five. In pre-Destruction times, she would only now be settling down to have children. A decade of mistakes behind her. Tested and failed relationships. Finally making progress in her career.

But in Ignis, she may as well have been a hundred years old.

A few of Zandra's journals sat on the bookshelf beside Imogen's vanity. Imogen swallowed, her eyes drawn to one in particular. Against her better judgement, she found herself removing it from the stack.

It was from just over a year ago. The weight in Imogen's chest grew heavier with every word she read.

Why is Charlotte so much better than me at everything? The only thing I've ever beaten her at is the climbing wall. Aren't twins supposed to be the same? The same genes? Same smarts? No matter how hard I try, I can never keep up with her. At anything. It's like she thinks at 3x my speed.

But I don't think it's always been like this?? Or did I just not notice because no one was comparing us? Sometimes being her sister is so hard. I worry about her too. What if I go Unruly? Who would take care of her then? She doesn't do ~~good~~ well on her own. She needs me. It's easier for Lynx to go Unruly because no one needs her.

Imogen slammed the book shut. She needed a clear mind, not a guilty one. She took in her reflection in the mirror. She objectively looked breathtaking. Young, like she was. Should she have dressed less conspicuously?

It didn't matter. Her presence would be missed regardless of her clothing. It would be *more* suspicious if she weren't dressed to impress.

Imogen took a deep breath and grabbed her final accessory. A small vial of a clear liquid. She stuffed it into her dress, between her breasts.

Go time.

Just a few minutes later, she was on Lawrence's arm, walking into the top floor of Princeps' Recreation Center. The glass walls offered a great view of both the city and Ignis' mainland.

No one bothered to check their names to confirm they were invited. "It's an honor, Two," the guard said, bowing.

"Thank you."

The space was already crowded. People gathered by the screen that would replay the introductions. Teaser snippets played. Zandra had done a mediocre job—well enough that people wouldn't be suspicious. They would, however, wonder what she had been discussing with Lynx and Five. Why she'd approached them before conversing with her Pairs. And why Lynx had left immediately after their conversation.

Maybe only Imogen was wondering the last part.

Think of the devil, because the first two people that Imogen saw were the pair of them.

Five wasn't with her Pair. On Princeps, she could be herself. She and Lynx were hand-in-hand, Five radiant. Imogen always found her to be much more agreeable with Lynx.

But while Five looked content, Lynx seemed preoccupied. Within a few seconds, she glanced to the side door multiple times.

She was either expecting someone, or had somewhere else to be. Interesting.

Imogen wasn't the only one watching her. Daniel Solace kept glancing her way, as if trying to decide if he'd brave interrupting her and Five. If they noticed him, they didn't reveal it.

Imogen pulled her gaze away, to shots of the luncheon, zoning in on the footage of Lynx. She had been eyeing the door there, too. Before her disappearance.

If Imogen didn't have a mission to accomplish, she would have figured it out. Followed her. Learned her secrets. Exposed her when it was beneficial.

One was already greeting the guests, promising them a season to remember. As they entered the throngs, Imogen overheard people placing bets. Most on *Charlotte*. They lowered their voices when they noticed Imogen and Lawrence within earshot, though some continued on obliviously. Like the group that she found herself stuck behind.

"Whatever happened on that stage…that's going to come out later. There's something wrong with her," a man said.

"But she had more than *double* the class' average! She was putting on a show. That girl is smart," a woman—the man's Pair —responded.

"She's going to be One someday."

"She'd be One this year if she was allowed to go above Four her first time running."

"I wouldn't be surprised if she booted Five from the Council at this year's election."

"Assuming she gets here."

"Of *course* she'll be here."

"I'd be happy to see Five out."

Even when Imogen was basically in their circle herself, the gossipers didn't notice her. "She thinks she's so much better than everyone."

"And, I know that we aren't required to fulfill our duties to the population, but it's an *honor*. The way she struts around with that Unruly—" The word's caught in the man's throat the moment he noticed Imogen. He bowed low. "Two. I didn't see you there."

Five's public approval had significantly decreased the moment Lynx had come into the picture. "That is apparent," Imogen deadpanned. "Best keep a tight tongue. You never know who may be listening."

She guided Lawrence away, toward better company. "I don't like them speaking of Charlotte this way," Lawrence murmured.

"I know. But there's nothing we can do about it. It's the price of greatness."

"I suppose," Lawrence said, not one to argue.

Imogen needed to leave soon enough that she had time, but late enough that she could campaign for herself with the election looming ever nearer. Votes would be cast a week after Pairing Season concluded.

She shook hands with various well-dressed people, assuring them that Charlotte would market their various products the moment she stepped foot back on Princeps. While she received much congratulations, she also was given a few, "I'm very sorry about, you know..."

To which she responded, "There's nothing to be sorry about. I have faith that Zandra will win the Conquest and be joining us in a few months." Lawrence remained quiet through it all, as he always did, speaking excitedly only when he saw someone wearing one of his designs.

Lawrence was having one of said conversations when Imogen felt a tap on her shoulder. "Excuse me, Two."

Behind her was an elegant woman Imogen immediately recognized—she had been in the class above Imogen and had been the Highest Pointer of her year. She hadn't chosen to go the political route, instead becoming something of a fashion influencer on Princeps.

"Daphne Phillips. My son Mace is a potential Pair with your daughter." She bowed.

"Yes," Imogen said. Daphne waited for her to continue, but Imogen kept quiet. She had no strong opinions about Daphne, and would remain as neutral as her emotions.

"Mace told me that he was very impressed with your daughter this afternoon," Daphne said.

"I'm impressed by her every day."

Daphne leaned forward, as if Imogen didn't know exactly what she was going to say. "I would be very happy if our children found a Pair in each other."

"If that is what Charlotte wants, then I will be happy as well," Imogen said, taking a page from Akil's book.

"You must admit," Daphne said as Imogen turned to leave, "They would be a powerful Pair. With your political power and my followers behind them."

Imogen hid the amusement from her voice. "I'm afraid Charlotte has already surpassed the need for help from either of us. But I will put in a good word regardless."

It wasn't wise for Imogen to alienate anyone, especially someone like Daphne, with so little time before the election. Maybe Charlotte didn't need allies, but Imogen certainly did.

"I'm sure the last thing you want to have is another conversation about Pairing a daughter," a voice said.

Imogen turned to find Daniel Solace behind her, his hands in his pockets.

"I don't want to waste your time," he said. A straight-shooter. Imogen appreciated that. "I only have a year left before I have to get Paired."

Imogen cracked a smile. "It seems getting Lynx's attention is going well."

Daniel remained serious. "We're genetic Pairs, but I've been having difficulties speaking to her with Five in such close proximity."

"I can imagine."

"*However*, my options are...limited. My only other option is a thirty-eight year old woman whose Pair passed four months ago. And I don't think any twenty-year-old's dream is to get Paired with someone double their age."

Imogen knew exactly where this conversation was going, but she waited for him to say it.

"*And* I despise the woman," he added.

Imogen had to hold back a laugh.

"I just wanted to ask—if Zandra wins the Conquest and we *are* genetic Pairs, would you be willing to set up a meeting?"

Imogen was sympathetic. "Do I have your vote at the election?"

"Of course."

"Then it will be arranged."

"Thank you." He bowed and disappeared into the crowd.

These events never failed to entertain her.

Imogen searched for other social climbers when she spotted Akil standing a few paces away. Based on his half-smile, Imogen deduced he'd been eavesdropping. "Two. Forgive me for not having spoken to you one-on-one before this."

"It's been a busy day."

"Thankfully, One and I have worked together long enough that he knew how to make my travel day as painless as possible." There were bags under his eyes—he was exhausted, doing his best to rally. "But it's been *especially* busy for you."

Imogen just dipped her head.

"I have four sons. I'm only as happy as my least happy child, and my second eldest—Timur—is leading the navy against the Union."

"You must not be very happy, then."

Akil offered a grim smile. "He loves it, somehow, which is a small mercy. I hope that Unruly isn't as horrible as everyone seems to think it is."

He was fishing. Why? The Council had tried to keep the extent of Luxor's knowledge of their Pairing program—and Unruly—to a minimum. But diplomats were always coming and going, so Imogen was sure he knew more than he claimed.

"Thank you," Imogen said.

"But I'm sure it's comforting that it isn't a complete enigma, with your position and all."

"I think it's hard regardless," she said, allowing an edge to creep into her tone.

Akil got the hint. "Certainly. I feel the same about my sons. It was nice meeting you, Two."

They both bowed.

Imogen had no desire to small-talk, but she had to time her exit perfectly. She'd wait until twenty minutes before the footage would begin. Then, she'd excuse herself to the restroom.

When the time finally came, she told Lawrence she'd be a few minutes—she had business to attend to. Per usual, Lawrence didn't ask questions.

It was a short walk to Main Square, and Imogen wasn't stopped by anyone in the streets. She kept to the shadows and doubted that any of them could see her face well enough to know who she was.

She hurried to Town Hall and punched in the code that only she and the other four members of the Council knew. Though she doubted that Five had kept it from Lynx, or Four from her Pair. The lock unbolted and Imogen slipped inside, waiting for the lock to slide back in place before making her way down the inside staircase.

There were only two ways to get to Unruly—water and tunnel. Imogen found the latter a much simpler commute.

Imogen's path was lit by the emergency lights. The quiet and darkness didn't disturb her. She was used to Town Hall's vast emptiness. Maddox would be aware of her presence by now. The Council member on duty would be notified via alarm if a presence was detected in the building.

Imogen kept her footsteps soft as she padded down ten flights of stairs. No one would hear, but Imogen wasn't one to tempt fate.

She felt the vial in her dress. She sent a murmur up to the heavens that nothing would go wrong.

At the bottom of the staircase was a bolted door. Imogen scanned her finger and the lock clicked open to a basic hallway.

Imogen took the first door—the only door—on the left. The Security Room. Inside, Maddox waited. He stepped away from the dozens of monitors that Imogen didn't bother to look at and gave her a stiff nod. Even now, he remained professional. Cold.

"Are we clear?" Imogen asked.

"Yes."

"Thank you," Imogen said, lightly touching his arm. He yanked it away.

How could he be so cold even now, when Charlotte was in danger? When *both* the twins were in danger?

"This is for our daughter," he said, "Not you. Go."

Not a day had gone by that Imogen hadn't loved Maddox. But the love was complex, with layers of regret, anger, bitterness, and resentment weaved within. She still wished they'd been Paired. She still wished she hadn't screwed up and lost him.

But she despised him just the same.

"You've been trying to speak with me for days. This is your chance."

"About the children!" he exclaimed, "But it's too late for that. Because you went ahead and put their lives—and *mine*—at risk for your ambition."

"I did this for *all* of us," Imogen retorted, "This is what we wanted. This is how we change the world."

"They didn't *agree* to do this, Imogen!"

"You said you wanted to help."

"I do, and I am. But that's the extent of this," he replied, gesturing between the two of them. "So *go*."

Lingering went against her better judgement. She intellectually rebuked herself, even as her heart begged her to stay.

She and Maddox never got moments together. Imogen had made sure of that, especially as they'd gotten older. They could never be seen together in public. Or private, for that matter. It could ruin everything.

Which was why she hung onto every moment she managed to steal away with him, though his contempt for her grew stronger with every interaction.

When Imogen didn't move, he continued bitterly, "You need to get going if you're going to change the world, don't you? I'm sure they've already noticed your absence."

There was nothing else to say. Imogen would not demand an audience from him. She wouldn't stoop so low. So she forced herself away, ignoring the plummeting in her stomach.

Imogen hurried down the hallway and opened the door at the end. The door to the tunnel.

The mile-long tunnel that connected Princeps and Unruly.

Even though Imogen had been through the tunnel a dozen times, it never seized to make her uneasy. Ten stories underwater, constructed completely of glass.

It was less unsettling in the night. Imogen could pretend she wasn't walking beneath hundreds of tons of water—she was surrounded by darkness rather than the eerie green of reflections of daylight.

Below the tunnel was the narrow air shaft, which Imogen always found herself staring at when she crossed, centering her in space.

She had two objectives: speak with Charlotte and administer the vial. With Maddox covering her back, she could pull this off.

Imogen took off her stilettos, picked them up, and ran. The cardio was needed, her body finally able to catch up with her emotions and her brain.

Within eight minutes, Imogen reached the other door. She was sweating, hair in her face, her makeup smeared. She'd need to clean up before reentering the party.

She didn't take a moment to collect herself before opening the door to Unruly.

This side was much different than the Princeps side. The hallway had been carved by the elements themselves. Others may have found that disconcerting, but Imogen trusted the naturally carved space more than the glass tunnel. Men made mistakes. Nature, whatever higher power—well, Imogen supposed she trusted *those* more than the corrupt leaders in Princeps.

She didn't look into the rooms she passed. She knew exactly where she needed to go.

Everything was going according to plan. She was going to pull this—

The hinge of a door creaked. Imogen froze, her heart rate tripling. There was nowhere for her to hide. The nearest door was four steps behind. There was no way to reach it before Lynx appeared in the hallway directly in front of her.

Lynx was just as surprised to see Imogen as Imogen was to see her. But Imogen masked her shock before Lynx could read it. Maybe Lynx would one day learn that trick.

"What are you doing here?" Imogen demanded, playing offense before Lynx could get her bearings.

"I could ask you the same thing."

"I was following you," Imogen lied, "And it's a good thing I did. So I will ask you one more time—what are you doing here?"

Imogen pieced together theories as she spoke. She wasn't sure if it was her own bias steeped in narcissism, but her mind immediately jumped to the sabotaging of Charlotte.

Lynx gained her composure quickly. "We could both just go our separate ways, Two, and pretend this never happened."

"You are in no position for negotiations."

"I know you just want to help Zandra. I don't know how or why, but she's my friend. Which means *I'm* not your enemy."

But Five was, and Imogen had a feeling that Lynx would be running home to tell her unofficial Pair about this immediately.

"And if you take me back," Lynx said, "You can't do whatever it is that you were planning on doing."

Lynx had gotten smart quickly. Had Unruly done that to her?

"High Society won't be happy to know that a reformed Unruly is back on Unruly," Lynx pointed out, "So I certainly won't be telling anyone I was here."

But Lynx could tell Five. Imogen was between a rock and a hard place—she needed to get to Charlotte, and she wouldn't have a better opportunity than now.

But Lynx must've been stuck between a bigger rock and a harder place, or she wouldn't be offering to pretend their encounter had never happened.

"Best be on your way," Imogen said. She had more power and

more experience than Five. She could deal with the repercussions of this later, if there were any.

"Thank you," Lynx said, relief coating her voice. A good sign.

Imogen thought about whispering a threat as Lynx passed, but decided instituting fear in the teen would make her more likely to go crying to Five. Imogen would process this when she had the time to give the predicament the thought it deserved.

Lynx all but ran out of the tunnel, back toward Princeps. Imogen made sure that she'd actually left before continuing onward.

When Imogen reached Door 19, she pressed her finger to the scanner, knowing Maddox would wipe the evidence in the security room, and turned the handle.

Inside were four reclining chairs in a diamond, each supporting a body.

Charlotte's was directly in front of her.

Her eyes were closed, arms and legs hooked into a metal contraption to prevent atrophy. An IV protruded from her arm and her eyes were obscured by the helmet that had tricked Charlotte's body into thinking she was in Unruly.

All Imogen wanted to do was unplug Charlotte from the helmet. But she couldn't. That would set off just about every alarm in Town Hall.

Charlotte's unmoving face looked peaceful. The tiny wrinkle between her eyes caused by stress—the one that Zandra had somehow managed to duplicate when she'd been playing Charlotte—was gone.

But upon further inspection of Charlotte's vitals, Imogen noticed that Charlotte's body was not at nearly as much peace as her face initially led Imogen to believe. Her heart pumped at twice its normal rate. Her blood pressure was high. And there was a slight tremble to Charlotte's hands.

It was too soon for this.

Imogen took the syringe out of her dress and plunged it into Charlotte's left arm. She didn't waste time waiting to see if Charlotte was relieved of her symptoms, instead setting off toward the opposite door, ignoring the rest of the unconscious teenagers. She didn't bother shutting it behind her.

The back room—the one that the Unruly believed was a tunnel to their new home—was instead filled with helmets and computers. Imogen rushed toward Computer 4, labeled *Alexandra Julia Galvin*.

Imogen used her retina to bring the computer to life. She clicked in sync with her heartbeat, until she pressed: *Pause Simulation.*

Then two options appeared: *Open Breakout Room* and *Eject Subject.* Imogen swiped the cursor toward the former, a click away—

"This is not your best moment, Two."

Hell.

Imogen turned toward One slowly, buying herself time to think of an acceptable excuse. But she couldn't. There was none.

"Trying to tell your daughter how to win the Conquest?" One said, gloating against the doorway. This was exactly what he had needed to seal Imogen's coffin.

"I could have done that before she was on Unruly."

Think, she told herself. But there was no talking or manipulating her way out of this.

Imogen leapt to her feet and charged toward One. Though One had size on his side, Imogen had taken combat classes since the twins had been born. She was prepared for a moment like this, when she couldn't rely on her intellect to get what she wanted.

Imogen had never killed someone. She'd *thought* about it plenty, but only for the sake of the greater good. She could've gotten away with murder and disposed of One plenty of times over, but it was a moral boundary she hadn't been willing to cross.

At least, not until now. Not when her daughters—and Ignis —were at stake. Saving them would be worth the blemish on Imogen's own soul.

Maddox would wipe the footage. No one would ever know it was her. She would be One within a week.

Imogen was less than a foot away from One when the laser reflected in her eyes. She stopped in her tracks.

One raised a remote, a smug smirk on his face.

Imogen lifted her hands. Dozens of red dots were trained on her body. She wracked her brain for leverage. When she found none, panic flowed through her veins.

"You should be grateful I reached you before I had to disqualify Zandra from the Conquest."

A threat. One still could do that—there certainly weren't enough checks and balances in Ignis' government to stop him.

Had Maddox been discovered as well?

One grinned. "I will discuss this with the other Council members tomorrow. You will be detained until then for breaking the law."

Imogen didn't say anything. There was nothing else to say.

"You know," One said, "I was talking to Five about the Pairing Season, and I think that we ought to shake some things up. Wouldn't that be fun?" She couldn't process his words before One tossed her some handcuffs, keeping his eyes glued to her as she snapped them into place. A few large men arrived from the room behind her to escort her out.

Imogen glanced at Charlotte's monitor as she was led back toward the tunnel—Charlotte's heart rate had significantly dropped and was nearly back to normal. At least Imogen had bought herself some time there.

It would be up to Maddox to fix this now. Imogen just hoped that he loved their daughters more than he hated her.

23

Charlotte's blood was on fire. It burned through her temples and into her brain. She could no longer ignore it—the pounding intensified with every beat of her heart.

She barely managed to find a tunnel to let the other Unruly in. Harris rushed toward her.

"What is this place?"

He spotted the other Unruly and Impaired in the shadows. Charlotte ignored him and went toward where Jeri had disappeared to. Her entire body shook, though from the headache or anger she couldn't be sure.

"Jeri!" Charlotte called, "I want answers!" She marched under a section of the wall until she was in Jeri's own torch-lit living space. It had an old mattress and some half-broken wooden chairs. The ceiling hung too low for comfort, but Charlotte supposed that people did what they needed to for privacy.

Jeri crouched in a chair, eating some sort of stew. Charlotte had no guilt interrupting her dinner. Or breakfast. Lunch? Whatever meal this was.

"I have no answers."

"Well, I have questions." Her excitement at the whole situation had already faded. She was *not* about to be stuck living under a pile of garbage for the rest of her life. Not when a mansion waited for her in Princeps. Jeri kept eating, so Charlotte fired away before the pain in her head made her vomit. "How do I win the Conquest?"

Jeri laughed, nearly choking on her stew. It had more than a hint of condescension beneath it, but Charlotte refused to feel stupid. "One of you always comes in here and asks that. Lynx won the Conquest last year, did she not?"

"Yes." How did Jeri not know that?

"She must've found it."

A voice sounded behind Charlotte. "Found what? Charlotte turned. Harris crouched behind her, sticking his head where it didn't belong.

"A way out," Jeri said, returning to her stew. "Leave me."

All Charlotte had to do was find a way out of there? She could do that. The only problem was—

"She's interesting," Harris murmured, not bothering to hide his eavesdropping.

"*And* rude," Charlotte grumbled.

"Well, you weren't exactly nice to her, either."

Why did he think he had the right to speak to her like that after what he'd done to her? "She isn't telling us anything!"

"This is her home. We're intruders."

Charlotte closed her eyes, swallowing a wave of nausea. "It's our home now, too. And she hasn't exactly gone out of her way to welcome us."

Harris said nothing, following her to the others. They were seated in the center of the junkyard, eating the same stew as Jeri. Charlotte sat amongst them, her legs basically collapsing beneath her.

Rae passed Charlotte a bowl. She needed to start searching for a way out—without Harris breathing over her shoulder. She could prove herself. She'd done it millions of times over.

Harris took Charlotte in as he ate. "Are you okay?"

"Why wouldn't I be?" She tried to stop her hands from shaking. Was she hungry, or was her body feeling the absence of Dust? Maybe it was a mixture.

"You look...pale."

"Can't be good if you're telling me that when we're surrounded by people who've been underground for decades," Charlotte joked, hoping her voice didn't betray her queasiness.

She'd never had a hangover before—usually the Dust seamlessly left her body. But she had heard Jayana talk about them. Charlotte just hadn't realized how awful they were.

Was there Dust down here? Would she be able to survive without it?

There must be, she assured herself, *If anyone has Dust, it's the Unruly.*

Charlotte finished her stew. She was still hungry, but there were no seconds. "Can you watch over them?" she asked Harris, "I need a minute alone."

Harris nodded. She was barely on her feet before he murmured, "Zandra?"

"Yes?"

He hesitated. "Don't get lost."

Not what he'd wanted to say. Charlotte just gave a curt nod, sweeping her gaze over the others one final time.

Their little group of Unruly stretched out on old pillows and blankets. They didn't look like troublesome teenagers—just tired, scared kids. Kids who had voluntarily exiled themselves because they didn't want to be Paired. Kids who *seemed* too young to be Paired.

Maybe she was more like these people than she'd originally believed.

No. She couldn't think this way. She would do better by giving the others the tools they needed to survive, but she couldn't think of herself as one of them. She would never win with that mindset.

Charlotte's gaze landed on Wade. His cheeks were stained with a stream of dried tears. She had no words to comfort him. He wouldn't win the Conquest. This would be his home indefinitely, until he was needed as a Pair for a future Low-Pointer.

She was about to turn when Wade met her gaze, rolled to his feet, and walked toward her. "Thank you for getting us here."

"We *all* got us here."

"But you did more than the rest of us," he said, "I mean, you climbed a freaking wall of garbage! That's so cool." He was trying to cheer himself up. "Do you think we're going to get out of here?"

Charlotte was silent. A thousand possibilities of what to say passed through her mind, but none of them felt honest or right, and she felt too sick to think clearly.

"*Yes*" was the simplest response. The one he wanted to hear. *She* would get out of here, but he wouldn't. At least, not for a while. It felt cruel to give him false hope.

"I'm not going to answer that," Charlotte said. She *could*, but she wouldn't.

"I'm glad you're here with us, Zandra."

Guilt nestled beside the nausea. But there was nothing she could do for him except convince him that he could survive down here. Then she would leave, and the Unruly would have to fend for themselves.

But her pep talk would have to wait. Because she needed to start figuring out how to win the Conquest *immediately*.

"I'm glad you're here, too," she said, "I have to run to find the bathroom."

Wade laughed. "Oh, I've been like five times already. Stomach issues, you know? It's been a rough day. Want me to show you?"

"That's—that's okay. Just point me there?"

Wade did. She circled toward it, then doubled around toward the opposite side of the junkyard campsite that they'd entered from.

The food hadn't helped her sickliness—she was still dizzy. How long did Dust hangovers usually last? She swallowed the rising acidic stew. She would be fine. She had no eyes on her. No one expected anything. She could feel terrible and not have to check her posture.

Dust or Conquest first?

Charlotte asked a straggling Unruly where she could exit camp. He pointed her toward a hole in the garbage mound.

"Thanks. So any chance—?"

He ran faster than Dust dissipated into the air.

Charlotte sighed and grabbed a flickering torch and ducked through the hole. This heap of things consisted mostly of old clocks. Each pile seemed to have a theme, though there were a few mismatched ones.

Would Dust be hidden in the mounds? She peeked inside, but the interior was a labyrinth of time.

Opposite the clock-wall was a twisting and forking tunnel through the stone—an escape from the garbage-camp, back into the natural tunnels.

Charlotte hurried forward, her torch casting long shadows on the stone. She went left with every fork. And just to be safe, she kicked a pile of rocks at the end of each one, because she didn't trust her dizzy brain to be able to find the way back on its own.

After several long minutes of walking, Charlotte began to hear the soft trickle of running water.

Was it water? Or were Charlotte's senses so deprived that she was imagining things?

She followed it anyway. The sound grew louder and louder, until the water was almost at a roar...

Charlotte reached a dead end.

How could that be? She swept the torch around the rocks, searching for some kind of opening. A boulder blocked the back wall. Charlotte peered around it—

A distinguished torch rested on the ground.

It wasn't covered in dust or debris. Charlotte felt the top. Still warm.

The base of the wall curved inward into an opening.

Someone was here.

Charlotte crouched and peered inside. A light blue glow reflected off the rock.

Her heart leapt. Could it really be so easy to get out?

Charlotte secured her torch between two boulders so it wouldn't meet the same fate as the other one and took a deep breath.

She dropped onto her stomach and shimmied through the tight opening, rocks scraping against her chest. But she didn't care —she was so excited that she almost forgot how sick she felt. She almost forgot that there were likely hundreds of thousands of tons of rock just inches above her head. She almost forgot that the only way was forward, because the tunnel was so narrow that there would be no way to turn around.

The tunnel sloped and widened, and confirmed that Charlotte had not been losing her mind—the blue light was certainly real and growing brighter with each inch she moved.

The tunnel opened into a cavern. Charlotte got to her feet. Perhaps in one bend, she'd be able to see the water, and where the light emitted from, even with her swimming vision. She turned...

And forgot how to breathe.

Blue lights covered the walls and top of the cavern, and a tall waterfall sent droplets of water ricocheting off the black stones.

They reflected the blue light, transforming into sapphires as they flew through the air.

The pool of water was wide, but Charlotte couldn't calculate how deep. She had an overwhelming desire to find out, even though she was sure it would be freezing.

She was giddy with awe. Maybe Unruly wasn't all bad.

"Isn't it beautiful?" a voice echoed.

Charlotte started. Enid sat on a rock in her sports bra and underwear, her eyes wide with wonder, hair resting on her shoulders. She sat on a retro denim jacket that she must've found back at the camp.

"What are you doing here?" Charlotte asked. She must've been cold, sitting there basically naked.

"Dunno," Enid said, "I just went for a walk."

Charlotte wasn't sure she believed that, but she didn't allow herself to overthink. Not now. She could do that when she was back under the pile of trash.

Charlotte approached, and Enid made room for her. "What do you think the blue lights are?" Enid asked.

"Glowworms."

"How do you know that?" Enid said.

Charlotte grinned, "Charlotte—my sister—paid attention in school. I guess I picked up more than I thought."

"Gotcha." They settled into a comfortable silence before Enid said, "What's it like having a sister?"

Charlotte frowned. Zandra was her best friend. She made life easier. More fun. But also more difficult. Charlotte often didn't understand Zandra, even as she protected her. It was complicated and hard, but also the best thing that had ever happened.

"It's...good," Charlotte finally said.

"That's it?"

"No," Charlotte admitted. But she didn't offer anything else.

"What's Charlotte like?"

The words came before Charlotte knew she was saying them. "She's under a lot of pressure. All the time. Mostly from herself. But it made her really insecure, and kind of gave her a superiority complex."

Here, under tons of rock and glowworms, Charlotte could see herself clearly—who she had been, and what had brought her to Unruly. There was no one to impress or perform for. Or maybe it was that—*here*—she *wasn't* Charlotte. Or even Zandra. She was someone else entirely.

Somehow, even though the cavern spun and her head throbbed with pain, things were sharper than ever.

"She sounds...fun?" Enid said. And Charlotte laughed, feeling an unfamiliar connection with her.

"She is, she is. I do really love her. I just...worry about her. A lot."

Charlotte touched the shark tooth necklace, thinking about Zandra. Wondering what she was doing at this very moment.

"Did you find that tooth?"

Charlotte nodded, then corrected herself. "Well, Charlotte did. On the beach when we were kids on Princeps. She made it into a necklace and gave it to me."

Charlotte remembered the day vividly. Zandra had wanted to find her own so badly that Charlotte had given it to her.

"How did you two end up in such different places?" Enid asked.

"I'm not sure that we did."

Enid cocked her head. "What does she think about Pairing?"

"She hates it." When Enid didn't respond, Charlotte added, "Deep down. I, uh, think."

"Do you think she would ever stand against Pairing?"

Something didn't sit right. "Why?"

"I dunno. She has a lot of power."

"See? Everyone wants something from her. Even the Unruly."

Enid marinated on that as Charlotte changed the topic, "What do you think of this place?"

"I think I can get used to it."

"Really?"

"Yeah. I mean, look at this. It's incredible. We can do whatever we want here."

"But...what's the point?"

"What do you mean?"

"We're not working toward anything. We'd just be...living."

"What, you need a mission or something?" Enid asked, "Like reproducing for the survival of humanity just so your kids can do the same?"

Charlotte took her in. There was a somewhat challenging look in her wide eyes. They looked more blue than hazel in the light.

Zandra would've liked Enid. Charlotte liked her—but also found her infuriating. She traced her fingers over a smooth edge of the rock, mulling Enid's words over. "Maybe a better mission than *that*."

"Our mission could be making this place less sad."

"*Our* mission?" Charlotte asked.

"Yeah, I'm not going to live with a bunch of depressed people for the rest of my life."

"Are you going to be their therapist, or...?"

"We can change this place. Show these people there's something to live for."

"And what exactly *is* there to live for down here?"

"I just told you!" Enid said, a hint of frustration in her voice as she searched Charlotte's face.

Fight or flight kicked in—she didn't like her face being studied so closely, at such close proximity. The nausea intensified. She needed to lie down. But she couldn't—she'd wasted enough time sitting on this rock already. She needed to find a way out. Enid was still staring—

Charlotte had offended her. She had no idea what to do. Say. She centered herself on her hands, feeling what her fingers had been tracing.

It was a carving. Letters. No, a *name*. *L-Y—*

LYNX.

"Look—"

But Enid cut her off, "You're trying to win the Conquest."

There was a shift in the energy. Once upon time—also known as yesterday—she would've been able to process both Enid's words and Lynx's carving at once, but her Dust hangover made it difficult to focus on just *one* thing, let alone two.

"Lynx was here," Charlotte mumbled, still disoriented, trying to ignore Enid's disappointment.

"Lynx Hillenbrand?"

Charlotte nodded at the carving. Enid studied it and ran her fingers over it.

Her fingers brushed against Charlotte's before Charlotte could react. Charlotte yanked her hand away.

Enid shrugged, "So? She was down here for a while."

So I must be on the right path!

"She was a friend of mine," Charlotte said.

"Before she sold out, I take it?"

"What?"

Enid blinked. "She gave up on what she believed in."

"Can you blame her?"

"You don't?"

"You didn't know her." Charlotte didn't either—not really—but that didn't matter.

"I did, actually," Enid said, an edge in her voice. Whatever closeness Charlotte had felt to her dissolved, as if it were never there at all.

"Well, it sucks here!"

"Look at where we are! This—this is *beautiful*. It doesn't suck!"

"Lynx did what she had to do," Charlotte said, "She found a way out."

"No, she decided to preach the opposite of what she actually believed in." Enid's face curled in disgust.

"You don't know that."

Anger filled Enid's eyes—and Charlotte got the sense that Enid *did* know. This was personal. Just as Charlotte's defense of Lynx—of *herself*—was personal.

"What did Lynx do to you?" Charlotte murmured.

"Don't put her on a pedestal, Zandra," Enid replied, confirming Charlotte's suspicions.

"I don't put people on pedestals." *She* was the one that was put there, and she'd never do the same to someone else. No one deserved that fate.

Charlotte stood. She needed sleep. She could come back here and enjoy the beauty when she wasn't fighting the urge to throw up.

Enid grasped for Charlotte's wrist before she could escape. "Hey, I'm sorry."

Charlotte shook her hand away, the familiar bubble of panic forming in her throat. But she didn't move. "It—it's fine."

"Before you leave—join me for a swim?" Enid asked, her voice mischievous, "I've been hyping myself up."

"Won't it be too cold?" But Zandra would've already been swimming. And there was something alluring about the grin on Enid's face as she hopped off the rock, her lanky limbs landing with much more grace than Charlotte would have anticipated, and half-ran toward the water.

Now Charlotte understood why Enid had been in her underwear.

Maybe the water would clear her head. And Charlotte *did* feel rather grimy. There'd be enough blankets back in the junkyard to sufficiently bundle up.

Charlotte stripped off her clothes. Enid went calf-deep, her whole body tensing with the cold.

"How bad is it?" Charlotte asked, already knowing the answer.

"Not—not bad," Enid lied.

Charlotte tip-toed forward, dipping a single toe into the water. It was numbingly cold, and Charlotte's heart rate was already increasing by the time she was knee-deep beside Enid.

"Nothing like cold water to make you feel alive," Enid said.

Charlotte couldn't agree. Zandra might have, but Charlotte was finding it harder to do what her sister would've done. Enid didn't know Zandra—and even if the others did, who would notice? Who would care? Who could they even tell?

"Not for me," Charlotte said.

"Well, what does make you feel alive?"

Dust. She pushed the thought away with the shame that accompanied it.

What *did* make her feel alive?

"I guess...spending time with my sister," Charlotte said, "When she isn't thinking about what other people think."

"That's sweet," Enid said, and Charlotte wondered if she'd shared too much. Been too vulnerable.

But before Charlotte could think of anything else to say—this hangover was *really* slowing down her brain speed—Enid dove in.

Charlotte stared. A moment later, Enid's head popped out, and she screeched with a mixture of adrenaline and glee. "It's *freezing*! Come on!"

Inspired, and before she could lose her nerve, Charlotte dove.

For a moment, Charlotte felt nothing. Then came the shock, knocking the air out of her lungs.

Charlotte resurfaced and gasped. Enid laughed. "Should we swim to the waterfall?

Charlotte would freeze if she just stood, so she nodded and waded after Enid until her feet lost contact with the bottom.

The current picked up as they closed in. Charlotte was about to suggest going back when Enid began stroking faster, heading straight for the roaring crash. She threw Charlotte a cheeky grin, her intention clear.

If Charlotte hated anything, it was losing. So she rose to the challenge. She'd win even when her head pounded stronger than the falling water.

Enid was a good swimmer. Charlotte suspected that her disproportionately long arms had something to do with it.

But Charlotte held her own for several long seconds, until the force of the waterfall kept her in place. She felt her fatigue, the exhaustion from the last few days—and her Dust hangover—deep in her muscles.

But Enid kept going, slow but consistent. Even when Charlotte finally allowed herself to be swept back by the current, Enid still fought. She looked powerful.

Charlotte got the sense that Enid could've been a High-Pointer had she wanted to be. It didn't take as much skill as others thought—just a quick wit, determination, and willingness to sacrifice. And Enid had them all.

She must not have wanted to be a High-Pointer. But *why*? Why did she call herself average? Why was she a Mid-Pointer in a family of Mid-Pointers?

Enid got within a few meters of the waterfall before allowing the current to take her back to the shallows. She looked *alive*, her inner feelings radiating onto her face and doused in cool blue light.

"We'd never be able to do this in Ignis," Enid said.

"I know." Charlotte's teeth chattered, and she knew her lips were purple, based on the way that Enid was eyeing them.

"Let's get out?" They climbed back onto the rock. "I would've looked for a towel if I'd known we'd be swimming."

"It's fine," Charlotte said between shivers. Enid searched her eyes. "Do you want my jacket?"

"No. It was worth it."

Enid grinned as if she had just won an Upgrade. It was contagious. "This has been really fun." Her skin was blue—not only from the light—and covered in goosebumps. "I feel like I could stay here forever." She reached a hand toward Charlotte's...

Charlotte jumped to her feet, flustered. "Yeah, yeah, it has. Been fun. Really nice. But I have to go."

"I—Are you okay?"

Charlotte looked away. "Yes." The cavern spun faster than Charlotte's thoughts. "I just need to get warm."

"I can walk back with you."

Charlotte threw her clothes on her still-wet body. She needed to get out.

It wasn't as bad as her usual panic. There was an escape. She could just crawl through the tunnel and be free. She wasn't trying to run from inescapable thoughts in her mind.

Just a person.

Even so, she needed to get out of the cavern, and she needed to get out *now*.

"No, don't worry," Charlotte said, "I don't want to disturb you."

She half-ran for the tunnel before Enid could protest.

She couldn't win the Conquest while trying to lead or help or even befriend the Unruly. Whatever this had just been—talking and swimming—had distracted her from her mission.

The light from Charlotte's torch lit the path through the

tunnel. The tunnel spun. What was wrong with her? She needed to get out. She needed help. She needed...

Dust.

When Charlotte reached her torch, she breathed. She had no idea what had happened back there, but she didn't like it.

Charlotte relit Enid's torch and propped it up. She'd keep searching in this haze, even as her body begged her to stop. To rest. To sleep.

Charlotte continued to the previous fork and went left, down a path she hadn't gone before.

"Ouch!" A sharp prick tingled through her left arm, almost making her drop her torch. Charlotte brushed her fingers over her skin. But it was smooth. Undisturbed. And there was nothing nearby that could have touched it.

Dust, dust, dust.

Charlotte stumbled forward, blinking rapidly, trying to get her eyes to focus.

To her pleasant surprise, after just a few blinks, they did.

Charlotte furrowed her brow. She was still a little woozy...but the world was rapidly steadying.

How odd.

Charlotte felt a little better with every step. She had no idea that hangovers could be cured so quickly. Maybe she'd be able to scour the tunnels all night after all.

Something about her quick recovery felt strange, but Charlotte didn't dwell on it. Maybe the cold water had helped.

Now that she physically felt better, the cold was much more biting. Her clothes were wet and coated in dirt from her tunnel crawl. She needed to change into something dry.

It was much easier to get back when the world wasn't spinning. Charlotte ducked back under the gate of garbage, back into the junkyard.

She found a pile of dusty clothes on her way back and began

sorting through them—she pulled on a down jacket and some much-too-large sweatpants. She wouldn't be caught dead in this outfit back in Ignis, but she knew Zandra would go for the comfiest clothes she could find. And Charlotte certainly wasn't going to complain about that.

Once she was bundled in three layers, Charlotte made her way back toward camp, just to make sure things were in order before she went out again.

Most of the kids were sleeping, and the few who weren't were speaking quietly amongst themselves.

Wade was among them and waved her over, his face lighting. "Zandra! Come join us!"

"Not now."

Wade looked hurt, but Charlotte could only process so much. She was still reeling from her encounter with Enid, obsessing over how to find her way out, and worrying about when she'd get her next Dust fix. She doubted Wade would be able to help with any of it, and the warm sense of fulfillment she'd felt as she led the Unruly to the junkyard was rapidly fading from memory.

She glanced around for veteran Unruly—the people who were supposed to be their mentors and guides—but she found none.

Except one, an older Impaired man covered in sores who offered her a cup of soup. "Have you eaten?"

"Yes," she said, "I—I'm new here."

"I know. I'm Owen."

"Zandra."

"I should offer this to someone else."

"Wait!"

He did, and Charlotte struggled to find the right words. "I—is there something that eases the pain?" She nodded at his sores.

"Who said it hurts?"

She was never going to find Dust. "I—I'm sorry, I—"

"Why would Ignis create medicine if everyone has a perfect

immune system?" The unspoken words were clear: *Except people like* me.

The nation wasn't built for the Impaired. Charlotte felt a wave of guilt.

"Do they ever take Impaired out of here?"

Owen shook his head.

"*Have* they ever? Was there a year where no Impaired came?"

"There have been years where none joined us." Those year must have been the ones in which the Impaired went to Luxor. "Have a good night, Zandra."

Charlotte looked around for her next target. Only two others sat in the clearing: Harris, and a twenty-something-year-old man sitting across from him, whispering quietly.

Interest piqued—and also worried that Harris was learning invaluable information without her—Charlotte hurried to join.

Harris cracked his knuckles as the man spoke. He tapered off at Charlotte's arrival, a little annoyed by the interruption.

"Zandra, this is Nickolas."

Nickolas stood to greet her. He was taller than Charlotte had expected, with a dark beard, long hair, and a scrawny body that Charlotte suspected had once housed defined muscles.

"Hello." He didn't quite look her in the eye. "Nice to meet you. Good night." He scurried away before Charlotte could say a word.

Harris sighed and ran his fingers through his hair.

"That was...awkward," Charlotte said in her best Zandra impression. "What did he have to say?"

"I was trying to see how often we get fed." *Not everything's about the Conquest.*

"How often *do* we get fed?"

"Not enough! Nothing here is enough! I didn't even get to ask *where* the food comes from!" He stood and began cracking his knuckles once more, his emotions radiating off of him like a heatwave. "They just send people here with nothing to live off of! Or for!"

"Pairing sure isn't looking so bad," Charlotte said glumly. Enid would disagree, but Charlotte was still cold and hungry, and only freshly feeling better after her Dust hangover. She wanted a warm bath and bed.

Right?

Yes. Yes, that was what she wanted. A warm bath, but no unblinking eyes noting her every move. She would get that on Princeps. Her brain was tricking her again, telling her that *maybe* she'd be happy here.

Except was she even anxious?

Yes. Charlotte was *always* anxious. Even when she wasn't, it was there, lurking. What would happen when the reality of her situation settled in and there was no Dust to be found?

"It's screwed!" Harris said.

"Well, what were you expecting?"

"I didn't expect anything. I just wanted to know. I wanted to know what needed to be fixed."

Fixed?

Harris was smart. He had a plan. Probably a better plan than Charlotte had, though that wasn't saying much, considering that Charlotte hadn't planned to come here at all.

"You're going to *fix* this?"

Harris exhaled and sat back down. She hadn't noticed until now that it was on an old microwave.

"That's why I came here."

He would need power to do so. He wasn't so arrogant that he thought he could come down here and singlehandedly fix it blind. Further proof he planned on beating her to the top.

"How?" asked Charlotte.

"I need to figure out exactly what *needs* to be fixed before I figure out how. Like, how screwed up is it that we send Impaired here at *ten* years old?"

"Very."

It was admirable, to want to take on the challenge of championing the people. Brave. Selfless. Something that Charlotte would've never even thought to do. Something that the Harris Charlotte had known—the one before he'd betrayed her—would sacrifice his future for.

But to do it, he would have to win the Conquest. But he wouldn't, because—no matter how noble Harris' intentions—Charlotte was either going to win or die trying.

24

Spas were a modern form of torture.

Zandra sat still while a person she couldn't see—because her eyes were covered by cucumbers, which was a complete waste of food—painted her face in some kind of liquid mask. She fidgeted, feeling just as trapped as when Imogen had locked her in the guest room.

She'd only been in the palace one day, but it felt like centuries. She was getting her *face painted* while Charlotte was probably fighting for her life on Unruly.

"I know this isn't totally your speed," Jayana said somewhere to the right. Wasn't *she* supposed to be getting a facial as well? How could she see Zandra fidgeting?

"I'm *very* relaxed," Zandra snapped.

"It's worn off, hasn't it." A statement—not a question. Why did Zandra never know what Jayana was talking about? "I haven't been able to find any here."

Zandra decided her best option was to feign comprehension, "Yeah, me neither."

Jayana lowered her voice, "I heard Jaxson got arrested at the delinquent party. Do you think that's why?"

Zandra's eyes snapped open, dislodging one of her cucumbers. An attendant rushed to replace it. "Jaxson got arrested?"

Jayana knew Jaxson too?

"Yeah. And I think he's the only one who...does what he does."

"You think so?"

"Maybe his Pair is taking over. She's done so a few times before."

Zandra heard her facialist step between them. There would be no answers for her. Thankfully, the woman began wiping the goo off of Zandra's face and removed the cucumbers.

"Thank you," Zandra said, jumping to her feet. Jayana also straightened. Zandra searched for something to ask that would give her a clue—

"So who's caught your eye?"

"Uh—" Zandra said, not expecting the turn in conversation. She had an "outing" scheduled with Atticus around noon, then another one with some boy whose name she couldn't remember. She wished she could just sit on the roof with her journal. It was still morning and she was already socially drained. How did Charlotte do this all the time?

"I have my eye on the prince," Jayana said.

Zandra hesitated a moment too long. "Oh?"

"His presence throws things off. You and him are the two who will be chosen for High Society. So one of us needs to get Paired with him. If you want him, speak now and I'll go for Atticus."

Zandra loathed the dehumanization, but couldn't ignore the anger at the idea of Jayana with Tiberius. She needed to speak up. She needed to tell Jayana to pursue Atticus.

But *why*? She wasn't even Pairing herself. She was picking out Charlotte's Pair for after she saved her.

Because Zandra *was* going to save her. She just needed to figure out how. Tiberius was beside the point.

"Yeah—ahem, go for it."

"Great. Then you have your pick of the rest of them," Jayana said.

"Assuming he likes you too." It took Jayana's raised eyebrows to realize that was *not* the proper thing to say. "He will, of course, I just want you to make sure that you have a...back up plan. In case he's doing the same thing. That we are."

This was so much work.

"Right," Jayana said as they approached a fork in the hall, "Well, I shall see you later. You're at Cav too, right?"

Zandra shrugged. She had no idea where she was going.

Zandra's alone time lasted two seconds. Eloise rushed down the hallway the moment Jayana disappeared, her simple gown billowing behind her.

"Charlotte!" Eloise said, "We must get you ready for your outing with Mr. Marquez. Come."

Why was she acting as if she was hours behind schedule when it had only been a minute since her facial had ended? Everyone in the palace needed to calm the hell down.

"Alright," Zandra mumbled, falling in step behind Eloise as Eloise scanned her face. Whatever the facialist had done must have worked, because Eloise nodded in approval.

An hour later, Zandra stood in yet another dress she hated, Eloise leading her toward a carriage outside the palace's front gates. It was too beautiful outside for a forced social interaction. A pair of monarch butterflies twirled past her. Zandra watched their flight.

"Good luck," Eloise said, "And remember—have fun."

The monarchs looped around each other, so familiar that they guessed the other's path of flight before it was made.

"Charlotte," Eloise rebuked. Zandra tore her gaze away.

"Right, yes."

Atticus was waiting for her outside the carriage. He gave her a smile that was neither warm nor cool—he didn't have an opinion of her yet. Despite everything Atticus had heard about her, it seemed he was going to make his own judgements.

"I was told to help you into the carriage, but you scored more physical points than I did."

Zandra grinned. "Do you want *me* to help *you* in?"

"I think I'll manage." But a hint of warmth appeared on his face.

Five was inside the carriage. She fixed Zandra with a glare. Zandra hadn't forgotten the promise she had made Five's mother, but she didn't want to compromise her situation. Five certainly wouldn't believe that "Charlotte" was sharing this information out of the goodness of her heart.

"Hello," Zandra decided to say.

Five gave a curt nod.

The moment Atticus was situated, the horses moved.

"Have you been to Cav before?" Atticus asked. So they *were* going there.

Cav was Ignis' finest restaurant and was said to have food as delicious as Princeps'. The Galvin family went almost every day when she and Charlotte were home from the Academy for the summer.

"Yes," Zandra said, "Have you?"

"This will be my first," Atticus said, and Zandra remembered that he was born in the LPC. "What's good there?"

The conversation got even more boring as the carriage rolled on, and Zandra realized that her first impression of him was both correct and incorrect. Atticus seemed to be a good person, but talking to him was like pulling teeth. They had nothing in common.

When they reached Cav a few long minutes later, Zandra was ready for the outing to be over.

They walked into the restaurant, Five "chaperoning" or, as Zandra decided to call it, *breathing down her neck*.

The restaurant was open and airy, with natural light and a light color scheme. The tables were spread out, with enough room so nearby diners would have difficulty eavesdropping. The restauranteurs did double takes as Zandra, Atticus, and Five arrived.

In a moment of nostalgia, Zandra glanced over at the table she always sat at with Charlotte and her parents.

Then she was the one doing a double take. There, at *her* table, sat Tiberius and Jayana.

Tiberius was nodding, fully invested as Jayana animatedly spoke. Zandra forced down her jealousy, chastising herself for telling Jayana that she could pursue Tiberius.

"So who were your friends at the Academy?" Zandra asked Atticus as they sat, "Any of the others here?"

Atticus hesitated, then finally said, "My best friend was Harris Alder."

"Really?" Zandra asked, her guard rising. She wondered what he knew of Harris and Charlotte's falling out.

"Yes."

"Do you know why he went Unruly?" Zandra couldn't stop herself from asking. She'd overheard the other girls discussing—judging—his decision before her facial. Zandra wondered if he and Charlotte had somehow learned to coexist on Unruly.

Atticus shrugged.

"Was it to win the Conquest or because he didn't want to get Paired?"

"Are you just looking for gossip?" Atticus asked, an edge to his voice.

"I'm sure you know that we were childhood friends."

"He was a curious guy." Atticus' use of the past tense, as if Harris was already dead, didn't go unnoticed. "Too much for his own good."

Was it petty to dislike Atticus just because he'd been friends with Harris?

She swallowed her questions at the unpleasant sensation of Five's eyes on the back of her neck. How was she going to make conversation with this boy through a whole meal?

She stole a glance at Tiberius as she adjusted her chair, expecting him to be fixated on Jayana...

Certainly not on her.

But his brown eyes met hers, and his face lighted. Zandra flashed a smile. He must've been able to see the desperation in her eyes, because he said something to Jayana and she glanced Zandra's way as well.

A moment later, both of them were walking toward their table.

Zandra didn't hear Atticus' next question. Not when she could hear Tiberius' approaching footsteps.

"Hello!" Tiberius said, "Jayana was just telling me that Charlotte would know what's good here."

Zandra glanced at Atticus—he also looked relieved by the interruption. Good. "Would you like to join us?" Zandra asked, begging Tiberius with her eyes to say yes.

She knew he would. He had told her that he was only interested in pursuing her—or rather, *Charlotte*—after all.

But Tiberius looked to Jayana first. She just shrugged, which Tiberius must have decided was good enough. "We would be honored."

Atticus pulled up a chair from an empty table too quickly, moving his so he'd be next to Zandra. Tiberius claimed the one on Zandra's other side by swinging his crwth over the back of his chair before pulling another up for Jayana.

"I've heard the most incredible things about Princeps," Tiberius said. Zandra internally groaned.

"I heard you turned down a pre-Pairing visit," Atticus said, "Why is that?"

"It didn't seem fair." Tiberius said too casually for Zandra to believe it true.

"So how does this compare to Luxor?" Zandra asked, not caring to talk about Princeps when there was a far more interesting world out there. "You said the parties were different. What else is?"

"Everything, really. But I don't know if it was just *my* life, or life in general."

"Well, what was your life like?"

"I always knew that I was going to leave, so—even though it was all that I knew—it wasn't *home*." Tiberius hesitated. "I know that probably doesn't make any sense."

"No, it does." Too much sense. She'd never felt that she belonged in either Ignis or Princeps. It was what had drawn her toward Unruly—the only other place she could access the possibility of contentment. Where she wouldn't feel the need to run.

"And we have much more music there," Tiberius said, "A restaurant like this would never be so quiet."

"There aren't many musicians in Ignis," Zandra said.

"You don't learn it in school?"

"The only people who learn are High Society and High-Pointers. It's a privilege."

"It's hard to learn as an adult," Tiberius said, "No wonder the music scene is...subpar."

Zandra imagined being in Luxor, dancing to a full orchestra with whomever she wanted, all day and night, with no one to answer to.

Maybe she *did* belong in Luxor. But it was a fantasy. Even if she did get Charlotte Paired with Tiberius, she doubted she'd get more than a visit to Luxor, if she was lucky.

Atticus and Jayana had begun talking amongst themselves. Zandra barely stifled a sigh of relief.

"Does Princeps have more music?" Tiberius asked. "You grew up there, didn't you?"

"I don't think it did. I haven't been there in years."

"It sounds amazing. My father told me that the ceiling of Town Hall is ten stories high! And that his living space is built into a cliff overlooking the ocean."

Was he as curious about Princeps as she was about Luxor? It was a gilded cage, just like Phoenix Palace.

Tiberius leaned toward her so the others couldn't hear. "He also told me that there's a tunnel between Princeps and Unruly. If you're still worried about your sister."

Zandra's blood froze. A *tunnel*?

That was her way in. It didn't matter how well-protected it was—she would figure it out.

It was a plan. An impossible plan, but that was still much better than *no* plan.

"Where?"

"I don't know. Under the water somewhere."

"Did he see it?"

Tiberius shook his head. Zandra gripped his arm. "You have to find out more."

He narrowed his eyes, too intense to be anything but genuine. "I will. I promise."

"Thank you," Zandra whispered.

She had to get to High Society. Now Princeps also held the key to getting Charlotte off Unruly.

She just couldn't mess up. She was a shoo-in. She and whoever she got Paired with.

Charlotte said she wanted to be Paired with Tiberius, but she hadn't seemed very excited about him when she had run into him as "Zandra". Should Zandra be trying to find her someone else? Someone she was more interested in? How would she even *know*?

Would Charlotte like Atticus? Maybe, but Zandra wasn't sure she was up for the challenge. Why did this have to be so complicated?

Zandra released Tiberius' arm, and turned back toward the others.

"Let's play a game," Jayana suggested.

Zandra nodded mindlessly. She wished she could ask Imogen for help. Imogen would've known.

No, Zandra corrected herself, *Imogen* had *known.* Akil had already learned about the tunnel and told Tiberius. Anger flared through Zandra's body. How could Imogen have manipulated them like that?

"I ask a question and then we all have to guess the answer for the person to the right of us," Jayana said. "Okay, the question is... what's something you think the person's done that no one else knows? I'll go first—Tiberius, I think that you used to seduce all the women in Luxor with that crwth of yours."

Tiberius laughed. "Certainly not all. There was only one who really caught my eye growing up."

He stole a glance at Zandra, and it filled her with both giddiness and guilt. *He never knew Charlotte,* she reminded herself. *And the fact that he thinks he did is weird.*

"Do tell," Jayana said.

"I think it would make her rather uncomfortable if she knew."

"It's not like she's here."

Atticus cut in, "Tiberius, it's your turn."

"I think that Charlotte has a side that she doesn't let anyone else see," Tiberius murmured.

Zandra laughed.

Jayana looked between them, then said, "Everyone knows that about Charlotte. That's, like, why everyone's obsessed with her. Because *no one* knows who she really is. Is that the best you can come up with?"

Tiberius' fist clenched and face darkened. Zandra opened her mouth to apologize on Jayana's behalf when Tiberius blurted, "Jaxson."

Zandra's mouth stayed open, but no sound came out. A heavy silence filled the air.

"Well, I certainly have no idea what you're talking about," Jayana said in a way that confirmed she was lying. Jayana glanced Zandra's way, no doubt expecting something clever to come out of her mouth.

But how *could* something clever come out of her mouth when she literally had no idea what was going on?

Atticus was just as confused, while Tiberius already regretted his words, "Charlotte, I—I'm sorry."

Zandra looked over her shoulder. Five was watching the entire exchange with raised eyebrows.

Whatever Tiberius had just said was *bad*.

"You can't go wrong with the fish," Zandra said, trying to get this train back on the tracks, hoping they could roll over whatever obstacle they had just hit.

Apparently it was too big to do so. "I have to use the restroom," Jayana said, fixing Charlotte with a pointed look.

"Um, same," Zandra said. She was finding it hard to keep her shoulders back, feeling trapped in *Charlotte's* body.

Jayana grabbed her hand as she passed. When they reached the bathroom, Jayana checked to make sure they were alone, then pulled Zandra into a stall and locked the door.

"I can't believe him. How the hell does he even know?" Jayana seethed.

How the hell *didn't* she know what was going on? The stall walls were too close together. Zandra fought the urge to open the door.

Jayana searched her face and sighed. "You're freaking, aren't you?"

"Just—just a little bit."

Jayana must not have believed her, because she sighed and rummaged through her pockets.

"I have a little Dust left. I was saving it, but I think you need it more than I do. I can't look at you like this."

Dust? It took Zandra a long moment to understand the word. She still wasn't exactly sure what it meant until Jayana shoved a baggy of powder toward her.

A drug.

Nothing made sense until everything did.

Jaxson. Why Charlotte had wanted to go to the party. Jayana's coded words.

Jaxson had been dealing Charlotte Dust.

And everyone knew it.

Except for her.

Since *when?* How hadn't Zandra known?

How many times had Charlotte *lied* to her?

First not passing on Lynx's message, now this?

Zandra turned and vomited in the toilet.

"Oh! Charlotte, darling, it—let me—"

Jayana gathered Zandra's hair and held it back. It was too much for Zandra to digest. She couldn't really remember what the drug did—helped people focus?

The next question came crashing down—was Charlotte so much better than her at everything because of the Dust?

Zandra flushed the toilet and stood. She felt everything— stupid, afraid, ignorant, ashamed of her sister despite being worried for her.

But she was mostly angry. Angry at Charlotte, at herself for not knowing.

And at Tiberius.

How could he just blurt Charlotte's secret out to everyone? In front of *Five*?

Everyone was going to know, if they all didn't already.

"Are you okay?" Jayana asked, concern in her voice. Zandra knew she'd be grateful to Jayana for handling the situation when she was able to feel something *good* again.

"No." She certainly was not.

"The Dust will help—"

"No!" Zandra repeated. She didn't want to be *near* the Dust. The stall walls were closing in. Zandra opened the door and rushed outside.

She thought that she'd known Charlotte better than anyone. And yet, some boy who had only met her *once* somehow knew about Charlotte's Dust habit!

Zandra beelined for the door. She was half inclined to demand to go Unruly so she could scream at Charlotte herself. She was over this ridiculous competition and its passive aggressive manipulation.

Tiberius stood when she rushed past the table. "Charlotte—"

She didn't stop. Not even when Five stood as well.

Outside the restaurant, a crowd had formed. Word had gotten out that she was here, and the people wanted a glimpse of the Highest Pointer of All Time.

They were going to get a glimpse of the Lowest Pointer of All Time instead.

Zandra could see no way through them. Her claustrophobia threatened to strangle her.

"Charlotte—" Tiberius said, coming up behind her, "I'm so sorry. I don't know what came over me—"

"Leave me alone!"

"Please, I just—it was stupid. I just wanted to show how well I know you—"

"But you *don't* know me! We've had *two* conversations, Tiberius. You know *nothing* about me."

Tiberius nodded, backing down. "I understand that now. But I would like to get to know you, if you'll allow me."

"I don't want you to know me, okay?! I don't want anything to do with you after that, and I certainly don't want to be your Pair!"

Tiberius stood, mouth agape, staring at her as if she had just shattered his entire world.

But she hadn't. Because he wasn't even living in the same world as she. He had a fantasy of Charlotte in his head. One that Charlotte would never be.

And one that Zandra *could* never be.

"I don't ever want to see you again."

"I'm sorry," Tiberius murmured, his voice cracking.

Then he was gone. Back into Cav.

All the people stared at her. Several had heard everything that had gone down.

Before Zandra could figure out what to do, Five came up behind her. "Enjoying yourself?'

"I want to go back."

"Sure," Five said. She gestured toward the carriage driver, who was able to see Five's long arms over the heads of the crowd. "You sure like a dramatic exit, don't you, Charlotte?"

Zandra didn't take the bait. Five waited for the carriage to stop before heading back inside. Zandra hopped in, ready to be alone, so she could properly release her emotion.

She was shocked when she saw that she had company.

Inside was Three.

What the hell was *he* doing in her carriage?

He smiled, but it quickly turned to concern when he saw Zandra's chin trembling.

"What's wrong?"

"What do you want?" Zandra said, too exhausted to remember to be Charlotte.

The carriage started rolling. "To help you."

"Everything is *perfectly fine*." Zandra wanted to fast-forward to a different day. This one sucked.

It got even worse when Three said, "Your mother has been detained."

Zandra's heart sank further. "Detained? How? Why?" Was she going to have to go rescue her mother as well? How was she going to do all of this alone?

"She was trying to help Charlotte on Unruly."

Zandra's mouth hung open. *Charlotte*. He'd said *Charlotte*.

Three knew. Did that mean everyone...? Zandra tensed, ready to fight. Was *she* about to be detained as well? Was her whole family screwed?

"No one else knows. And your mother is tough. She'll be fine until she finds a way out." Sensing her unease, Three added, "I'm here to help you,"

Zandra wanted to believe him. Hell, if it had been two days ago, she would have. "Why?" Surely he wanted something in return. Another thing she'd learned during her short day in the palace was that people didn't do things out of the goodness of their hearts.

"Because you need a friend."

Zandra scoffed. "Fine, you want to help me? Get my sister out of there."

"I can't."

"There's a tunnel. But you knew that, didn't you?"

Three ignored the question, though he didn't seem irritated with her. "I promised Imogen I would help."

"You must not've done a very good job, if she's detained."

"You. I promised to help *you*."

"To what end?"

"To get you to Princeps," he said.

Zandra was just getting another Imogen. A pawn in another political game. He was probably only keeping her secret so he could expose it when it suited him.

But at least that meant that she *had* more time. If Charlotte were here, she would already be figuring out what she could use as leverage against him. "So what's Plan B?"

"Charlotte wins the Conquest and you and your Pair get sent to Princeps."

"That's an awful plan!" Zandra exclaimed, "Hoping for the best? That's all you got? What if Charlotte gets *killed* before then? Or has another mental breakdown, with no one to help her?"

"It's all we can do for now," Three said.

"Then what the hell are you even doing here?"

Three pulled a phone—a communication device that only some in High Society had—out of his coat pocket. "Press any button, it'll ring me directly. If you run into any problems, call me and I'll help."

Zandra had half a mind not to take it. To tell him that she didn't need his help.

But it wasn't true, so she took the phone.

"What just happened in there?" Three asked in a moment of silence, after she'd pocketed it. He wouldn't understand. No one would. The person Zandra thought she'd known better than anyone had a side that she hadn't shared.

"It's hard to be someone else sometimes."

"I know," Three replied darkly. He wasn't just saying that. He *did* know.

Even though Zandra was livid at Charlotte, Charlotte still

needed her help. And she needed to get to Princeps to do that. She hoped that her meltdown wouldn't be the difference between getting chosen for High Society and not.

Charlotte was popular. Far more popular than any of the other candidates, and more powerful than all of them except Tiberius. She and her Pair would be the second couple chosen. She just couldn't mess up again.

But Tiberius had messed up even worse. He had let Five know about Charlotte using *Dust*.

If Five let the word get out, she would tarnish Charlotte's reputation forever. Zandra wouldn't be able to get to Princeps. She would be shamed.

How could Charlotte have done this? How could Charlotte have wasted the points Zandra gave her to get *Dust?*

The harsh truth hit Zandra like a freight train. Both of them could've been Mid-Pointers. But Charlotte would rather she be the Highest Pointer of All Time, and Zandra the Lowest.

Charlotte would rather have points than be with *her.*

New tears pooled into Zandra's eyes that she angrily blinked away. She couldn't do this now. Not in front of Three. She would wait until she got back to her private quarters.

"I have to escort you to an announcement."

Of course there was a freaking announcement today.

Five needed to be stopped. And the only way that Zandra could think to do that was with Three's help.

"There's a problem," Zandra whispered. The words like cotton in her mouth. "I guess that Charlotte had a...Dust problem." She paused for a moment, watching Three's eyes widen in surprise. She supposed not *everyone* knew about it. "And I think Five just found out."

~

Three would speak to Five. Zandra hoped it would be enough, though she doubted it, unless he had some very juicy blackmail. Zandra had calmed down slightly when they pulled back up to the palace. A crowd was already beginning to form in preparation for the announcement.

The carriage stopped in Phoenix Square. How could something she used to see as imposing and beautiful, filled with unknown secrets and adventures, now feel like a crate in the Union?

Zandra hurried toward the palace gate. This was a side entrance, not the main one, but it was just as well-protected. She wanted to run back to her room and compose herself before whatever stupid announcement was announced. She doubted it had anything to do with her—it was probably about an Upgrade. Or someone important on Princeps was pregnant.

When she reached the gate, guards cleared the way for her. Eloise waited behind them. "So rude of One to cut your outing short!" she exclaimed, gesturing Zandra up a staircase.

Zandra's stomach dropped. The announcement was going to be exciting. Shoot. "What is this about?"

"I don't know," Eloise said, glancing back at her. She stopped short when she saw her face. "Oh my...what happened here?"

Zandra glanced down at the marble staircase, but it wasn't clean enough to catch a glimpse of her reflection. It must have been bad, because when they got to the top of the stairs, Eloise licked a finger and started brushing at Zandra's cheek. Charlotte would've flinched in disgust—at both the touch and the saliva— but Zandra didn't react.

"What's wrong, dear?"

"Nothing."

Then they were joined by One, who took in her appearance with raised eyebrows.

Screw you, Zandra thought.

"Are you ready to speak?" One asked, an underlying delight in his voice.

Zandra blanched. *She* was speaking? Every time she thought this day truly couldn't get any worse...

"May I inquire what I'm speaking about? Um, *as to* what I'm speaking about?"

"There will be a screen. Just read it."

Shoot. Shoot, shoot, shoot. "But what if there are...technical difficulties?"

"There won't be."

Eloise kept dabbing at Zandra's face as they continued toward the balcony. Maybe this would be a benign announcement. Maybe nothing bad was going to come of it. But Zandra knew better. Hope for the best, prepare for the worst.

One stopped just short of the balcony doors. The square had filled even in the few minutes since Zandra had been outside.

"Where is Five?" One asked Three, who approached behind.

"She was escorting the other Pairing candidates back," Three responded.

Had Three intercepted Five when Zandra had rushed inside? One made an impatient noise. Zandra normally wouldn't have noticed the gleeful glint in his eye, but a day in Charlotte's shoes had done wonders on her perception skills.

Eloise finally got ahold of some makeup. As Zandra closed her eyes, she pretended she was all alone in Luxor, wandering through the streets, with no one wondering or caring who she was.

She thought about the Barrenlands, and what lay on the opposite side. A village grew in her mind. Huts by an oasis. Nomads traveling in an out, walking through the sand until they reached lush mountains, where adventure waited.

No. She needed a plan. She couldn't disassociate. She couldn't give up, no matter how bad things were.

It was just Eloise, the guards, One, and Zandra. She needed to figure out what she was announcing. Lynx's entrance disrupted her thoughts. One's eyes flickered her way. "Where is Five?"

"I haven't seen her," Lynx said.

One grumbled something under his breath and began pacing. Even the guards seemed disturbed by his mania.

Lynx stopped beside Zandra. "How are you, Charlotte?"

"Fine," Zandra said. She had no trust left to place.

Lynx leaned toward her so no one else could hear. "I just wanted to let you know that if you need anything, I'm here for you. I know how hard it is when everyone's expecting something of you."

First Three, now Lynx? People were trying to get in her good graces. Something was coming. And Zandra was going to be the one announcing it.

"Can you tell me what's happening?" Zandra asked.

"I don't know," Lynx said. She appeared candid.

This was her chance to ask what Lynx had told Charlotte to pass on. Her chance to assemble some of the many missing puzzle pieces.

But Five swept inside a moment later, and Lynx took a step away from Zandra.

"Finally," One grumbled, opening the balcony door to a cacophony of cheers. "Five, read the screen and introduce Ms. Galvin."

Five smirked at Zandra. Yes, this was going to be very, very bad.

"I want to know what I'm saying."

"We don't have time for this," One said, "Just read."

Five stepped onto the balcony. One shut the door behind her so they couldn't hear the introduction, then ushered Zandra in line.

Zandra glanced at Three. He gave her a small nod.

When the doors opened and Zandra heard the applause, she

didn't balk. These people were fools—they didn't know what or who they were cheering for. They didn't know that she was the Lowest Pointer of All Time.

They didn't know that she could say whatever the hell she wanted.

She loved the view. She could see everything—Ignis, the Barrenlands, Princeps, *everyone*. Despite her heavy emotions, she was weightless over the world, both conflicting emotions existing at once.

Zandra fled into her thoughts. She didn't look down into the people—she didn't care to see who was staring as she plastered one of Charlotte's half-smiles onto her face.

The screen was small and hidden by a podium from the rest of the people. They'd all think she'd been briefed.

Their ignorance was alarming.

Even after the crowd had fallen silent, a few voices called, "I love you, Charlotte!" What was it like to love someone without knowing them? How could so many do it?

Zandra looked ahead at her electronic cue cards and started reading.

"Greetings, Ignites."

More applause. She hadn't even said anything interesting.

"We've gathered you here today to inform you of an exciting new change to Pairing this season."

Zandra paused, allowing the words to sink in. The next words flashed. Zandra read them to herself, not saying them aloud.

This would *not* be good for her.

But this was the way it would be, whether she announced it or not. So she shared her knowledge with the rest of the people, "Due to a deficit in leadership on Princeps, this year High Society will only be letting one Pair join Princeps, rather than the usual two."

How One had decided a lack in leadership equated to admitting only one couple, Zandra had no idea. It made *him* look bad. He was the leader, wasn't he? But it meant Zandra had to get Paired with Tiberius, because *he* would be the one joining High Society regardless of Charlotte's points. This must've been Imogen's punishment. She wasn't just getting detained.

"The Council has consulted. This is what's best for Ignis. Upgrade competitions will remain the same, as will the Conquest."

More cheers. These people would cheer for anything. But there must've been people out there who knew, if this were true, Upgrades would be cut next.

Zandra put her hands up for silence. "This is not the only announcement, I'm afraid. There has been a troubling discovery that has personally affected me, which is why I asked One if I could deliver it to you personally."

Zandra pieced together what One had put her up here to say. And why *she* had to say it.

She had to make a split second decision. An *impossible* decision.

Zandra froze. There was nothing to fight and nowhere to run. She glanced inside. One wore a Cheshire grin. Five gloated. Lynx had a poker face that she certainly hadn't been capable of one short year ago.

Three gave her a nod. *Do it*, his eyes said, *Trust me.*

But Zandra didn't trust him. She didn't trust anyone except herself.

If she didn't do what she was told, there was no way she'd be able to save Charlotte. That was her priority. Save Charlotte so she could tell her how pissed off she was.

"Imogen Galvin, formerly Two—my own mother—was caught trying to infiltrate Unruly." The crowd gasped. Zandra continued, "Not only was this incredibly dangerous, it was also an act of treason. Imogen used her power for her own personal benefit."

Zandra's words were a knife in her own heart. The people were silent, and the silence was deafening.

"I renounce Imogen as my leader—"

The next words said, *And as my mother.*

Zandra skipped them. "—And all of Ignis should as well. She will be replaced in the next election in three months' time.

"I know this is a difficult time for us, with the constant threat of the Union looming, and more and more teenagers choosing to go Unruly," Zandra said, "But we will remain together and strong. Thank you."

Zandra felt ill. She hated being a puppet, hated feeling as though she had no power, hated the guilt that already wracked her gut from having betrayed Imogen.

Zandra turned. Three was frowning. And Lynx—Lynx was gone.

If only it were that easy for *her* to flee. Before Zandra could move, a female voice yelled, coming from some sort of voice amplifier, "How long have you been on Dust?"

Silence. Only the rapid beating of Zandra's heart.

The oasis beyond the Barrenlands flashed back into her mind. A well beside a lake.

Zandra forced it away. *Think, think, think.*

She needed time. Time and advice. She hadn't been trained for this. Charlotte would've known what to say. *But only because she was on Dust.* Charlotte had cheated at this. At *life.*

Zandra willed herself to do it on her own. She was capable. The smartest Lowest Pointer ever, probably. She could do this.

There was murmuring, but Zandra put her hands up. She was in control. She would say what *she* wanted to say. They couldn't control her voice. Her words.

"Excuse me?" Zandra said, searching the crowd for the interloper.

"How long have you been on Dust?" This time Zandra spotted her.

Greta. Five's mother. Zandra compartmentalized.

"I am *not* on Dust," Zandra said in her most intimidating voice, allowing a hint of her anger to leak through her vocal chords. "Perhaps you should check your sources. And I'm happy to *prove* I'm not on Dust with a drug test. If there are no other wild accusations, I think that is all.

"Thank you all for your support, and I will see you soon," Zandra finished, dramatically turning away, her dress flaring behind her.

Murmuring gave way to claps and cheers. Even though she had subdued the masses for now, it was only a matter of time before someone found proof.

And then everyone would know the truth. In the meantime, Zandra just had to make sure she got Paired with Tiberius so she could rescue her selfish sister.

25

For the first time since he'd learned of Charlotte's existence, Tiberius was unsure they would be Paired.

The doubt ate at him, so overpowering that he could barely manage to play a mournful lament on his crwth. Had he deserved it? Probably. His jealousy had blinded him, but that didn't make it hurt any less. If anything, it hurt more—he had been stabbed by his own knife, with no one to blame but himself. There was no anger to be externally directed.

His knife oozed poison into his soul.

This wasn't what love was supposed to be. Love was supposed to be effortless and easy, not painful, difficult, and confusing.

He did know Charlotte. She just didn't understand the extent of his knowledge yet. She didn't know that she had been his muse for the past five years. He hadn't even had the chance to give her the crwth bow he'd had made for her in Luxor.

He was singing the pains of unrequited love when a knock on the door interrupted him. Tiberius almost ignored it—but what if it was Charlotte? What if she was here, to work things out?

He couldn't seek her out. He knew that. She'd told him to

stay away. The ball was in her court. If she was here and he *didn't* answer—

"Tiberius," a barely-decipherable voice called, "Can I come in? I want to make sure you're okay."

The pitch of the voice made his heart stop. It was high and soft—female. Not his father or Leon.

Was he even ready to speak with Charlotte? What would he say to her? What would *she* say to *him*? But his hopes were shattered when he realized who the voice belonged to. "I'm sure that today was hard for you."

Jayana Triller.

Tiberius put down his crwth and walked to the door on autopilot. He wasn't sure what compelled him. Maybe morbid curiosity. Maybe because he knew it would be better for him not to be alone. Maybe he really could use a friend right now.

Jayana was in the same outfit as before, one that he hadn't failed to notice hugged her body, highlighting its best aspects. It was a strategy, he knew, one that didn't work on him since he was so single-mindedly focused on Charlotte.

"Hi," Jayana said.

"Hi," Tiberius echoed. Rogue tears still streamed from his eyes, but he didn't care who knew that he'd been crying. If he hadn't been in turmoil, he wouldn't have been human. Men in Luxor weren't taught to stifle their emotions.

"May I come in?"

Tiberius moved away from the door. His room was tidy, though not by any of Tiberius' own doing. He gestured toward his balcony. It was a temperate night, with a fresh ocean breeze. It would be good for him to get outside as well—he needed to remember that the world existed beyond his pain.

"You can sit anywhere," Tiberius mumbled, not possessing the energy to be his usual chipper self. Jayana did just that and studied him, a hint of pity in her eyes. Some people hated pity, but Tiberius felt validated.

"I can't imagine being you right now."

"It isn't my best day."

Jayana studied him, tilting her head. He wondered what kind of read she was getting on him, and if it expanded beyond his current state. "Do you miss home?"

No one had asked him this question since he had arrived. Tiberius hadn't even considered it himself. *Did* he?

Before he could decipher the answer, Jayana added, "And your family?"

"No," Tiberius said. He was the runt of the litter. His brothers were constantly on him about something, always telling him to put away the crwth and take up more useful hobbies. Yes, Luxor men did cry, but they still had some toxic ideas surrounding masculinity. "I mean... My brothers are...I love them, but it's nice to be my own person for once."

"I have a brother too," Jayana said, surprising Tiberius. Only four percent of the Ignis population had siblings.

"Older or younger?"

"Younger."

"Is he in the Academy?"

Jayana looked away, and Tiberius immediately wished he hadn't asked.

"He's not...well. And he hasn't been—almost his whole life, actually." The only way people got sick was if they were Impaired. Before Tiberius could ask, Jayana continued, "He got into an accident—but he still..." Her voice trailed off, her sentence too hard to finish.

"Oh," Tiberius said. He hated how stupid his voice sounded, "Well, if there's anything I can do to help him—"

"There isn't," Jayana interrupted, "The only thing that might be able to help are some of the doctors on Princeps, but my family are Mid-Pointers, so there's not much hope for now."

Jayana wanted to get Paired with him for her brother. So she could go to Princeps and get him the help he needed.

Tiberius had no reason to believe she was lying. Her words, her posture...everything about her was genuine. And, Tiberius realized, he *did* like her. As a friend, anyway. Maybe if he hadn't been so obsessed with Charlotte his entire life, he would have felt even more.

This was his chance to get to know his other potential Pairs. Maybe it was a good thing. Yes, it would be hard to overcome a lifetime of fixation, but Tiberius would do it.

He had to.

He just couldn't do it now. Now, he needed to mourn.

"Sorry," apologized Jayana, "I didn't mean to make things heavy."

"I think I made things heavy first by bawling my eyes out."

Jayana laughed. It was a soft laugh, with a hint of vibrato beneath it.

"Do you want to talk about it?"

He *did*. And Jayana knew Charlotte in a different way than he did. Maybe she could offer some context. "Sort of."

Jayana studied him for a long moment. "I love Charlotte, I really do. But I don't really know her."

"What do you mean?" He'd deduced from his information that Jayana and Charlotte had been thick as thieves.

"No one does. She doesn't let people in, or let them know what she's feeling. She doesn't trust anyone, Tiberius, so no one trusts her."

Tiberius wanted to stick up for Charlotte. He *wanted* to, but wasn't sure how. Because there was nothing he could say to counter Jayana's words.

Jayana took in his blank face and changed the subject. "What were you playing just now? It sounded beautiful."

Tiberius perked up a bit, then went inside to fetch his crwth. "Wait here. I'll show you."

A moment later, he was plucking the sad melody on the strings. He hummed along in places, singing a few of the words he had written in his head.

When he was finished, there were tears in his eyes again. He glanced up at Jayana, a little self-conscious.

Her eyes were wide. She was enthralled in a way Tiberius knew only he himself had ever felt about his music. In the way that he had hoped Charlotte would react.

But Charlotte hadn't and Jayana *had*. Maybe that meant something.

"That was really beautiful," Jayana whispered, her voice soft as if afraid to break the spell of the music.

"Thank you." He was trying to figure out what to say next when a loud knock sounded on the door.

Tiberius jumped to his feet. "Oh, uh, I—"

"I should go."

"You don't have—"

But Jayana was already rushing back inside. Tiberius followed her in.

"Is this your only door?"

"As far as I know."

Tiberius half-expected her to ask if she could hide in the closet. But instead, Jayana took a deep breath and composed herself, then nodded at him to open it.

He did.

And there stood Tiberius' father, King Akil.

Tiberius had expected that. Akil likely wanted to debrief the speech with his son.

"Your Majesty," Jayana said, bowing in Tiberius' peripheral vision.

"Hello, Father."

Akil did a double take, though he didn't seem displeased at Jayana's presence. "Miss Triller," he said with a bow.

"I'll be on my way," Jayana said.

The moment she was out of sight, the pain crashed back onto Tiberius' shoulders.

Akil stepped inside and closed the door. He took in Tiberius' appearance.

"Are you okay?" he asked gently.

Tiberius inhaled his mucus and nodded, unable to look his father in the eyes.

Akil's voice grew firm, though not unkind, "This is how the game works, son. Pairs fall from grace. People embarrass themselves. You cannot get attached."

Anger exploded from within Tiberius' gut. "You—you were the one who showed me who she was five years ago! And now I'm supposed to just—just *forget*?"

Akil nodded. "Charlotte is particularly...unideal now that Imogen has been imprisoned."

"So I can't get Paired with her just because her mother did something wrong?"

"And she's an addict."

"She said she isn't!" Yes, she'd most certainly taken Dust before, but Tiberius believed her when she said she wasn't on it. At least, not any more.

Hell, he *hated* Pairing. Why was love a political game? Shouldn't it be based in feelings? Shouldn't he be Paired with the person he loved the most?

Were genetic Pairings *that* important for the future of humankind, that love could only exist within a system? Why did it matter if people were Impaired? If everyone was Impaired, wouldn't no one be?

"These women," Akil said in a condescending tone that Tiberius immediately hated, "are politicians. They lie. They charm. They cheat. And Charlotte is the *best* of them, which means she's the *worst*. Everyone is out to be *your* Pair, since you're the only one who can give them a ticket to Princeps. You have the power here."

Tiberius had never had the power. His brothers had the power. His father.

But he didn't want it. He would much rather curl up by a warm fire with Charlotte and his crwth.

Charlotte, who now hated him. *Rightfully*, after he'd betrayed her trust.

"I *want* to be Paired with Charlotte."

Did he, though? Tiberius felt his unflappable belief cracking. The only thing he was certain of was that Pairing was a horrible, corrupt system that went against everything he believed.

Akil took him in. "What was Jayana doing in here?"

"I don't know. Listening to my music."

Akil surprised him with a nod. "Good. She's the Highest Pointer who hasn't fallen from grace. She's a good choice."

"Doesn't that just make her the second-best liar and cheater?" Tiberius asked.

Akil frowned with sympathy, but not enough to stop him from saying, "Go on outings with everyone. And if someone else catches your eye...then we will revisit this conversation."

Tiberius looked away, feeling his heart—the best part of himself—rip into shreds.

Akil's exterior cracked for the shortest moment. "This isn't what I wanted for you."

Then he fled like a coward, Tiberius' dream of playing the crwth by the fireplace retreating with him.

26

Things were happening quickly for Lynx Hillenbrand.

She hadn't expected this much drama in two days, but she was prepared. She hoped, anyway.

Imogen was out of the picture. But anyone who thought she'd stay that way was stupid.

It kept Lynx out of the woods for the moment. Yesterday, some of her simulation equipment had broken down and she'd had to sneak through the tunnel to replace it, barely avoiding One after her encounter with Imogen.

Today, before Charlotte had finished speaking, Lynx had chartered a private boat from the mainland back to Princeps. She was confident that Charlotte would find a way into High Society even with the new rule. Even with One sabotaging her at every turn.

The problem was going to be getting Zandra there. Lynx would only admit to herself, but she enjoyed watching Unruly. She'd missed Zandra.

Maybe a tiny piece of herself missed Unruly, though she knew that was ridiculous. She didn't miss being brainwashed. Watched. Manipulated.

So when Lynx got home to the mansion she shared with Five, she took out the portable simulation unit she'd stolen and logged into Unruly.

27

Charlotte woke with a tinge of a headache to the sound of whispering voices.

Yesterday had been fine. She'd felt well—*great*, even. No one wondered where she had been. No one cared. No one ogled at her. She'd been underground more than a day and no idea how to get back into the sunlight...but she barely noticed when she was consumed by her mission.

She did, however, notice that she could once again hear her heart rushing through her temples.

She'd spent the previous day searching every crevice just to reach more dead-ends and confusing turns. The tunnels were complex, but through her stone-pile tracking system, she was confident she had explored every pathway. So how was there no way out?

I need Dust.

Especially if it was going to take her a while to get out. The Conquest usually ended shortly after Pairing Season.

But Charlotte needed out *now*. Every minute she wasn't there was another minute that Zandra could be messing up her life.

She needed to get back if things were ever going to be the same again.

But first, Dust.

But the Unruly quieted when she tried to speak. How did Harris converse so easily with them? What was he learning that she wasn't?

Charlotte grunted as she lifted her head, her neck sore from the springy, uncomfortable king mattress. Her head ached like a lesser version of her Dust hangover. She was probably just hungry and dehydrated. And lacking Vitamin D.

Today she'd search even harder than before.

For both the exit and Dust.

Charlotte turned, almost yelping when she saw that she was not alone—a body lay still on the other half of the mattress.

Enid.

There weren't many sleeping options, so the Unruly took what they could get. Charlotte stared. Enid's resting face was at peace. Her hand twitched subtly.

Charlotte had avoided her the previous day, even though Enid had gone out of her way to intercept her.

Enid stirred and Charlotte looked away. When she went still, Charlotte stole a glance. Enid stared through bleary eyes, a crooked smile on her face. "Hello," she said.

Why did she feel as if she had been caught redhanded? And why did Enid look so amused?

"Hi," Charlotte replied, inching away. She ought to get moving. She needed to leave this hell.

Because she *certainly* wanted to. She would be crazy not to.

You are *crazy,* a voice in Charlotte's head whispered.

No, she wasn't. She had just—the anxiety had gotten the better of her. She would undo it all.

You don't want to, the voice continued.

Charlotte shut the thoughts out.

"What did you do yesterday?" Enid asked, propping herself onto her elbows with a huge yawn.

"Wandered. I wanted some alone time."

"Did you get it?"

"Yeah. It's nice not feeling like someone's watching my every move."

Enid tilted her head. Charlotte got the sense that she understood. But *why*? Enid had been the definition of average.

So why did she seem like the most extraordinary person to Charlotte?

"It's worse than being stuck underground, isn't it?" Enid said, "It's like even if you just breathe the wrong way, people will know everything that's wrong with you."

"Yeah. Exactly." She wouldn't have been able to say it better herself. She felt...seen. Not *seen* in the way she hated—in an *understood* way.

She and Enid stared at each other. Charlotte felt the air between them across the mattress, both too far and too close at the same time. When she realized that she was noticing the air, Charlotte leapt to her feet.

"I have to go."

"Where?" Enid said, "Stay. You're not bothering me."

Charlotte gestured toward the continuing indecipherable whispers from the other side of the wall. "They're calling me. I'll, uh, see you later."

Charlotte almost tripped over her own feet for what she was sure was the first time in her life, not slowing until there was a substantial barricade of junk between them.

Why did Enid have this effect on her? It was making her weak.

The voices grew louder, until she could make out the words.

"Enid's freaking awesome," Rae's voice said from behind yet another mountain of antique telescopes, lamps, tables, and grandfather clocks. Charlotte noted that this junk-wall consisted of a random assortment of items, rather than adhering to a theme. "How is she so chill, but also, like, a boss?"

A hint of jealousy. Because *she* wanted to be the best, Charlotte was sure.

"Yeah," Wade agreed, a hint of uneasiness in his voice.

"She's like how I expected Zandra to be," Rae continued, "How Zandra *was* before she left and wandered all day yesterday."

Charlotte paused, jealousy morphing into something darker.

"I don't know what all the hype was with Zandra," Killian's voice said, "She literally wouldn't even tell us where she went. Screw her."

"She's definitely just trying to win the Conquest," Rae said.

Charlotte's breath constricted—even the Unruly wanted to watch her. Wanted to know her, and what she was up to. Why couldn't they just care about themselves? Why did everyone want to judge her, even when she *wasn't* her?

They didn't deserve to have her lead them. She'd walked around for one day and they'd turned on her after she'd corralled them here. After she'd comforted them. Climbed a *wall* of *garbage* for them.

At least their words dissipated the remaining guilt she'd had about leaving them to fend for themselves.

"Enid said we should give her a chance..." Wade reasoned.

"Maybe she should give *us* a chance. I swear, she's no different than her stuck up sister."

Killian grunted in agreement.

"It's a little weird how similar they are," Wade agreed, "But I like Zandra."

"She blew you off the other night," Rae said, "I had hope for her the first day. The wall thing was cool."

"Enid was the one who did that. We should be giving her credit instead," Killian said. "And I *would* have done it, if she hadn't just jumped up without consulting us like that."

"She helped me, though," Wade said.

"Grow up, Wade," Killian muttered.

Charlotte turned around the barrier to find the three of them huddled in a circle. Killian had the audacity to laugh, while Wade looked at her with wide eyes.

"Hi, Zandra," Rae said, "Sleep good?"

Sleep well! "Yeah, until I was woken by what a disappointment I am."

She gave Wade a nod, a silent thanks for standing up for her. He didn't seem to know how to react. But Rae—Rae suddenly found a telescope in the garbage-wall very interesting.

Would she know if there was Dust down here? Would Killian?

"Did you all go to Jaxson's party?" she asked.

Rae turned, perplexed by the shift. "Yeah?"

"What's his deal?"

"Jaxson's deal?" Killian said, "What does it matter now?"

"Well, it's not like there's a lot going on down here."

"There's a lot more interesting things than *Jaxson*," Rae said.

"So you knew him?"

Rae shrugged. "Just that he wanted to be a High-Pointer for some reason."

Killian and Wade shrugged. Of course they didn't know. Dust was a High-Pointer vice.

What if there was *no* Dust on Unruly?

I have to get out of here. Quickly.

"Are you done interrogating us?" Rae asked.

"Never mind, then," Charlotte said, turning.

She wasn't the Zandra they'd been expecting. They'd been hoping for a hero. A leader. Someone they could look to for hope and guidance.

Instead, they'd gotten someone obsessed with leaving and making sure *she* was the only one who made it out.

But the people who mattered loved her. The people with power. These Unruly—

Are the ones with the power down here.

But the real issue was that they were catching on. They knew she was too similar to *Charlotte*.

She didn't know what they'd do if they learned, and she didn't want to find out. And if *she* was struggling, Zandra would be close to slipping, if she hadn't already.

Hang in there, Zandra, Charlotte thought, *I'm coming back.*

Charlotte stepped into the main clearing. It looked as it always did, with a few sad Unruly milling about. Charlotte spotted Jeri across the way, eating some porridge, and decided to try her luck again. She pasted on a smile as she approached. "How are you this morning?" Charlotte asked, though she had no clue whether or not it was morning.

"Fine," Jeri said, already exasperated.

"How's breakfast?"

"Fine."

Charlotte took a deep breath. "I think we got off on the wrong foot. I was just scared. And didn't know what I was getting into."

"It's fine."

Charlotte knew the woman knew more words. She considered walking away, but if she was anything, it was persistent. "Where does the food come from?"

"It's all food from the mounds," she said, nodding at the towers of stuff. "All stored goods. We ration it."

Charlotte's eyes widened. "How long will it sustain us?"

"Maybe one more month."

One month? That was it?

She'd gone to Unruly right when Unruly was about to die.

"What happens then?"

"I can't see the future," Jeri snapped.

"So we're just gonna starve down here like we're in the freaking Union?!"

Jeri clenched her jaw and looked down at her food. Charlotte took it as her cue.

How could the Council just let the Unruly starve? Surely they knew! One of the Conquest winners *must* have told them. Was her own mother that cruel? Or were they waiting until the last moment, then coming in to save the day?

Time was of the essence in more ways than one. She had to win.

Charlotte did a loop around the clearing. She needed information. But every wizened Unruly she caught the eye of immediately looked away. She looked for Owen the Impaired man, but he was nowhere to be seen. Why was it so hard?

She tried speaking to a few of them, but Unruly and Impaired alike scattered before she could get a word in. Frustration consumed her—why were they all so afraid of her?

Charlotte's mood soured. She hated this.

It got worse when she spotted Harris speaking with Nickolas yet again, this time on torn up pre-Destruction sofas. Nickolas gestured at an old paperback in his hand.

Charlotte didn't want to risk angering Harris again, but she saw no other option. Once again, Nickolas scattered as she approached. Thankfully, Harris didn't seem to mind this time around.

That should have frightened her. It meant Harris was getting somewhere.

"I'm starting to think it's me," Charlotte half-joked.

"It's not." Charlotte didn't believe him, especially after what she had just heard from the others, until Harris said, "I knew him from before."

"Really?" Charlotte asked, "From where?" Kids didn't

interact much with people so many years older. Charlotte doubted she'd ever spoken to anyone above Five's year.

"The Academy," Harris replied, which Charlotte found odd. They must've become friends after she and Harris had stopped talking.

"What does he think about it here?"

"They all hate it. Every last one."

It was cold on Unruly. And dark. The reprieve of freedom would wear off, especially if she didn't have a mission. Soon she'd be miserable just like everyone else.

She needed help, especially if she was going to do this without Dust. She could outsmart Harris at the end. "Haven't they tried getting out?"

"Yes," Harris said, eyeing her warily.

"And none of them have figured it out? Even the ones who have been here for years?"

"Most have given up."

"How? It's not like they have anything else to do!"

Harris scoffed, though she could tell his anger wasn't directed at her. "You don't get it, do you?"

"Enlighten me."

"Even if they got out, where do they go? Their Conquests have already been won. And the Impaired don't even *get* a chance to begin with. They figure they'll just wait until they get selected to get Paired with widows and stragglers. And the Impaired— well."

Charlotte intellectually understood, though giving up wasn't her style. Not at all.

Harris cracked his knuckles. He knew more than he was telling her. Something she needed to win.

"You said you want to fix Unruly? Let's break it instead."

Harris had no idea where she was going. He didn't ask—just

waited for her to explain. Yes, they would be a good team. They always had been.

"Two people have never won the Conquest together, have they?" she asked, "I need to get back to my sister, and I've basically mapped these tunnels already. You clearly want a spot in the Council, and you're not going to beat Charlotte out unless you do something crazy. This can be it."

Harris *still* wasn't sold.

"Who better to endorse you when we get out than Charlotte's own sister?" There was no way he could refuse. He didn't need her knowledge of the tunnels—he could figure that out himself in one day. But the endorsement from "Zandra"—that was a guaranteed win over "Charlotte".

"You wouldn't do that."

"I care more about being with Charlotte than whether or not she has power. Yeah, she'll be pissed, but I'll get to *see* her be pissed."

Harris cracked his knuckles again, looking at the top of the cave. "How do you propose this works?"

Charlotte released a breath. She was going to have to be the first one to offer information. So she said, "There aren't any obvious exit spots."

Harris nodded. "That's because apparently there was a big cave-in just after Lynx left. Did you see that?"

Charlotte nodded. There had been a big pile of rocks at the end of a particularly wide tunnel, but she had thought nothing of it. "I know the spot."

"Nickolas said we can probably find something here to blow through it."

He nodded at the towers of things. Charlotte internally groaned, but Zandra would've been thrilled by a treasure hunt. So she smiled wide. "Cool. So we start now."

"You really want to get out of here, don't you?" Beneath the joke, a question. *Why?*

"There's only a month supply of food left," Charlotte murmured.

Harris nodded. He already knew this, of course. "We're trying to keep it under wraps."

"Who's *we?*"

"Nickolas and me. He told the others not to mention it. How'd you find out?"

"So you don't think that everyone has the right to know they're going to starve in a month?" Personally, she agreed with Harris—it would cause too much chaos, too much in-fighting—but Zandra would've told the entire population by now, hoping that one of them would be able to think of a solution.

"Don't you think it would be wiser to fix it rather than start massive panic? We don't need people fighting to the death over mouthfuls." His brows were furrowed, two stress-wrinkles forming between them.

"For someone with one of the lowest community scores, you really seem to care about *this* community." There was no accusation in her voice, just curiosity.

Harris looked away. "For someone who claimed not to care about points, you sure know a lot about mine."

Charlotte just smiled, internally rebuking herself for the slip.

"I had stuff going on," he said when Charlotte didn't pry. Harris' community points had dropped after their friendship had ended. He offered nothing more, though she suspected it had something to do with her.

Charlotte nodded in silent acknowledgment of his past trauma, whatever it was, then said, "So what kind of stuff are we digging for?"

"Explosives. Shovels. Matches. Drills. Anything that could be used to blast or dig through stone."

"You know how to create an explosion safely?"

"No."

"Great. Want to start over there?" Charlotte asked, pointing at a mountain away from the main clearing. She'd named it *The Gardening Wall* in her head—lots of pots and hoes. Maybe it would have a drill and shovels. And it was far enough away from the traffic that every Unruly wouldn't wonder what they were doing.

"Seems like an ideal spot."

Charlotte assessed before they reached the bottom of the mound. The thought of sorting through garbage for days looking for equipment sounded like torture.

Harris started looking for handholds to climb the moment they got there. Charlotte raised an eyebrow and asked, "What are you doing?"

"We should start at the top."

"Why?"

"So we don't topple the whole thing. It's less dangerous this way."

Charlotte looked into the mound, taking in the wheelbarrows and garden tools. "But we're looking for small things. Shouldn't we start by looking into the crevices and holes?"

"I don't know how efficient that will be," Harris said, still climbing. "How will we know whether we've looked through it or not?" He lifted himself up a few more feet, balanced on a lawn chair, and held out a hand. "Are you coming?"

"I don't want to go to the top," Charlotte blurted before she could stop herself.

"I thought you loved heights."

"I—do," she lied, "I just hurt my leg the first day. I can't climb."

Harris looked down at her quizzically, then jumped back to

the ground, landing on his feet. It was easy to tell he'd gotten a high physical score.

He peered at her leg. "What's wrong with it?"

"I hurt it in the fall. It's not that bad, though, it just needs a little longer."

"Okay. Then we'll start down here."

"I can fit into small spaces," Charlotte said, masking her relief, "But I'm going to need you to help me lift some stuff so I can squeeze under."

"Sounds good."

Charlotte soon remembered what a great team the two of them made. They shifted things around, Charlotte's headache growing increasingly worse, until there was a large enough hole for Charlotte to shimmy into.

At least, she *hoped* it was large enough. But she'd rather be stuck in the pile than fall off the top of it, of that she was certain.

Harris just had to lift a disjointed diving board up, then she would go inside. "You ready?"

"I think that's more important for *you* to answer."

Harris grinned, then said, "I'll admit, I'm impressed by you, Zandra."

A bubble of discomfort crept into Charlotte's stomach. But she summoned the courage of Zandra. "Are you?"

"Yes. More impressed by you than Charlotte, even."

That touched Charlotte for a reason she couldn't quite put her finger on. She should have been offended, but...it felt like a compliment.

"I won't tell her you said that," Charlotte said, "And you're probably the second coolest High-Pointer I know."

"But the coolest Unruly?" he joked with a smirk.

Charlotte's voice caught in her throat. Maybe he was. He'd shared his information with her, he had been nothing but kind, he was already regaining her trust...

But she'd be a fool to trust him again. Were people capable of change? Was he sorry for what he'd done?

She had every reason to say yes. That he *was* the best Unruly. But an image of Enid appeared in the back of her mind, swimming toward the waterfall.

This good-natured question shouldn't have provoked such unease. "*I'm* the coolest Unruly I know," she managed.

"Fair." His dark eyes were full of warmth. Charlotte felt safe in them. Something she *never* felt toward anyone except Zandra. Not even her own mother.

She had to repress it. He couldn't get in the way of her winning the Conquest. She couldn't fall into this trap again.

In a perfect world, he would have never betrayed her. She would have gone to the palace, and she'd have finally realized that she was happy with him. They'd have been Paired, and would have lived together on Princeps again, just like they did when they were children.

But they wouldn't have been *them* if they hadn't gone Unruly. Harris wouldn't have wanted to help the Unruly. Charlotte would have been more firm in her beliefs.

Maybe Harris wouldn't have backstabbed me in the first place.

The Charlotte and Harris in that reality were two very different people from the ones digging through outdoor supplies in a cavern underneath a forbidden island.

"What?" Harris asked.

"What?"

"You're looking at me strangely."

"Oh." That was all she offered, so Harris just grinned and rubbed his hands together.

"Okay, I'm in position," Harris said, stepping behind the diving board.

"Let's do it." She slid into position.

Harris lifted the wheelbarrow and Charlotte crawled into the hole. Her knees scraped against something metallic beneath her, but she barely noticed. She was on a mission, and Charlotte *thrived* with a mission. She didn't have to think—she just had to enact the plan.

Harris lowered the wheelbarrow with a grunt. Charlotte was surprised by the darkness—torches lined the side of clearing but only a few splotches of light seeped into the eye of the junk pile.

"I need more light." She didn't dare move until she could see for fear of hurting herself or dislodging something wedged precariously into the structure.

"On it."

Charlotte squatted for several long moments, listening to her breath. Even beneath this mound, she felt powerful in the action.

Light flickered into Charlotte's enclosure, giving her enough confidence to start moving.

"What do you see?"

"Lots of the same." It was cramped, a hodgepodge of items balancing upon each other. Charlotte managed to crawl between them, careful not to disturb anything until she was certain the entire structure wouldn't come crashing down on her head.

She pushed through deflated plastic pool toy, her back brushing past the bin of a tractor.

Beyond the tractor were more shadows.

"Do you think they have working flashlights somewhere?" This wasn't going to work. They were going to have to do it the original way—by climbing up to the top and slowly moving down. And hope that these garbage-walls were built of something that would get them past the cave-in.

Charlotte did *not* want to do it that way.

"I can go check," Harris called.

"Let me just...try moving some things around."

If she could move the inflatable pool toy she'd crawled under and the chair behind it, Charlotte could get more light. Enough to look through a sizable portion of the rubble.

She hadn't even begun when she heard Wade's voice. "Zandra?" he called.

Charlotte sighed and just kept working, frustrating bubbling, her head pulsing to the beat of her heart.

Harris' voice murmured, "Zandra, I think someone's, uh—"

"Just...tell him I left," she whispered. She eyed a gap to the side of the chair, which didn't seem to be an integral piece of the junk pile's structure.

Charlotte placed her feet on the chair and pushed, fueled by her aggravation.

"Zandra," Wade's voice called again, "I don't know if that's you over there...but I'm sorry about the others. I think they're just scared like—like the rest of us. Even Killian."

Charlotte trusted that Harris would handle him. There was only a month of food left. The time for comforting the other Unruly was over.

The chair refused to move. Charlotte's quads and core burned. Heat coursed through her body.

Nothing.

Charlotte gritted her teeth, resentful. Why was this so *hard*?

She pushed again. Before she knew it, her pent up emotion exploded in her gut, as if the valve had been broken by the unmoving chair. She was unable to contain it any more—they all should've gotten Paired! Then she wouldn't need to be worrying about a whole population of people starving! She wouldn't have to feel guilty about leaving them!

She wouldn't have to worry about if she was ever going to get another dose of Dust.

Every thought that she hadn't realized she'd been wrestling with materialized. If she pushed hard enough, it would all go away. The feelings, the darkness—it would expel through the exertion.

She grunted, attracting the voice of Wade, now much closer. Was he in the pile too? "Zandra! What are you doing in here?"

"Get out!" she gasped, "You're in my way!"

The chair moved—Wade's fingers appeared under it, lifting.

And beneath his fingers, under the chair...

Powder.

Dust?

Charlotte's body reacted before her brain. She released her legs and reached—

Wade's balance was thrown by the shift, the chair collapsing onto its side with a thud, releasing a chemical smell as it crushed the powder.

Chlorine.

Time froze, during which Charlotte saw her fatal mistake. The chair had been supporting a massive section of the wall.

The world came crashing down.

Charlotte didn't have the luxury of falling unconscious. No. She watched the whole thing unfold through acute pain and hazy eyes.

Just before the major debris fell, Charlotte was knocked sideways, giving her a clear view of Wade.

Her throbbing head was forgotten in Wade's horrified eyes. The image would be branded into her heart and mind forever, the kind of invisible wound that no one could see, but hurt far worse than anything that could leave a physical mark.

Time stopped.

Some things were too painful, too horrible, to leave a trace. The silent, internal assassins never did.

A wagon fell between them. That was the last time she'd see Wade. She knew it.

Something landed on her arm, still outstretched toward the

chlorine, trapping her in place, forcing her to watch as an engine fell from above.

This was it. She was going to die.

If time slowed before, now it stopped.

Charlotte felt a wave of sadness. For Zandra. For Lawrence. For Harris. Even for Imogen.

For her future. She could have changed the world if she wanted to.

And she realized she did—really, actually—want to.

How had she gotten here? How had she let herself chase a life —become obsessed with a life—she didn't want?

Leading the Unruly on their first day had felt more meaningful than any points she'd ever accumulated. Now she would never get the chance to do it again. Her body would be buried beneath the rubble, forgotten.

And sweet Wade was the one who would pay the price for her sins.

Harris would tell the others. She hoped he didn't tell them that she was brave. Charlotte Rachel Galvin was no martyr. She wanted him to be honest—she had died selfishly, trying to get back to her life on Princeps.

A life she had lied about ever wanting.

In the next life—if there was one—she would do things differently.

Charlotte closed her eyes. Not embracing death—not at peace —but with a promise on her dying lips—she would do better if she ever got another chance.

She waited for the pain. Surely pain came before death.

But nothing happened.

Was this it? Nothing?

The rubble stabilized.

Charlotte was afraid to open her eyes, but she did it anyway.

She could make out the outline of the engine, which had gotten caught on a tractor, inches from her face.

She was alive.

"ZANDRA!" Harris called, "ZANDRA!"

Charlotte's voice was hoarse, "I—I'm here."

Her arm was still trapped, but she was alive to keep her promise to make a difference.

C harlotte had no idea how long it took them to pull her out of the rubble, only that Enid and Harris led the charge.

There was nothing she could do except wait and trust—two things she'd never been good at.

But maybe it was time to give them both a try.

She yelled to the others for an update on Wade, but no one responded.

That could only mean one thing.

"We're going to get you out," Harris' voice kept saying. Charlotte believed him. Maybe it was stupid of her, but she didn't have the energy not to.

Enid ordered people to move things. Charlotte was in good hands. Her body ached, especially her head, but the pain felt far away, like it didn't quite belong to her.

What was probably hours later, the engine lifted away and flames lit Charlotte's vision.

"Wade," Charlotte said again, "Is Wade okay?"

Her arm was still trapped. Enid lowered herself and raised whatever had landed on it with a grunt.

It was bruised, but would heal. Charlotte didn't even feel it.

Harris and Enid helped her to her feet. She tried to shoo them away, but neither moved.

"You might be in shock," Harris said when Charlotte took a staggering step away.

"Where's Wade?"

Enid bit her lip and looked away. But Harris met her gaze. "I'm—he...didn't make it."

Charlotte's stomach dropped. "No. That—that can't be." Harris and Enid remained silent. "Let me see him."

"That's not a good idea," Harris said.

The moment she was out, Charlotte shrugged Harris and Enid away. "I didn't—I just...I just wanted to get out of here."

Charlotte looked at her hands. Something about them was wrong. The color.

She was stressed enough for her body to have a blue hue. It wasn't just the lack of light.

It was easier to focus on that than that Wade was gone.

All because she needed Dust.

Half of the Unruly seemed to be there. She'd never seen so many gathered in one place. Jeri, Nickolas, Owen, Rae, Killian.... Charlotte couldn't look into any of their eyes. Being the object of attention was shameful.

She glanced at Enid, hoping for some support. Or solace. Anything that wasn't judgement.

But Enid's face was angry. "You didn't think that moving the foundation of the walls might be dangerous? It's a miracle you weren't killed, too!"

"Back off," Harris said.

But Charlotte shook her head. "She's right."

Jeri finally stepped forward. "Which is why, for the safety of all of us here, the two of you are being imprisoned."

Harris looked around, mouth agape. "Imprisoned? Don't you think that's a little harsh?"

"For involuntary manslaughter."

In any other situation, Charlotte would have found it odd

that Jeri was finally stepping up. Her paranoid mind would have dissected the meaning.

Or maybe Jeri just drew the line of caring when people died.

Someone grabbed Charlotte's arm and she pulled it away. "I'll go. Just don't touch me."

Harris shook his head at the men who grabbed his arms. "This is insane. We didn't know that was going to happen! We were trying to help!"

"Aren't you supposed to be smarter than that?" Rae piped up from the crowd, "Weren't you the Highest Academic Pointer? If anyone should've known better, it's you."

And Charlotte. The two of them probably had more Academic points than all the other Unruly combined.

Enid said nothing. She agreed with Jeri. Would she even look at Charlotte again if she knew what had really happened?

Charlotte agreed, too. So when she was escorted into a natural cave with a single torch, a mattress, a bucket, and bars to lock them in, she didn't protest.

The same couldn't be said for Harris. Even after their captors left, he yelled at the bars, "What is this? The Union? Where's my trial?"

"Stop," Charlotte murmured, plopping onto the mattress, ignoring her pain and headache.

"This isn't—"

"I *killed* someone, Harris!"

Harris took in her downcast face. He sighed and sat beside her. "That wasn't your fault."

He would think differently if he knew about the Dust.

"It *wasn't*," Harris insisted, "Okay?"

She was at a crossroads. She could either hate herself and let the guilt and eat her alive, or she could change. And Charlotte was nothing if not productive.

She would change.

She'd tried everything. Tried and failed. She'd *killed* somebody.

She wasn't going to win the Conquest. She wasn't even going to try.

Despite the heaviness, a weight lifted off her shoulders. Maybe what mattered was down here. Maybe she could find food *down here.*

She touched Zandra's shark tooth necklace. She would be more like *her.*

When Harris finally tired, he slumped beside Charlotte. "I'm sorry I didn't include you."

"What?"

"Growing up."

"Oh." She'd always thought that Zandra didn't want to join them, though she'd never bothered to ask.

"I just...I thought Charlotte was going to be my Pair, you know? We were going to both be the Highest Pointers and live happily ever after."

"Harris—" Charlotte said, too drained for this conversation.

"No, let me finish." She could tell he needed to. "And then I did something stupid—just because I was worried about her— and I lost her. Forever. But I'm not sorry I did it. And I don't think I should tell you—"

"You told Imogen she was doing Dust. I know."

Harris was stunned. "She—she told you? I thought you said—"

"I lied," Charlotte lied.

"I know I betrayed her trust, but...even if she hates me now, it was worth it. It got her off of it."

Guilt consumed Charlotte's heart.

"Both my parents are on Dust. Did you know that?"

Charlotte shook her head, surprised.

"I guess it was fine for a while—years, really—they were more productive and got into High Society, but then...I don't know. They stopped being themselves. They were using so much that nothing really...affected them any more. They stopped caring. *I* had to take care of *them*."

Charlotte had never experienced the negative side effects of Dust.

"It's why my community points were so low. There wasn't time for me to do anything else except...pick up the pieces. I couldn't let that happen to Charlotte. Even if it meant she hated me for the rest of my life."

Charlotte rubbed her eyes, just listening. Not thinking, not judging.

"Are you okay?" Harris asked.

"Just...go on."

"What happened after doesn't matter. What matters now is... maybe I was chasing the wrong Pair."

Charlotte's breath hitched. The familiar unsettlement, the one she felt with Enid, flowed through her body. But there was nowhere for her to run this time. She was trapped—

"You're smart and noble. And what happened to Wade wasn't your fault—"

Charlotte put up a hand, stopping him. It *was* her fault. And she couldn't deny it, or hide, anymore. She had to face it.

Her head pounded a little harder, heart pulsating through her eyes.

"Harris," she said kindly, "You don't know you're talking about."

"Yes," Harris insisted, his brown eyes wider than saucers, "I do, and—you know what, damn these Unruly who don't want our help! We were trying to save them, and what do we get in return? Locked up? Let's win the Conquest together, and we can live on Princeps and get Paired, get them some food, and never think about this place again—"

"Stop, Harris! Just stop!" exclaimed Charlotte.

Harris stopped with his mouth wide open. Charlotte noticed that he wasn't cracking his knuckles for once.

She couldn't leave. Not with him, not with anyone. She had to stay and honor Wade.

Harris pulled away, embarrassed, realizing he'd gotten lost in the fantasy.

Charlotte forgave him. She really did. But she didn't want to be Paired with him. Charlotte exhaled, exhausted. She had nothing to lose. "I *am* Charlotte, Harris."

A blankness wiped his face. Like he didn't know how to react.

No, Charlotte realized, he *couldn't* react.

For the briefest of moments, there was nothing in his eyes. Charlotte was afraid she had broken him.

But a noise from outside the cell door snapped him out of it. Enid stood there with food.

She had heard the whole thing.

28

Lynx logged out of Unruly immediately after Charlotte revealed that she wasn't Zandra to the entire simulation.

There wasn't time to panic. The Council was still on Ignis' mainland. They wouldn't have been notified yet.

There was time to undo this.

Lynx felt many things, none good and all confusing. But her personal feelings didn't matter. The mission came first. It always did. It had to.

There was no time to report. She jumped into action immediately.

The only place Lynx could think to go was the one place she knew she shouldn't. But she had no other choice. They needed both twins on Princeps, and this would damn them both.

Lynx was hurrying down the grand stairs when Five entered the mahogany double doors and stepped into the foyer.

From Lynx's point of view, she and Five had a complicated relationship. A part of Lynx loved Five. There was lots to love about her. Five was the reason that Lynx had won the Conquest.

The Council all watched what went down in the simulation.

Lynx had been nowhere *near* winning—but Five had broken every rule to crown Lynx the winner.

When Five had "asked" her to be her unofficial Pair, Lynx couldn't deny her. Not when she was the only Conquest winner who had simply been...chosen.

Claimed.

Not that she would have. Lynx genuinely liked Five.

She was trusting. Kind to the people she cared about. Thoughtful. Ruthless.

Lynx cared for Five. She appreciated Five for seeing her. For loving her.

But she hated Five, too. For seeing her. For loving her.

For giving Lynx no choice in the matter when she'd plucked her out of the simulation.

Now Lynx knew. She pictured Five watching her in the simulation and wondered how similar it was to Lynx watching who she now knew was Charlotte.

No. It was different. Very different.

Lynx was a romantic at heart, which was a new discovery—she had never pictured being Paired with a man, and had simply thought that Pairing wasn't for her.

Then she'd realized, in Unruly, that things could be different. She just needed to stay there.

Now her personal happiness was irrelevant. Unimportant.

"Why'd you leave before the end of the announcement?" Five asked.

"I have to go, but I'll tell you when I get back," Lynx said as she reached the bottom of the stairs.

"Where?"

"Later," Lynx promised, giving her a quick peck on the cheek as she threw on a pair of shoes.

"You missed the best part of the announcement," Five said, "Charlotte was outed for using Dust."

Lynx froze. *Holy hell.*

Now that it was public knowledge, she supposed it didn't matter that she'd revealed it in Unruly. At least there was that.

"Dust?"

"I always knew she was a cheater. It was the only way for her to be that good. And it was too easy to prove." Of course Five had something to do with it.

If Lynx hadn't just learned it was Charlotte herself in the simulation, she wouldn't have said, "She's under so much pressure, Five. Did you really have to do that?"

"Kids were going to try to get that many points and not realize that it's impossible without cheating."

No time, no time, no time.

"You're right." It would have been fine to argue—they'd had much bigger differences of opinion that they'd agreed to disagree on. Despite Five's flaws, she was much more openminded than she led on.

But those discussions went on for hours. Lynx had seconds.

Five gloated. Lynx hated when she got competitive. "Bye."

"Love you."

Lynx didn't repeat it. She never had. Five didn't pressure her to or expect it, which Lynx appreciated.

Lynx built her plan as she hurried toward Town Hall. No one spoke to her. Though no one would dare to openly complain about Lynx and Five being together on Princeps, that didn't stop the hostile stares.

But she was protected by the fifth most powerful person in the nation, so they left her alone.

Lynx took the steps of Town Hall three at a time, pulling out a small piece of plastic that had Five's fingerprint on it. It scanned and the lock unbolted. Easy.

She ran down the interior staircase until she was in the basement, where a few *cells*—locked artificially lit rooms—were located. The only thing that differentiated them from hospital rooms were the steel bars that divided the living space from the door.

Lynx had only heard of six people being kept in this prison. The first, a man who let it slip that High Society were allowed to have an *unofficial Pair* so long as they only reproduced with their *official* one. The second, third, fourth, and fifth were all High Society citizens who'd attempted to reproduce with someone other than their Pair. The last was a woman who'd told a Mid-Pointer on Ignis that the Conquest winners were allowed five years to recover after Unruly before they were required to get Paired.

Though she still had four years, Lynx felt the seconds ticking down. The special treatment from her unusual "victory" of the Conquest only went so far.

She told the guards she was passing a message from Five. That was always enough to get her in. Everyone knew that Imogen and Five didn't get along, so the guards assumed that nothing good was coming of her visit.

Imogen sat on the bed, writing on a blank sheet of paper that she hid at Lynx's approach.

Lynx knew that others thought her young. And, to them, young was synonymous with stupid. But Imogen was the only person who actually made her feel that way. Lynx could feel her own lack of political experience in Imogen's presence.

"Charlotte and Zandra—" Lynx began. But Imogen leapt off the bed and across the room. Lynx jumped back before Imogen could reach through the bars.

Imogen tilted her head toward a camera in the corner of the cell. Of course. In Lynx's haste, she'd forgotten.

She wondered what Imogen didn't want the cameras to hear. Imogen couldn't've believed their goals aligned. Lynx nodded at the paper that Imogen had been scrawling on.

Imogen furrowed her brows, ripped off a piece, and handed it and a pen to Lynx.

Lynx scribbled, *Charlotte announced in the sim that she's Charlotte and on Dust. 10 mins ago, maybe no one knows yet.*

Imogen paled as she snatched the pen back, blocking the camera with her body, and wrote. *Find 3. Tell him. Go now. Charlotte needs Dust.*

Dust. Lynx had no idea how addicted Charlotte was, but she supposed it was bad if Imogen was tasking her with getting Charlotte more.

That wasn't good.

Lynx sprinted away while Imogen...ate the paper. That was one way to hide the evidence.

Where the hell would Three be? Lynx hadn't interacted with him in months. She didn't even know where his mansion was.

She thought that Three and Imogen hated each other. How were they aligned in this?

She hoped that One, Four, and Five all had better things to do than sit and watch what was going on on Unruly all day. They *had* to.

One of Three's workers was in the security room, and they didn't have the clearance to watch the simulation or look at the cameras unless an alarm sounded. That was good. Though the entire Council could watch what was happening on Unruly in the security room, One was the only one who had a portable unit. It was him she needed to worry about.

She wondered if the time would be better spent finding One and distracting him than getting to Three. But what if Four or Five decided to take a trip to the security room and log in during that time?

What would Three even be able to do? Did he have the ability to wipe the footage, enter the simulation, and talk to the Unruly? To tell Charlotte to pretend what was said...wasn't said?

Lynx asked a ceremonial guard outside the main steps of Town Hall where Three lived, telling him she had an urgent message. He would assume it was from Five and not Two, of course.

Assumptions were the best disguise. Lynx had gotten away with countless punishable crimes because of them.

Then Lynx ran for the twins' lives.

29

Maddox was still reeling from his discussion with Zandra when he got a knock on the front door.

He didn't give much thought to it as he sat in the library, pretending to read beside his Pair, Clara.

Maddox loved Clara. Even though, like the majority of the population, they hadn't been able to reproduce.

She didn't know his secret. And at this point, it would only be cruel to reveal.

He needed to go to the security room. If Charlotte was addicted to Dust, she would need another hit soon. No wonder Imogen had been obsessed with reaching her. It wasn't just to tell her not to reveal that she wasn't Zandra.

If only he knew where to find it. He'd never seen Dust. Hadn't even know of its existence until he'd been elected. It was apparently to help the Impaired and, according to One, was being tested in Luxor. Here, it was used recreationally.

Illegally.

Clara glanced at him. "Want me to get it?"

He was always the one who answered the door—he always had been—though it didn't stop her from asking.

Maddox shook his head. He could use some distraction.

He'd spoken in formal settings with Charlotte before, when she had been honored for various awards, but that was his first conversation with Zandra.

His heart hurt for her. He had no idea what would happen if it came out that the twins had switched places. He just knew it would be bad. How could Imogen be so stupid?

Imogen. Though Maddox generally wasn't one to blame, he couldn't help but hold her accountable. She had sacrificed their daughters.

He wished he could cut ties with Imogen, but their mutual occupation—and the twins—made it impossible. It was made worse by the knowledge that she was still in love with him.

Meanwhile, Maddox had never hated her more. A hatred so profound, it could have only been born of soured love.

It was impressive that the hatred was still growing after everything she'd put him through. Each time he thought it couldn't grow stronger, Imogen found a way to commit yet another near-unforgivable sin.

Maddox supposed a small blessing from Imogen was that her actions had greatly expanded his capacity for forgiveness.

But this was the point of no return.

There was a part of him that would always remember what it was like to love her. The version of her that existed eighteen years ago.

But that love was just a memory now.

Maddox had been the Highest Pointer of his class, though nowhere near the Highest of All Time. He had won marginally, pulling out the victory with only days to spare.

Imogen had been in the Top Twenty, though Maddox had long forgotten her exact ranking. Somewhere in the bottom third.

Clara had been the seventh highest of the class. Above Imogen.

At Phoenix Palace, Maddox and Imogen's connection had been deep. Profound. They shared a passion—and attraction—based in their desires to lead. To change Ignis. To see Princeps. The only reason that Imogen wasn't the Highest Pointer of her class was because she had scored below-par in physical points. Imogen had been clumsy back then, something she'd spent years remedying.

Imogen was ambitious. Far more so than he. It drew Maddox to her. *She* was the one who would be ruling the world, not him. It was a passionate romance, one that the Five at the time, and all the other overseers of Phoenix Palace, would never see. They would only see the small talk in the hallways, when all Top Twenty had a mandatory event.

No one would see their nights, when they'd sneak out to sleep beneath the stars in the gardens, or stroll along the beach in the dead of night as they plotted just how they would change the world.

But Imogen's ambitions had left her guarded to the point that Maddox was never truly sure who she was. And when Maddox had voiced it, she'd said, "And you never will. *No one* ever will."

Her ambition was also what drove him away.

Years later, Maddox would learn that she meant it—with one exception. She *would* show her true self to *him*, against her better judgement, long after it was too late.

Imogen wasn't going to Princeps unless she was Paired with him. But that wasn't possible.

Because Maddox and Imogen were not genetic Pairs.

Their genes were never supposed to have merged. Their daughters were not supposed to have been born.

Despite that, Imogen had assured Maddox that she actually loved him—that they would find a way to be together—and Maddox believed her.

Until she'd sabotaged Clara.

Maddox and Imogen were doomed from the start. Both of them knew they would have to find genetic Pairs. And Maddox had found a friend in Clara. Clara was kind, emotionally intelligent, calm, content—the opposite of Imogen. He confided in her platonically, enjoying his first ever female friendship. He trusted her more than he trusted Imogen, despite loving Imogen in a very different, much more intense way.

Which was why he believed Clara when she told him that Imogen had threatened her one night, warning her to steer clear of Maddox.

Though Imogen had never admitted it, it was something Maddox was certain she would do, just as he knew Clara would never lie about such a thing. It confirmed Maddox's deepest fear, that Imogen only loved him because she believed that he could somehow get her to Princeps with his ranking.

Their end had been painful, scorching Maddox's heart as he succumbed to his intellect. Even then, Maddox still wanted to be with her. But it would only end in more pain.

Maddox had publicly chosen Clara before learning that Imogen was pregnant. He still remembered the moment that she'd told him, three hours after his announcement, just before he got whisked away to Princeps.

The words still reverberated through his mind. *Impaired. It's Impaired.*

"I don't know what to do!" Imogen had cried, "It's Impaired! I don't want this, Maddox!"

Maddox hadn't known what to do. He was only seventeen. "I'll revoke my Pairing proposal to Clara. You don't have to do this alone," Maddox had told her. "I can tell them I made a mistake."

But Imogen shook her head. "If anyone knows...there's no way we'd get into High Society. And this baby...it'll be sent Unruly. You know that."

"I meant," Maddox said, "I can do something that will keep me from getting selected for Princeps, so I can stay here with you. No one has to know it's mine. Maybe it won't—maybe no one will be able to tell."

"No," Imogen said, "You're not giving that up for me."

They could live good lives on Ignis. Not together, but near. Near enough to be a family. But Imogen had made him swear an oath of secrecy.

That had been one of the biggest regrets of Maddox's life.

Imogen had never spoken to Lawrence before they decided to get Paired. Maddox had rarely interacted with him at the Academy—all he knew was that Lawrence was incredibly intelligent academically and artistically, but lacked brains outside it.

The only reason Imogen and Lawrence had been chosen to join High Society as the second Pair was because her pregnancy had been discovered at her monthly fertility appointment. And it wasn't just any pregnancy—it was with twins. The first born since the Destruction, as far as Ignis knew. One and that year's Five had made an excuse about Imogen's exemplary behavior at Phoenix Palace, and Imogen's pregnancy wasn't announced publicly until several months after her residency on Princeps.

Imogen told Lawrence that they were his. She told everyone that. And everyone believed her. There was no way *twins*—the first twins since the Destruction—could be *Impaired*. Maddox just hoped and prayed that when they were born, their Impairment wouldn't be obvious to the naked eye. That all the rumors of what the Impaired looked like weren't true. Maddox and Imogen could help them with any other less obvious impairments they might have.

And no one would know.

But when they reached Princeps, Maddox was cut from the picture. He and Imogen didn't speak once during her pregnancy. Maddox tried. Tried and failed. He told himself that Imogen was just trying to protect them.

Maddox had worried endlessly about the health of his children through the pregnancy. He kept waiting for something to go wrong. He barely slept during those nine months.

Then they were born. Healthy. Not grotesque.

The first month after their births, Maddox couldn't find a way to visit. He had been turned away from Imogen's door several times, until Lawrence—who he had never seen stand for anything—threatened to report him. He just wanted a glimpse. Did they look like him? Did they have his eyes? His even temperament?

Were they going to live through the winter?

He saw pictures. They had his eyes and nose. They were smiling. They looked happy.

They were perfect.

What had he done wrong to go through the torture of not being able to see them? To have the woman who he was still in love with keep his children away from him? To have the entire population talk about *his* children, without knowing they were his?

But then he wondered what he had done right, that he had two Impaired children who were healthy?

It was about two months after the twins' birth, on a stormy night, when Maddox woke to a pounding on his door.

Maddox jumped to his feet and rushed to it. The reason he never let Clara answer the door—he was hoping one day Imogen or Charlotte or Zandra would be there, waiting.

Something that would never change, no matter how many years passed.

For the first time, rushing to the foyer had paid off. There on his porch was Imogen, sleek hair plastered to her face, her face wet with what may have been tears or rain.

"I can't do this, Maddox!"

Maddox closed the door behind him and stepped into the rain, putting an arm around her as he hurried her into a copse of trees, away from any potential prying eyes, dread filling his body.

"Charlotte won't stop screaming until I hold her while standing. I can't—I can't do this. And Alexandra's afraid of the dark."

Maddox sighed in relief. Those sounded like regular baby problems.

"It's okay. It's okay, Imogen."

Imogen burrowed her head on his shoulder, holding onto him as if he were the sole life raft on a sinking ship.

Maddox sometimes forgot how young they were. Especially Imogen. She seemed ten years older than eighteen. That moment, he saw her as she was—a terrified girl.

"I don't want to be a mother. I can't do it."

"You can. You will be a fantastic mother."

"Not if I want to accomplish my dreams."

"You can do both."

"I can't."

Not knowing what else to do, Maddox just held her.

"Our duty to Ignis is to rebuild humanity," Maddox said after a few minutes of listening to the rain, long after his clothes were soaked through. "And you—*we've* done that. We should be proud."

"They're *Impaired*!" Imogen cried. The way in which she said it—like it was a bad thing—made him pull away.

"Yes, but they're *perfect*." Anything that came from him and Imogen was bound to be.

"Just because we don't see it yet doesn't mean that it won't become apparent."

"So what if they're a little different? They're *still* perfect."

He meant it, fury toward whomever had ever decided that the Impaired didn't have a place in Ignis ignited.

Imogen began pulling herself together. "I falsified the gene test—merged mine and Lawrence's on the computer."

Maddox flinched. He wanted the world to know they were *his*. He wanted to scream it from the rooftops.

But he couldn't. Not if he didn't want them sent Unruly at ten years old.

"Good," he finally managed.

"I didn't want this," Imogen said, lifting her head so she could look at him.

"I want it," Maddox said. But it was impossible. "I want it all. To help you. To protect them. To tell the world that the Impaired are just as worthy as the rest of us."

"No one can ever know," Imogen stated.

"But people *could*. After the twins are...established."

Imogen mulled this over. "After they've achieved more than we have. And they've both earned their way to Princeps."

Maddox smiled. "Imagine the shock when the rest of the nation finds out they're Impaired. It would change the whole world."

It was a dream. Nothing that could ever be a reality.

Imogen looked conflicted, but Maddox squeezed her hands. "We could do it. If the girls want it, of course."

Imogen frowned. He would make no progress with mending things with her today.

But he had seventeen years.

Imogen wiped off her eyes as the rain slowed to a drizzle. Maddox raised her chin and helped.

Imogen stared into his soul. "I wish we could switch places. I wish you could take them."

He didn't know it at the time, but that was the moment that his love for her became tainted. Learning she didn't *want* them.

The years that followed confirmed it, permanently damaging Maddox's heart.

Imogen visited him several times over the next years, always when she couldn't handle her predicament. When she had no one else to turn to. No one else who would understand.

But every time she made a burden of what he desired, Maddox found himself despising her more. And each time, the door got just a little heavier as he opened it, until he stopped altogether.

M addox opened his front door.

His thoughts snapped back to the present when he saw Lynx on the other side, unable to hide her twitching.

He would have been less surprised if Imogen had somehow escaped from prison. He would have been less surprised to find Zandra there, demanding more answers.

Not Lynx.

"Charlotte just announced that she's not Zandra. I went to Imogen, she told me to find you. I don't think the others have seen yet."

Questions flooded his thoughts. But there wasn't time to voice any but the important ones. "Who did she tell? How long ago?"

"Twenty minutes? Harris and Enid."

Maddox threw some shoes on. No time to tell Clara where he was going. He rushed outside, the door slamming shut behind him.

He and Lynx took off running, Lynx matching his pace. She had been training with Five. "Imogen said she needs Dust."

Maddox scowled. There wasn't time. "She's going to have to live without it for a little longer."

Lynx grimaced. "What's the plan?"

Maddox was still making it. "Town Hall. We have to get to the security room."

"I think the simplest thing is to is erase the footage and then run interference. Go in and tell Charlotte—"

"No. It's time to end this."

Lynx wasn't following, but Maddox didn't expect her to. He explained, "She needs to win the Conquest *now*. We get her out of there."

"It's...not looking great for her."

"I'll fix it."

"It's been three days," Lynx pointed out.

"Then she'll be the fastest person to win."

Lynx was quiet. Mulling it over as he was. "One won't let it happen."

"We're not giving him an option."

"How?"

"She wins the way everyone else wins. By choosing her Pair."

Maddox hadn't figured out the details yet. He just knew that his daughter was in danger and the longer she was on Unruly, the longer she was in danger.

Lynx was silent for a long moment. "I need to do something. Do you need me?"

"Just...if it doesn't work, keep helping them. Can I trust you with that?"

Lynx gave a grim nod. "Of course."

Maddox was out of breath, and decided not to waste any more on talking.

"Good luck." Lynx peeled off down a different alley and Maddox sprinted for Town Hall.

Maddox slouched with relief when he realized that he had gotten to the security room before the rest of the Council.

He dismissed his lackey, and told her not to have the next three shifts clock in.

As a Council member who had witnessed many years of the Unruly simulation, and had been monitoring the security room for a decade, it was simple to find where Charlotte confessed she was Charlotte—and that she'd done Dust—and delete that moment off the computer. He caught up to the present using *2x* speed, keeping the silence that followed and trimming out the following moments that would have given her identity away.

When Maddox was caught up to the present, he sighed and mentally prepared to do something so violating that he was disgusted by himself.

He hoped his daughter could forgive him when this was over.

30

Charlotte and Harris didn't speak for several long moments. All Charlotte could comprehend was the painful thumping in her sinuses. The cell spun.

Then Harris said, "I knew you were too much...like you."

Charlotte had her doubts, but she didn't want to be a jerk and say so. "I'm sorry. I'm sorry for how I've treated you these past years."

Harris put his head in his hands and rubbed his eyes, trying to wrap his head around her revelation. "How did you end up here?"

"You know when you don't really want what everyone tells you that you should want, so you distract yourself so you don't have to think about it?"

"Not really," Harris said.

"I...broke," she murmured, "I couldn't do it any more. I couldn't pretend to be perfect."

Harris took her hand and Charlotte once more felt the urge to run. "Your imperfections are what make you *you*. You can be the Highest Pointer—be yourself—and not be perfect."

Charlotte wasn't sure that was true, but she remained silent.

She was too aware of Harris' palm, and how she wasn't sure if she loved it or hated it.

How could she not figure out something as simple as that?

"Do you think that Enid is going to tell the others?" Charlotte asked, gently removing her hand. She wasn't sure why it mattered to her, just that she wasn't ready for the others to know. She had buried this side of her identity—the Unruly side—for so long, that the thought of everyone suddenly knowing that she was *her*, and not on her own terms, felt wrong.

Enid wouldn't do that, right? Not without consulting her.

"I don't know," Harris said, "I thought I understood these people, but now...I don't know. We were supposed to be free here."

They sat in silence, Charlotte worrying about what everyone would think once they knew she wasn't the Lowest Pointer—but the Highest. Would they treat her differently? Scorn her? Outcast her?

She'd already done that herself by killing Wade. A fresh wave of horror passed through her body at the thought. *Change,* Charlotte reminded herself, *You're going to change.*

And every time she thought of Wade, she would remind herself to be accountable to it.

"I meant what I said," Harris interrupted her thoughts.

Charlotte looked at him. Had he been sitting that close the whole time?

"About us," he continued, "You've been *you* this whole time down here. I was right. We can still win this together. We can win a life on Princeps."

Charlotte wondered how, in pretending to be Zandra, she had internally found her truest self. The self she was right now, in this moment.

Harris hadn't seen *her* yet. Not truly. She wasn't the mixture of herself and Zandra that she was pretending to be.

Before Charlotte could reject him, Enid returned.

Charlotte's heart skipped a beat. She searched Enid's face for clues of what she was thinking. If she had told people. If she still hated her.

But Enid was emotionless.

And she had a key.

Harris leapt to his feet. "What's going on?"

"I'm giving you a chance," Enid said, "Everyone's asleep and there's garbage from the wall all over the clearing. I'll help you clean it."

Harris glanced at Charlotte out of the corner of his eye.

"Okay," Charlotte said. She knew what Harris wanted to do. And even now, she felt herself being pulled in that direction. Away from here.

Remember Wade, she reminded herself, *Be better.*

Dust, her brain responded, *You need to get out to get Dust.*

"And please don't run off," Enid said, as if reading her mind, "I don't want to get locked up in here, too."

Charlotte imagined being locked in this cell with the two of them and a mirthless smile appeared on her face. *That* would certainly be something to see.

"I won't," promised Charlotte. Harris tilted his head—Charlotte wasn't particularly known for her honesty. That had always been more of Zandra's thing.

Harris gave a brisk nod. Enid looked at him for a long moment, then must've decided that it was enough.

"Come on," she said, unlocking the door, "Follow me."

Charlotte and Harris walked a pace behind Enid. Harris raised an eyebrow. *What's the plan?* She shook her head, the only way she knew how to tell him there was no plan. That she was going to stay down here until she was sure the Unruly had enough food.

And maybe after that.

I don't need Dust. I don't need Dust.

She would look after the others, help instill hope in them with Enid, swim in the waterfall...

Maybe she'd send a message up with Harris to give to Zandra. To tell her that she was okay, and she hoped Zandra was too.

Charlotte felt a pang of guilt. Zandra hadn't asked for any of this. Hadn't asked to be thrown to the sharks of Phoenix Palace.

She hoped Zandra was faring better than Charlotte had in the role of Highest Pointer. Maybe she was—Zandra was far stronger than Charlotte had ever been.

The clearing was littered with garden hoes, lounge chairs, portable heaters, wheelbarrows, and pots. The collapse of the wall of outdoor items had made the clearing look fundamentally different—less easy to navigate and more likely to cause injury in the darkness.

"I think we should start piling it over by the original wall," Enid said.

"Okay," Harris said, "Want to help me over here, Char—Zandra?"

Enid dragged a wheelbarrow toward the pile. Charlotte went to help her. "In a minute."

Harris nodded and starting gathering items while Charlotte joined Enid, piling random items into the wheelbarrow as they passed.

"Tomorrow morning I'll tell them it was you two who helped."

"Thank you."

Enid looked her in the eyes. "I think you're selfish, you know."

"I know," Charlotte knew it too. But coming from Enid, it stung even more.

"Why do you even want to get out of here so badly if you chose to come here in the first place?"

"I don't."

"Doesn't seem that way."

"I belong here. I knew that before, but I forgot for a second."
I don't need Dust.

Enid's eyes widened in surprise. But then she shook her head. "You don't. Not if you don't care about the rest of us."

"I know," Charlotte said, "But I do care. About the others... and you. It just took me a minute to realize that."

Harris was on the other side of the clearing, carefully picking something up, trying and failing not to look too excited about it.

He turned back and met her gaze. He raised what he held.

Charlotte swallowed a gasp.

Dynamite.

He hid it behind his back and tilted his head to one of the walls.

Then he disappeared around it.

Charlotte swallowed. Was she making a big mistake? Was this a sign that she should go with Harris? Win the Conquest, increase awareness, bring back food? Get Dust?

No. *Remember Wade. I don't need Dust. I don't need Dust.*

Harris could get help on his own. He didn't need Charlotte. Neither did Zandra.

The Unruly *did.*

Enid had been speaking, but Charlotte hadn't heard a word. "What?"

Enid dropped the wheelbarrow and stepped toward Charlotte. "I said, what do you mean?"

She searched Charlotte's face, trying to see what she had originally seen in her when they first arrived. Charlotte wanted her approval. To let her know that she wasn't as bad as she seemed.

"I'm not going to try to win the Conquest."

Now that the words were in the universe, Charlotte felt as if she could manifest them. She had someone to hold her accountable.

I don't need Dust.

A weight lifted off her shoulders. She was stepping into a new era. A more honest life.

Enid looked something between shocked, troubled, and touched. "Really?"

"Yes," Charlotte murmured. Enid took another step toward her. Something in Enid's demeanor revealing it was against her better judgement.

They stood just a little too close together. Charlotte's heart raced, speeding up as the rest of the world slowed down.

Then Enid leaned in and kissed her.

Charlotte felt nothing.

No heartbeat.

No pain.

No joy.

Just nothing.

Charlotte's brain stopped for what may have been a moment or hours.

She felt absolutely nothing.

Then her brain went into overdrive.

Fight or flight?

She froze. Her body tensed up as her brain overflowed with questions.

Why were Enid's lips so wet? Why did Charlotte feel like she had to close her eyes? How was she supposed to breathe? How did people enjoy this? What was she supposed to do with her hands? Was her nose positioned weirdly? Had she ever noticed the positioning of her nose before this moment? How long was too soon before she could pull away? Would it be rude to pull away now? Did she care if she was rude? Would she relax if she didn't pull away? Why did her head still hurt? Why was she thinking about her headache?

Enid sensed the stiffness of Charlotte's body and made the

decision for her, breaking apart. "Are you...I—I'm sorry, I didn't —I thought—"

"No," Charlotte said, "No, no, you did nothing wrong."

Run, run, run, Charlotte's mind begged.

"I thought you were—"

Charlotte looked into the distance. She couldn't say anything —her flight response had consumed her.

Enid waited. When it became clear that Charlotte had no words, Enid gently touched Charlotte's shoulder and said, "Why are you so tense?"

Charlotte's mind, which was usually so good at processing, was utterly blank. She had no idea if she should be offended by the question.

"I'm not—I have to go." So Charlotte ran, gripping Zandra's necklace, the cavern beginning to spin again.

She didn't know where she was running. She just needed to be anywhere else.

One thing was abundantly clear. She wasn't the way Ignis wanted her to be. She knew in her gut that it didn't matter if it was Enid *or* Harris—she would have had the same reaction if it had been Harris who had kissed her. She wasn't ready for Pairing. For romance. For any of it.

Even Unruly couldn't fix her. She could earn all the points in the world, but it was no use. Because she didn't know how to love. Not in the way that Ignis wanted. Not in the way she wanted. Not in the way that Enid wanted. Or Harris.

She was going to be alone forever. And even though a part of her could finally rest and find peace in that realization, there was another part that was overwhelmed with sadness. That longed for companionship in a way that she knew no one else wanted or could give her.

She was alone. The Highest Pointer turned Lowest Pointer.

The one who couldn't be Paired or Unruly. The only person who didn't belong anywhere.

You will be okay, Charlotte told herself, *You have yourself.*

She was all she needed—and despite her actions, despite how messed up she was, she felt a deep internal empathy and understanding. She was falling, but she would catch herself if no one else waited at the bottom with outstretched arms.

Once she outran her feelings.

I don't need Dust. I don't need Dust. I don't—

Charlotte reached the wall of the junkyard, where the opening that she had entered and exited the tunnels had been, but found that the collapse she'd caused had blocked it.

It was rather poetic.

She wiped the snot dripping down her face, feeling like a caged animal. She wanted out. She wanted her head to stop pounding.

She wanted—

Zandra. She wanted to jump into her twin's arms and stay there forever. Because even if Zandra didn't understand, she would support her. Love her. Accept her.

So she climbed, ignoring her fear. She noticed once again that her arms weren't blue despite the stress. She didn't think anything of it.

Up, up, up—

"Charlotte?"

She stopped her ascent. "Harris."

"What are you doing?" There was alarm in his voice. Enough for Charlotte to start climbing back down. She jumped the last few feet and Harris steadied her.

"I don't want what you want."

Harris took her in. Charlotte wasn't sure he understood, but he seemed to realize now wasn't the time to ask. He nodded, and Charlotte loved him all the more for it. "That's okay. Now *what's wrong*?" Before the words were even out of his mouth, Charlotte threw her arms around him.

"I am," she whispered.

In all the years they'd known each other, she had never embraced him.

It took Harris a long moment for his shock to subside. He squeezed her shoulders. He cared about her. Even when she had cut him out of her life—when he had only been trying to help her —he'd *still* cared. "You aren't to me."

"I don't feel things like other people do."

"That doesn't mean you're wrong."

"Then what am I?"

"Special."

"I'm never going to be what they want me to be. Or feel what they want me to feel."

"No one does. Everyone just pretends to."

"That isn't true."

Harris squeezed her shoulders. "Well, maybe you will feel it at some point."

Charlotte grew frustrated. "You don't get it! I'm not going to find the right person! I don't have a Pair, Harris! I'm unpairable. I'm not capable of it."

"You haven't even tried, though," he said gently, "Maybe you just need to find yourself first."

He was just trying to be helpful. He was trying to understand. But she didn't want people to understand—she just wanted to be validated. For someone to tell her that yes, she was unpairable, but that she would be okay despite it.

But no one would tell her that. Because it wasn't true. Not in Ignis.

Maybe Harris was right. Maybe she just needed time. But if that were true, it felt a millennium away. Like she would need to live a thousand lives before it came to fruition.

"I don't want a Pair," she admitted, "I don't want a Pair, or a kid, or a mansion, or to be One."

"Then what *do* you want?"

I want—no. I don't need Dust.

She wanted to feel something that wasn't anxiety. She wanted peace. She wanted to be loved for who she was, not what she accomplished. "I want to be free."

"Then you want to get out of here?" Harris asked gently, showing her a shovel he had propped against the wall. The dynamite was next to it, along with a match box. "Somewhere you won't be locked up?"

Yes! Charlotte internally screamed. But to where? Things wouldn't be better for her on Princeps. Here, she could do what she wanted. She would smooth things over with Enid and find peace. She could honor Wade. Live a life without expectations.

She couldn't run anymore. She had to face her problems. Face her fears. Face her faults. Face her past.

"No," Charlotte forced herself to say. She allowed herself to feel the anxiety. She accepted its presence. Accepted that it was part of her, but it wasn't all of her. That they could co-exist together.

And for the first time in her life, she felt power over it. By not trying to control it, it stopped having control over her.

A flicker of hope cut through Charlotte's agitation.

And then everything went wrong.

Charlotte didn't know what was happening. Suddenly, she was no longer in control of her body.

She tried to move her mouth, to use her vocal chords, but... nothing. She tried to move her legs, to take a step forward, but her body didn't respond.

Panic swelled in her gut. What was happening to her? Why was she frozen?

She tried calling out to Harris for help, tried to tell him with her eyes, but he was blind to what was happening. How wouldn't he be?

"No?" Harris asked, a hint of sadness in his voice.

No! Charlotte wanted to scream, *Help!*

But instead, her mouth moved of its own accord. "No," it said, "I want *us* to go. I don't want a Pair. I want you."

Charlotte's voice came out of her mouth, but the words did not belong to her. Her internal panic increased, but not her heart rate. How? What was happening to her?

"You were right before. About everything. We need to win the Conquest together," Charlotte found her vocal chords speaking again, "And I do just need time. To get to know you again."

What the *hell* was she saying?! She tried to budge, to fight, but her body betrayed her.

The terror she'd had the first day of Pairing Season was nothing compared to the terror coursing through her veins now. Charlotte had never felt so out of control. So scared.

Was she possessed? Having a psychic break? Was she in a nightmare?

There was no way to express it. Her soul was stuck in a body that didn't feel like her own.

She didn't know what to do. She didn't know how to fight it.

So she just watched, trapped in her own body, as Harris grinned, took her hand, and started digging.

31

Zandra had gotten a good night of sleep. Eloise must have put something in her tea. That, or she had used up every droplet of energy that her body had to offer, giving it no choice but to shut down.

She had gone straight back to her room after the announcement. She wasn't a planner. She wasn't a manipulator. She didn't think twelve steps ahead like Charlotte.

Zandra journaled for a few hours before collapsing. About Tiberius, and what he had done, and how he made her feel. About Charlotte, and how Zandra was realizing that she had been taken for granted by Charlotte. But she would stay the course anyway.

Only when all her thoughts were on paper did she manage to close her eyes. She tried to come up with a plan, but she didn't have enough facts. Eventually, she gave up and hoped her brain would work better in the morning.

Zandra could have slept for another three days, but Eloise came rushing into her room at noon.

She pulled the blinds open and Zandra groaned at the light.

"Five more minutes," she mumbled, shielding her eyes.

"I let you sleep as late as you can," Eloise said.

Zandra supposed it was time to figure out what the hell she was going to do. She wasn't a coward or a hider.

"I want to see my mother," Zandra said to Eloise.

"I'm afraid that's out of my control. And you have an outing—"

"It's a basic right, isn't it?"

"One that I don't have the power to give you." There was compassion in Eloise's voice, but the words were final.

She felt claustrophobic. But it wasn't the room. It was this ridiculous life that she'd been thrown into by her own mother and sister. It was constricting her. Strangling her from the inside out.

Zandra eyed the cabinet in which she'd placed the anti-anxiety medication that Imogen had given her. She supposed she could use a boost today. Right? Especially if today was going to be anything like yesterday.

Zandra waited until Eloise gave her privacy to throw one of the pills into her mouth. Then she pulled out Three's phone. This was a low-risk request—and if Three couldn't grant it, she would have her answer about whether or not to trust him.

She pressed the call button and put it to her ear, pacing around the spa. It rang. Once. Twice. Three times. Four.

There was crackling on the other end before Three's voice said, "Hello?"

It was strangled, like he was heavily exerting himself and on the verge of collapse. But Zandra didn't care. Whatever he was stressed about could wait.

"It's me," Zandra said. She hoped he was smart enough to recognize her from the sound of her voice, because there was no way she was saying either *Zandra* or *Charlotte*.

"Is—everything okay?" he rasped.

"I need to see my mother."

There was a long pause. Then, finally, "I can't do that—but—I can pass her a message if you'd like."

"Bull," Zandra said, "Since when are children not allowed to visit their incarcerated parents? I want to see her and I'd bet my father's life that you could figure out how to make it happen." Her father's life felt like it held the most weight—she wasn't willing to bet her own, or Charlotte's, and she was too angry at Imogen for it to mean anything. Hence, Lawrence was offered.

There was more crackling, then Three said, "Okay. I'll make it happen."

Zandra sagged with relief. Imogen would know what to do. She always did. Even if Zandra didn't trust her anymore, a plan from Imogen was better than waiting to be admitted into High Society. And she may have overlooked something.

She was sure Tiberius would take her back. Zandra would have to look past his loose lips.

As for the Dust rumors, that's all they would be. Because Zandra had never touched Dust in her life.

It was ironic that she was the "rebel." If only Ignis knew.

When Eloise returned, Zandra's eyes drifted toward her reflection and landed on the circles under her eyes. Beneath the mirror were the loose pieces of paper she had written the night before, as well as the anti-anxiety medication.

When Eloise turned away to get her dress, Zandra stuffed all of it into the top of her corset. It was so tight that it wouldn't budge. If Eloise noticed the missing items, she didn't comment.

In an attempt to draw attention away, Zandra asked, "So who is this outing with?"

"Mace Phillips."

"Can I have one with Tiberius instead?"

"You think I have anything to do with the scheduling?"

Zandra hadn't thought about it, but she supposed not. It must've been...

"Where's Five?"

Eloise sighed. "Charlotte, I do not know any more than you do."

Zandra was silent throughout the rest of Eloise's preparation. She let Eloise do what she wanted, as if she were a doll. She was past caring.

Or the anxiety medication was working.

It must've been. Because, as Zandra ran herself through the plan, she felt confident. She would find Tiberius. If she couldn't ditch Phillips, she would get him to help her. And then she would apologize, even if the thought made her want to vomit.

But did it? Why was the idea of spending time with Tiberius much more digestible than spending time with Phillips, even after all Tiberius had done?

It didn't matter. She would play nice with Tiberius. And then on Princeps, he would be Charlotte's problem. It raised a myriad of negative emotions, but she told herself not to feel them.

To her surprise, she didn't.

Zandra narrowed her eyes. This anti-anxiety medication was no joke. Her mind felt clear. Yesterday had been a nightmare, but today was the day she fixed it.

Eloise clasped a tight necklace around her neck. Zandra fidgeted, feeling as if it were cutting off her windpipe, like a noose.

She missed her shark tooth.

A knock interrupted Eloise's finishing touches. Zandra jumped to her feet, ready to get this day started. Was this how her sister lived her whole life? How could Imogen and Lawrence not have noticed that Zandra had anxiety as well? Because she must have, if she was reacting so well to the medication.

Five waited at the door. Zandra had never been happier to see her. "I want to see Tiberius," she said before Five could get a word in.

"I'm here to escort you to your outing with Mace Phi—"

"I know, but I need to see Tiberius instead."

"That's not possible."

"I'm sure you can make it happen."

Five smiled at her with shark-like malice. "You will go on your outing with Mace Phillips."

This wasn't the way to get what she wanted. Five was unflappable. So Zandra nodded, put on her sweetest smile—one that she had never used in her entire lifetime and didn't even know she had —and said, "Of course, Five."

Five turned, not waiting to see if Zandra followed. Zandra flashed Eloise a grateful look, then rushed after Five through the maze of the palace.

The outing with Mace could barely be called an "outing". It was a walk through the palace gardens, where Five would follow a pace behind. Didn't she have better things to do? Why was it always *her* that Five babysat?

Phillips was charming. He picked her an apple from a tree— Zandra spat it out the moment she tasted the sour, then rebuked herself for her lack of poise.

Phillips talked her ear off about all the fun things they were going to do in Princeps together. He showed her his double-jointed wrists.

None of it mattered. Even if Zandra thought he was perfect for Charlotte, she wouldn't be choosing him. He was doomed. Didn't he know that? The only boy going to Princeps this year was Tiberius.

Maybe that was something she could take advantage of.

She almost felt guilty for thinking it, but she *could* help him. And he may as well help her in return.

"Phillips," she interrupted him carefully, soft enough that Five couldn't hear, "This is unproductive."

Phillips stopped, his hands curling and knuckles whitening. "Excuse me?"

Zandra took his arm and pulled him forward. Five subtly closed the gap behind them.

"Tiberius is the only one who's joining High Society now," she whispered, deciding full transparency would be the wisest way forward, "I need to see him."

Phillips gazed ahead, sour as the apple. "I don't see what this has to do with me."

"Get rid of my babysitter and I'll find a way to get you to Princeps after I'm Paired with Tiberius."

A glint appeared in Phillips' eyes, then he fell over into the bushes, dry heaving, and screaming at the top of his lungs. With Five's attention on him, Zandra ducked into the trees.

Tiberius was sitting with Jayana in the empty library, teaching her to play the crwth, when Zandra opened the door. A pit formed in her stomach as she fiddled with her constricting necklace. She tried to convince herself that it was only because this meant it would be harder for her—*Charlotte*—and Tiberius to get Paired. *Not* for any other reason.

"Hi," Zandra said, self-conscious about how straight she was standing. She was acutely aware of her entire body. Her arms dangled. She could see a strand of hair on the side of her face... She focused all her attention on her left foot, which was hidden beneath her ridiculous dress. No one could see it, so it didn't matter that it was just awkwardly...there.

"Charlotte," Jayana said, surprised, "What are you doing here?"

"I have to speak with Tiberius," Zandra said, a hint of apology in her voice. "It's urgent."

Tiberius looked at her, then shook his head. "It can wait until after my lunch with Jayana." His voice was formal, but not cold. Even so, Zandra felt the wall he had built between them—tall and strong. It would be difficult for Zandra to summit.

"I'm really sorry, but it can't," Zandra said, "I don't know when I'm going to be able to see you next and I really, really need to apologize."

Was she being a terrible friend to Jayana? Probably. But Zandra and Jayana had never really *been* friends. She didn't know the depth of Jayana and Charlotte's friendship and she decided the less she knew, the less guilty she would feel about screwing Jayana over.

"Then you can do it in front of both of us," Tiberius murmured.

Tiberius could barely look at her, and Zandra sensed he was having as hard of a time as she was.

"No," Jayana said, jumping to her feet. Anger radiated off of her, making Zandra take a step back. "I'd like to take a walk, anyway."

"Jayana—" Tiberius said, rising as well.

She softened when she looked at him. "It's okay. Really. I'll be back in a few."

Tiberius opened his mouth to protest, then glanced at Zandra and closed it. Zandra took that as a good sign.

The moment Jayana was out of earshot, Zandra said, "I shouldn't have said what I said, but you also shouldn't have said what you said."

"I know," Tiberius murmured, "And I'm sorry. I really am. But would you be saying this now if I weren't the only person who could get you to High Society?"

She admired his honesty. "Yes. I was livid at you, Tiberius. I still am. But I don't want to be. So before I pursue anything further, I need to know...why did you mention Jaxson?"

Tiberius finally looked at her, his eyes deep with guilt. He wanted to fix things between them. "I didn't know. I thought he was just a boy from your past. I didn't realize he..." Tiberius lowered his voice. "I didn't realize he dealt you Dust."

Tiberius had inadvertently revealed Charlotte's secret out of jealousy—that was easier for her to forgive than outing Charlotte as a drug addict.

"I'm not on it now," Zandra confirmed, "And I can't really tell you why Dust was *ever* in the picture. But it's not anymore."

Her words were misleading but truthful. And Tiberius believed her. Zandra could tell by the way the wrinkle on his forehead relaxed with relief. "So what do you say?" Zandra asked, "Can we start over?"

A grin overtook Tiberius' face, and Zandra's heart beat a little faster. "I'd like that."

"That makes me...very happy." She meant it. She was ready to get to know Tiberius again. "I shouldn't have interrupted like that."

"Well, it saved me a lot of overthinking," Tiberius said. "This whole Pairing thing is a bit ridiculous, isn't it?"

Zandra was surprised. No one talked down about Pairing, especially not in the palace.

"We wouldn't have met if not for it," Zandra pointed out. Though that wasn't exactly true. She and Tiberius would never be together, no matter how much she loved his goofy lopsided smile and his persistence. He was *Charlotte's* Pair.

"Maybe we would've found each other regardless." He was keeping it light, though Zandra knew his feelings ran deeper.

For *her*. Or whatever this version of herself she was playing. Would they continue for Charlotte when they switched back? Would he even know the difference?

He was her way to Princeps. That was it.

She couldn't wonder about what Tiberius' childhood was like. Or his opinions about the war with the Union. Or what he liked to do for fun when he wasn't playing his crwth. Or what his brothers were like.

She couldn't think about what came after she swapped places with Charlotte.

"That's what Zandra would have said," said Zandra.

"And what do *you* say?"

"I—I don't know."

Tiberius studied her. "I'm sorry about your mother. And what they made you say about her. That couldn't have been easy."

Zandra frowned and bit her lip, unsure of what to say.

"We have power," Tiberius whispered, sensing her unease, "We have a lot separately, but even more together. We could get her out."

His words rang true. Right now, she was chained to Five and One, using her power as a weapon in their game. She had done the same for Imogen and Charlotte all her life.

"We could fix everything that's wrong with Pairing."

"I have to save Zandra." Yes, she wanted to speak out against Pairing. If it were only her own life on the line, she would have done it then and there. But it wasn't.

Tiberius frowned, and Zandra immediately realized her mistake.

"Right. And you have to get to Princeps to save her." *But you're* not *just using me, you claim.*

"I can fix what's wrong with Pairing after she's safe," she lied. Because Charlotte sure as hell wouldn't do so.

"Have you ever thought," Tiberius said, keeping his voice soft and kind, "That maybe she doesn't want to be rescued?"

His words shifted something within her. She hadn't. Because Charlotte had been so against Unruly. Zandra hadn't even considered that the predicament had been anything but Imogen's fault.

"I—yes," she lied again.

"Maybe you need to stop living for her and doing what you think *she'd* want you to do," Tiberius said, "And start doing what *you* actually want."

"Would you do anything for your brothers?"

"No," murmured Tiberius much too quickly.

How could Tiberius not understand that siblings had to look out for each other when he had his own? That they were the only people who could ever truly know each other, because they had always known each other? Because they had done everything together?

"Why?" Zandra asked, trying not to judge him.

"Because they're their own people who make their own choices. And sometimes I don't agree with them, but I don't change who I am to try to fix them."

Zandra didn't agree. No. Charlotte was part of her. If she had to change who she was to save her, then she would change.

Right?

"I suppose you have a point. I'm just...not used to thinking that way."

Sympathy appeared in Tiberius' eyes. "Maybe you just need someone to help you expand your mind to new ideas."

"And you think you can?"

"Yeah," he said with a lopsided grin.

Zandra guffawed, and all remaining tension eased as they basked in each other's presence.

"I know speaking against Pairing would take a lot of bravery. And risk," Tiberius said, "But there's nothing we can't do together."

She needed to leave in a good place with him—it had been so up and down that she wasn't going to let it go bad.

She could get used to how analytically this anti-anxiety medication was making her think.

"I should go get Jayana, but I'm going to think on it."

"Yes," Tiberius said, "I appreciated this, Charlotte."

"I'd like to see you again soon. But I don't think Five will be arranging it—"

"I'll make sure we do."

Zandra grinned. He escorted her to the door. She'd thought she'd need to do more to rebuild his trust, but Tiberius appeared to be satisfied by the apology.

She started back toward the garden, nodding at Leon. Five certainly had realized that Phillips had been distracting her, but Zandra couldn't imagine it would be difficult to talk her way out of.

But as Zandra passed the balcony overlooking Phoenix Square, she stopped in her tracks.

Jayana was out there with Phillips, speaking to a small but growing crowd below, "I've seen it with my own eyes, and someone on Dust is *not* who should be joining High Society. Not when so many other women have put in the work."

The door was open, each soft word hitting Zandra's ears like poison.

Instead of standing there dumbly as she usually did, Zandra searched for Five. She must have been behind this.

Sure enough, Five leaned against a pillar where the crowd couldn't see her and she could make a hasty exit if anyone asked what was going on.

Think like Charlotte. Options rushed through Zandra's brain. Should she go out there? Should she *get* out of there?

Something buzzed in her pocket. Three's phone. Relief flooded through Zandra's veins as she hid behind a pillar opposite of Five's.

"Three," she said, "I need help, Jayana is saying that she's seen Charlotte do Dust—"

"Are you alone?" the voice on the other side said back.

Imogen.

Tears sprang into her eyes. "Mom," she whispered, her voice cracking, "Mom, I miss you so much. And I don't know what I'm doing. I hate it here. I—I want to go home."

Zandra put her knuckles into her mouth to spot herself from audibly sobbing. She waited for her mother to sooth her. To help her. To tell her everything would be alright.

"You're strong. You will get through this."

It was what Zandra needed to hear. If Imogen believed she could do it, then she would. She would do it for her family. Zandra inhaled the snot back up her nose and nodded, then remembered Imogen couldn't see.

"Okay," she said, "But please—I need help."

"Jayana said she's seen *you* do Dust?"

"Yes. Just now, to everyone. But it—it doesn't mean anything, does it? They can drug test me."

There was silence on the other end that made Zandra uneasy.

"Have you taken any of the anti-anxiety medication I gave you?"

Zandra's ears started to ring.

No. It couldn't be.

But Zandra finally understood. She understood exactly why Charlotte had always been so much smarter, faster, *better*.

Charlotte was none of those things. Dust had just made her seem that way.

"Yes," Zandra found her voice saying. It didn't feel like her own. It felt like it belonged to someone else altogether.

"Then you have to say it was Zandra. Charlotte has done that before. I'm going to make a few calls and get those rumors circling right away."

Zandra's heart shattered into a million pieces.

"They won't drug test you. They'll believe you."

Zandra didn't say anything. The Dust was numbing her feelings, numbing her heart. But she *wanted* to feel the pain. She *wanted* to feel the anger. She wanted to scream. To ask Imogen why she'd chosen Charlotte and not her. To ask why she had decided to screw one of her daughters over. To ask why she had lied to her face.

To ask what had made *her* unworthy of Imogen's belief.

But Zandra instead hung up the phone, not wasting her breath.

Time slowed.

Zandra put a hand on her heart, making a personal promise. If no one else would defend her, she would do it herself. Even through the layers of pain, she knew she was worthy. She knew none of this was her fault.

She would be a scapegoat no more. Charlotte had made her decision without giving a damn about what happened to Zandra. So had Imogen.

She brushed the smeared make up out of her eyes and took off her strangling necklace, throwing it to the floor. A janitor heard the gemstones clatter on the marble and met her eyes, alarmed.

Zandra didn't care. She strutted toward the balcony and stepped up to Jayana's side, overlooking Phoenix Square.

Jayana's words, which Zandra didn't care to listen to, trailed off. Jayana stared ahead, fury radiating off of her body like heat.

Zandra looked down, taking her sweet time. The crowd had grown, though it was nothing like it had been the day before.

She heard her name whispered, along with the word *switched*. Imogen must have gotten her call through. One day she would figure out how, within two minutes, Imogen had convinced the entire city that Alexandra Julia Galvin had a nasty Dust addiction.

"Yes," Zandra said, silencing the whispers, "I have taken Dust. But you know why?"

The people were enraptured.

"Because you all expect me to be perfect. And I'm not. No one is. What do you think really happened at the Season Opener?"

There weren't even murmurs. Zandra had the attention of the entire crowd.

"I *broke*. Because I didn't want to do *this*—" She gestured at the crowd, "Anymore."

She stared, taking in as many faces as she could.

"So screw Ignis for making us have to do everything right just so we aren't forced to be with a stranger for the rest of our lives! Screw Pairing!"

Her words echoed, bouncing off the buildings, reverberating into the world. Warning Zandra that there was no going back, as if hoping she would understand the consequence of what she had just done if she heard them repeated back enough times.

The silence that followed was even more deafening. But Zandra didn't stick around to listen to it. She briefly met Jayana's wide eyes, then turned.

Tiberius was standing halfway across the balcony behind her. Zandra almost had to take a step back when she saw his face. His brown eyes spilled with love, warmth, respect.

Zandra had no idea how much she needed that right now.

Before she could move, he met her at the edge of the balcony.

"I choose you," he breathed.

Zandra gaped, not believing her ears.

Tiberius raised his voice. "I choose you, Charlotte Rachel Galvin. I choose you to be my wife. Will you have me?"

Tiberius had never used her. He didn't need her. He admired her bravery. And, though she had only known him for a few short days, he had already proven himself more trustworthy than her own family.

He picked her despite her imperfections. Despite that she was likely about to be hated by most of Ignis.

Despite the fact that she had just acted like an Unruly.

And, despite everything that she had just said—or maybe because he hadn't used the word *Pair*—Zandra found herself nodding.

"Yes. I will."

32

One didn't remember his name before the Council.

He had been Five. Two. Then One. And One he had stayed.

He needed to get rid of these pesky twins so he could remain that way. He'd worked too hard.

He'd been the Highest Pointer of his year. He'd learned to read lips. He had done his duty to the future of the human race by producing a High Society son who had given him a now-teenage grandchild.

Being One was his life. Protecting Pairing was his mission.

He'd been One for so long, he was the only one who knew where Dust came from. He was the only one who knew the true reason for the war with the Union. He was the only one who knew that when Ignis' technology broke down, it would be gone forever. It was why the final memory download for the Unruly was during Final Chance, and not *on* Unruly—it was too risky to unplug and transport the technology. A risk that wasn't worth taking just to download the Unruly's final moments before entering the simulation. Especially when no one even knew *how* to access the citizens' downloaded memories anymore—they only knew how to upload the memories into the simulation. And Four monitored the Unruly closely on the boat ride, ensuring they didn't speak with each other, to keep it as clean as possible.

It would make One's life so much easier if he could access the memories. So he studied. He read. He quizzed the smartest people on Princeps. If the remaining engineers didn't have the knowledge to reproduce something as simple as *cameras*, they certainly weren't going to figure out how to duplicate the more advanced technology.

He wasn't making much progress, but he would keep trying until the day he died.

Ignis needed him. And if he wasn't One or, heavens forbid, on the Council at all, he didn't even know the name he'd return to.

Imogen and her twins were a danger to the order he'd devoted his entire life to. Imogen knew it. Three knew it. Five knew it, though to a lesser extent. Pairing was the only thing keeping the human race from extinction. Genetic matching led to higher birth rates. It gave the people purpose, and kept them orderly. It was a perfect system, greater than any individual person.

Thankfully, One had the power to destroy the Galvins. He just needed to take them all out with one blow.

Yes, Charlotte was already coming to Princeps with a prince on her arm, but her downfall was imminent after she'd shot herself in the foot with her speech against Pairing. But the *symbol* of Charlotte was more meaningful than Charlotte herself, and would need to be disassembled carefully.

Unruly was necessary for the survival of the human race. When the chosen Unruly were brought back to Ignis to be Paired when there was an odd number of graduates, when someone's Pair died, or when someone didn't have a genetic Pair in their class, their memories were wiped—but not the feelings. Not the lack of hope.

And that lack of hope would convince them not to doom their children to Unruly by birthing Impaired children. Because the Impaired didn't get a second chance go back to Ignis. It had worked for generations, and would continue to, so long as he fixed the technology reproduction issue.

Four was easily bendable. Two was imprisoned. Three was only in the Council because One let him be.

Five was *his*.

Which was how One found himself knocking on Five's mansion door the moment he knew she'd be back from her chaotic day at Phoenix Palace.

One had also just returned—he'd announced to the mainland through gritted teeth that Tiberius and Charlotte would be the Pair that joined High Society as early as that night.

One hadn't *wanted* to, but he had to keep his alliance with Luxor intact. Ignis needed Luxor more than Luxor needed them. A little Dust, and some consulting on implementing Pairing? Luxor's military protection from the Union and retrieval of Ignis' Impaired was hardly a fair exchange. One didn't need Akil to decide he was going to use his military *against* Ignis—he'd bit his tongue and befriended the man because he couldn't imagine what would happen if Akil decided he'd have a more fruitful alliance with the Union.

So he'd given the speech. Charlotte would arrive in under an hour, when he'd give another speech in Main Square.

Five was flustered when she answered. One didn't blame her. Her position was the one in jeopardy—she was the lowest in the hierarchy and One could take it away with a snap of his fingers.

"I would like to speak to you privately."

"Here? Lynx is home, somewhere," Five said.

The only relevancy Lynx had was that she was the *only* one of the fifty six living Conquest winners who hadn't *technically* won the Conquest. She knew more than One would have liked her to, but thankfully the Unruly weren't the sharpest spears in the armory. She was just Five's arm candy. Heavens knew she needed it to make up for her own lack of beauty.

Despite the risks, retrieving Lynx worth it for the power he now held over Five.

"That's fine," One said, stepping around her into the foyer and sitting in one of the chairs near the base of the stairs. "Sit."

Five obeyed. She always did.

"You are aware that your position is in jeopardy in the upcoming election, I'm sure."

Five scowled, but nodded.

"I want you to be my Two," he told her, "And then One when I retire."

She was the perfect candidate to do his dirty work. If things went wrong, it would be easy to manipulate the situation so only she fell, and she hadn't been playing the game long enough to know how to stop that from happening.

"I'm flattered," Five said, keeping her voice neutral. But One could tell by her higher cadence that she was elated by his words.

"Imogen doesn't care about the future of humanity. She doesn't even care about her children. She only cares about herself. We can't have a leader like that."

Five opened her mouth, probably to point out that Imogen was imprisoned, but then thought better of it. "So how can I help?"

"We can't let Zandra win the Conquest. And I have too many things to attend to...to *monitor* the situation."

Their interests were aligned, and One knew Five wanted nothing more than to make sure Zandra Galvin never set foot on Princeps.

33

All Five wanted was to be freed from her debt to One, even though it would never happen.

She should have been kicked off the Council for what she did last year. But One was smart. She wanted to choose the Conquest winner because she wanted her for herself? Fine—but at what price?

Five didn't even know, just that her decision got more expensive each day.

She pretended to mull One's words as they sat in her foyer. "What are you proposing?"

"Full discretion, firstly."

"Of course."

"I have access to the simulation program that allows the admin—in this case, you—to add external obstacles to make it harder for the user—Zandra—to trust her Pair and get out."

"I assume," Five said, "The others on the Council can't know about this."

They could overthrow him if they discovered what he was

doing. She assumed that's why he was having *her* do the dangerous part.

Will we be even after this?

Five knew better.

One nodded curtly. Five said, "And how do I make sure they don't see me down there?"

"You're a smart woman," One said, "Figure it out." He slipped her a piece of paper with her instructions.

Two minutes later, One was gone.

She had a rough plan of what she would do. She'd create a physical obstacle that would push Zandra toward Enid and away from Harris.

Five just needed an alibi. So she went to the only person she trusted in all of Ignis.

Lynx had been behaving strangely since the start of Pairing Season. Five knew to leave Lynx alone in these moments, but Five's patience was running thin and her anxiety growing thick.

Five had struggled during her Pairing Season. All her potential Pairs were far too shallow. They cared more about her too-big teeth and lopsided eyes than the fact that she was absolutely brilliant.

She had known long before that she would never feel anything for men. Even the one boy who genuinely seemed interested bored Five out of her mind. Five had chosen him as her Pair anyway, but only spoke to him when they had to attend events together. Five got the sense that he was happy in his Princeps mansion—he wouldn't have been able to join High Society without her, after all—so Five didn't feel guilty.

But watching Lynx in the simulation...it had only taken Five a day to fall for her. When Lynx hadn't even *tried* to win the Conquest, Five took matters into her own hands.

She'd almost lost everything for it, but One had been merciful. Five had assumed it was because she'd only been on the

Council for two weeks, and in High Society for a month. She was still learning.

Now she knew that Lynx's retrieval had been the most expensive decision of her life.

Lynx had taken a week to mull Five's proposal to be her unofficial Pair over while Five wooed her, before finally moving in.

But lately Five sensed Lynx straying, as if Lynx were falling out of love with her. Had Lynx decided that she no longer wanted to look at Five's hooked nose? She'd *never* ask—her appearance was the one thing she was insecure about, and if people knew that, it would be used against her. Vulnerabilities were exploited in politics. So Five made sure no one ever knew what mattered to her, or frightened her, or made her happy, or kept her up at night. She never went to visit her parents in the LPC. It was best that people forget she came from there altogether. She'd already made her lack of dislike of the Unruly clear through her affiliation with Lynx—the last thing she needed was everyone knowing her mother had lived on the island as well.

It made life lonely, but safer.

Five trusted Lynx—all the *what ifs* were in her head. It was what brought her to Lynx's study, where she knew her Pair liked to write and think.

Only Five knew Lynx was an adept poet. She'd only read a few of her pieces, but almost half of them had brought her to tears. It was how Lynx coped.

Five knocked gently. "Lynx? Can I come in?"

Lynx had spent the last night in the study, "writing feverishly." Five didn't know what that meant, but there had been scattered pieces of paper around the room.

No response came from within, so Five knocked harder. "Lynx?"

Another long moment passed before Lynx opened the door

with unkempt hair and smelly breath. She was in the same clothes as the day before.

"Hi!" she said, mania laced in her too-peppy tone.

"What are you doing?"

"Writing," Lynx opened the door further, inviting her in. It was even messier than it had been in the morning.

"Are you okay?" she asked, more than a little concerned.

"Yeah, yeah," Lynx said, "I'm just...in the flow."

"Have you been outside? Or even out of this room?"

"Yeah, a few times. I'm fine, don't worry."

Five did worry and didn't believe her.

"How's your day?" Lynx asked, tidying up some of the papers that were scattered throughout the room. Five moved to help her.

"You heard that Tiberius and Charlotte are getting Paired, I'm sure."

Lynx dropped the stack of papers she was holding, eyes widening. Based upon *that* reaction, she hadn't. "What happened?"

Five filled her in, and Lynx shook her head. Five was irritated to see that she was impressed.

"Only she could admit to taking Dust and somehow get an invite to High Society in the meantime."

Though Pairing Season wasn't officially over, tonight would come the announcement that Tiberius and Charlotte would be moving to Princeps and joining their brethren in High Society. The other teens would stay in Phoenix Palace, still monitored by Five, until the season was officially over. Five would be off to the sidelines, doing unimportant work, while the others, including Charlotte, prepared for the election.

"She's an issue!" Five protested.

"Why?"

"If Charlotte ousts me from the Council, we are even *further* from helping other people like us," Five said, "Why can't you see that?"

Lynx kept picking up papers, purposefully avoiding Five's eye. Why was she so determined to hide her thoughts? They were supposed to share their hopes and dreams and fears.

But Lynx never did. Her guard was up, now more than ever.

"Maybe she would be *on* our side, if we talked to her," suggested Lynx.

Ridiculous.

Lynx read her sour expression. "You told me that Zandra is one of us. And Charlotte loves Zandra more than anyone."

"Last I heard, Zandra was choosing *Harris*," Five said, "If she can just choose to be like everyone else, she isn't *one of us*."

It was an argument they'd had before. Five stood beside her point, but she could feel the conversation growing heated. Lynx scowled, "We should be helping her, not allowing someone like Harris to win, who shouldn't have even gone there in the first place."

Lynx had a point, but Five was in this for the long game. For the greater good. They weren't going to be able to help *every* Unruly. And if Zandra was the one who was sacrificed, Five wouldn't lose sleep over it.

"I need your help," Five said, changing the subject.

Lynx took a deep breath, and Five took Lynx's hands, feeling her drifting. Was Lynx trying to anchor herself to Five despite the current, or was she willingly allowing the waves to sweep her out with the tide?

"I will always help you, Five." She meant it, easing Five's worries.

"One actually just gave me an assignment," Five said, watching Lynx to gauge her reaction. Lynx gave none, so Five continued, "And I need you to be my alibi, if things go wrong."

"Of course." She squeezed Five's hands, and Five felt a wave of appreciation. Here she was, questioning Lynx's devotion, as Lynx promised to cover for her with no hesitation.

Maybe Five herself was the problem. It was a thought she'd never had before—about anything—and one only Lynx could make her ask.

"What are you doing for him?" Lynx asked as Five dropped her hands and prepared to go to the security room.

"It's best if you don't know," Five said, heading for the door. "Thank you, Lynx. I love you."

Before Five reached the door, Lynx murmured, "Five."

Five glanced back at her, hoping—

"Don't get involved with the twins. It won't end well." Five couldn't stop her nostrils from flaring. She just kept the course, barely hearing Lynx's final words of, "Be careful."

Lynx should have known by now that Five was always careful.

34

If Five were a careful person, she wouldn't have let Lynx know what she was planning. How could someone who'd graduated with double the academic points be so much stupider than her?

It was easy to piece together that Five was off to hack Charlotte's simulation. One must have given her access.

Lynx had to warn Maddox before Five arrived.

Why couldn't Five realize that the Galvins were much better allies than enemies? Why was she so insecure that she had to feel threatened?

Lynx packed her simulation equipment into a backpack, just in case she needed it, and waited until she heard Five leave before sprinting down the stairs.

Five wouldn't run. She had to look casual as she walked through the streets for the passersby. And she wouldn't take the most direct route—she avoided even walking past the Princeps Clinic until she had to go in for her monthly fertility visit.

Lynx would beat her there.

She sprinted through side streets, weaving through the few people she saw out and about.

Until she turned a corner and rammed into a man.

"Sorry!" Lynx said, stumbling. She made to move around him—

"Lynx!" Daniel Solace stood before her. "Don't be sorry, I'm glad—"

"I don't have time," she said. But Daniel grabbed her shoulders—not hard enough that she couldn't break free, but enough to know that he wouldn't be denied.

"*Please*," he said, "Just a minute. I'm begging you."

"I don't *have* a minute," she said, shoving his hands away.

"I *need* to get Paired with you!"

"That isn't my problem."

He stood in her path, not budging. "It's *going* to be your problem in four years, Lynx. Don't make me get Paired with an old hellish narcissist. We went through the same thing—"

But they hadn't. The other Conquest winners didn't know it was a simulation. They didn't know they'd been manipulated into thinking Pairing was the only way.

"Fine. If you get out of my way, we'll sit down and talk for real. I swear it."

Daniel stepped aside and Lynx bolted past.

She had two minutes at most. She took the stairs three at a time to the security room and scanned Five's fingerprint with shaking fingers.

Maddox was inside, electrodes on his brain. Sweat soaked through his shirt and he struggled to focus on her.

"Lynx?"

She wondered what it was like to be Charlotte. To control her. It didn't sound pleasant.

"Five is coming. To mess with Unruly. You have to stop her."

Maddox closed his eyes. Doing...*something* in the simulation. His outfit indicated he'd been here the whole night, even when Charlotte was sleeping, watching just in case. "She's...almost there."

"And it will all be for nothing if Five isn't stopped," Lynx said, "So stop her. I'll take over."

Sweat dripped down Maddox's brow. He didn't brush it away. He didn't move at all.

"I...can't do that to her," he mumbled, a hint of protectiveness in his voice.

"You don't have a choice." She respected that he didn't trust her enough to just hand over the job. "If she sees this, it's over."

Maddox's eyes glazed. Lynx nervously realized that that would be her soon. Based on Maddox's appearance, it wasn't going to be easy.

Lynx waited for the electrodes. Maddox must've needed to find an appropriate moment to pass the baton to her.

When he did, he acted quickly, as if woken from a long hibernation. He unclipped the electrodes from his head and put them onto hers. Then he lifted the helmet and ushered her under. Lynx barely registered the sweat-soaked padding.

"Say as little as possible," he said, "Make it seem like she's in love with Harris."

"I know." There was no time for doubt. No time to wonder whether or not she'd be able to do it.

Maybe that was good. Best not overthink.

"It's hard. Very hard," Maddox warned.

"Okay."

"I'll be back as soon as I can. Just hold on until then."

He pressed a button on the computer and Lynx found herself torn between two worlds. If she opened her eyes, she could still see the outline of the security room.

She closed them.

Then she was Charlotte.

The anxiety hit her like a tsunami.

Screams for release. Pain and horror and a lack of control.

Lynx was blinded by it. Charlotte wanted to wail for help, wanted to let Harris know that this wasn't *her*.

It took every ounce of Lynx's strength not to let that happen. She'd never felt anything so potent before. She wasn't sure how Charlotte could stand it at all.

Lynx's body temperature rose. After a few moments of adapting to the pain, Lynx was able to focus on what Charlotte was looking at. Harris. He was shoveling rocks out of the pathway, clearing a path through a cave-in.

A stick of dynamite was beside him.

He turned toward her and spoke. His voice sounded far away, as if underwater. "What are we going to tell them when it's both of us?"

Attempting to speak made Lynx vomit in her mouth. *What's happening!* she —*Charlotte*—wanted to say.

It must have been horrible, being trapped in your own body. What she was doing was unforgivable—if Charlotte knew, would she be able to look at her the same way? If she knew *any* of the things Lynx had done?

"We'll tell them it's both of us," Lynx said in a voice that wasn't her own, "And that we're going to be Paired."

Harris looked at her. Lynx swallowed Charlotte's cry.

"What about Enid?" Harris asked.

Charlotte's emotions cut through Lynx's pain like a knife. They were twisted and contradictory—she wanted to run *from* Enid, but also *toward* her. Enid would understand that something was wrong. Like she'd be able to break through to her.

She wanted Enid here more than she wanted Harris. Much more.

It made Lynx's heart stop. She felt her control slipping, lost in the maze of Charlotte's feelings, her own emotions bleeding into Charlotte's, until she wasn't sure where hers began and Charlotte's ended. She needed to get back in touch—needed to find her way out—

But Charlotte's will grew stronger. She pushed back. Pressure built up in Lynx's head, behind her eyes, and just when she thought she couldn't take it anymore...

Her head split open and she slipped off the cliff of Charlotte's mind.

"Help," Charlotte gasped, "I'm not—this isn't real!"

"What?"

Lynx could no longer feel Charlotte's consciousness. She'd been ousted, merely a bystander. Charlotte had won.

Which meant everything was ruined.

L ynx didn't know what to do.

She hadn't realized how ill prepared she was for everything to go wrong.

She couldn't even begin to formulate a plan. They needed Charlotte to get into High Society if they wanted to see any change. She needed to jump into action to make that happen—

But all she could think about were Charlotte's mixed emotions toward Enid.

Lynx had never felt that way about someone before. Infatuated. Obsessed. Bewitched. But also terrified. Nauseated. Like if Enid touched her, her skin would crawl and she would need to scrub herself raw.

Why? And how? How could Charlotte feel all of that at the same time?

It unsettled her.

Focus, Lynx ordered herself. Could this be undone like Maddox had done before? What could she do right now?

Five was going to do everything in her power to get into the security room. They wouldn't be able to control Charlotte through the Conquest unless they took Five out of the picture.

Did Lynx have it in her to lock Five up? *Yes*—but that would lead to an entirely different domino effect.

Since she no longer had the ability to do anything except watch, Lynx paced and pulled out her phone, about to make an emergency call to a woman whose name she didn't even know—

"I'm here on behalf of One," Five's muffled voice sounded from outside the door, "to make sure everything is running smoothly."

Lynx froze, the call forgotten. She knew that tone. Five suspected something was fishy.

Maddox replied, "And *I* told *you* that everything is under control. This is my job, Five."

"Go take a shower, Three," Five shot back, "You need one."

Lynx pulled up footage of the hallway security camera. Maddox blocked Five's path to the door.

"Move, Three," Five ordered.

"If One wants to supervise, he can come himself."

"Get," Five growled, sending a shiver down Lynx's spine, "Out. Of. My. Way."

A glint in the camera behind Maddox's back, out of Five's sight. A knife.

He wouldn't.

Would he?

If Lynx went out there, would he hurt her too? Would Five kill *him*?

Lynx had a single moment. There were only bad options and no time to think them through.

She couldn't let Five get hurt. Not on her watch.

One's password—the simulation's admin password—had already been inserted by Maddox. She had full control.

So Lynx prayed to the heavens, to whatever god looked upon her, and did what she knew there would be no coming back from.

She inserted the other code she'd been given by the nameless woman and pressed, *GO LIVE*.

Unruly was live-streamed to all of High Society.

35

Charlotte ruminated over every strange occurrence on Unruly.

The prick in her arm, followed by suddenly "feeling good". Someone injected her with Dust. Her anxiety not turning her body blue. The lack of control—someone was using *her* body to get what *they* wanted.

It was terrifying not knowing *who* or *what* or *why*. She didn't need answers—she just needed to be resilient.

Was *this* the Conquest? Having the mental strength to hold onto control?

It didn't matter. She just needed to stop it. So despite her harrowing panic, Charlotte fought as if her life depended on it. Because it very well may.

There was a lapse in the grip on her body while Harris dug through the tunnel's cave in—where Lynx had escaped. She pushed harder, trying to move her hands. To speak. She was so close...

The pressure came back.

But this time it was different. This consciousness pushing

against her own didn't know what it was getting into. It was startled, with curiosity and a drop of pity.

Charlotte could beat it. She knew it. She'd never met a game she couldn't win, especially when her opponent felt something as demeaning as *pity*.

Charlotte had spent too much of her life being used. That was over. No one would ever use her again.

Harris turned toward her from where he was digging. Charlotte could barely hear his words over her invisible battle. "What are we going to tell them when it's both of us?"

Charlotte screamed, but nothing came out. She tried to push air out of her diaphragm to form her own words.

But Charlotte's voice still wasn't her own. "We'll tell them it's both of us. And that we're going to be Paired."

"What about Enid?"

Enid. What would Enid think about this? Would she have realized what was going on inside of Charlotte? How didn't Harris know?

She longed for Enid, but knew it was good that she wasn't here. Enid wouldn't understand—she would tell Charlotte she was making excuses by leaving.

Or she would believe Charlotte. Believe that Unruly wasn't what it seemed.

Maybe Enid would've been able to help Charlotte in a way that Harris couldn't. Maybe she would have understood.

But Charlotte didn't actually *want* to see Enid again. She had been too vulnerable. She had let Enid see too much of her.

The tension of her opponent slacked. There was a distraction.

Charlotte jumped on it, using every fiber in her heart. She pushed internally, punching, pulling, concentrating, searching for herself. She tried with all of her might to clench her hands into fists...

And they did.

Then it was over. The pressure within her head—her soul—disappeared.

Charlotte collapsed on the ground, struggling for air as Harris hurried toward her, concerned.

"What's wrong?" Harris asked.

Charlotte dry heaved onto the ground, her shirt lifting as she crouched on her hands and knees.

Her eyes settled on her stomach. Something looked wrong—

There was a mole on her stomach. *Zandra's* mole.

Charlotte gaped at it. "I'm not—this isn't *real*."

"What?"

Charlotte took a long moment to collect herself, straightening to conceal her—Zandra's?—mole. "This isn't real," she repeated.

"I'm...not following."

"Something about this is wrong," Charlotte rasped, leaning on him, "Unruly isn't...actually what we think it is."

"Well, what is it, then?"

"I don't know! But we have to get out of here. Get *everyone* out of here."

Harris just blinked, bewildered. But he was bright—he'd understand soon.

"We *are* getting out of here," Harris said, "We're winning the Conquest."

"I don't think this is how we win the Conquest."

"I'm still not following."

Charlotte wished she felt well enough to figure out exactly what was going on. She wished she had Dust to help her through it.

"This is fake. And my mother...she knew it. She knew it, and she sent me here. Imogen is a monster and Ignis is being lied to. Because they're afraid they'll lose power without Pairing."

The Unruly were certainly being watched. She wouldn't have been possessed otherwise. Charlotte's skin crawled. She'd said that she and Zandra had switched. It didn't matter if only Harris and Enid knew about the swap, but *everyone*? The Council?

"It's not safe for us here," Charlotte said to Harris, "They're listening."

"Ch—"

"*Zandra*," Charlotte interrupted, trying not to do even more damage.

"Okay." He was doing his best to hold it together for her, but she could sense his frustration, "Who's listening to us, Zandra?"

At this point, they had already heard her say it was fake, so what more did it matter? "They did something to us. With the brain scans."

Harris touched her arm, concerned, but Charlotte pulled it back. "Did something fall on your head when the wall collapsed?"

Harris wasn't going to understand. Which meant that the task was her burden to carry alone, as it always was and always would be. And despite the weight, Charlotte would stand to bear it.

36

Charlotte's simulation was broadcast on every screen and monitor in Princeps.

Harris' face—from Charlotte's point of view—stared down every person in High Society. Lynx rushed behind the desk in the security room, ignoring Harris' face staring down at her on every screen.

An alarm beeped, drawing Five and Maddox inside, neither injured.

"What the *hell* is going on?" Five shouted, "What did you do, Three!?"

"This wasn't me!" Maddox said, panic in his voice.

That was when it dawned on Lynx—this had *not* been the right move. No. It had been a very, very bad move. Perhaps the worst she could have made.

She'd protected Five, but at what cost?

"But we have to get out of here," Charlotte's voice whispered through the speakers. "Get *everyone* out of here.."

At the cost of *Charlotte*.

"What the actually living hell!" Five screamed over whatever Harris said in response.

Lynx put her knees to her chest, thoughts racing.

"I don't think this is how we win the Conquest," Charlotte's voice said.

"Now!" Five snarled, "Stop this, Three!"

"I *am!*" Maddox shot back. Lynx could hear him typing at the computer.

"This is fake. And my mother," Charlotte said, "She knew it. She knew it, and she sent me here. Imogen is a monster and Ignis is being lied to."

Five and Maddox were quiet, as if time had frozen. Lynx could barely hear the clattering of Maddox's fingers on the keyboard over the thumping of her heart.

"Because they're afraid," Charlotte whispered, "they'll lose power without Pairing."

The calmness of Five's next words startled Lynx further, "Stop, Maddox."

"I beg your—"

"I want to hear what she has to say."

Charlotte was digging Zandra's grave. Enough damage had already been done that Five was going to let Charlotte nail her sister's coffin before she shut the broadcast down.

"No," Maddox said. He stopped typing. He must've been about to stop it—

Five attacked. She rammed Maddox into the wall, the chair behind him clattering to the floor beside Lynx's hiding place.

Lynx peered out from beneath the desk to find Maddox pinned, Five's hands wrapped around his throat.

Maddox was strong, but not as strong as Five. He fought with the heart of a lion, and managed to free a hand—

Maddox punched Five in the face.

Lynx rolled out from under her desk. She couldn't watch

Maddox get killed, and she cared too much about Five to see her get hurt.

Five didn't loosen her grip, even as Lynx yelled, "Five, stop!"

Five grunted in surprise. Charlotte's voice seeped into the back of Lynx's brain through the broadcast, though she didn't process the words. "They did something to us," Charlotte said, "with the brain scans."

Maddox and Lynx locked eyes. He pleaded for help.

Lynx did what she had to do, even though she didn't want to. She charged into Five, grabbing and thrusting her away from Maddox. Maddox immediately recovered and hit the *STOP BROADCAST* button.

Harris' face disappeared off the screen.

Five faced off against Lynx, trembling with rage. Not just rage —betrayal. Lynx swallowed her guilt. She and Five were on different sides of this war. It was for the greater good. If anyone could understand that, it was Five.

"Did you do this?" Five demanded, her voice cracking.

Lynx didn't know what to say. Didn't know what she *could* say. Except...

"Help me," she whispered, "Help me do away with Pairing."

"You—you lied to me. About everything."

"Not everything." But even Lynx didn't fully believe her own words.

"I don't understand," Five murmured.

Maddox stepped in between them. "Lynx has obviously been tampering with Unruly and we need to put her in custody."

"You're not putting her in custody," Five snapped, "*You* were the one who was monitoring."

"You assaulted your superior, Five."

Maddox had a point. Five had a point.

Lynx had nothing.

She said the only thing that might save her. "We are *all* going to be screwed if we're found here. So let's just pretend that none of this happened and run while we can."

Lynx's words rang false. Five scoffed, fighting back tears.

Lynx had *never* seen Five cry. She'd thought Five incapable. "Get out," Five snarled at Lynx and Maddox.

"I'm on duty," Maddox said, "I will stay."

"Your funeral," Five said. Then she strutted out the door. She couldn't bear to be seen like this. That was the only reason she'd leave.

There was so much Lynx wanted to say. She wanted to call after her. To explain herself. To get Five on her side. Because she *could* get Five on her side—she just needed to make her understand. But understanding took listening, and that was something Five would not do right now.

The moment Five was out of earshot, Maddox hissed, "What have you done?!"

"I made a mistake," she said, remembering his knife. Would he have used it on Five? Would he use it on *her*?

"One will be here soon," Maddox said, "Just...go."

"What about you?"

"I will deal with this. Say we were hacked."

"By the Union?"

Maddox put his hands through his hair. He looked like he'd aged a decade overnight. "I'll think of something." He was too calm. Too quiet.

Lynx stared at him, her feet glued to the ground.

"Stop trying to help, Lynx," Maddox said, "You've made things bad enough."

But Lynx couldn't stop. Not when she had mistakes to correct.

37

The announcement that Tiberius and Charlotte would be the Pair to join High Society came via One shortly after Tiberius' Pairing proposal.

Tiberius hadn't let go of her hand since Zandra had said yes. Zandra didn't mind. She felt comfortable with him. Safe. As safe as she *could* feel with anyone after her concept of trust had been completely shattered.

Zandra didn't know how long it would take to rebuild. If it was even possible.

She stood numbly at Tiberius' side, anchoring herself to his warm hand, enjoying the brush of his crwth callouses against her palm. She was coming down from the Dust, her brain returning to its normal speed, her stress more acute. But she liked being sober. She appreciated her mind at its natural speed.

Jayana passed them, looking away. Zandra felt nothing. No guilt, no regret, no pity, no anger. At least she hadn't made the mistake of trusting Jayana. That'd been Charlotte's fault.

After One's speech, Tiberius and Zandra paraded through Ignis' streets. It wasn't the usual merry event that she had witnessed in prior years. Zandra noticed the scowls. The mutters. The whispers.

She was grateful for Tiberius' guard, Leon.

She couldn't wait to get out of there. Not that she was sure she was going to anything better.

At least she would be closer to saving Charlotte. She couldn't wait to rescue Charlotte and tell her *just* how infuriated she was.

But now, switching places didn't feel quite right. Not when she was with Tiberius. It was going to be harder to let go than she was telling herself.

She had to give up her happiness for Charlotte, which she vowed to never do again. Not that this contentment was maintainable. Her relationship with Tiberius was built off a lie.

When would he discover that he'd been Paired with the wrong sister?

There was no reason for her to stay here. She *had* to go Unruly. If she hated it, she could win the Conquest, and come back and watch Charlotte and Tiberius live happily ever after.

So many great options.

She focused on boarding the ferry. She breathed in the humid salty air and washed Imogen and Charlotte from her mind.

Zandra's spirits couldn't help but be lifted. She hadn't been on the water since she had been transported to the Academy as a child. The wind whipped through her hair.

Zandra made her way to the stern of the ship and watched as Ignis grew smaller in the distance. She looked at the horizon and saw farther into the Barrenlands than she'd ever been able to see before.

Tiberius joined her and flashed his lopsided smile. "I like this choice."

"What?"

"Not standing at the bow."

"I just...want to see how small it really is. When we're not engulfed in it."

"I'll be honest. I didn't particularly like Ignis."

"Neither did I."

They stood in comfortable silence, their shoulders touching as they leaned against the railing.

"I've been waiting to leave for as long as I can remember," Zandra murmured.

"Really?" His big brown eyes were so curious. So lost in her, like she was the only person in the world. The only person he cared about.

Before she knew what she was doing, she had grabbed his face and pulled it toward her own. Their lips touched. Zandra's heart soared, and a giddiness spread through her body. She allowed herself to be lost in the moment, to bask in his closeness, until he pulled away.

"I know we have a lot of work to do," he said, "A lot of trust to build...and to rebuild. But I'm willing to do it. To fight for us."

The lightness left Zandra's body. He would hate her if he knew. *She* hated what she was doing to him. *Could* she and Charlotte just switch back when Zandra rescued her? Would Tiberius know the difference? How *wouldn't* he?

Tiberius glanced at their trunks packed on the side of the ship, then motioned for Zandra to wait. A moment later, he reappeared with a long wrapped parcel.

"I had this made for you on Luxor," he said, "I meant to give it to you sooner, but now feels right."

Zandra swallowed and opened it. Inside was an intricate, beautiful crwth bow not unlike the one that was fastened to Tiberius' instrument strap.

"Carved from Luxor's finest pernambuco, by our best carpenter," Tiberius said proudly. "It also shoots these tiny arrows." He opened a hidden compartment on the bottom, revealing a few darts inside.

"I—I love it," Zandra managed, barely able to keep her voice from shaking.

You're just like Imogen, a voice in Zandra's head whispered.

She took the bow and hung it around her shoulder, exactly how he wore his. He beamed, glee radiating off his body.

Zandra hoped he wouldn't blame Charlotte. That he would place all the blame on Zandra, so he and Charlotte could start anew.

It would be painful for Zandra, but she would be okay. She had lived her entire existence for others until now—this was the final sacrifice before she reclaimed her life for herself.

"I...will fight for us too," Zandra said, almost choking on her own words. "But first I have to find the tunnel."

"*We* have to," Tiberius said, taking her hands and placing them in his own. "We're a *we* now. And we will. Together."

What it was like to be an individual? An "*I*"?

"Would you like to go to the bow now?" Tiberius asked.

Ignis was far enough away that Zandra could see the Barrenlands surrounding the entire city. Maybe looking forward would be better. Tiberius led her by the hand past the few crew members to the front of the ship.

Would her childhood memories of Princeps match its reality? Would it feel familiar, as if she were returning home, or completely foreign?

She would go Unruly before she could figure it out.

Zandra inhaled the ocean air, still grasping Tiberius' hand. She took a picture in her mind and willed this moment to last forever.

But forever could only last so long. And when the end came, no matter which path Zandra took, her heart was going to be shattered.

She should've been more careful. But she'd already come this far—it was too late to stop caring about Tiberius. May as well enjoy her last moments.

"Do you remember Princeps well?" Tiberius asked.

"Not really," Zandra replied, "It's all gotten murky. The memories and the rumors blended together."

"I think coming to Ignis was similar," Tiberius said, staring at the colorful architecture of Princeps. "I knew so much about it, had looked at so many pictures, but I didn't *really* know anything about it." He paused for a moment, and Zandra knew what was coming next, "Kind of like how I felt meeting you."

"What surprised you?" Only to let her sister know how to behave before Tiberius' memories of Zandra were replaced with the real Charlotte. Until he didn't know the difference.

"Your humility. I thought you would have a bit of a superiority complex. How could you not?"

Zandra laughed.

"And your boldness. You don't follow the rules, despite your points indicating you do."

It was the pieces of *her*—of Zandra—that he was surprised by. Maybe he'd known Charlotte better than he thought. Maybe he really did know everything about her.

Tiberius was grinning. "What?"

"It's just...thank you."

They stood in silence, taking in the view. Tiberius' eyes were set on Princeps, but Zandra found hers drawn toward Unruly.

She had never seen it from this angle. It was still obscured by the barren cliffs. Was Charlotte crouching in a crevice, hiding from wolves? Had she formed an alliance with any of the others, like Rae? Had she and Harris reconciled?

Zandra frowned, her eyes, mind, and heart on Unruly for the rest of the ferry ride, nervous anticipation growing.

I can always trust myself, Zandra reminded herself. She would be okay, whatever awaited her on the other side.

Zandra expected a crowd to be awaiting them, even if a silent one.

But there were only two people on the beach.

Zandra knew Lynx well enough to know that something had gone horribly wrong.

And Tiberius knew his father well enough to think the same.

38

When the broadcast cut out, silence filled Main Square. No one knew what had just happened.

One needed to claim this. They had to believe it was *he* who had let them glimpse Unruly. He made his way toward the stage, the one that Charlotte and Tiberius were to be presented on in just a few short minutes.

"Thank you all for being here," One said to his people, "The Council greatly appreciates it."

People were too confused to applaud. Their whispers met his ears, their nudges his eyes.

"I'm sure you're all wondering about the footage that was just shown."

One looked down into the crowd, trying to connect with his people. Akil pushed through the crowd, heading for the harbor. He and One needed to greet Charlotte and Tiberius. But this was the more pressing issue, even if Akil's alliance was the most important. One would be late, then apologize for this embarrassing display.

"Zandra Galvin is insane," he announced, "This was caught by our monitors."

Most of the crowd were appeased, but some were not buying it. One could see it in their eyes. Maybe it was the way the view had been from Zandra's eyes—blinking when she blinked, the view shifting whenever she moved her head.

But One knew the power of mob mentality. He would just have to appeal to their emotions. "I thought it was imperative to share this troubling footage with you before the arrival of Charlotte. She will be a powerful presence in our community, but she is biased when it comes to her sister. Now you see the truth. Do not allow yourself to be brainwashed by celebrity. Especially after Charlotte's outburst earlier...I'm afraid some of her sister's madness may have rubbed off on her, if she so callously speaks ill of the system that has given her everything."

One didn't like giving statements about other people. It was bad optics. But he saw no other option here, if he wanted to nip this problem in the bud.

"Zandra's mental state has disqualified her from The Conquest," One decided, because he might as well take Zandra out of the picture while he was at it. "She will be kept on Unruly indeterminately until she is needed to be Paired with a Low-Pointer."

The crowd was difficult to read. Zandra was an Unruly Low-Pointer—which meant most of his audience didn't care whatsoever about any of this. But another group—a smaller portion—knew better than to believe Zandra was any Unruly Low-Pointer. She was an anomaly in a family of high achievers. She was the forgotten one lost in the Galvins' scandals, making her all the more interesting.

The underestimated were always the ones who launched successful sneak attacks. They were the most dangerous of all.

One would double security at the tunnel and lock down Zandra's body, lest Imogen send someone to save her.

One reminded his people of what mattered. What he believed with all his being. "We are here—happy, fed, *unable to get sick*, because of *Pairing*. We have safety and order. Those without order, without Pairing—like the Union and the Unruly—they threaten the very existence of our race. Without Pairing, we wouldn't have rebuilt after the Destruction. Without Pairing, we would degrade into chaos. We would look like the Union. Which is why it's so important to stop them before they create yet *another* Destruction.

"This is a reminder of the insanity of the Unruly. This thinking is how we die."

He reclaimed the people. A lack of choice was what kept them safe. One knew it. They knew it. The concept of Unruly gave them the illusion of autonomy, which was enough to keep them satisfied.

But this speech was a bandaid on the wound. Charlotte would find a way to publicly redeem herself. Then she'd want Zandra out of there, and set her sights on the Council to ensure it, and she'd learn Unruly was a simulation.

All with royal power on her side.

One would destroy her in due time. When he could create maximum damage. Right now, he just had to make sure today didn't go even *more* off the rails.

One scanned the lips of his people, searching for answers as he jumped off the stage and began pushing toward the harbor.

"What did she mean about it being fake?" someone mouthed.

"One was right. She wasn't stable," was the response.

"None of them are, to go there rather than getting Paired."

Satisfied, One hurried away to welcome his greatest rival onto his island.

39

The beach was a more romantic entry onto Princeps, one on which the Pairs chosen for High Society had been disembarking for decades.

Tiberius tried to help Zandra off the boat, but she shooed him away and jumped down herself.

She was too worried to enjoy the soft Princeps sand in her toes, or to take in the newness of the land. The smell of the pine trees and the cooler air were left unnoticed by Zandra.

Zandra hurried toward Lynx as Tiberius approached his father, Leon on his heels. "What happened?"

Lynx threw her arms around Zandra, squeezing tight. "You did it."

Zandra's arms hung limply at her sides. "Where's One?" she asked. He was supposed to have been waiting with his entourage.

"We have to go before he comes," Lynx whispered.

"Where?" She glanced at Tiberius, whose brow was furrowed beside his father.

"Let me just make sure Akil doesn't—"

"Lynx," Zandra said, "*What happened?*"

Where was their welcoming committee? Why was Lynx helping her?

"We have to get Charlotte out of Unruly."

Zandra gaped. Could it really be this easy? Could Lynx really be waiting to take her to her sister?

Wait.

Lynx had called Charlotte by her real name.

"You knew this whole time?" First Three, now Lynx? Did *everyone* know?

"No," Lynx said, "I just learned. But if we're getting Charlotte out, it has to be now. They're going to be upping security, if they haven't already. This is our only shot."

"Who *are* you, Lynx?" She searched Lynx's face. She looked like the friend Zandra had grown up knowing. But how *could* she be after experiencing Unruly and vouching for Pairing?

Lynx's next words knocked the air out of Zandra's lungs. "I work for the Union."

Zandra's mouth hung open.

The *Union*? The barbaric junkyard country that was always on the verge of attack?

Lynx read the horror on Zandra's face. "It isn't what we've been led to believe it is. They're—they're free there."

"You've *been* there?"

"No."

"Then—"

"The Union is the world we talked about. The first Council was so afraid of losing their power that they spread false rumors. We don't have time now, but I promise I'll explain later. We have to go save Charlotte."

"But...the war," Zandra murmured, trying to piece it together.

"They're fighting to stop Pairing, not to get more land."

Zandra's mouth hung open.

"Do you know why the Destruction actually happened?" Lynx asked.

"Well, now I'm assuming I don't."

"Because what is now Ignis already had the technology to Pair people whose offspring would have perfect immune systems. And when the last pandemic swept through the world, everyone wanted it. But the old Ignis knew it was unethical, so they didn't share it."

"And that's what caused the war. Pairing was the problem, not the solution," Zandra breathed.

"Exactly."

Zandra head spun. What should she believe?

Maybe what I want to believe.

She wanted to believe in hope. In freedom. In a better world.

A world without Pairing. Where she and Tiberius could be together. A world where no one was a High-Pointer or a Low-Pointer.

So she did.

Zandra thrust her trust issues aside. It didn't matter what Lynx had been up to, or what her agenda was. The magic words had been uttered—saving Charlotte—and Zandra needed no more.

But there were logistics. She tilted her head toward Akil, Tiberius, and Leon. "What about them?"

"That's up to you," Lynx said, "But they can't know about the Union. And we need to hurry."

"But...if they did, Akil could stop the war!"

"He knows, Zandra," Lynx said, "He's already picked his side."

Tiberius' feet were still in the water, his hair disheveled as he frowned with worry, his tunic blowing in the wind. His posture looked uncannily similar to his father's.

Zandra was blindly trusting Lynx. Would Tiberius? Should Zandra lie? What was one more with all the lies she'd already told?

Zandra hurried toward them, leaving Lynx behind her. "King Akil," she said with a bow, before addressing Tiberius. "I have to go. Will you come with me?"

"Go where?" Akil demanded, "You should go straight to your mansion after that broadcast."

Zandra filed that away. Of course another drama had unfolded.

"Of course I'll come," Tiberius said, not bothering to ask where they were going.

"Tiberius—" Akil started.

"It's done, Father," Tiberius said, "I have a Pair, just as you wanted. And I love her. I go where she goes." He gazed at Leon, "And now that I'm here, I don't need protection anymore."

He *loved* her? Yes, they had chemistry. Yes, she enjoyed being with him. But *love*?

She was doing to him what had been done to *her* by her family. She was using him as a pawn for her own benefit.

Zandra's skin grew hot. This wasn't who she wanted to be. How could she do this when she knew how painful it felt? When Tiberius said he *loved* her?

If they truly were about to save Charlotte, this could very well be their last moment together.

Tiberius took her hand and led her toward Lynx, who fidgeted impatiently. "I take it we're going with her?" he said, stepping away from Akil. Leon made to follow, but the king stopped him. "Whatever this is, my father can help us—"

"He can't. Not with this."

"He's a good man. He'd—"

"Tiberius," Zandra interrupted, "There's something you have to know."

This was the stupid move. The move that Imogen and Charlotte would never make.

It was why she had to make it. *I will not be my mother.*

"Okay." He stopped. His eyes were innocent. Hopeful. Confident in her. He grabbed her other hand. "Tell me."

"I'm not who you think I am." She made herself look at him. She needed to see the hurt—she wouldn't give herself the privilege of looking away. She didn't deserve that luxury, and she wasn't a coward.

"I don't care that you did Dust."

"It's not that."

"Or about Jaxson, if something went on between you."

"Tiberius—"

"There's nothing we can't get through, Charlotte. I believe in us—"

"I'm not Charlotte!"

Tiberius stared, unable to digest her words.

"I'm not her. But I—I don't know, I think—no, I *know*—I have feelings for you. And I'm so, so sorry. I can't hurt you any longer."

Tiberius' eyes darted from her left to right eye, unable to decide where to look, as if they represented herself and Charlotte —identical, but seeing the world from completely different angles.

"I..." he trailed off, his voice pained. It broke Zandra's heart. "You're Zandra?"

Zandra nodded. The look on his face made her wish she could take it all back. Demand that Charlotte take her own place in the palace, just so Tiberius wouldn't feel this way. "I did it for my sister."

"Why?" Tiberius said roughly, removing his hands from hers.

"Because she...she was having a—a breakdown, I guess" Zandra said, "And I—I thought I had to."

"You don't *have* to do anything. My father told me I *had to* get Paired with someone else—not you—but *I* didn't listen." His eyes were watering, and he did nothing to stop them. Zandra fought the urge to brush them away as they fell.

Her voice was hoarse. "I'm so sorry." There were no excuses. "I really, sincerely am."

Tiberius turned back around to where his father had stood moments before. But he and Leon were disappearing into the streets beyond.

"He was right," Tiberius murmured. He wiped his eyes, snorting his mucus back into his nose.

"*Guys*," Lynx called, urgency lacing her words.

A hardened look masked Tiberius' sorrow. "So where are we going? To find Charlotte?"

"You're still coming?" Zandra asked, relieved.

"If we're going to find Charlotte, yes," he said, "She is my Pair, after all."

Air refused to enter Zandra's lungs. Her blood screamed for oxygen, but there was none to be had.

Breathe, Zandra told herself, *Just breathe.*

She did. She gasped with an intense delayed reaction.

Tiberius stepped forward, as if to make sure she was okay, then thought better of it.

Zandra took one more second to recover, her heart in her throat. "Okay. Let's save her."

"Wait," Tiberius said. "The crwth."

Zandra had almost forgotten it was strewn across her back.

"I would like it back."

Zandra swallowed and unbuckled it, then passed it to him. Tiberius wordlessly strapped it beside his own.

This was the best response she could have hoped for. He still wanted to be with Charlotte. This was a win.

As they rushed toward Lynx, Zandra decided that if this was a win, she'd never be able to bear losing.

~

L ynx led them through the winding back streets at a swift run.

Zandra wanted to take in her surroundings. She wanted to see what matched with her memories from childhood.

But all she could focus on was keeping up with Lynx in her restrictive gown as Lynx delivered her instructions. "You have to get into Town Hall without being noticed."

"Is there a back entrance?"

"Not that I have access to. Use this."

Though he was in good shape, Tiberius was the slowest. Maybe it was because he refused to abandon his two crwths, even when Lynx suggested he put them down. Zandra had a feeling it was the only thing tethering him to his sanity, and there was no time to argue, so the crwths came with them.

Lynx passed a piece of plastic to Zandra. "It's Five's fingerprint. It'll scan."

"What are you going to do?" Zandra asked, stuffing it into her corset, trying not to break stride.

"Get inside," was all Lynx said, "Turn left. Go down the stairs. The tunnel will be guarded, so you can't get through that way."

"Then how are we getting there?"

"Make another left," Lynx said, "And you'll see the air duct."

"The *air duct*?"

"Crawl through there, then you'll be in Unruly. They're

gonna be on your tail. Only Charlotte can come back. You've been disqualified from the Conquest."

"Since when?"

But Lynx kept going. "You'll see the cavern. Five's fingerprint will work."

"Do I stay on Unruly?"

Lynx slowed for the shortest moment. "No. Then you sail north twenty miles. The boat is at the end of the hallway."

"What hallway?"

"We don't have time. But it's *you*. Not *we*. If we're going to fix this place, we need Charlotte here."

Zandra frowned as they ran. Princeps was much cleaner than Ignis. Not a single piece of trash lined the glimmering cobblestones. The doors were colorful, the buildings sturdy. The disparity in wealth between Princeps and Ignis' mainland was already apparent.

Ignis *needed* to be fixed. But would she really be able to part with Charlotte so soon after they reunited?

Zandra couldn't stay. And she didn't want to. She wanted to see what the Union *really* looked like. What if it was actually a paradise, with rivers and trees and lakes?

The thought intellectually excited her, but her split with Tiberius weighed on her soul, making it difficult to feel positive emotions. How long it would last? Was the weight of it even heavier for him?

Zandra heard the voices before she saw the people. Lynx stopped at the end of the alley, keeping to shadows. The sun was low—soon they'd be shrouded in darkness. Until then, they would have to remain inconspicuous.

Beyond the people was a towering building with a single bell tower. Zandra remembered it well, and seeing it again helped clarify her childhood memories. Town Hall.

Monitors were spread throughout Main Square, the flashing

bright colors catching Zandra's eyes. When she realized what was playing, goosebumps rose on her skin.

Clips of her and Tiberius. Them on the balcony. Them at the party. At Cav. Him asking her to be his Pair.

Zandra was thrown by how happy she looked. How *smitten*. She thought she'd done a better job hiding it, but she was just as taken with him as he with her.

In her peripheral, Tiberius clenched his jaw and muttered, "They're going to notice us."

"We'll need a distraction," Lynx said, "When I do it, you sneak in."

Lynx slid her backpack off one shoulder and rummaged through it. Zandra spotted equipment—electrodes and computer screens—but what Lynx pulled out was a piece of paper. She scribbled something onto it, then handed it to Zandra.

"This is for Charlotte. Give it to her when you get her out."

"What?"

Lynx didn't meet her gaze. "Just...give it to her, okay? Three will wipe the footage. Good luck. I'm proud of you."

"What are you—?"

But Lynx rushed into the crowd, shoving people out of her way, yelling, "Zandra was right! Unruly isn't real!"

Everyone turned toward her, enraptured. Zandra and Tiberius exchanged a look. Even though she had broken what was between them, she had him for a final mission.

"Now?" she asked, stuffing the piece of paper into her corset, with the other stuff she'd put in there what felt like a hundred years ago. No time to read it.

"Now," Tiberius agreed.

They hurried for the crowd, both keeping their heads down.

When they were in the throngs, Zandra found herself separating from Tiberius as the people of High Society craned their necks. She waited for him, then grabbed his hand and resumed pushing.

They were going to be in full view of everyone when they climbed the steps. But Lynx had positioned herself so that no one would be looking directly at them. Zandra couldn't quite make out Lynx's words over the thumping of her heart.

She just needed to get inside. Then she could get to Charlotte. She didn't know what she was going to say—what could even be said—when they were finally reunited, but she knew a weight would be lifted off her shoulders.

Zandra and Tiberius reached the stairs. Zandra glanced back —Lynx was swinging from a statue, her head above the crowd. No one looked their way.

"Now!" Zandra took the steps two at a time, feeling naked. The bell tower's shadow obscured them, though not well enough. All it took was a curious wandering mind and they'd be spotted and recognized.

Zandra reached the top. She spotted the scanner and pressed Five's fingerprint to it.

The door unlocked. Zandra opened it and slipped inside.

Safe. She'd made it.

Tiberius was a heartbeat behind her when someone yelled, "The prince!"

Zandra saw the heads turn through the slit door. Her heart stopped.

Tiberius didn't turn. "Save your sister, Zandra," he whispered.

"But you—" Before Zandra could finish the sentence, he pasted a warm smile on his face and turned toward the crowd, waving to them as he subtly closed the door behind him with his foot.

Silence met Zandra's ears.

She was alone. It felt right. Like fate knew she was the only one who could save Charlotte. The only one who cared to.

Her eyes adjusted to the dim light. She was in an entrance hall like one from a pre-Destruction church. It struck her that perhaps this *had* been a church pre-Destruction—it matched the description of gothic-style Roman Catholic. So she sent up a prayer and hurried to the left.

It was as Lynx had described. A staircase. She descended as quietly as she could manage.

At the bottom, she heard voices. She crept down the final steps and peeked around the corner.

The guards were facing to her side, blocking the entrance to the gray tunnel. Zandra held her breath and slowly moved left, making no sudden movements.

When she was clear and no alarm sounded, she broke into a quiet run down the barren corridor. She looked around. Lynx had said she would easily spot the duct...

When she did, she wanted to vomit.

It was halfway up the wall and she would have to shimmy on her stomach. Her legs shook. She didn't want to do this. She *couldn't*.

But she had to. She had to conquer her fears for her sister.

Zandra swallowed and tried to open the vent. It didn't budge, screwed in.

She looked around, searching her pockets. Nothing.

Then she remembered that she still had at least four pins in her hair, despite trying to remove them all. She fished through her tangles, grasped one, and shoved it into the screw. Her hands shook. She forced them to be still.

"C'mon," Zandra muttered.

She twisted. It loosened and Zandra pocketed it.

Then the other one. Within a few seconds, she had the vent opened. Her path was clear. If it could be called a path.

Zandra wiped her sweaty palms on her stupidly inefficient gown. She couldn't waste any time bemoaning her situation.

She was going to be *so* mad at Charlotte when she saw her.

Zandra hoisted herself into the vent head first. She inserted her torso, then her legs.

She couldn't turn around to close the vent. Would someone notice? Would anyone think anything of it?

Already she was hot, sweaty, and miserable. And she wasn't sure if she was imagining it, but the vent seemed to get even smaller ahead.

Zandra trudged forward on her forearms, breathing deeply to ease her anxiety. It didn't work. A balloon of panic in her stomach threatened to pop.

How was she going to get out? Would the other vent be screwed in too? What if she got stuck and couldn't go backward?

She'd think about that later. She was already in here. She just needed to keep putting one forearm in front of the other.

So that's what she did. The islands were about half a mile apart. So it would be a long crawl. Longer than Zandra cared to think about.

She passed the first vent that led below into an empty room, with bars splitting it at the center. A prison cell. Zandra looked at the size—she would've been able to escape through the vent if she had to. It relieved some of her anxiety, even though she would just be stuck behind the bars.

The next vent she passed led to a room almost identical to the first. Zandra mentally broke the crawl into sections—she'd just have to make it to the next one.

She reached the third vent. But this room, though similar in size, was different.

It was occupied. There was bed and a toilet. A blanket.

And a woman.

Zandra narrowed her eyes at the top of the woman's head.

Then her eyes widened.

It was Imogen.

Zandra felt too many things to track or keep count of. Anger. Joy. Relief. More Anger. Sadness.

She pressed her face down, not knowing what to do. She couldn't see any guards beyond the cell door.

"Mom."

Imogen's neck snapped up toward the vent.

"Charlotte?" she stammered, startled and confused, "Zandra?"

"Zandra," Zandra said, pressing her face down.

"How...?" Imogen looked up, her voice trailing off as she met Zandra's gaze. Imogen collected herself and decided she couldn't waste time on the *how*. "What are you doing?"

"I'm going to rescue Charlotte," Zandra said, "From Unruly."

"Zandra," Imogen said, meeting Zandra's eyes. "We don't have much time. If you kick out the vent, I'll catch it before it clatters. We can save Charlotte together."

The vent was too high for Imogen to reach on her own, especially without the proper tools. This was the break Imogen needed.

Zandra wondered what she looked like through the bars. She wondered if Imogen could only see the reflection of her eyes. If her mother could see the distrust on her face.

"And what will happen after that?"

"We'll figure that out when we get there."

"*We?*" Zandra scoffed. "When have *we* ever decided anything?"

"Zandra—"

"You—you used me as a doormat. A doormat for Charlotte to step on."

Imogen shook her head, so self-assured that Zandra questioned herself for a moment. "This was the only way to get both of you to Princeps."

"And why the hell did it matter if we both got to Princeps?" Zandra demanded, "I—I never wanted this! Any of it! All I wanted to know was what my options really were—"

"What do you think Final Chance is, Zandra?"

"Who the hell cares!"

"It was to *process* your memories in order to make Unruly as terrifying as possible. If I'd told you more, it would have made Unruly worse."

Zandra was too angry to be confused. "And then you tell me to claim Charlotte's addiction? What kind of mother does that?"

"Because," Imogen said, "you're the only ones who can save your people."

"What the hell are you talking about now?"

Imogen paused for a long moment, as if she were debating whether or not to shatter Zandra's world. "Why do you think I put Charlotte on Dust?"

"Because you needed her to be the best and you didn't think she could do it without cheating."

"Because she couldn't *breathe,*" Imogen said.

"No. Her anxiety was just an excuse to you."

"It wasn't anxiety."

"Well, then what was it?" Zandra snapped, patience wearing thin.

"Allergies."

Zandra barely knew what that word meant. Some pre-Destruction ailment...?

She realized just as Imogen said, "You and Charlotte. You're Impaired."

Zandra waited to feel some sort of way about it—it was a life-altering revelation. But Zandra found, even as things were pieced together, she didn't particularly *care.*

"Well, who's my father, then?" Zandra asked, emotionless. She cared about Imogen presumably cheating on Lawrence, though now wasn't the time for the conversation. When Imogen didn't respond, Zandra said, "It's Three, isn't it?"

Nothing.

Zandra scoffed and Imogen murmured, "I wanted you both to be here, and then to ask if you wanted to let the world know. To fight for the Impaired."

"It's not *asking* when you've already decided for us!" Zandra exclaimed a little too loudly. "I'm in a freaking air duct!" Imogen shushed her, but Zandra barely managed to lower her voice. "I trusted you. I thought you wanted what was best for me."

She wondered what Imogen knew about the Union. And Lynx and Unruly and everything else that had gone on.

Imogen looked down, obscuring her face to Zandra. "I want to help the Impaired! But we need all three of us in order to do that."

Zandra was unmoved. "What, you want to tell everyone that the reason you were a terrible mother is because we're Impaired?"

Imogen didn't respond.

"Thought not. And we're going to get rid of Pairing altogether. Without you."

"It's not possible."

"No one's Impaired if everyone's Impaired," Zandra pointed out, seething.

"We will sort this all out," Imogen promised, "And I swear I will make it up to you."

But Zandra shook her head. "It's a little late for that, Imogen. Have a good imprisonment."

"Zandra, please—"

"Goodbye, Mother."

"I have been trying my best, Zandra," Imogen called after as

Zandra began moving, "You can't save Charlotte. It will ruin everything!"

Zandra trudged forward, leaving Imogen's empty promises for the walls of her cell. Zandra knew that once she had the chance to properly dissect what she had just done, she would feel guilty, sad, upset. But in that moment, all she felt was empowered by taking her destiny into her own hands.

Soon the euphoric feeling was absorbed by the silence of the duct. The restriction of her dress. The coolness of the air.

She was Impaired, but she felt nothing about it. She didn't even really know what that meant. Was it why she had always felt *different*? Why she wanted something different than everyone else? Or did that have nothing to do with being Impaired?

Did this mean that when she was exposed to other Impaired people in the Union, she might get sick? Charlotte already was on Unruly—would she be healthy?

Zandra would find out soon enough.

The duct got darker.

The next vent she passed gave her a new view. One she was both relieved and terrified to see.

She was above the tunnel to Unruly.

It was translucent—a tube cutting through the deep green of the ocean, beautiful and terrifying. All it would take was a small change in pressure for the whole tunnel to explode.

Zandra's anxiety increased. She tried to distract herself from how stuck she was. How cemented in her journey. How if she got stuck, it could be days before someone found her in there, if they found her at all.

Zandra brought her mind to Charlotte. It had only been a few days, but it felt like they had been separated for millennia. Would Charlotte have changed? Would she have changed as much as Zandra had?

Somehow Zandra doubted it. She felt like a different person.

But if Unruly was as terrible as they were led to believe, how could she have not? Lynx had changed, though Zandra supposed that Lynx had been on Unruly much longer than Charlotte. And what had Imogen meant about their memories being processed?

There was the matter of how Charlotte was going to react to being Impaired.

Not well, Zandra already knew.

She wanted to sit down with Charlotte and exchange everything that had happened, but Zandra knew that—even if there was time—she wouldn't be able until she forgave Charlotte. Even after that, their friendship and sisterhood would never be the same.

Zandra's forearms chafed and burned. She wanted out. Would this tunnel ever end? Would she be crawling forever?

Thoughts of Tiberius came next. What would he have said to the crowd on those stairs? She didn't think anyone had noticed the door. What would he say about her absence?

It's not me anymore, she reminded herself. When she was out of this tube, Charlotte would take her rightful place back. At Tiberius' side.

It made Zandra's own sides ache. She despised that Tiberius could make her feel this way.

Another vent came and went. Another. Another.

Zandra looked down, glimpsing the water. Before Lynx had told her about the Union, she'd thought herself doomed to—or gifted with—a lifelong trip to Unruly. She was furious at herself for not being thrilled about her impending exile. For being hung up on Tiberius. This was her dream. This was the life she'd always wanted.

You will be grateful when you heal, she told herself.

Another vent. Another. Another.

Would this be what the Union was like? Crate after crate after crate? Or would it be beautiful and unique, no building quite the same?

Zandra tried to let her imagination run wild, but instead, all she could think about was the length of the damn air duct.

She tried to focus on the mystery of Lynx. How had she even gotten involved with the Union in the first place? Who had recruited her?

Where was the end of this cursed duct?

Zandra's heart rate increased yet again. Heat overtook her. A hot flash. *I need to get out.*

She was going to die in there if she didn't find an exit. She would have to go down the next vent she saw. She would—

Wait. Was the duct *lightening*?

Zandra looked up from her raw forearms. Ahead was the other side.

She had no idea how long she'd been inside the hellish tube— she guessed almost an hour—but the heat left her body at the sight of the exit vent, leaving only the sweat behind as proof that it had ever happened.

There wasn't enough room to spin, so Zandra would have to punch out the screws. She hoped she was strong enough.

But first she needed a look. Her first look at Unruly. She was here. At the place that had tantalized Zandra her entire life.

She looked down, excited—

Below a was gray-white hallway. Zandra was a little disappointed, but then she supposed that she wasn't going to be dropped in the middle of the wilderness.

No guards were in sight, but neither was the tunnel entrance. What would she do if—*when*—she encountered resistance? *Were* there even guards on Unruly? She supposed the less people who knew about it, the better the secret was kept.

Zandra shook the vent, thinking that maybe it was so old that it would just fall off.

She wasn't so lucky.

Punching at the vent was going to hurt, but she had no other choice. She needed to get out. Now.

Zandra ripped the frills off her now-useful dress and wrapped the fabric around the knuckles of her left hand. She wasted no time before issuing the first blow.

CRASH! The vent shook, but didn't budge.

She hit it again. CRASH! It rocked again.

CRASH! CRASH! CRASH!

Soon Zandra was releasing her emotions on the vent. Cathartic, yet terrible. Even though she knew it would take a lot of time, effort, and work to come to terms with the revelations of the past few days, she let herself believe that if she punched hard enough, the anger would fly from her body like the vent from its hinges.

When the vent finally did clang to the floor, Zandra was surprised to find she felt better. It gave her hope that she could internally get back to normal in time.

She was proud of herself. She never would have thought she'd be able to crawl in that small of a tunnel for so long. She felt more certain in her ability to save Charlotte.

The peace slowed Zandra's adrenaline, allowing the pain from her hand to course up her arm and into her brain. Her knuckles were bleeding through the dress fabric. She kept it wrapped. She could inspect it later.

Zandra didn't know how to exit the vent except by going head first. She managed to turn onto her back before wiggling her upper body out.

She looked for something to grab on the wall above her, but there was nothing. So she gripped the top of the vent and lifted her upper body.

Her left leg slipped out easily. She lifted her right, expecting it to come out just as quickly, but she was met with resistance.

Her dress was caught on the side of the opening on one of the dislodged screws.

Zandra's sweaty hands slipped, and before she knew it, she was falling head-first to the ground.

There was nothing she could do except brace her hands so her head didn't absorb the impact.

Gravity conquered the dress, ripping it a millisecond before Zandra's already-wounded hand took the brunt of her weight. She rolled onto the floor, not quite feeling the pain.

Then everything was quiet. Zandra was too shocked to properly take stock of her injuries. She didn't think she'd hit her head hard enough for a concussion.

But *holy hell*, her left hand *hurt*. It throbbed harder than anything she'd ever felt before.

Zandra turned onto her right side, but didn't allow herself to inspect the damage. She hid her bloody hand beneath her dress. It was better than an ankle—at least she could stand and walk.

So stand and walk she did. She had a sister to save, and very little time to do it.

Zandra knew better than to assume that no one had heard the crash. She got to her feet, still shaking. Half her dress was hanging from the vent. She stood on her tiptoes and stuffed the remnants into the duct, then placed the vent back over the hole. It was lopsided, but it would do.

Zandra started down the hallway, deeper into Unruly. Lights flickered. Dust had settled on the ground, giving the air a musty odor.

The ceiling was uncomfortably low, though Zandra doubted she'd ever feel truly claustrophobic again after the vent. Maybe exposure therapy really did work.

Zandra ran, gripping her hand. Within a minute, she spotted the first doorway. And another after that.

And another.

Like the vents in the duct, they were identical and evenly dispersed. Zandra was determined to leave no stone unturned, so she turned left and tried the first door.

It was locked. Zandra fumbled around, digging into her bosom, past the message from Lynx, the Dust pills, and loose pages of her journal, until she found the plastic with Five's fingerprint. She marveled at how good a corset was for storing things.

She pressed it to the small scanner beside the door. It beeped and she threw the door open.

Zandra balked, stopping in her tracks when she saw what was before her.

Four teenagers—all her age—in chairs, their heads in helmets and electrodes on their temples. Two of the teens' limbs were being moved by a machine. All of them had IVs in their veins.

Zandra recognized a boy she'd seen at the party.

This was Unruly?

What was being done to them? Were they merely on ice until they were needed for Pairing?

It made sense. Maybe that was why no Unruly in the LPC could remember what had happened.

Zandra swallowed her nausea. She had to reach her sister.

She didn't want to leave them, but this was the best way to help. One thing was clear—the Unruly needed saving. And Zandra promised herself that, when she had more resources, she'd come back for them.

Zandra raced away into the next room on the opposite side of the hall. These Unruly were older. From Lynx's class. They had been there for a year.

The nausea increased.

Even before she opened the door to the third room, Zandra knew it was the one. Her sixth sense—her twin sense—sparked.

The moment she burst inside, Zandra's eyes landed on her sister.

Before she inspected her, Zandra rushed to the camera in the corner and ripped it from the wall, then crushed it. Just in case Maddox couldn't wipe it.

Charlotte's eyes were closed, but Zandra could see her eyeballs moving rapidly beneath the lids. She otherwise looked peaceful. Her body was still, the IV dripped into her veins...

Her vitals monitor told a different story. Her heart was racing and her blood pressure was high.

Zandra wanted to throw her arms around her. She wanted to apologize for leaving her—for letting Imogen do this to her. *No,* Zandra corrected herself, *I have nothing to be sorry for.*

So, seeing that there was no big red "EJECT" button in sight, Zandra ran over to the machine and unplugged it.

And Charlotte's eyes snapped open.

40

A war was coming. One greater than the skirmishes between the Union and Luxor.

"Unruly is a simulation!" Lynx screamed, "I've been in it myself!"

Whether it'd be a civil war or a world war as tragic as the Destruction, Lynx did not know. She just knew that there was no way to do away with Pairing without one.

Just as she knew that this was the end for her. If not her life, then her mission. Her freedom.

Charlotte and Zandra were the ones Ignis needed. They needed The Highest Pointer and The Lowest Pointer of All Time —the twins of the country's second-in-command, the twins that they'd spent the past seventeen years watching grow up—to bring Ignis together and show the nation there was a better way to live. A way where the human race survived and Pairing wasn't needed.

Like the way the Union lived.

No one would listen unless it came from them. They meant far more to the future than she did. The twins were both supposed to be on Princeps, but Zandra going to the Union wasn't the worst possible scenario. If Lynx was imprisoned for the rest of her life—if she were charged with treason, or killed—it wouldn't be in vain, as long as Zandra managed to save Charlotte.

Charlotte.

Lynx had been surprised by her. Even pretending to be Zandra, she had come across as the most authentic person Lynx had ever had the pleasure of knowing. If Lynx could even say she knew Charlotte.

Because Lynx was the most *inauthentic* person she knew. Not that she blamed herself for that. She would do it all the same way again, minus releasing the simulation information. She'd let her soft spot for Five get in the way.

Lynx hopped onto the statue of First One so the crowd could see her. She didn't look toward Town Hall. She couldn't draw attention toward Zandra.

"It's immoral," Lynx continued, "We sit here and force *kids* into Pairing. And for what? To repeat the cycle? There's a different way to save the human race!"

She didn't tell them how. This wasn't the time or place. Already, her voice could barely be heard over the protests. But Lynx screamed anyway. "No more Pairing! NO MORE PAIRING!"

"No more Pairing!" Daniel Solace's voice boomed through the crowd.

The next second felt like an eternity before another joined, "No more Pairing!"

Two people. Lynx held her breath, waiting—

But before more people could add to the chant, Lynx noticed the attention of the people divert. The crowd near the base of Town Hall was turning.

Eye-level with her was Tiberius, Zandra nowhere in sight.

Lynx prayed that she had made it.

Tiberius silenced the people with a gesture and said, "Hello."

Lynx could barely hear him and wasn't going to stick around for more. Maybe this was her chance to escape. To get out of here and go to the Union.

But before she could jump down, she spotted a familiar head protruding above the others, pushing toward her.

Five.

Lynx jumped down and began pushing a path through the people behind her. But it was clear within seconds that she didn't have the ability to bulldoze through people like Five did.

She had only gone two feet before she felt Five's hand grip her shoulder.

It was pointless to try to fight, but she did anyway.

"Stop!" Five said as Lynx tried to twist away, accidentally hitting the man beside her. "I'm trying to help you!"

Lynx stopped and turned, meeting Five's gaze. Five was livid at her, yes, but Lynx knew her well enough to see that she also was angry at herself.

For what she was about to do.

"I'll hide you," she said, "But you have *a lot* of explaining to do."

"I need to leave Ignis, Five," Lynx breathed. But Five shook her head.

"Not until I know what's going on. C'mon, we have to get you out of here."

Maybe it was because Lynx knew that having Five as an ally could be the tipping point, or maybe it was because of her affection for Five—but Lynx found herself falling in step with her unofficial Pair.

She had done her part. Now the future was in Zandra's hands.

41

Nothing was real.

Tiberius had been warned. By everyone. By his father, the other boys, Jayana...even Zandra herself.

He'd chosen Charlotte, but he'd gotten Zandra. He had fallen in love. But with whom? The version of Charlotte that existed in his head? Or Zandra?

Neither. It was Zandra *pretending* to be Charlotte.

How? How could he have been so blindsided?

The possibility that the real Charlotte had nothing to do with this kept him together. That she was an innocent victim of this scheme. That, when she got off Unruly, she would be exactly who Tiberius expected her to be.

He was falling into the same trap as before. But it was the only path he knew. So he would hope.

Watching the videos play to hundreds of people in the square of him and Zandra made his heart hurt. Deep down, Tiberius knew Zandra had been telling the truth. She had fallen for him, too, against her better judgement.

He didn't want the real Charlotte. He wanted the one who

would lie to the entire world to save her sister. The one who had stepped up and said screw Pairing.

Zandra had told him the truth, despite having *everything* to lose. Tiberius was the only thing keeping her safe from One's wrath—and she'd *still* told him. That had to have meant something, right?

Stop. He couldn't want her. He *shouldn't*. Zandra had used him *and* his feelings. Pursuing her would just lead to more lies and pain.

Was he on the wrong team? Was he on any team at all?

His angry fist built with pressure.

He would meet Charlotte, the person he'd been destined for his whole life. And if she wasn't who he envisioned in his mind, he would go home. Shamed and Pairless.

When he and Zandra climbed the steps to Town Hall and he was spotted, he made a split second decision. He would let her go and bring Charlotte back to him. Or she wouldn't, and his decision would be made for him.

Zandra needed to try to save Charlotte. If she didn't, Tiberius and Zandra would remain in this toxic, unsurvivable limbo.

Tiberius shut the door to Town Hall behind Zandra as inconspicuously as he could.

He stood in front of the people—the people who weren't his, despite him having been promised to them.

They looked for Charlotte. They didn't care about him. They didn't know what had been done to him. They only cared about *her*.

They wanted a perfect love story. They wanted to know that Pairing *worked*.

Tiberius' anger built as he faced the people. He couldn't lie to them. He didn't have the energy.

How had Zandra lied to the crowds time and time again? How had she lied to *his* face time and time again?

He wasn't sure what it was about the eyes on him—the exposure—but it made his confidence in Zandra shatter. He was a fool. He had done this before, more times than he cared to admit. It was time to stop putting expectations on people and stop believing they cared for him as he cared for them.

"Hello," he said, hating the strangers and their parasocial relationship to him.

Like your relationship with Charlotte.

The rage couldn't be contained in his fist. Not this time. It began climbing up his wrist, into his forearm, through his elbow. Would he be able to stop it before it reached his heart?

He was up here alone. Embarrassed, no Pair in sight, a failure at his one job.

One rushed up the steps toward him, an artificial smile on his face. Akil was nowhere in sight. "You were tricked by her too, weren't you?"

And because Tiberius no longer believed in love, and humanity, he nodded.

"It has happened to the best of us. By their whole family. We can stop them from hurting anyone else. And then I will let you get re-Paired."

The offer was tantalizing. To choose someone without having any prior knowledge or expectation. To form a bond with someone based on who they were rather than what he believed them to be.

He wished he could let go of Zandra and Charlotte, and find someone that he placed no expectations on.

He wished he could have listened to his father.

But he couldn't let Charlotte go. Not yet. Not when there was still hope.

He would stay with One, but he would play his own game. Not One's, not Zandra's, not his father's.

"Okay."

42

Maddox watched the havoc of Main Square unfold from the safety of the security room.

He was all-seeing down here. He'd watched Zandra climb into the air duct. He deleted the footage, pride for his daughter blooming in his chest.

He watched Lynx go rogue. Despite her idiotic decisions, his heart ached for her. There would be no coming back from this. Lynx was bright. The Union would miss her. He would miss wiping the surveillance whenever she snuck onto Unruly to do whatever it was she'd been assigned to do.

Maddox had tried to control Charlotte in the simulation again, but she had somehow destroyed his ability to. It had made Maddox proud, if not a little terrified. Though she seemed to be going out of her way to act "normal"—which hopefully meant she would behave appropriately until Zandra got her out.

Maddox paced around the room, waiting to jump into action the moment he was needed. Wherever the chaos demanded he go.

He narrowed his eyes when he saw One whisper to Tiberius just outside of Town Hall, his hand gripping Tiberius' shoulder.

Maddox zoomed in on them. Tiberius nodded, then spoke. Maddox had no way of hearing what was said.

Then they went inside.

Wait, was Tiberius—he *couldn't* have. Could he?

Tiberius hadn't know Zandra very long. That probably made it easier to betray her.

Maddox rushed to the monitor that showed the interior of Town Hall. Were they coming here? Were they going to stop Zandra?

Maddox would stand in their way if so. One would reach his daughters over his dead body.

But instead of heading for the tunnel to Unruly, One, Tiberius, and the guards turned toward the hall of empty rooms.

Mostly empty rooms.

Imogen.

What did One want with her?

Before Maddox could determine, his breast pocket vibrated.

His heart raced. Zandra must've gotten stuck in the duct.

But when he saw the Caller ID, a different kind of concern overtook him.

The Union.

Maddox swallowed and opened the phone with shaking hands. "Hello?"

"Password," came a woman's demanding voice. She was efficient and never wasted time.

"Tree frog."

"You alone?"

"Yes."

"Delete all footage from Unruly and the security cameras, then turn all cameras off."

"Okay." He did as he was told, knowing this would nail his coffin politically, but trusting the Union had a plan. "Done."

"Good. You need to kill One. Now."

A chill rushed through Maddox's body. He had never killed someone. When he'd agreed to work for the Union in an attempt to eradicate Pairing, they'd assured him that he could fulfill his duties to them at least *somewhat* ethically.

And now they wanted him to *murder* someone?

One didn't deserve to die. He was doing what he thought was right, just like the rest of them.

"I'm not doing that."

"He will hurt your daughters if you do not," the voice said. How could she be so emotionless? So matter-of-fact? "And countless more will die. He will hurt the entire next generation with Pairing. So what is more important, Maddox? Your personal moral code, or the lives that will be saved on the battlefield? What do you want your legacy to be?"

Maddox pulled the phone from his ear and cursed under his breath. If he was going to do this—which was a big *if*—he needed answers. And he didn't have much time.

"Why now?" Maddox whispered into the phone.

"If he's gone, Charlotte will be able to ascend. He has enough power and knowledge to wipe all of you out, which—if he's smart, and he is—he'll be leaking tonight, while the ground is still shaking.

"Make the right decision or everything will be ruined, Maddox. Good-bye."

The call disconnected and Maddox bolted for the door.

He had a thirty second sprint to make a decision. He had a gun beneath his coat. The only gun in Ignis, as far as he knew. It had been supplied by the Union, and he'd vowed never to use it.

The cost of his soul was worth a better world, wasn't it? It was selfish of him not to kill One.

Maddox made up his mind. He would do it.

He didn't want Tiberius to see it, and it couldn't be in the hallway. Nowhere near where the guards could see.

Maddox reached the guards at Imogen's cell before One and Tiberius.

"You're dismissed," Maddox said, "Go home."

"We only take orders from One," the bigger of the two responded.

Footsteps approached from behind. Maddox internally rebuked himself for wasting his element of surprise.

"Fine," Maddox said, striding past them. He would deal with them later. After whatever happened...happened.

After I kill him.

The gun was heavy against his chest. He'd never imagined he'd use it. It was like a bodyguard—there as a last resort, but never actually expected to be used.

Maddox stepped into the sterile room and laid eyes on Imogen, who paced on the other side of the bars keeping her in captivity.

Their eyes met. Hers were puffy, with large bags beneath them. She'd been crying. Maddox had always thought she'd looked most beautiful when she cried. He hadn't seen her tears in over a decade.

"Maddox," she breathed, "You're here."

Maddox reached for the bars. She met him there and placed her hands over his.

He didn't pull away. He let her intwine their fingers together. Maybe it was because *he* was the one who was about to need forgiveness, or maybe it was because she looked so much like she had the day she'd banged on his door in the rain seventeen years ago, but a ray of affection penetrated through the hate.

"I screwed up our children," whispered Imogen.

"People screw themselves up," Maddox replied, "And our daughters *aren't*. They're...perfect. Better than we are...but I don't think you're allowed to take credit for that."

Imogen sighed. Maddox basked in the peace. The tranquility

that he knew was about to be shattered by the presence of One. He pretended he was back in Phoenix Palace eighteen years ago, standing with Imogen before things had gotten complicated.

The sound of One's arrival broke the fantasy. Maddox closed his eyes and put his hand inside the jacket. His fingers wrapped around the cool metal of the gun, burning his fingers.

Maddox turned slowly, removing his hand from Imogen's.

One was gloating. He would die gloating.

He must've left Tiberius outside with all the guards, because he came unguarded. Unprotected. Unarmed.

Maddox would have to live with killing an unarmed man.

"Fancy meeting you here, Three," said One, "I would've thought you'd be in the security room digging your grave."

Imogen spoke, but Maddox couldn't hear over the pounding in his head.

Do it now. There's no better time than now.

Maddox began pulling the gun out of his coat. It was heavy in his hand.

One's voice felt a million miles away. "I'll tell you both what's going to happen, and you're going to do it—unless, of course, you want to be the greatest scandal in all of—"

One spotted the gun. The smile faded from his face.

Maddox snapped it into position, safety off. Now that it was clear what he was doing, there was no going back.

He held it there. One froze. Imogen froze.

Maddox froze.

Several long seconds dragged by.

"If you're going to shoot me, boy, get on with it."

Maddox's hand shook. He couldn't do it, but he *had* to. He'd passed the point of no return.

One stepped forward. So did Maddox. "Stay back!"

One didn't. But he didn't move forward, either.

"Put it down, Maddox," Imogen said behind him. How?

How could he put it down now? "We'll talk this out, One. We'll come to an agreement."

One took another step.

Then another.

Another.

Until he was looking down the barrel. Maddox's entire body shook. One wasn't evil, but Maddox *would* be if he did this. Wouldn't he? Or was he evil if he didn't sacrifice One for the greater good?

One had a family. A grandchild.

Maddox lowered the gun. It wasn't even pointed at the floor before One moved forward.

The next moment was a blur.

Maddox processed many things at the same time. A cool sensation in his chest. Imogen's scream. One's snarling face inches from his own. A metallic taste in his mouth that bled into his nose, smelling the same as it tasted.

The chill in Maddox's chest morphed into pain. He looked down—there was a flash of silver as One jerked forward. The pain thrust deeper, into Maddox's back.

Then it erupted through his veins.

Maddox fell backward, into the steel bars separating him from Imogen.

The chill left his body. One's shirt was flecked with the most beautiful shade of maroon Maddox had ever seen.

Only when Maddox slumped against the bars and saw the liquid color gush down his body did he process what had happened.

One wiped the silver blade on his maroon-speckled jacket. He sounded as though he were speaking underwater as he took the jacket off, threw it next to Maddox, and exited.

Arms were around him, trying to help him from the other side of the bars. Trying to stop the blood flow.

"Stay with me, Maddox," Imogen said. "Stay here."

The pain was as muted as his vision. But one thing was clear through his exhaustion. "I—forgive you," he choked.

Imogen's hands left his chest to cradle his head. They were wet and sticky.

"I love you," she whispered, kissing his forehead.

"Take—care—of—our—girls."

"I will. I promise. I'll do it right this time."

That was all Maddox needed to hear to allow peace to consume his body.

Maddox inhaled his last breath in the arms of Imogen Galvin. No exhale followed.

43

For the first time in her life, Charlotte felt claustrophobic.

Usually she found comfort in confinement. Enclosed spaces meant no one could see or judge her. But now she was trapped in a reality she didn't understand. She didn't know who was watching, or what the eyes were searching for.

Her withdrawals were getting stronger. She didn't know why. She had gone days without Dust before and hadn't felt this way. Why was it so bad? Was it the stress?

After Harris' reaction to her reveal—and now that Charlotte had somewhat calmed herself—she decided not to say more to him until she could explain what had happened.

As if she *knew*.

So Harris continued onward, as if the Conquest weren't rigged. She felt as far away from him as she'd been during their years of not speaking.

"Are you sure you're okay?" Harris asked time and time again as they dug, Charlotte going through the motions in the hopes that it would keep the anxiety at bay, as movement so often did for her.

"Yes," Charlotte lied every time, compulsively touching her stomach, disturbed as her fingers ran over the ridge of Zandra's mole.

Beneath her confusion, she was still terrified that she would be controlled again. And if she had been controlled, had Harris? Had the others been? What kind of games was High Society playing, and for what purpose?

If it even is *High Society.*

She felt a kernel of comfort knowing that Harris was here with her. That she wasn't in this alone, even if he didn't understand.

She wasn't sure where the two of them stood. She'd told him she was broken—he'd accepted her, but then she'd been possessed, and now he seemed to think they would be Paired when they got out.

Charlotte struggled to push down the panic. *I don't need Dust. I don't need Dust. I need—I* don't *need Dust.*

She would pretend. She would become a chameleon until she knew more. She was an observant person—she would remain on guard and pray that she had scared away her possessor for good.

They dug. And dug. And dug. Preparing the optimal spot for the dynamite explosion. With every second, Charlotte became more confident that she'd remain in full control of herself, and also more anxious about her imprisonment.

She wondered about Enid. Was she thinking about Charlotte? Was she as thrown by Charlotte as Charlotte was her?

Would Enid figure out that Unruly wasn't what they believed? At some point, Charlotte was sure. She was smart and curious, but Charlotte wished she could warn her now.

She wished she could tell them all.

Getting out was how she would help them. She wouldn't abandon them. Not like she had with Wade.

Wade.

Was he actually dead? If this wasn't real, then Wade's body wouldn't have been crushed. Right?

She couldn't be sure, but a flame of hope kindled in her soul, rejuvenating her.

This hope became her companion as she dug with Harris, cold sweat dripping down her brow.

"I think this is where we put the dynamite," Harris announced when they couldn't move any more rocks.

"Okay."

"Have you thought about what you're going to do first when we're off this island?"

"Have you ever been so focused on behaving a certain way that you forget to do what's right?" Charlotte asked.

"I don't know," Harris murmured, grabbing the sticks and the matches. Charlotte's stomach did a somersault. So many things could go wrong.

"I'm going to make sure I do what's right," Charlotte decided. *I'm going to find out what's going on here and make sure that* no *Unruly is left behind.*

"Don't be so hard on yourself."

"And don't tell me what I want to hear. I gave up on you after one mistake."

"It was a pretty big mistake." He met her gaze. "But I'm glad we're here now. And I'm going to make it up to you."

He was too close to her, though not by any fault of his own. It was simply that Charlotte hadn't noticed until now.

A prickle of unease spread through her.

Harris put the dynamite on the ground. "You should get out of here."

"I'm not letting you light it."

"I'm not letting *you* light it."

Charlotte didn't move.

"You were the one who went in last time," Harris pointed out. "It's my turn."

"I'm not—"

But Harris was already bending down. "There's no point in both of us being in harm's way."

"Well—"

"I *will* stop you if you try," Harris said, clearly meaning it. "Let me make up for some past mistakes."

Charlotte sighed. She could say the same thing. But she could see that Harris needed this, so she backed off.

"Thank you."

She crouched behind a boulder a safe distance away.

Harris opened his mouth and closed it, gazing at her.

"Don't leave me in suspense like this," Charlotte said.

"I love you," Harris said.

Charlotte's head spun, and this time it had nothing to do with her withdrawal. "Stop acting like you're going to die," she murmured.

Harris grinned. "I just wanted you to know."

"I know," she said, not knowing what else to say. She loved him too—just not in the same way. And it felt wrong to confuse him further.

And there were far more pressing matters at stake.

When Harris was satisfied she was well-protected, he lit the end of the fuse. Charlotte held her breath as the flame licked the wire—

Before Harris had even fully turned, everything exploded. He flew through the air, an inferno behind him. Before Charlotte could further process, before she could feel any horror, the world went black.

She panicked. She was dead.

...*Was* she dead? Could dead people think?

A voice drifted through her ear and into her brain, "Charlotte? Charlotte?!"

The voice was comforting and familiar. *Zandra's* voice.

Yes. She was dead.

Her shoulders shook, but the darkness continued. It took Charlotte a few more seconds to realize that her eyes were closed. She would open them to her first glimpse of the afterlife.

She snapped them open, gasping as if resurfacing from underwater, though she had been breathing just fine.

Zandra hovered over her, her freckled brow creased with worry. Charlotte watched it relax as Charlotte came to.

"Can you hear me?" Zandra asked, "Are you okay?"

Charlotte threw her arms around her sister, her IV ripping out in the process. "I'm sorry," Charlotte whispered, clinging to Zandra, tears falling, "I'm so, so sorry."

The world spun, and Charlotte clung to Zandra to stop from falling over.

She was alive. Alive and free of Unruly.

Zandra had saved her.

Charlotte touched her stomach. No mole. She sagged with relief.

"It's okay," Zandra said, "I'm here now." She took in Charlotte's haggard face, then pulled a bag of pills out of her corset. Charlotte's anti-anxiety medication. "You've been on, like, a *ton* of Dust. Can you function without it?"

Charlotte stared at it blankly before everything made sense. Dust. *That* was why her withdrawals had been so bad.

Imogen had been *drugging* her. Charlotte choked down the hatred to deal with later.

She wanted the Dust more than anything. She *needed* it. She deserved it, after all she'd just been through.

Harris. Where was Harris? What had happened to him?

Wade.

They might be okay.

Zandra said, "I don't really know how it works or how much you need it—"

Charlotte took the Dust into her hand. It would be so easy to lift it to her lips. To make the headache and the nausea and the guilt fade away.

What happened to Wade hadn't been her fault. It was Imogen's. Imogen was the one to blame. So it wouldn't be her fault if she took the Dust.

She desperately wanted to. More than anything.

Her hand shook. It would be so easy. She needed her head to be clear for whatever came next. She needed—

I don't need *Dust!*

If she didn't do it now, she never would. Before she lost her resolve, Charlotte dropped the pills and crushed them beneath her foot.

The moment the powder dissolved onto her shoe, she regretted it. Could she lick it? Should she—?

"We need to get going," Zandra said, not realizing the significance of what had just happened. But her voice anchored Charlotte, reminding her of what she was fighting for.

"I left you," Charlotte murmured, her voice breaking, "I left you all alone."

Zandra didn't soothe her this time, as she always did. Charlotte pulled away and took in her twin's face. They both searched each other's eyes, trying to understand what the other had been through. Finally, Zandra said, "How bad was it?"

Charlotte didn't know how to respond. "How long has it been?"

"A few days."

Time had worked the same in the simulation. Charlotte took off her various monitors and fluid bags. It must have been a simulation. Her body had been in the chair while her mind had been underground.

"We have to find someone," Charlotte breathed, shaking, trying not to think of the Dust crushed beneath her foot, "We have to look through these rooms—"

"No," Zandra said, "We have to go."

"What?"

"We don't have much time," Zandra said, already heading for the door, "I have to get out of here and take the boat north."

"What are you talking about?"

"There's another place. A better place. That the Council was hiding. They're how we get rid of Pairing. I'm going to drop you off at the vent, then you can...take your life back."

Charlotte felt bile rise in her throat. She shook her splitting head. "I can't go back."

Zandra looked at her, then said, "What do you want, Charlotte?"

"What do you mean?"

"What do you want your future to be?" Zandra asked, a steeliness in her voice that had never been used on Charlotte before. What had happened? What had she been through? How had she gotten here, and so quickly?

"I don't want to be Paired," Charlotte whispered, "I don't want anyone to have to be Paired."

Zandra nodded, as if she knew that. Charlotte felt exposed. Was it that obvious?

"This is how you do it, Charlotte. They need the Highest Pointer of All Time to tell them that Pairing isn't the way."

Charlotte was about to ask *what* "the way" was when Zandra answered, "I'm going north to find out what is. And then I'll let you know."

They were a team. This was how they saved everyone in Unruly.

"Let me come," Charlotte breathed. Now that her old life was so close, she felt her former anxiety pressing in, already eating away at her resolve. She was already regretting crushing the Dust. "I want to go. Or—or you can stay here, and keep being me, if you want—"

"You think I *wanted* to be you?"

Charlotte felt like a fool.

"You lied to me!" Zandra exclaimed, "About everything! You took away *my* future! You hid the Dust, you hid Lynx's message." Zandra reached into her corset and pulled out a piece of paper. "But I'm not like you. I'm giving you all the information I have time to give. Which is *no* time, by the way." She shoved the paper into Charlotte's chest. "Here's *your* message from Lynx. I'm not going to keep it from you like you did from me."

Charlotte didn't care to read it. "I know, Zandra."

"No," Zandra said, "You *don't*. I've lived my whole life for you. And you used me. I love you, Charlotte, but you don't love anyone but yourself."

Charlotte certainly didn't love herself in that moment.

"You can come with me," Zandra continued, "If you want. But that's not going to help anyone. *Or* you can go back and fix your mistakes. You want to stop Pairing? This is how you do it."

Charlotte had said—she had promised—she was going to make up for her mistakes. And already she was backing out.

Reclaiming her life was going to be the hardest thing she'd ever done. She looked at the paper to avoid Zandra's disappointment. Her hands trembled as she opened it. She had no idea what Lynx would have written to her.

The handwriting was messy from haste, but still decipherable: *Be the last Unruly. Come back and help me help people like us. -Enid*

Charlotte had to read it three times before she understood.

Enid hadn't been Enid. Enid had been *Lynx*.

Charlotte's blood turned to ice. She hadn't seen Enid on the ship. She hadn't known her before Unruly. The familiarity—she'd carried herself like *Lynx* carried herself.

The "belowdeck" Unruly had been spies possessed by High Society.

Charlotte's heart thumped. Everything she had said to Enid had been to *Lynx*. Enid had tricked her. She had manipulated Charlotte's feelings.

And yet.

Yet.

The letter. *Help me help people like us.* Maybe it hadn't all been a lie. Charlotte had been lying to her, too, about who she was. Had what Lynx been doing been so different?

She supposed it would come down to what, exactly, Lynx had been lying *for*. Or who.

Charlotte felt both a pang of excitement and dread at the thought of seeing Lynx again. She couldn't imagine what their future held, just that it was nothing good.

Charlotte pulled her mind away, back to her twin, though her body wouldn't obey so easily. It continued trembling.

"You're right," Charlotte finally said to Zandra, folding the paper into the pockets of the white graduation clothes she was still wearing, "I do want to stop Pairing. And I will. I'm going to be better."

"Good. There's something else I need to tell you. Don't freak out, okay?"

"I think we're long past that point."

Zandra took Charlotte's shoulders, her face kind. "We're Impaired."

Her heart raced. She wasn't supposed to be Paired. Neither was Zandra.

Their genes were compatible with no one, and the Impaired on Unruly—they weren't actually covered in boils and sores.

Relief crashed over Charlotte like a waterfall. She didn't *have* to get Paired. She didn't have to do anything.

They can send me to Luxor. But she knew she couldn't. She had a duty now.

"Only Imogen and Three know, I think."

"Is *he* our—?"

"Yes. What are you thinking?"

"I'm thinking that we can stop the Impaired from getting sent Unruly," Charlotte murmured. She pictured all of them—people like her—torn from their families at ten—either hooked up to the simulation or exiled to Luxor. It made her sick.

"That's what I'm thinking, too."

Charlotte finally swallowed her shame and allowed herself to properly look at Zandra. Her hand was wrapped and bleeding. Her dress was torn. But she looked more aware and certain than Charlotte had ever seen her.

"I missed you so much," Charlotte murmured.

Zandra softened. "Me too."

"And I'm going to miss you when you go."

Zandra squeezed Charlotte's hand. "I'll be back, okay? I'm going to drop you off at the vent. Just climb through and...don't mind who you see as you pass."

Charlotte made a note to ask Zandra what that meant before she left. But first...

"I need to find some people."

"I told you, there's no time." Zandra started stripping out of her ripped dress to switch outfits.

"They know," Charlotte said, "They know we switched."

"No, they don't," Zandra said. Charlotte wanted to ask *how*, but that was not the most important issue at the moment.

"Then I have to find them. I promised."

She had to reach him. Charlotte peeled off her graduation

clothes and threw them at Zandra, who passed her the itchy shredded dress. Charlotte was going to miss being comfortable.

When Zandra took off the ridiculously tight corset, she passed Charlotte the loose pieces of paper that fell out. "These might help you with what you missed, but they're not going to be easy to read. I was kinda mad at you.... So what are you going to do with these people you have to save?"

"You're going to take them."

Zandra pulled on Charlotte's shirt, then helped Charlotte into the corset. Charlotte passed her the shark tooth necklace and Zandra brightened as she threw it around her neck.

"Is it Harris?" Zandra asked, squinting at her as she took the bloody bandage off her hand and wrapped it around Charlotte's.

Charlotte just nodded.

Zandra shooed her through the door. Charlotte ignored the guilt of leaving Rae and the others, mentally promising herself she'd come back for them.

The hallway was too quiet. The calm before the storm.

"I think I know where they are."

Zandra sighed. "Thirty seconds. That's all."

Charlotte glanced at the doors. The one they had exited was labelled 19. So she hurried down the hallway in the opposite direction of where she knew the boat was.

Door 20. She tried the handle.

"Here," Zandra said, pressing a piece of plastic to the scanner. Charlotte could hear the fear in her voice—this was taking too long.

It unlocked.

Charlotte busted the door open, hoping to see Wade, Harris, and two others in chairs in a room identical to her own.

She wished she had hoped to see *only* them.

Surrounding them were One and Tiberius, and two guards armed with spears.

Charlotte stopped in her tracks.

They'd been too late.

Zandra was behind her, still obscured from One and Tiberius' views.

This was the moment Charlotte made things right. Charlotte turned and whispered under her breath, "Go north. I love you."

Zandra still had the plastic, but Charlotte trusted she would understand that this was how they saved *both* of them. And all of Ignis.

The confusion on Zandra's face evaporated when she heard One's voice beyond the door, "There's no point in running, Charlotte."

Charlotte slammed the door behind her, praying Zandra would go. Hoping she would see that this was the only opportunity she'd have to get out.

If One and Tiberius were curious as to why she had locked herself in a room with them, they didn't show it. One was too busy basking in his victory, his grin like a snarl. For some reason, he was wearing a guard's tunic, and his trousers had a dark stain on one side.

"Charlotte Galvin," One said, "I'm *quite* disappointed in you."

Tiberius searched her face.

"And I *you*," Charlotte said, her attention on Wade, whose heart monitor was still beeping.

He was alive.

Charlotte sagged with relief, despite the fact that One had her surrounded.

She glanced at Harris. He was right there, just out of reach. Heart also beating.

But she and Harris may as well have been a hundred miles away. There would be no reaching him.

"Do tell me why," One said.

"Unruly is a lie."

"These children *chose* this."

"The Impaired didn't."

"The Impaired aren't here," he replied.

Charlotte frowned. Were Jeri and Owen and the others not hooked up to the simulation as well?

"Despite my disappointment, I am merciful. I will offer you clemency like I did for your Pair," One said, nodding at Tiberius.

Tiberius fidgeted, playing with his instrument strap. This wasn't the boy she'd pulled out of the heart of the party in the LPC. He'd been hardened.

One continued, "Starting with the honor of waking the winner of the Conquest."

One gestured toward Harris. Had lighting the dynamite secured his victory? Or had they picked him randomly?

Charlotte glanced at Wade in her peripheral. Had his consciousness been shut down when she'd "killed" him, and now he was waiting for someone to wake him up?

Too many questions and too many possible answers. Nothing was certain, except that Zandra needed more time to get away. If One didn't know the twins had swapped as Zandra had claimed, he likely believed that she—Charlotte—and Harris hated each other.

"Would you like to do the honors?" One said, nodding toward the cord connecting the electrodes from Harris' head to the computer.

Wade's cord was right next to Harris'.

Charlotte walked toward Harris as slowly as she could, easily lowering the mask of her former self onto her face. She would have to make sure that it stayed just that. A mask. She couldn't return to her old ways.

One would be in for a rude awakening when she and Harris showed a united front, though she hoped Harris would know to hide it so they could use it against him when it would hurt the most.

Yes, it was going to be difficult to avoid slipping into old habits.

One gestured impatiently Charlotte held her breath. She needed her old friend. She trusted him. She needed him in this house of vipers more than anyone.

Charlotte reached for the cord in slow motion. When Harris got out, they could stall even more. He would follow her lead.

Her hand was inches away when a loud, *WoooOOO* overpowered her ears.

The alarm.

One glance at One's face confirmed it was the alarm for the boat. Zandra had reached it. She was on her way to freedom.

Charlotte ripped Harris' cord out of the computer.

She didn't wait to see what happened before doing the same to Wade's.

One shouted, but Charlotte couldn't hear him. She was too busy glancing between Harris and Wade, watching as their eyes twitched.

Harris came to first.

Charlotte had to stop herself from running toward him. One couldn't know—

Harris looked around, confused and struggling to focus his eyes.

"Charlotte?" Harris whispered groggily as his eyes focused. Charlotte expected them to be filled with warmth. With a secret acknowledgement or understanding of what they had been through.

She didn't expect his lips to curl into a snarl.

Before Charlotte could react, Harris grabbed her shoulders and pinned her to the wall, his IV ripping through his skin. "Get the *hell* away from me, you psychopath!" he spat, "Or I will *kill you!*"

Shock rippled through Charlotte's body like an earthquake, right through the center of her heart, splitting it in two.

Terror was the aftereffect.

She tried to push him away, but he overpowered her, a rabid hatred in his eyes. "She's *dead*! She was my Pair, and she's dead! And it's *your fault* for not making her choose Pairing!"

Beyond him, Charlotte saw One smile. He had known this would happen. Because Harris' Unruly had been completely different than her own.

Everyone was in their own personally simulated hell.

Tiberius' words from the party suddenly made sense—*no* Impaired were sent Unruly. They were all sent to Luxor. The Conquest meant *choosing* Pairing—and resisting the temptation to stay.

Then watching your Pair die.

And the only reason Charlotte hadn't extraordinarily failed was because she'd been controlled.

44

*Z*andra had never driven a boat before—or *any* vehicle, for that matter—but she was sure she could figure it out. She hurried up to the cockpit and scanned Five's fingerprint on the boat's dashboard.

The engine spurred to life. The Unruly transport boat was massive, but the cavern door that led to the ocean was even bigger. The button to open it was right beside the engine starter. Zandra eyed it, swallowing her guilt at leaving Charlotte. This was *her* life now. And she had to live it to stop Pairing.

She pressed the button.

WoooOOO! WoooOOO!

The door ascended. Zandra yanked the lever as hard as she could.

The boat jolted into the side of the cave. Zandra lurched forward, catching herself with her hands to stop herself from falling overboard.

Zandra hissed through her teeth as pain erupted in her injured hand. Zandra leapt to her feet and got back behind the wheel. She reversed and righted her course.

Maybe it was harder than she'd expected.

Sunlight reflected off the indigo water. Zandra had never appreciated the sun so much following the duct experience. She didn't even mind being blinded by it.

Zandra rammed the boat into the other side of the cavern, denting the side.

"Shoot!"

She hoped none of her accidents had been severe enough to sink the ship. But this was her only option. Freedom—her life—was so close.

Excitement overpowered the pain. She had done it. She had chosen herself. And she was about see the world, as she had dreamed her entire life.

A yell startled her.

Two armed guards stood at the top of the staircase, heading toward her.

She had to go *now*.

She attempted to right the boat, overcorrecting once more. The guards flew down the stairs.

"Come on, come on, come on," Zandra muttered, pushing the throttle as they jumped for the boat.

The first guard made it, the second landing in the water.

A spear was thrust an inch from her face.

45

I t was Charlotte.

Actually Charlotte.

Tiberius didn't know how he knew, but he was certain.

This was not the woman from Phoenix Palace, and he couldn't bring himself to feel anything for her.

Unruly being a simulation...this place was messed up. And it bled into its citizens. There was no *right* side. No good options.

Where had Zandra gone?

It doesn't matter. She can go wherever she wants.

When the alarm sounded, he knew it was because of her. The guards rushed out with a single tip of One's head. Charlotte took the distraction to wake two of the boys.

When one of the boys attacked her and One did nothing, it was time to make a decision. Tiberius had to pick a team.

"And it's *your fault* for not making her choose Pairing!" the attacker said.

He unstrung his crwth, rushed toward the boy, and knocked him upside the head.

The boy fell to the ground, unconscious.

Charlotte stared into Tiberius' eyes, panting as she rubbed her neck. Tiberius felt nothing.

Then everyone was talking.

"What are you doing?" One demanded.

"What's happening?" the other Unruly boy asked.

"We have to get Wade out," Charlotte whispered.

One moved toward Tiberius, but Tiberius unstrung his other crwth—Charlotte's crwth—a dart in the bow before One had taken two steps. "Stay there," he ordered One.

"Your father will not be pleased," One said, stepping forward.

"No," Tiberius said, "He certainly will not be." And he fired a dart into One's leg.

46

Charlotte, Tiberius, and Wade beelined through the hallway. Charlotte grounded herself in her stride, fighting down nausea. She should've taken the Dust—

Stop.

When they reached the cavern, a guard was already on the boat with a spear to Zandra's throat.

Tiberius fumbled with the bow with trembling hands. "I—I don't have the best aim from this distance. I don't want to hit her—"

Charlotte snatched the bow and loaded a dart. Even in her state, she was confident. She'd been the highest physical pointer. She'd won the archery competition.

On Dust. You're not on Dust now.

She shook for a second. No. She could do this without Dust. She steadied herself, aimed...

Fired.

It launched into the man's shoulder. He shrieked, and Zandra pushed him onto the dock, grabbing his spear.

"Wade," Charlotte said, "You need to get down there *now*. Trust me."

"I—"

"You'll get put back into the simulation if you don't. This is your only option!"

Wade saw the desperation on her face. He nodded and bolted down the stairs.

Charlotte glanced down. Zandra stared at her.

I love you, Charlotte mouthed, *Be careful.*

Zandra put her hand on her chest and mouthed back. *I know. I love you.*

Then One was there, backed up by a dozen guards. "Don't let her get away!"

Wade hopped into the boat just as the cavern door began sliding downward. Zandra gave Charlotte a final glance, then gunned it.

Charlotte watched as the ship flew out of Unruly, wishing she could have been the one fleeing with Zandra. But instead, the guards escorted her back to her old life to deal with the consequences of a lifetime of terrible decisions.

47

The last image Zandra saw of Unruly was Charlotte and Tiberius being swept away by One's guards.

Her last moment of eye contact with Charlotte lingered—she hoped Charlotte could see the pride in her eyes.

I will find a better world for you, sister.

The boat tossed forward into the ocean, and Zandra embarked on the adventure she'd dreamt of her entire life, just to a different place than she'd thought.

To the Union.

Charlotte and Zandra's quest to save Ignis continues in:

Impaired

Coming 2027

ALSO BY BECCA MANN

Outside the Lanes: A Pro Swimmer's Story of
Resilience, Reinvention, and Redefining Success

ACKNOWLEDGMENTS

Unruly has been through so many drafts and variations the past five years, and I'm so grateful to all the people who helped me get it to where it is today.

First, to Eva Fabian for reading every single draft of this, for countless story-problem FaceTimes, and for pitching me fresh ideas whenever I got stuck. Unruly wouldn't be Unruly without you.

To my mom, who championed this book even when I wanted to give up on it. Thank you for always believing in me, my work, and my vision. And for everyone who was wondering—my mother and Imogen could not possibly be more different.

To all my friends who gave wonderful feedback and love to this book: Michelle Askew, for giving the best story notes of anyone I know; Rachel Mann, for telling me when things don't make sense; Ashley Wall, for my unofficial MFA in grammar; Declan Grogan, for always being excited to read my work; and Michael McGuire, for answering every question I have.

And to you, my readers—thank you for coming along to Unruly.

ABOUT THE AUTHOR

Becca Mann is a writer and 7x USA Swimming National Team member. She graduated with a BFA in Writing for Screen and Television at the University of Southern California after becoming the only person to consecutively swim the triangle between the Hawaiian islands of Maui, Molokai, and Lanai. She is a 2x National Champion and has represented Team USA at four World Championships. Her other work includes a sports memoir titled *Outside the Lanes* published by Blue Star Press and Penguin Random House. In her free time, you can find her at karaoke or skateboarding down The Strand.